THE CHOCOLATE SHOP

by
J.J. Spring

RIVER
POINT
PRESS

Belleair, Florida

ISBN: 978-0-9853408-2-7

Published in the United States of America by RiverPoint Press.

To June Elizabeth and Theodora Pearl

*A daughter's relationship with her mother is
something akin to bungee diving.
She can stake her claim in the outside world
in what looks like total autonomy—
in some cases, even divorce her mother in
a fiery exit from the family—
but there is an invisible emotional cord that snaps her back.*

Victoria Secunda

CHAPTER ONE

June

Laura wanted Mickey to die.

Tonight.

Now.

She had it all planned. They'd relax on the sofa in front of a roaring fire, watching the flames dance and crackle, snuggling together under her grandmother's time-softened green and white patch quilt. The red wine stain on the quilt from New Years Eve when they'd made love on the same sofa had faded away and almost disappeared.

And now her husband was about to fade away and disappear.

She would take his hand, mercilessly scabbed by needles searching for a vein, and entwine her fingers through his. Their interlocked hands would act as one and empty the medicine vial of tiny white pills into the glass of Chivas, his favorite. They'd enjoy their last hour together, her head nestling into the hollow space where his neck met his shoulder. She always considered that spot her private property. She would breath in his scent, and if she remained still she'd be able to feel his heartbeat tickling her cheek.

Then a final toast. He would drink the whiskey from his favorite cocktail glass, the one with the etched Orioles logo. They'd reminisce using the shorthand developed by every husband and wife over decades of marriage.

Remember when . . .?

He'd become sleepy. She would gently rub his neck right behind his ear . . .

Then a lingering last kiss.

Goodbye my darl—

"Mother?"

Laura's eyes sprang open. Had she dozed off? She glanced at Mickey asleep in the narrow hospital bed squeezed next to her chair. With so many twisting tubes and wires connected to his shriveled body he more resembled a monster from an old black and white horror flick than her husband.

"You were mumbling in your sleep," Brooke said. "Something about white pills and the Orioles." Without looking up from her phone she rotated her hips in an unsuccessful attempt to find comfort in the battered gunmetal chair.

What was her daughter talking about?

"Maybe you should go home and get some sleep," Gracie said. "I can stay with him for a while."

"Sleep's overrated." She yawned, and her eyes caught the old Baltimore Orioles baseball pennant hanging over the hospital bed. *Orioles logo . . . whiskey glass . . . white pills . . .* Her dream flashed before her eyes.

"You okay?" Gracie asked.

White pills . . . She gasped. Oh my God. She could not, she *would* not permit her mind to visit that awful place ever again.

Gracie pressed. "Laura?"

"Yes, yes, I'm fine."

Her aunt responded with a skeptical expression, then hoisted a pink tote bag to her lap. Short and wiry in stature, Gracie colored her hair red and wore it below her shoulders in a wavy style more suited to a young starlet from the forties than a woman of seventy. A Kurt Vonnegut quote in green script decorated the side of her bag: *"Tis better to have loved and lust, than to let our apparatus rust."* Laura shook her head and took a deep breath. The thick, stifling hospital air smelled of must, of decay. Of death.

For the millionth time she wondered why God would spare the evil people of the world—serial killers and terrorists and child molesters—while the good man lying next to her faced certain death?

Mickey moaned again. Eight months earlier he'd been diagnosed with "distant" esophageal cancer, meaning the cancer had spread away from the tumor to his lymph nodes and organs. The cancer had been hiding there for some time, undetected, slowly eating away, bite by tiny bite.

At first it had been hard to think the words—*my husband's dying*— much less say them. Now, after witnessing him wither away for the past many months, the vocabulary of death came easily. Hope arrived early but departed long ago leaving her with the heartbreak of seeing the man she loved suffer the quiet torture of a lingering death.

Mickey's treatment plan combined palliative care along with active treatment, but the pain medication never seemed to be enough. When she begged for more, the doctors furrowed their brows and explained how they were limited by dosage protocols. What BS. She'd considered transferring Mickey out of Annapolis General to a hospice facility, but Delaware offered the closest available bed, and in-home hospice care couldn't provide the constant attention he required.

For the last few weeks Mickey had been begging her to end his life. She, of course, wouldn't hear of such a thing. Lately, however, the dreams had come. The Chivas Regal and the white pills in the Orioles glass. She loved him so much, and it broke her heart to see him suffer. But she wouldn't do it. Laura Beckman followed the rules, and the rules were pretty clear that a wife should not murder her husband.

Brooke pulled a hip flask from her back pocket.

Laura lowered her voice to a harsh whisper. "What do you think you're doing? This is a hospital, and your father's lying here barely alive."

Brooke ignored her, took a drink, then passed the flask to Gracie. After raising it toward Mickey in a silent toast, Gracie helped herself to a healthy swallow.

Laura closed her eyes and tried to control her emotions. She didn't need this stress, not now. She heard a gurgle from the bed. Mickey's eyes fluttered. She stood quickly. "I'm right here."

He tried to talk, but with the breathing tube obstructing his airway the sound blurred to a ragged rasp. Mickey attempted a weak smile, then his eyes found Laura. He lifted a corner of the blanket and made dabbing motions in the air.

"What's he doing?" Brooke asked.

Laura smiled to herself, and her mind drifted back almost thirty years . . .

At the beginning of the second semester, Laura, like almost all of the students at Bollen except for maybe the nerdy engineering majors, tried to schedule her classes so Friday afternoons were clear. An early December snow dump left no uncertainty about how that afternoon would be spent. She, her best friend, Megan, and three other girls strapped their skis and snowboards on top of Megan's old blue Ford Explorer, and they drove north to Massanutten for a few hours of night skiing.

On the first run down Rebel Yell Laura caught an edge and twisted her ankle. Despite Laura's strong opposition, Megan decided to remain with her at the lodge bar while the others skied. The crowded bar made maneuvering between tables difficult. Laura had taped an ice bag around her ankle and propped it up on a chair while she and Megan enjoyed their hot-buttered rums.

A good-looking guy with thick, curly black hair and soft brown eyes attempted to squeeze by. Someone bumped him from behind, and he spilled beer down the front of Laura's sweater.

"Sorry." He grabbed a handful of napkins from the dispenser and attempted to blot the beer from her sweater. A moment later, he realized he was dabbing her breasts and froze. "Sorry. I'll be happy to pay for the cleaning." Their eyes locked, and the attraction was instant. "How about you let me buy you ladies another round?"

Laura smiled. "Only if you promise to keep your hands to yourself."

He offered a goofy grin, and held up his pinky finger. "Pinky swear." After letting him twist in the wind for a few moments, she laughed and hooked her pinky finger into his. At that very moment he was bumped again, and this time spilled beer down the front of his ski jacket. Laura pulled more napkins from the dispenser and dabbed the beer from his jacket.

Megan laughed. "You two are the Dabbers."

Laura rode back to college with him, and they became inseparable. From then on, throughout their dating and married life, before going to sleep each night they'd hook pinkies and say, "Love you, Dabber." One of those private little moments in a marriage that only has meaning to the husband and wife, something anyone else would consider plain silly . . .

Laura reached over and stroked her husband's hand. Almost all of the flesh had been replaced by scabs from the IVs. She hooked pinkies with him, then peered deeply into his eyes and whispered so only he could hear. "Love you, Dabber." He nodded and slipped back into a restless sleep.

Brooke headed for the door. "I need a cigarette."

"Great idea, your lungs will love it."

Brooke ignored her and walked out.

Laura sighed and settled back down. Truth be told, she felt relieved without Brooke in the room. Her daughter created tension, and that was the last thing Laura needed now. Her life had been defined by stress since Mickey's diagnosis. Seemed like years ago, not months. Second opinions and third opinions and tests and treatments and, in the end, the inevitability. She lightly rubbed her husband's arm and wondered where all the time had gone. They'd married young, both still in college, and their life together had been good. Not great she supposed, but good. More than good. The few bumps along the way had mostly been caused by their rebellious eldest daughter.

"If I say up, she says down. If I say, black, she says, white," Laura mumbled. "Why does Brooke have to be so damn headstrong?"

"Sounds like her mother," Gracie said. Before Laura could respond, Gracie stood and announced, "I'm going for a walk down the hall, check out the scenery. There's nothing more sexy than a man in white coat with a stethoscope around his neck. You take the ugliest man in the world and put him in a white coat, and I'm telling you—"

"Go. And don't be surprised if those men in white coats take you away in a tight white jacket."

In a moment she was out the door.

Mickey's eyes opened again and found Laura. He made a writing motion with his hand. Laura grabbed the note pad and pen from the table and set the pad in front of him. She flipped through the pages where he'd already written until she found a clean page. She placed the cheap Bic pen in his right hand and wrapped his fingers around it. The ridges made it easier for him to grip with the IV stuck into the back of his hand. He wrote the word, "please," in half cursive, half print. The handwriting of a young child.

Mickey locked eyes with his wife, then jerked his head toward the wall next to the bed. Laura's eyes followed his gesture to the control panel for the ventilator equipment barely keeping him alive.

Laura studied the panel as she'd done countless times. Several switches, including the one controlling power to the machines. *The Magic Switch.* One flick of that . . .

"You know I can't, sweetie." She stroked his head. The baldness still felt strange. Over the past weeks and months she'd watched his hair fall out and his skin change from a healthy tan to a pale, almost translucent parchment.

Mickey's hand struggled to form an image on the paper pad, a crude heart that more resembled a lima bean.

"It's lovely, Honey."

The thick plastic tubes turned his attempted smile into a snarl. He convulsed and emitted a ragged cry that ripped across Laura's heart. Mickey's eyes pleaded with her. He flipped the tablet back and forth in frustration. Laura didn't need to be reminded what had been written all over the previous pages—the single word, "please."

Desperate, Laura's gaze returned to the ventilator's control panel and noticed the manufacturer's identification plate. RxTron, Eden Prairie, Minnesota. Eden Prairie. Sounded so peaceful. *Flip the Magic Switch, and you'll float away to Eden.*

Mickey's beseeching eyes locked with hers. He took the blanket corner again and made dabbing motions in the air, these much more rapid than before.

She gasped and bit her lip to stem the tears.

She couldn't do it.

CHAPTER TWO

August

Laura walked Anna down the front porch steps to the Uber car waiting at the curb.

"Sure you have to go so soon, baby?"

Taller than both Laura and Brooke, Anna was the apple of her mother's eye. Over the years Laura's friends at the club had watched Anna grow up and excel—she'd been junior club tennis champion three years running—and Laura took great pleasure showing off her younger daughter whenever the girl returned home to visit.

At twenty-six, two years younger than Brooke, Anna's light coloring drew from Laura's side of the family while her older sister's dark complexion, dark hair, delicate features, and slim build took after Mickey. He always said Anna's warm smile could melt an iceberg, and Laura loved it when strangers assumed she and her beautiful daughter were sisters. Not bad for a woman in her mid-forties. Well, technically late forties, but her friend Helen advised that any woman who hadn't yet reach fifty could still be considered in her mid-forties.

Anna tilted her head toward the handsome, sandy haired young man waiting in the back seat. "Sorry, but Brandon and I have to be at work tomorrow morning."

Brandon worked for the same Chicago financial consulting firm as Anna, and was the first male her daughter had brought home since high school. Laura thought, maybe this is the one.

Anna wrapped her mother in a tight embrace, and Laura had to bite her lip to stem the tears. "You gave an amazing eulogy," Laura whispered. "Everyone said so. Your father would've been so proud."

"I'll call every night, Mom. Promise." Anna gently pulled away. "And don't be too hard on Brooke. People grieve in different ways." She waved to everyone on the porch, then entered the backseat next to her man. A moment later the car drove off, heading north to the airport in plenty of time for Anna and Brandon to make the seven o'clock flight back to Chicago.

Laura climbed back up the stairs to the small group gathered on her wide porch. After the funeral service the official reception took place in the Chesapeake Country Club's richly appointed Blue Heron Ballroom. The place had been packed. No surprise given the many friends she and Mickey had made over the years. Afterwards, a few of Laura's closest friends and relatives joined her back at the house on Eastgate, and the last couple of hours had been spent reminiscing about Mickey in a less formal setting. Now, most everyone sensed it was time to go.

The McGinty twins stood and each opened her arms for a good-bye hug. Alicia and Helen were very close friends who, along with Laura, had effectively run the club's Ladies Association for years.

"Again, so sorry, dear," Helen said.

"How are you holding up?" Alicia asked.

"Not too bad under the circumstances, but I'm really going to miss him." This was the same response Laura had offered repeatedly to the line of guests at the reception. While sincere, she'd said the words so often they came out more rote than she intended.

Helen said, "And don't worry about Brooke's little incident at the reception. Everyone in the Association knows you've done your best, and I'm sure there will be no adverse repercussions."

Images from just a few hours earlier flashed through Laura's brain—her inebriated daughter stumbling into the buffet table knocking over the candles, the tablecloth catching fire, the smoke alarm blaring, the guests screaming, the bartender lifting a huge cut glass serving bowl and dumping fruit salad on the flames, Brooke curled up on the floor in a pile of melon balls sobbing her eyes out. The suffocating embarrassment layered on top of her near debilitating grief over the loss of Mickey had been almost too much to bear.

Alicia patted Laura's hand. "Absolutely no repercussions at all. We understand."

"Thank you."

Helen lowered her voice. "Listen, Laura, now's not the time, but when you're ready we do need to call a meeting of the Symphony Ball Committee."

Laura was mildly surprised her friends would bring up club matters now. They probably wanted to distract her from her grief for a few moments. "Of course. Soon as things settle down."

"Unless you don't feel up to handling the responsibilities of the chair, given the circumstances," Alicia added with an expression of exaggerated concern.

"No, no. The chair duties will help take my mind off things." She'd been vying for committee chair over the last two years, and she certainly had no intention to step down now.

Alicia's face brightened. "Actually, I had a great idea for a theme. Garden of Eden. What do you think? I'm seeing mango colored table linens and—"

"For God's sake, Alicia," Helen scolded. "Now is not the time."

Garden of Eden. The magic switch.

Suitably chastised, Alicia walked quickly down the porch stairs to their car with Helen trailing close behind.

Gracie mumbled in a voice everyone else on the porch could hear. "Idiots."

The late afternoon shadows on Eastgate Avenue had substantially lengthened. Everyone had left except Gracie, Mickey's older sister, Nora, and family friend Everett Tisdale. Laura still wore her black dress despite Nora begging her to change clothes, even to the point of suggesting Mickey would've wanted Laura to be comfortable. Nora may have been right, but what would anyone passing by think if they saw her lounging around in jeans and a T-shirt?

Laura couldn't really reminisce about her husband at the funeral or reception. Even during the more intimate front porch gathering she'd deferred to others who wanted to share their memories of Mickey Beckman. Gliding idly back and forth on the slatted wooden swing in the company of Gracie, Nora, and Everett, she finally had the opportunity to spend the last couple of hours talking uninterrupted about Mickey recounting a seemingly endless string of "remember when's." Part of her feared if she failed to list each event in their life together, the big stuff and the little stuff, that omitted piece of him would somehow be lost forever.

Finally, she'd talked herself out.

The rhythm of the swing and the warm summer air seasoned with the sweet fragrance of her backyard tea roses had a calming, even hypnotic effect. From her vantage point she could see almost halfway down Eastgate Avenue. The tall leafy oaks and tulip poplars lining each side created a broad green canopy across most of the street. Tiny irregular specks of late afternoon sunlight filtering through the swaying leaves mesmerized her as they danced and darted up and down and around the shadowy pavement. How she loved this street, how she loved this house.

She and Mickey moved to Eastgate when the girls were young. She'd entertained in their huge backyard on numerous occasions, and word of a function at the Beckmans spread quickly throughout the club. Everyone kissed up to her for an invite, and Laura liked that, she liked it a lot. The street had changed little in the past two decades and continued to offer its residents a reassuring stability. Laura prized few things in life more than stability.

The screen door squeaked open, and Everett Tisdale emerged from the house carrying a tray of drinks along with a small platter of homemade chocolate fudge cookies. Ten years older than Mickey, Everett had been a friend of the family for decades. A small, nervous, whippet of a man, he'd lost his wife a few years earlier. Everett wore round, rimless glasses that kept slipping down his nose. He'd recently taken to dying his hair coal black and combing it over his bald head with styling glop smelling of burnt taffy.

"Sure as hell's about time," Gracie said.

"I'm moving as fast as I can."

"You didn't put water in it, did you?" Gracie asked.

"No water. Wild Turkey on the rocks." He handed her the bourbon and passed fresh glasses of iced tea to Nora and Laura.

Nora selected a cookie. "Chocolate's my only guilty pleasure. Always makes me feel decadent." She took a bite. "Delicious, Laura."

"Anna made them," Laura said. "Old family recipe."

Everett set the tray on a small table, then headed toward the glider, only to see his path blocked by Elvis, a big, fat, long-haired, gray and white lump. The moment Everett stepped over the dog Elvis shifted in his sleep, tripping Everett into Laura. Reflexively, she reached out to fend him off, but Everett folded inside her arms, almost as if his loss of balance had been choreographed.

"Oh, so sorry." Everett slowly extricated himself.

"That's all right," Laura said. "I trip over Elvis at least once a day myself."

Everett sat on the two-person glider next to Laura, crowding so close that a third easily could have joined them.

"I thought the club did a fine job, an excellent tribute to my brother," Nora said.

Nora's father remarried a younger woman late in life, and Mickey had been a pleasant surprise. During his formative years, Nora, over thirty years his senior, acted more like a mother than a big sister.

"Except for the end," Gracie said.

Nora sighed. "Poor child."

"Poor child, my butt," Laura said, "Her behavior was an unmitigated disaster, and to have all my friends witness the spectacle." She closed her eyes. "It'll be all over the club by morning."

"You can't allow yourself to become worked up, dear," Nora said. "And deep down you know she loves you."

We're off to find the morning glories . . .

Laura's eyes widened, and a chill washed over her. *Why did that stupid song pop into her head? Must be due to the stress.*

She took a deep breath. Nora was right. Hardly the first time. For years Nora had assumed the role of family peacemaker, and Laura felt very fond of the woman. Tall and gangly as a young woman, Nora's age and her past battles with cancer caused a permanent stoop, and her once thick silver hair had dulled. But her Wedgewood blue eyes continued to reflect an intelligence and engagement in the world around her that belied her fragile physical condition.

"Nora's correct," Laura said. "I can't allow myself to stress out. Besides, Helen and Alicia said there would be no repercussions."

"Who gives a damn what those snooty country club bitches think?" Gracie said.

"They're my friends."

"They're all empty bra-slips if you ask me."

"I don't immediately recall asking you."

Nora said, "We should be concentrating on how to help Brooke."

"She's beyond help," Laura said, "and she's been beyond help since . . . you know."

"That was a long time ago."

Laura sighed. "I'm sure it's mostly my fault. When she was born I knew absolutely nothing about parenting."

"Nobody knows crap about parenting," Gracie said. "Seventy-three percent of children born to child psychologists are on Ritalin."

"You just made that up."

"Maybe I did and maybe I didn't."

"Tom hasn't remarried," Nora said, changing the subject. "Maybe someday he and Brooke can reconcile. I'm sure Jennie would love having her mother and father back together."

Laura huffed. "Never happen."

For a few moments no one spoke, each withdrawing into his or her own thoughts. Laura watched a landscaping truck drive by. A few houses down a couple of boys tossed a football back and forth in the front yard. On the other side of the street a mean little dog strained at his leash, dragging Laura's reclusive neighbor down the sidewalk. A normal late summer day on Eastgate Avenue. Except, of course, the day was anything but normal.

Laura took a sip of her tea and closed her eyes. Her mind drifted back over the last months. She'd never really thought much about death. She'd been a young adult when both of her parents died within a year of each other. They were less than fifteen years older than she was now. When she mentioned her thoughts to her friends at the club, as expected, they brushed her off with assurances that today things were different. She enjoyed excellent health, there'd been great medical advancements, blah blah blah.

But watching Mickey die brought it all home. Great medical advancements hadn't helped him, they'd only prolonged his death. Mickey knew he wasn't going to recover. He accepted his death and wanted to leave this world on his own terms, but the doctors wouldn't help that happen. Eight states had legalized doctor-assisted suicide—she'd checked it out online—but Maryland wasn't one of them. Weren't slow torture and humiliation outlawed by the Geneva Convention?

She opened her eyes and sat up straight. "I need to ask a big favor."

Nora said, "Of course, dear."

"Anything," Gracie said.

Everett inched even closer to Laura on the glider. "You know I'm here for you."

Laura hesitated only for a moment. "I don't want to go like Mickey."

"Inhumane," Nora agreed.

"My Janie, she had a living will," Everett said, "but it only works if the doctors agree death is imminent."

"Imminent should be when we say it is," Gracie said.

"I'm not sure you understand," Laura said. "When I say I'm ready, you've got to help me go. On my terms."

"Ditto for me," Nora added.

Everett held up his glass of iced tea. "A pact." Everyone clinked their glasses, then drank.

Nora eyed Laura with concern. "You look tired. Maybe you should get some rest."

"Do you want me to stay with you tonight?" Gracie asked.

"No, no. I'll be fine."

But of course she knew she wasn't fine, and she wondered if she'd ever be fine again.

CHAPTER THREE

Laura slipped on the garish purple nightgown Mickey gave her for Valentine's Day a few years back—it had been his favorite—and crawled into her side of their king-size bed. Mickey was finally gone. Toward the end she'd actually found herself talking to the cancer cells invading her husband's body, begging them to hurry the heck up.

Over the last few days the controlled chaos—Anna arriving, friends streaming through laden with food, service arrangements, reminiscing—left little time to dwell on the finality of Mickey's death. During his lengthy hospital stay she believed she'd become used to his absence, but tonight felt different. The house somehow seemed more barren, more empty. Her eyes watered and she bit her lip. No more tears. She needed sleep. She rolled over facing Mickey's side and closed her eyes.

The tears came anyway.

An hour later she lay on her back, staring at the ceiling, unable to sleep. For the umpteenth time her head lolled to the left. Mickey's side. As long as they'd been married, Mickey always slept on the left. The neatly made brocade cotton spread appeared stark and vast, a white plain extending away from her to a distant horizon. She pulled back the spread and slowly ran her fingers over the sheet. It felt cold, hard, like a smooth white slab of marble.

Maybe reading would make her drowsy. She rolled back and turned on the lamp, then selected a travel magazine from the short pile stacked on her bedside table. After several articles failed to hold her interest, she gave up and thumbed through the pages quickly focusing on the photos. She was about to flip a page when her eyes caught an ad seeking contributions to the National Make-a-Wish Foundation. Laura always thought highly of the Foundation's efforts to help dying children fulfill a last wish. She resolved to send a check tomorrow.

She tried another magazine, this one about gardening, but couldn't concentrate. She grabbed theTV remote. Mind-numbing, she needed mind-numbing. After surfing through a bunch of channels she landed on a local cable station broadcasting a program describing Annapolis life in the Fifties and Sixties using old photos and home movies contributed by long-time residents. After only a minute or two a commercial for a local marina interrupted the programming. Some bozo and a blonde bimbo spilling out of her bikini stood in front of a sailboat and sang, *"Don't be sassy, Boat at Massey, Massey Mareeenahs!"* Who writes this stuff? She tapped the off button, turned out the light, rolled onto her side, and scrunched her head deep into the pillow.

But try as she might, sleep still wouldn't come.

An image of Megan Foster filled her head. Her body snapped tight.

Laura, are you sure . . . ?

It'll be fun . . .

Oh, my God. Why now?

C'mon, Megs, try it . . . Try the damn grape punch . . ."

Every nerve in her body burned like a lit fuse. *Why now?* She fumbled through the blanket folds until she found the remote and quickly turned on the TV again. She needed to fill her brain with something else, *anything else*. She could not permit her mind to drift back to that night.

The local channel still aired the retrospective of Annapolis. The screen showed a grainy home movie from the Sixties, giggly girls crowding to enter the Circle Theater where the Beatles' "Hard Day's Night" played.

Home movies.

She hadn't seen those old family tapes for years. She rolled her feet to the floor, flicked the light back on, and shuffled into the closet. In the corner she found the tapes inside a rumpled cardboard box. Most of the recording had been done on eight-millimeter, but some time back Mickey had converted many to DVDs.

She pulled one out and saw they weren't marked. A year earlier Mickey said he needed to catalogue them "one of these days." Keep putting something off long enough, and you'll eventually avoid having to do it because you'll be dead.

She popped the disk into the old DVD player, crawled back into bed, and hit the play button on the remote. The colors of the grainy images converted from the original eight-millimeter film had faded to dusty pastels. But she couldn't take her eyes off the screen—a montage of clips taken from different times in their lives.

The tapes were out of order, but this one showed Mickey standing in front of his furniture store. Must've been shortly after it opened. So young and handsome and full of life. Mickey pointed proudly to the sign above the storefront. The camera operator—was it Everett?—panned too quickly and the image was momentarily blurred before it focused on the newly painted sign. A voice off-camera said, "At least they got the spelling right." It was Everett. The camera panned back to Mickey. "Wave," ordered Everett. Mickey complied, waving like a homecoming queen. Where was I? Laura wondered.

The next clips covered other snatches of life with the Beckmans over the years, although it gradually dawned on Laura that she was absent from most all of them.

The image jumped to the next clip. *There I am.* On the screen, Laura and Mickey, dressed in formal attire, walked up the grand stairway to the club entrance. "The king and queen of the Spring Fling," Everett's voice announced. He was getting better with the camera.

In the next clip, Brooke wore an Orioles jersey. She must've been about ten. Laura smiled, remembering the argument she'd had with Mickey about naming their baby daughter. He wanted a boy and planned to name him Brooks Robinson Beckman after his boyhood hero, the Orioles Hall of Fame third baseman. They'd decided not to learn the baby's sex in advance, but both had a feeling it would be a boy.

When she'd given birth to a girl, Mickey quickly purchased a baby name book from the hospital gift shop and learned that by adding an "e," Brooke was a perfectly suitable girl's name. Laura resisted, preferring to call the baby Anna after her mother, but in the end Mickey prevailed. When the second child arrived there was no argument, and they both welcomed Anna Holly Beckman to the family.

The footage showed Mickey and Brooke outside the baseball stadium, part of the crowd streaming in for the game. "Who's going to win today?" Everett's voice elevated over the crowd noise. "The O's!" Mickey and Brooke shouted back in unison. "Brooke, are you ready to run the bases before the game?" asked Everett.

"Ten and under and I'm ten!" she responded with glee.

"Wish I were ten so I could run the bases," Mickey added. His voice was soft, and there was a wistful look in his eyes.

"It's Kids' Fantasy Day, and you, sir, are no kid," chimed in Everett. Mickey gave the finger to the cameraman. Everett laughed. "I'm recording that."

"What's that mean, Daddy?" asked Brooke innocently.

"Means the O's are number one." Heavy laughter from Mickey and Everett. A second later Brooke flashed the finger. Mickey doubled over in laughter. Oh, that man could laugh.

Laura couldn't take her eyes off Brooke—so happy, so full of life. A small slice of her heart ached for a reconciliation with her daughter, her firstborn, but she hadn't reached the point yet where she could forgive Brooke for what she'd done to Jennie, to Tom, to all of them. Maybe someday.

The tape ended and Laura considered putting in another but decided she would do that tomorrow night. She clicked off the TV. As she reached to turn out the light her gaze fell upon Mickey's notepad from the hospital. She kept it beside her bed. It was silly, she supposed, but those were the last communications from her husband, and she couldn't bear to throw it away. At least not now.

She picked up the tablet and it flipped opened to the last page where Mickey had drawn the lima bean heart. Laura's eyes glistened as she slowly traced the heart with her finger. "My darling." She kissed the heart, his last written message to her. "I love you, too, Dabber, and I miss you so much." She slowly replaced the tablet but it slipped to the floor. When she retrieved it, the tablet opened to the page where Mickey had written the crude "O." She stared at the "O" for a few seconds, then slid the tablet over to Mickey's side of the bed.

"Who's going to win today?"

"The O's!"

"Ten and under and I'm ten!"

"Wish I were ten so I could run the bases."

Wish I were ten . . .

She hesitated. She had a thought. A crazy crazy thought.

Wish I were ten . . .

Was she out of her mind? Maybe.

She reached for the phone and dialed quickly. After five rings Gracie answered with a "Hello" that was so slurred with sleep, Laura was worried she wouldn't make it to the end of the word.

"It's me."

"Do you know what time it is?"

"Of course I know what time it is." She paused and traced her finger around the lima bean heart.

"Listen, there's one last thing I need to do for Mickey, and I need your help."

CHAPTER FOUR

September

The nighttime crowd at the Slippery Clam consisted almost exclusively of blue-collar locals. Tucked between a marine hardware store and a rooming house, the Clam's location on King George Street was off the beaten path, away from the bustling, tourist infested Annapolis harbor area. A heavy oak bar ran the length of the space. Scratched and battered by time and rough men, the bar faced a string of cheap tables alternating with a few booths lined up along a chipped burgundy wall sorely in need of paint. Faded black and white photos of working boats and working men hung over the tables. Several years back, a stray tourist had recommended putting a ficus plant near the front door. Mike, the owner, threw the guy out, making clear there would be "no fuggin' ferns and fans in the Clam. Ever."

Brooke had been bartending at the Clam for a while now. She'd tried office work, even lasted almost eight months as a receptionist for a dental group, but the nine-to-five life wasn't for her. Never had been. Her dad had repeatedly offered her a job at the furniture store, but she declined. She knew she'd be subjected to daily harassment from her mother about how she couldn't measure up. She liked the Clam. Mike always treated her fairly, and that was all she could ask.

Her regulars consisted mostly of watermen, commercial crabbers, oystermen, charter captains, and others who made their living from the bay just as their ancestors had done for centuries before them. They formed the last front of resistance against the invasion of t-shirt shops and fudge companies and stores with names like Old Navy and Banana Republic. Her customers treated her like a sister or daughter. In many ways they'd become her family.

Linda Taylor, the singer booked for the last three months, took a break and found a seat at the end of the bar. "I want you to come up for the next set."

Brooke mixed Gossling dark rum and ginger beer in a tall glass of ice and set the "dark and stormy" in front of Linda. "Not sure I'm in the mood."

"Come on, you know you have a great voice. Your customers will love it."

Yeah, Brooke knew she had a good voice, but it was her voice, or more accurately her delusions of generating fame and riches from her voice, that ruined her life. She once had it all. A handsome, caring husband, an up and coming lawyer destined for success who adored her. And Jennifer, her pride and joy. Yet she pissed it all away over an impossible dream that, she now knew, even if it had come true would've made her much worse off in the long run.

"I'm serious," Linda said as she drained half her glass. "You could've made a decent living doing this."

"Been there, been done in by that."

"Don't be so hard on yourself. Everybody screws up. It's in the human genome."

Brooke wasn't exactly sure what a genome was, but she was quite certain she'd screwed up big-time. While Linda checked her phone for messages, Brooke's thoughts wandered back to that time many years earlier. It wasn't that she'd disliked the role of loving wife and mother, but she'd felt she needed something more. She wanted to prove she had an identity of her own, not only as the daughter of

Laura and Mickey Beckman, not only as Anna Beckman's big sister or the wife of Thomas Marshall, but her *own* identity—that of a famous singer. A *star*. She shook her head. What could be more trite than the poor woman trapped in her marriage, yearning for her own identity? Pathetic.

Brooke drew a couple of beers from the tap and set them in front of two grizzled watermen, then lit a cigarette. Most of the patrons smoked, and thankfully the anti-smoking police hadn't found them yet.

Linda turned off her phone. "You ever think about going back to it full-time?"

"No way."

"I'm serious," Linda pressed. "It's not only your voice. A lot of people have good voices. And a lot of people have pain. But only a few can sing their pain."

"Is it that obvious?"

Linda laughed. "Honey, I could listen to you singing the 'Hallelujah Chorus' and I'd know you've had troubles, probably man troubles."

Brooke drew the soothing smoke into her lungs, then nodded. "Nail."

"Nail?"

"We're talking a long time ago."

"So what happened?"

Brooke hesitated. She liked Linda and they got along well, but they were hardly close. "Maybe another time."

Linda finished her drink, squeezed Brooke's shoulder, and returned to the stage. Brooke poured herself a beer. Most owners had strict rules about bartenders drinking on the job, but Mike was understanding, and all this reminiscing . . . She lifted the glass . . . and froze. Booze was not her friend. When she'd first returned from

the West Coast her dad twisted some arms to force a few attempts
at reconciliation with Jennie and Laura, but the advanced pressure
made her drink, and the meetings had always ended badly. *So what
happened?* Linda's question had unearthed a basket of memories
and regrets. Like zombies rising from the grave they stalked her,
and no matter how hard she tried they couldn't be destroyed.

First one hand, then the other completely encircled the beer
glass. She squeezed as hard as she could, strangling the monsters.
Her knuckles whitened, but the zombies kept coming. She emitted
a tiny gasp, then dumped the beer into the sink.

Linda started her set with the old Kris Kristofferson tune, "Me
and Bobby McGee," made famous by Janis Joplin back in the sixties.
The song had become an anthem of sorts for those who found that
the call of the road never quite measured up to the dream.

Brooke stared at the remnants of the beer froth slowly disap-
pearing down the drain. Her daddy was dead. Who knew how her
mother would react over time? She'd probably bury herself even
deeper in her club activities and volunteer work, continuing to
project the smiling, vivacious image everyone had come to expect.
Tall, blonde, blue eyes, skin tanned from days on the tennis courts,
the attractive woman whose photo regularly graced the local society
pages.

Yes, to the outside world Laura Beckman would continue as
before. But what would her mother be feeling now, alone in the
house and away from the public glare? Brooke honestly didn't know
the answer. Could her father's death bring mother and daughter
closer together? No. Too much time had passed, too many doors
now locked from both sides for Laura to re-kindle a relationship
with her daughter. Well, re-kindle was the wrong word; it assumed
the relationship had been kindled in the first place.

At the end of the song, Linda pointed to Brooke. "There's a beautiful woman with a beautiful voice standing over there, and with a little encouragement, I'm sure we can get her up here."

The applause was louder than Brooke expected. Oh, why the hell not? She strolled over to the tiny stage and joined Linda at the microphone. As Linda strummed her acoustic, Brooke accompanied her in the Bonnie Raitt classic, "Love Sneakin' Up on You." Brooke heard her own voice meld with Linda's and liked the sound. Judging from the rapt expressions on the faces of the customers, they did, too.

Then Brooke closed her eyes and detached from the audience and even from Linda. For a few precious moments she lost herself in the music and found an elusive peace.

CHAPTER FIVE

Laura surveyed the crowd at Camden Yards. "I don't think there's an empty seat."

"That's because they're playing the Yankees," Gracie said.

"How do you know that?"

"I know lots of stuff you don't know I know."

Bright orange official Orioles rain jackets heavily dotted the crowd due to the cool temperatures and a forecast for light showers.

Laura, Nora, Everett, and Gracie sat in Mickey's seats, seven rows up from the rail along the first base line. Laura had intended to sell the seats when Mickey became ill, another item on the list of things she hadn't gotten around to yet.

Laura remembered when Mickey dragged her to a game shortly after they were married. An image of him dressed in orange and black, eyes bright with excitement, alternatively watching the players warm up and studiously examining the lineup card, flashed in her mind. So much energy. So much life. She took a deep breath and murmured to herself, "Love you, Dabber."

She'd tried to enjoy the experience for his sake, but remembered finding the game oppressively boring. Not to mention the occasional outbursts of profanity from the fans, including the women. Since graduating from college, Laura had never used the F-word. Not even on the golf course where, she'd been advised, God granted special dispensation. After that initial experience at the ballpark, she'd always begged off.

The rain held, and most of the fans had removed their orange rain jackets. But Laura kept Mickey's jacket zipped tight over a slight bulge in the front of her jeans. Everett sipped from a giant white plastic soda cup bearing the Orioles bird logo. She held his gaze and nodded. He dumped the few remaining ice cubes from the cup onto the concrete at his feet, then ran a napkin around the inside of the cup to dry it.

She tried to calm her nerves and concentrate on what lay ahead, but some yahoo sitting behind her with his granddaughter blared a radio in her ear. She needed to concentrate. Timing was important. Gracie suggested waiting for the end of an inning when the play-ers—*Auggh!* The jerk just increased the volume. She turned back to the offender. He seemed vaguely familiar.

"Pardon me, sir, but would you consider reducing the volume on that thing?"

"I forgot my earbuds, lady," he responded. "And I need to hear the play-by-play."

Laura had the uncomfortable feeling this insufferable man was checking out her chest like an adolescent schoolboy. She instinctively crossed her arms. He had dark, thinning hair, green eyes, and a stupid rakish grin.

"Is this better?" His voice sounded like sand mixed with syrup. He turned the volume knob up as loud as it would go, then quickly lowered it. "Ooops." The man and his friends laughed uproariously.

"I'm hesitant to embarrass you in front of your granddaughter," Laura said, "but I find your behavior—"

"Granddaughter? Hey, Kelli, she thinks you're my granddaughter."

He took a deep swig of beer that dribbled down his mouth, then planted a big sloppy kiss on the girl.

"God help us," Laura whispered.

Everett stood up and puffed out his chest. "Sir, I find your behavior reprehensible."

"I couldn't agree more, buddy. I find my behavior reprehensible, too!"

Kelli giggled. "Oh Arlo, you're so funny. You should be on TV."

"I *am* on TV! Right Sam?" The three of them laughed again.

Everett whispered to Laura, "Maybe this wasn't such a great idea."

Kelli laid another long, sloppy kiss on Arlo. He pulled off his orange Orioles jacket and dropped it to the concrete floor. "Getting hot, and it ain't the weather. You're giving me a woodie, baby."

Laura was aghast.

"Oh, my," Nora said, blushing at the display.

Laura whispered to her friends, "If I don't do it now . . ." They nodded their agreement.

Wide-eyed with fear, she unzipped her jacket, then her jeans. She could hear the surprise in Arlo's voice behind her.

"What . . .?"

She could feel him peering over her shoulder as she reached inside her clothing and removed a freezer bag that had flattened to the contours of her body.

Everett handed her the giant plastic Orioles cup. She opened the bag and, with her hands shaking, tried to pour the contents into the cup, but Mickey's over sized jacket, flapping back and forth in the breeze, interfered with her attempt. In frustration, she handed the bag and cup to Gracie, pulled off her jacket and tossed it over the seat.

"What the hell you doing, lady?" Arlo asked. "What's in that bag?"

Laura ignored him. She quickly zipped up her jeans, then with Gracie's help finished depositing the bag's contents into the cup.

"What about the guard?" Nora whispered, pointing to the security man at the bottom of the steps. A metal railing and a concrete wall with a drop of about five feet separated the first row of box seats from the playing field. A security guard stood at the bottom of the steps of each aisle to prevent exuberant fans from running onto the field.

"We need a distraction," Gracie said.

Before Laura could respond, Gracie stood up, turned back to Arlo, and screamed, "Take your hands off me!"

"What the hell you talkin' about you old biddy?"

Gracie raised her voice even higher. "And what are you doing with that poor, innocent little underage girl?"

"She ain't underage, she's twenty-four."

"Nineteen," Kelli corrected him.

"Nineteen?"

"My birthday was three weeks ago. Remember, you gave me that special adult birthday present?" She winked at him.

He turned back to Gracie. "She's over eighteen and she sure ain't innocent."

The security guard came up the steps to investigate. "What seems to be the problem here?"

Gracie turned on the tear spigot and pointed an accusing finger at Arlo. "This—this *hooligan* tried to squeeze my bosoms."

"That's ridiculous," Arlo said.

Gracie turned to the guard. "I'm sure if you check you'll see he's a registered sex offender." She elbowed Laura in the ribs.

Without the guard noticing Laura rushed down the aisle carrying the cup to the railing.

A loud crack pierced the night air. Arlo, the security guard, and every fan in the stands stood in unison and watched the ball fly off the bat of Orioles first baseman Crush Cameron. The field lights illuminated the white ball against the night sky as it soared toward the short right field fence.

Laura reached the railing and quickly crawled through, then slid down the brick wall. She was on the field.

A crescendo of cheers washed down on Cameron as his ball cleared the fence for a home run.

Laura walked briskly toward the playing field, her heart in her throat.

The security guard finally spotted her. "Hey!"

Laura started jogging toward first base, maybe forty feet away.

The security guard hurried after her. More security personnel ran toward her from other parts of the ballpark.

On the field, Cameron had rounded first base and was heading for second on his home run trot.

Another security guard leaped over the railing and chased Laura as she approached first base with the urn. The Yankee first baseman yelled at Laura. "What the hell you doin', lady?"

Laura struggled to catch her breath. "My husband's last wish." The Yankee paused a moment, then nodded her forward. She touched her foot to the base then, tilting the cup, streamed Mickey's ashes behind her as she jogged toward second, following Cameron.

"Stop!" the security guard shouted.

When the chasing guard reached first base, the Yankee stuck out his foot, sending him sprawling. "Ooops."

The fans cheered Laura as she ran toward second, the ashes trailing her overhead. Hearing the cheers, she became energized and her pace quickened. She held the cup higher. When she reached second, the umpire grabbed her. Forty-four thousand people rained down boos on the ump.

"Please, my late husband always wanted to run the bases and—"

"Sorry," the ump said sympathetically.

Cameron, who was halfway to third, heard Laura's plea. He paused, then jogged back to second. He smiled down at Laura and gently eased the cup from her grip. "Maybe I can help." He turned back toward third and, holding the cup high over his head, jogged to third, then headed for home, streaming Mickey's ashes behind him. The crowd screamed its approval as he hit home plate, then ran out to Laura and returned the now empty cup. "Sorry for your loss."

As security personnel led her off the field, she mouthed a tearful "thank you" to Cameron.

The guards escorted her through the concourse under the stands. "What you did constituted criminal trespass and I'm afraid we have to take you to the magistrate," said a guard. Club policy." A group of reporters caught up with her, shouting questions. As she passed fans waiting in line for concessions, they spontaneously cheered and applauded, so she had trouble hearing the reporters' questions.

"I wish Mickey were here himself," she said to no one in particular. "Seems like the only time an adult gets a last wish is in the movies."

Gracie, barely able to contain her excitement, forced her way through the crowd carrying Laura's orange jacket. "You were amazing out there. How are you doing?"

Laura paused for a moment as she considered Gracie's question.

"Actually, I'm doing rather well.

CHAPTER SIX

Arlo Massey awoke feeling his bladder was about to explode. He'd gone, what was it? Only four hours earlier? Must be all the beer he drank at the game. Maybe he'd try to wait a while longer. Used to be he could hold his water as long as it took to drink, sleep, and screw, in rotating order through ten, twelve hours. God, he hated getting old; he was now closer to sixty than fifty. But wasn't sixty supposed to be the new forty? Or was it forty-five? Who the hell knew?

He checked the clock on the table—4:00 a.m.—then glanced over at the sleeping girl lying next to him. Kelli didn't seem to care about his . . . maturity, and having sex with young women made him feel not so old. They were toys, and when he played with them, even for a little while, it took his mind off Jake.

He tried the best he could to slip out of bed without waking the girl. No need to remind her that while more than vigorous in all the ways that counted, he still had a maturing man's bladder.

His shaking foot hit the deck, the boat lurched, and he fell against the small dresser, banging his shin hard.

"Ouch."

Kelli lifted her head, squinted at him, and slurred, "Baby . . .?"

"Sorry, darlin', thought I heard a noise and got up to check it out."

Her mass of tangled bottle-blonde hair plopped back down on the pillow, and she returned to dreamland.

A few hours later, he scrambled up some eggs in a galley cluttered with dirty dishes, empty beer bottles, and surfaces mottled
with various unidentifiable substances. Thumb tacks pinned two
faded photos to a cabinet over the small sink. One showed Arlo
free-falling through the clouds with a goofy smile, giving the photographer the finger. In the other, an eleven-year-old boy guided
a sailboat alone through frothy waves. The photo captured him
grinning as the wind blew his thick, sandy hair back from his face.
Arlo tapped the photo of the boy, and in his daily ritual repeated to
himself the Irish farewell: *May the wind be ever at your back, may
the sun shine warm upon your face. Fair winds and following seas,
son. I love you.*

He glanced out the porthole down river, then returned to whipping the eggs.

Kelli, wearing earbuds attached to her phone, sat at the pull-out
table painting her nails and bobbing her head to the music. He kept
a collection of nail polish bottles in a basket under the sink, leftovers
from female visitors over the years, and the girl had selected yellow
because she said she felt sunny. Good. No need to struggle trying
to carrying on a conversation. She wasn't wearing a stitch and appeared quite comfortable. He would've been naked, too, except he'd
learned the hard way when frying eggs a man needed certain protec-
tion, and he kept a stained chef's apron handy for such occasions.

Kelli was a typical wharf rat—girls who hung around marinas
like groupies looking for a ride. Most understood the price of admission and didn't hesitate to pay. They loved boats and the men
who owned them. More than a few ended up the trophy wife of a
rich old fart with a big boat. Arlo had no intention of making Kelli
or anyone else a wife, trophy or otherwise.

His gaze fell on the orange Orioles rain jacket tossed over the chair next to her. Crazy night.

After they finished eating, Arlo took Kelli up on her offer of a goodbye quickie, then sent her on her way. He dressed and disembarked just as Sam Hacket approached. Sam worked for Arlo as his marina manager and had been instructed the boss wasn't to be disturbed before noon.

They set out on their daily inspection, walking along the ten piers making up the marina. Each pier had a row of both powerboats and sailboats berthed tightly against each other on each side of the walkway.

"Saw the wharfy you were with last night heading over to Cavanaugh's slip," Sam said.

"Cavanaugh could use an upgrade," Arlo said. "That brunette I saw hanging around him yesterday was so ugly she could turn a funeral up an alley." Sam laughed. They both checked the lines of the boats with practiced eyes. A marina had the responsibility to make sure the lines were tight enough to keep the boats from bumping into each other, while leaving enough slack to account for rising and lowering tides. Most owners rarely took their boats out unless it was a new purchase. The old saying was true: the two happiest days of a boater's life were when he bought the vessel and when he sold it. They waved to a few owners out staining teak or otherwise fiddling with this or that, and with a boat there was always plenty of this or that.

"Boy, last night was wild," Sam said. "That woman running around the bases? Have to admit, took balls."

Sam was right. The woman—the driver's license in the pocket of the orange jacket indicated her name was Laura Beckman—did have balls. He couldn't picture Lorraine ever doing something like that. The lovely Lorraine. Up until Jake had come along, by any measure they'd had a good marriage. She managed the marina books while he handled operations. But a problem birthing Jake had resulted in her not being able to have more children. After that she changed, became more moody, withdrawn. He suggested adoption and even offered to pay for a shrink, but she showed no interest. And gradually she showed less and less interest in him. Despite almost daily temptation from the local wharfies, he remained faithful to her. He loved his wife and held out hope that her problems were a hormonal thing, and she would get better.

Then they lost Jake. She rightly blamed him. Soon after that she left. His wife and his son, the two people he loved most in the world, gone.

"Boss? You okay?"

"Yeah, fine."

"So, you want to head down the Corral next Tuesday? It's ladies' night, but then again . . ."

Arlo joined in. "Every night's ladies' night!"

They moved to the next boat, a thirty-five foot Grady White. He glanced up to see a young woman sailing past the marina, alone on the water. She was close enough for him to notice the smile on her face. The familiar image of Jake sailing down the West River toward the Bay filled his mind. Turning, waving . . .

He squeezed his eyes shut, opened them quickly, and took a deep breath. For some reason this time the image took longer to fade away.

He crouched down and tightened the stern line on the Grady.

CHAPTER SEVEN

The sunlight filtering through the lace curtains dappled the round kitchen table with dancing spots of light, creating the impression the weathered oak was somehow alive. Laura didn't notice. She sat, almost frozen, completely uninterested in the cup of coffee resting in front of her. *Did she really do that? In front of all those people? My God.* Her mind clashed into itself. She'd not only violated the law—in and of itself momentous as she'd never even had a parking ticket—but she'd also shattered her own rules of appropriate conduct. And yet . . . *and yet* she found herself feeling guilty for not feeling guilty, not too much anyway.

She sighed. Okay, it happened. It's over. Nothing of the sort would ever happen again. She reached for her cup.

She heard the front door open, and Gracie's voice reached her from the living room even before the door closed.

"Front page!"

Gracie entered the kitchen waving the *Baltimore Sun's* morning edition high in the air. A large photo above the fold showed Laura rounding first base, streaming Mickey's ashes behind her.

Gracie sat down and jabbed her finger at the photo. "Did you see this?"

Laura rose and poured her aunt a cup of coffee. "Of course I saw it. My copy of the paper's sitting right there in front of you."

"How does it feel being a celebrity?"

"I'm not a celebrity, and I don't want to be a celebrity."

As if on cue her phone dinged, and she checked the text. Anna: *Hey, Mom, just saw the Sun's front page online. Wow! Daddy would've been so proud!* Laura showed the text to Gracie.

"Do you realize some shepherd in Tibet might be looking at your photo online at this very moment?"

"I'm not sure there are shepherds in Tibet, and if so I doubt they read the *Baltimore Sun*."

"Everybody's all wired up now, even shepherds. They sit on a rock watching their sheep and checking their cell phones for the latest news. What the hell else are they going to do all day? By the way, love your outfit."

Laura wore an oversized Crush Cameron Oriole jersey autographed with the inscription: *"To Laura —Hell on the base paths!"* She rubbed her eyes. It'd been a long night. She'd been taken to a magistrate who manned a tiny courtroom in the bowels of the ballpark itself. The guard told her most newer sports venues contained a courtroom where a magistrate could deal swiftly with drunks and disorderly fans. After a long wait and a short story, the magistrate took pity on her and released her with a very mild admonition to remain in the stands at all times. A very long night, but also a very… what? Satisfying night? She sat down with a sigh, and stared at the Orioles cup resting in the middle of the table next to the half-empty urn.

Gracie covered Laura's hand with hers. "How you holding up?"

"Okay, I guess. Although, I'll admit I've been wondering, after Mickey being so much a part of me, what am I going to do with the last half of my life now that he's gone?"

"Do what you've been doing, only without Mickey," Gracie said.

After last night, Laura wasn't so sure that would be enough.

They heard the front door slam, and looked up to see Brooke enter the kitchen waving her phone in the air. "I had to confirm it with my own eyes."

Gracie said, "Good morning, dear."

Brooke's gaze fell on the Orioles cup next to the urn. "I'll be damned. When Mike texted me this morning, I thought he must be kidding. It couldn't be, not my mother. Then I saw the story. The photo sure looked like you, but no, that was impossible. Laura Beckman would be the last person in the world to engage in such *inappropriate* behavior. Yet the article identified the base runner as Laura Beckman of Annapolis, Maryland. Could there be another Laura Beckman? One who would do such a crazy thing? I'll be honest, Mother, I'm at a loss for words."

Laura couldn't tell—was her daughter actually approving of her actions? She didn't know how she felt about that. "You're sure talking a lot for someone who's at a loss for words."

Brooke again waved her phone in the air. "You may be interested in knowing you've set the Twitterverse aflutter. The photo has been re-Tweeted a zillion times so far; people all over the world have seen it."

"Including Tibet," Gracie added.

Laura lowered her gaze, her voice softened. "All this . . . it wasn't my intention."

Brooke took a seat. "Then please enlighten me. What the hell were you thinking? Those were my Daddy's ashes you emptied out in front of 40,000 strangers."

Her daughter's accusatory tone bleached the conviction from Laura's response. "It's what he would've wanted."

"Really? Did you ever ask him what he wanted?"

Laura felt defensive, and she didn't like it. "Of course I asked him. I was his wife." *Did she? Did she ever ask Mickey what he liked?*

What he really wanted? "As a matter of fact, I was watching some old home movies, and your father expressed a wish to—"

"Home movies?" Brooke interrupted with a cold laugh. "Did you ever ask yourself why you're barely seen in any of those *home* movies? Could it be because you were never *home*? Where's Laura?" Brooke turned back and forth melodramatically, then walked to what the family called Mom's Trophy Wall in the dining room.

Laura was very proud of her trophies—first place low net eighteen hole Ladies Club Championship, 2018; Tennis Senior Doubles Championship, 2016, that had been with Alicia; and about a dozen more trophies in both golf and tennis going back over twenty years. And then there were her plaques—Chair, Scholarship Ball, 2017; Vice-Chair, Ladies Tennis Association, 2015; Certificate of Appreciation for charitable work from the mayor's office—she had a bunch of those. And of course, her Volunteer of the Year Golden Crab awarded nine months earlier by the mayor himself. This year she was the chair of the most prestigious event at the club, the Symphony Ball. She'd already cleared a place for the expected "thank you plaque" in the middle of the top shelf.

And then there were the photos. Lots of photos of her and her friends winning this, or coming in second for that. She was drawn to the pictures of her, Alicia and Helen. The eyes of her two friends seemed to stare right through her.

Brooke gestured dramatically. "Here she is. Ladies Bridge Champion; Golf Low Net Winner; blah blah blah. And of course, the Golden Crab. Oh, and let's not forget all of these Certificates of Appreciation. Everyone sure does appreciate Laura Beckman."

For what seemed like forever, but was only a few seconds, no one said a word.

Then the phone rang, piercing the silence.

Startled, Laura jumped up and headed for the phone on the counter. She paused, glanced at her daughter, then veered out of the kitchen into the den.

Brooke watched her mother close the door. She knew if only Gracie were present Laura would've taken the call in the kitchen. Thanks for being so trusting, Mom.

"Would you like some coffee?" Gracie asked.

"No, thanks. I better be going."

"Honey, what your mother did last night took a lot of courage. She doesn't really deserve your criticism."

Brooke didn't respond immediately. She couldn't shake the image of mother's crestfallen expression as Brooke returned from her little performance at the trophy shelf. Had she ever seen her mother look so vulnerable? Her voice softened. "I just never knew her to do anything so . . . I don't know. So crazy."

"From the time your mother was born, through high school and half of college, she was quite rebellious, and always seemed to find herself in trouble."

"Sorry, very difficult to believe."

"She was arrested twice for smoking pot under the football field stands. And once in high school she was suspended for a week. She put itching powder in the cheerleaders' briefs right before her school was to play in the Virginia state basketball championships."

"My mother?"

"In high school, she wasn't a full-fledged goth, but she hovered around the edges. Pink hair, black lipstick. So on the day of the game she and her best friend Megan snuck into the girls locker room before the "Perkies" arrived—that's what Laura called the cheerleaders because they were always so perky—and slipped itching powder into their briefs. An hour later the arena's full of screaming fans as the Perkies run out onto the floor waving their pompoms, ready to begin their routine. Except they can't perform their routine because they're scratching their crotches. The more they scratched, the more it itched. So the girls are rolling around on the floor, itching and scratchin,' scratchin' and itchin,' and the fans are howling with laughter. The whole thing was broadcast live on the local cable TV station."

"You're talking about the same Laura Williams Beckman who happens to be my mother?"

"The very same."

"And I'm just hearing about this now?"

"Not something she's proud of. She . . . changed during college."

"Yeah, and I know what it was. Motherhood. Me. I was born between her sophomore and junior year. Very ironic, don't you think? My birth's what flipped her from someone like me to someone who detests someone like me. She became a . . . what did she call them? A Perky?"

"You had nothing to do with it."

"I'm listening."

"Not my place. And I'd appreciate it if you don't say anything to her about what I've told you."

The door opened, and Laura emerged looking distraught. "Channel 13 wanted me to appear on their afternoon talk show."

Gracie's face brightened. "Coffee with Cassie? I love Coffee with Cassie."

"I told them, no. Last night was personal, private."

"Not too private," Brooke said. "Your little jog in front of thousands of strangers was broadcast across the entire region." She glanced at Gracie, lowered her eyes, and consciously softened her voice to make up for her harsher tone earlier. "But . . . for what it's worth, what you did? I think it was kind of cool."

Laura appeared too stunned to speak.

Brooke stood to leave. Her gaze fell on the urn. Suddenly, out of nowhere an image flashed through her mind. Coming downstairs in the morning, taking her mother's hand . . . skipping around the kitchen island, stopping in front of her dad . . . *We're off to find the morning glories . . . And you, and you, and . . .* Where the hell did that come from? Her eyes brimmed with tears. Shit, why couldn't she do a better job of controlling her emotions?

"Are you okay, sweetie?" Gracie asked.

Brooke wiped her eyes on her sleeve. She had to get out of there. She mumbled, "Still some ash left. If it's all the same to you . . . " Before Laura could respond, Brooke picked up the urn and clutched it tight to her chest. Without another word, she headed toward the door.

In the living room she ran into Nora entering the house.

"Brooke, dear, you appear a bit out of sorts."

She switched back to her default smart-ass tone. "Didn't you know? I'm always out of sorts."

She left, but took pains not to slam the door.

CHAPTER EIGHT

Laura stood motionless, her emotions jumbled, and watched her daughter leave. *What you did? I think it was kind of cool.* Laura couldn't remember Brooke ever characterizing anything Laura said or did as kind of cool.

Nora walked into the kitchen. "Brooke seemed upset. Remember, honey, she's your first child."

Laura's voice hardened. "She may've sprung from my womb, but from the beginning Brooke was always daddy's girl. Now she's turned into a drunk, she can't hold a real job, she tossed her family aside—"

Gracie interrupted. "For Mickey's sake, you need to forgive her."

"The alcohol, okay, maybe I could deal with that, but she abandoned her husband and daughter and ran off with that musician. Got up one day, decided it might be fun to be famous. She abandoned her family and took off without a second thought."

"I'm sure she had second thoughts," Nora said.

"I'll never be able to understand. She abandoned her *family.*" Suddenly, Brooke's words echoed in Laura's brain. *How the hell would you know? Did you ever ask him what he wanted?* A sneaking thought entered her mind. Could *she* have abandoned her family, though she lived in the same house? *You were never home, you were never—*

The doorbell rang.

Laura, with Gracie following, walked through the living room and peeked out the front window to see Helen and Alicia standing on the porch. A shot of acid instantly poured into her stomach. *They'd seen the newspaper.* She forced a smile and opened the door.

"Come in, come in."

"No thanks," Helen said.

Laura immediately noticed both women appeared uncomfortable. Something was up. In a synchronized quick-draw motion that would've made Annie Oakley proud, both women whipped their phones out of their back pockets and thrust them forward, inches from Laura's face. The *Sun* cover was displayed on both screens.

"Have you seen this?" Helen asked.

"Yes, I've seen it."

Helen said, "Those are your husband's *ashes.* I'm sorry, Laura, but that is so inappropriate."

Alicia pronounced, "It might go viral."

Laura wasn't sure how many hits it took for something to go viral, and doubted Alicia knew either.

"We're so worried about you, dear," Helen said, "and we—"

"All of us, not only me and Helen," Alicia interjected.

Helen gave Alicia a look that said, close your trap. "Right. All of us in the Association think it may be better for all concerned if you give yourself more time to grieve . . . privately."

"And not have to burden yourself with the Symphony Ball Chair," Alicia added, unable to help herself.

Helen couldn't look Laura in the eye. "Or . . . other Ladies Association activities."

"But I'm vice president," Laura responded, trying without complete success to keep the desperation from her voice. "And who else would chair...?" Before she finished the question, Alicia's expression gave her the answer.

While Alicia was struggling to formulate a dissembling response, Helen made it unnecessary. "Alicia," Helen answered, a brightness in her voice that garnered an evil eye from the new Symphony Ball chair. "Just until, you know."

Laura intentionally paused long enough for the two ladies to show visible discomfort. "I believe I understand."

"We'll all do lunch real soon," said Helen as she backed away. Both ladies couldn't scurry down the walk fast enough.

"That would be nice," responded Laura, not bothering to hide the sarcasm. But the ladies had already turned their backs and were practically jogging to their car. They both jumped in, and Alicia drove off. As they passed, Helen waved, Alicia didn't bother.

Laura closed the door. She couldn't believe it. She'd been iced. Gracie came up behind her. "You heard?"

"Scrawny-assed bitches," Gracie responded with a scowl.

Laura shook her head in disbelief. "We've been friends for years." How could her friends turn on her so quickly? Not only Alicia and Helen, but apparently the whole Chesapeake Country Club Ladies Association. She could imagine the phones and texts buzzing this morning as soon as the *Sun* hit the front porches. Laura knew exactly what happened because, she had to admit, she would've been one of the first to grab for the phone. *Can you believe what she did? Embarrassing to the club. Her husband's ashes? So inappropriate.* No doubt Alicia had orchestrated the whole thing. She'd wanted to be the Symphony Ball chair for years, but had always been voted down for the simple reason that she couldn't manage her way out of a paper bag.

Gracie asked, "Why didn't they just call?"

Laura knew the answer. "Because they wanted to see my reaction in person so they could report the juicy gossip in excruciating detail."

"You must be crushed," Gracie said, in a sincere attempt to be sympathetic.

As Laura closed the door she realized, curiously, that she really wasn't all that crushed. Her own reaction unnerved her. Aside from Mickey, the Symphony Ball chair had been the most important thing in her life over the past year. Perhaps she'd made a mistake. When she stepped back and considered what she'd done the night before she could easily see how she'd embarrassed her friends. Maybe she deserved to be iced.

Laura and Gracie returned to the kitchen to catch Nora with her head in her hands. When she saw them, Nora quickly lifted her head and tried to smile. "Good news or bad news?"

"Good news," Gracie announced. "The country club bitches blackballed Laura."

"Because of last night?"

"Who gives a crap what they think," Gracie said.

Nora turned to Laura. "I know how important your club activities have been to you over the years."

"Helen said I needed more time to grieve. Maybe she's—" Laura halted in mid-sentence as she read trouble on Nora's face. "Nora, what's wrong?"

Nora averted her eyes, then whispered, "It's back."

Laura and Gracie sat down quickly and each took Nora's hand. "I'm so sorry," Laura said.

"So it's back, so what?" Gracie said. "You knocked it into remission before, and that's what you're—"

Nora interrupted her. "No, not this time. Six months, that's what the doctors said."

"Doctors don't know crap," Gracie said. "Ellen had this woman on her show last week from Kansas or Oregon or someplace like that, and she was given three months to live. That was over two years ago."

"No." Nora's voice was firm. "I've had a good life. I will never forget the pain the last time, and I swore back then, never again."

The room fell silent. Laura didn't know what to say. The silence quickly became awkward.

Laura rose from the table. "Uh, how about some more coffee? Nora?"

"Remember the porch?"

"Not sure I know what you mean," Laura replied although she knew exactly where Nora might be heading.

"We made a pact, the three of us and Everett. What I want is for you to honor our pact."

More silence as Nora's words sank in. Gracie spoke first. "Six months gives you plenty of time to really think about what you're considering."

"No. This time I intend to control my life up to the very end. I elect to go out on my own terms and on my own schedule." Nora held Laura's gaze. "My schedule is now."

Laura's voice softened. "I know what we said on the porch, but I honestly don't know whether I could ever really do what you're asking."

"You were the one who brought it up," Nora said with an uncharacteristic touch of defiance. "Remember, you said you didn't want to have a long, lingering death like Mickey, and you asked us to help you go if you were ever in that situation. And we all agreed." She turned to Gracie. "Right? We all agreed?"

"She's right," Gracie responded. "A pact."

Laura couldn't remember Nora ever appearing so solemn. "All I'm saying is you really need to think this through."

"I have thought it through."

Laura turned away from the table and allowed her gaze to move around the room because she feared if her eyes found Nora's she'd burst into tears. A pact? My God, what had she done? If she'd only kept her thoughts to herself on the porch they wouldn't be having this conversation.

"Nora, Mickey's funeral had just occurred, I was distraught, emotional, even a little unhinged."

"Are you saying you want to suffer, you want all of us to suffer like Mickey?"

"No, of course—"

"Laura, look at me."

Laura forced herself to hold Nora's gaze. Those Arctic blue eyes were clear, nothing to indicate confusion or disorientation.

Nora covered Laura's hand with hers. "I need you."

A rapid-fire slideshow of images flashed through Laura's brain: Mickey in the hospital bed wired up like a grotesque science experiment; his face twisted in pain; his lima bean heart; him dabbing in the air with a corner of the hospital sheet; and the notepad pages, each containing a single word—please. She lowered her gaze and didn't speak for what seemed like forever.

What would Mickey want her to do?

Nora's life, Nora's choice.

She took a deep breath, raised her head, held Nora's gaze, and slowly nodded.

CHAPTER NINE

Laura used a serrated kitchen knife to slice a poppy seed bagel, then lathered one of the halves with smoked bluefish spread. Admittedly one of Laura's guilty pleasures, the fish spread was well worth the forty-minute drive south to the local market in the sleepy waterfront town of Galesville one morning a week to replenish her supply. Made fresh daily, the bluefish spread regularly sold out by noon.

She took a bite, and the taste of the smoky fish melded with the warm texture of the fresh bagel inside her mouth. Delicious. She sipped her coffee. Years earlier she'd developed the habit of limiting herself to two cups of high-test and then switching to decaf so she could continue drinking throughout the day without jangling her nerves. A nice balance—the watchword for most of her entire adult life. But now, after her ballpark escapade, that life felt out of balance, and what she found herself contemplating broke the scale.

Four days had passed since Nora invoked the pact, and Laura had gone back and forth in her own mind a million times—should she follow through or push Nora to seek further medical advice? At Gracie's prodding, she'd purchased an "assistance device" on Amazon. Who knew there was such a thing? Her thoughts were interrupted by the doorbell.

Coffee cup in hand, she opened the door and was shocked to see the disgusting man from the ballgame standing on her porch.

In one hand he held an orange Orioles jacket and a driver's license. Was that her license? In the other he clutched a small UPS package.

"Good morning, Mrs. Beckman."

"From the baseball game the other night. Sadly, I remember you."

"Our jackets got switched. I would've kept yours, but Cal Ripkin himself autographed mine, and it's worth some bucks. Oh, and here's a UPS package that was sitting on your porch."

As she reached for the package she forgot about her cup and it tipped hard, spilling coffee down the front of Arlo's shirt.

"*Shiiiit!*"

"Oh, I'm so sorry."

"And here I was expecting some sort of thank you."

Fortunately, she'd filled her cup fifteen minutes earlier so the brew wasn't scalding. Still, she could see the pain on the man's face. "Please, come in. Let me find some ice for that." Arlo didn't move, eyeing her warily. "If you apply ice to the burn right away the pain will diminish." Arlo grimaced and followed her into the kitchen.

Laura dumped the jacket and package on the table. She nodded to a chair. "Have a seat, Mr.—?"

"Massey. Arlo Massey."

Laura found a plastic bag in a drawer and filled it with ice from the freezer. She checked Arlo's shirt. The coffee stain covered almost the entire front. "You'll need to remove your shirt."

Arlo complied, revealing a bright red spot on the left part of his chest. She handed him the ice bag. "Hold this on it."

Arlo took the ice bag and gingerly dabbed the ice against the burn. "Cold."

"Ice is cold? Stop the presses."

"A word of advice, Mrs. Beckman. Sarcasm is not becoming—"

Without thinking, Laura clasped his hand holding the ice and pressed it hard against the burn. He yelped. "What the hell . . .?"

"You need to cover the whole wound or it won't work. You're not a crybaby are you, Mr. Massey?"

Laura observed that after the initial shock, judging from his expression, the pain from the burn had subsided. Apparently, he wasn't going to give her the satisfaction of admitting it.

Laura felt a little guilty for her behavior. Yes, the man was a total jerk, but she'd caused the burn. "I'm very sorry this happened, Mr. Massey. Why's that name familiar?"

Arlo's expression immediately brightened. "You've probably seen my commercials." He sang, "Don't be sassy, boat at Massey. Massey Mareenaahhhs!"

She remembered. The idiot on late night cable. "No, I'm sorry. I'll find your jacket." She turned toward the living room.

Arlo called after her. "Maybe Wrestlemania? I'm a local sponsor of Wrestlemania."

Laura ignored him and opened the coat closet. She pulled out the matching orange jacket, and returned to the kitchen.

"Look under the collar," Arlo said.

Laura peeled up the collar and, sure enough, there was an autograph from the Oriole icon. She reached into the pockets. "Just make sure I didn't leave anything in here . . ." She removed a condom in a foil wrapper and held it by the corner as if it had been dipped in the Ebola virus.

"It's a condom, Mrs. Beckman."

Was that a brief glint of embarrassment on his face? "I know what it is."

"Hasn't been used, so go ahead, take it. My gift to you."

Laura dropped the condom back in the pocket. Arlo shook his head. "Suit yourself. So, I have to hand it to you, running around the bases, trailing that dust . . . er, I mean the remains. Worth the price of admission. What was your husband's name?"

"Mickey."

"A big O's fan, I assume?"

"That's correct. I've made a mess of your shirt. You can't wear it like that. Do you have another shirt in your car?"

"No. I wasn't expecting someone pouring scalding coffee down my chest."

"It was an accident, and it wasn't scalding." Now what? The only shirts in the house belonged to Mickey, and the idea of offering one of her husband's shirts to this man . . . but she could see no alternative. She caused the spill. The shirts were bound for Goodwill anyway. "I'll see if I can find something from my husband's closet you can borrow."

"Thanks."

She hurried out of the kitchen. Arlo's voice followed her.

"Hey, the return address on this package says Sleep to Peace Society. Isn't that one of those suicide—?"

She ran upstairs so she wouldn't have to respond.

Once on the second floor she entered the master bedroom and opened the door to Mickey's closet. The last time she'd been in this space had been to select a suit for his viewing. She breathed deeply to settle herself. They'd remodeled a small bedroom into two walk-in closets, and over the years they'd rarely strayed into the other's space. Although there was that one time long ago when she'd surprised him the morning of their seventh anniversary. He'd been rushing to dress for work. She'd walked in straight out of the shower and given him an early anniversary present right there on the carpeted floor. She remembered Mickey reporting the salesmen at the store teased him when he'd arrived an hour late with a goofy smile on his face. It never happened before or after. Maybe I should've given him a morning surprise more often. Of course, that was many years earlier when they were both young. Once they reached middle age, he wouldn't have wanted to do anything like that. Or would he? *Did you ever ask him what he wanted?*

Her eyes fell upon his glasses, his keys, and some spare change lying on the dresser in the closet. The glasses were the worst. For years she'd peered through those windows into his eyes, into him. She turned away. Why was she here again? Oh, yes. A shirt for the obnoxious man sitting in her kitchen. She ran her hand gently across the row of shirts stopping when her fingers brushed the sleeve of a blue pinstripe, one of her favorites. She pressed the sleeve to her cheek and her eyes welled up. She couldn't help it. She felt dizzy. She took a deep breath, grabbed the dresser and collected herself. She wouldn't allow herself to faint.

She spotted a pink shirt with white collar and cuffs. It had been a gift from Brooke for Father's Day a couple of years earlier. Laura never particularly liked it. Pink didn't project authority. She pulled the pink shirt off the hanger and headed downstairs.

Entering the kitchen she saw Arlo shaking the UPS package. She handed him the shirt. "Here, Mr. Massey, put this on."

"Thanks, and please call me Arlo." He set the ice pack down. Laura gave him a dish towel to dry himself off. He pushed back from the table and stood. The man was taller than she'd remembered— maybe a smidge over six feet. He slipped on the shirt. "Your name's Laura. I remember from the license."

"I don't believe we'll be seeing each other again, Mr. Massey, so there should be no need for first name familiarity."

"No problem. And look, I should've said this earlier, but sorry for your loss."

Laura's eyes bore into him. "I wish he'd died sooner."

"Oh?"

"I tried to end it, but they brought him back to life."

Arlo nodded toward the UPS package. "I know losing the old man must've been tough, but I'm not sure that's the answer."

"It's not for me."

"None of my beeswax. Sorry." He headed into the living room with Laura following. She opened the door quickly. "Thank you for returning the jacket and my license, Mr. Massey," she said, her voice cool.

"Forget about it." He walked out onto the porch, turned and waved. Their eyes met and held for a split second. Then she heard a young woman's voice coming from the street.

"Arlo, hurry up. I'm hungry."

A girl in her early twenties dressed in tight shorts and a revealing tank top waved to Arlo from a small convertible.

He walked briskly to the car. "I'm coming, Babycake Two."

"Hey, Babycake One, that's what you said this morning." Her laugh was more of a screech. "Get it, Babycake One? You said—"

Arlo cut her off. "Yeah, I get it." He turned to Laura and shrugged. Could that be embarrassment she saw on his face? Probably not. He hopped in the car and they drove off.

Laura slammed the door, returned to the kitchen, and tore a bigger bite out of her smoked bluefish bagel than she intended. Babycake One? God help us. Chewing hard, she spotted his coffee-stained shirt. Should she toss it in the trash? She supposed she could mail it to him. Then her eyes fell on the UPS package and she immediately forgot about Arlo Massey and Galesville's famous bluefish spread.

The moment Arlo pulled away, the girl turned up the music on her phone, closed her eyes and bopped in her seat to the beat. Arlo handed her a set of earbuds he kept rolled up in a cupholder.

She asked, "You don't like Purple Roach?"

Arlo assumed Purple Roach was responsible for the wailing coming through his speakers. He loved young women, but their music was crap. "Put 'em on."

The girl pouted, then complied, and the noise mercifully stopped. Arlo's thoughts drifted to Laura Beckman. She was actually kind of hot. For her age, of course. But the bitchy attitude, he could do without that. And the package from the Sleep to Peace Society, that was strange to say the least.

The pink shirt fit him surprisingly well. Still, for some reason wearing her dead husband's shirt weirded him out. One of these days soon he'd need to return it.

Hopefully, she'd be in a better mood.

CHAPTER TEN

Laura parked the Lexus in front of Nora's apartment building. Anchor Cove was a large assisted-living complex made up of six red brick buildings, each four stories high. Laid out like a college campus with wide expanses of lawn and well-maintained landscaping, the Cove offered a range of living options from normal apartment residency with communal dining to full-blown nursing care. The facility was located not far from the hospital, allowing an elder resident to move in at the lowest assistance level and progress through to death in a hospital bed. Actually, many residents never reached the last stage and died at the Cove. Nora reported that ambulance visits were almost as frequent as the mailman, and the weekly newsletter reported deaths as routinely as upcoming dinner menus. Nora still lived in "A" Building—the lowest level of assistance.

Laura's attention turned to the UPS box resting on the passenger seat. Was this as nuts as it seemed? She answered her own question. Yes. She decided she'd leave the box in the car, go inside, and persuade Nora to forget the whole thing.

She stepped out of the car just as Gracie, driving the Lamont, pulled in next to her. In her twenties Gracie had a wild romance with a young D.C. lawyer who drove a powder blue 1964 Triumph TR-4. She'd found this one on Craigslist a couple of years earlier and paid entirely too much for it. The top was torn, both fenders displayed multiple dings, and the car only started when the ambient temperature ranged between 75 and 82 degrees. Any day Gracie drove her "Lamont"—she named the car after her lover—Laura didn't need to watch the Weather Channel to learn the temperature.

Gracie climbed out of the Lamont and closed the door very gently. She spotted the package in Laura's car and stiffened.

They'd spent the previous evening on the front porch, sharing a bottle of cabernet, going back and forth about what Nora was asking them to do. They finally decided they should do everything they could to convince her to change her mind, but if she persisted, they had an obligation to be there for her.

That was then.

Laura said, "I know what we agreed last night, but I've decided we can't go through with it. We need to go in there and convince her this is a big mistake. A huge mistake. The mother of all mistakes."

"I don't think she'll change her mind."

"We have to try."

Gracie didn't respond, focusing her attention on the box.

"I see the wheels turning," Laura said.

"Everything up to this point has been theoretical. Maybe if she actually sees the device she'll come to her senses. At this point we don't have much to lose. If we abandon her she'll try something else and put herself at risk for a botched attempt that will leave her far worse off."

Gracie was right, they couldn't abandon her. Laura nodded her approval and retrieved the Box of Death from the front seat, taking pains to handle it with care.

They entered the building and made their way to Nora's apartment. Nora told them she'd leave the door open so she wouldn't have to jump up when the doorbell rang. As soon as Laura and

Gracie stepped inside, Nora called from her bedroom down the hall. "In here."

Laura supposed Nora's bedroom fit the stereotypical image of an old lady's bedroom. Small room. Single, dark mahogany four-poster bed, wallpaper and bedspread covered with tight floral prints, and yes, doilies on the nightstand. Where did one buy doilies nowadays? Were there doily stores? Propped up by a mound of pillows, Nora leaned back against the ornate headboard watching *The Bridges of Madison County* on cable. Laura spotted a small plate of chocolates on her bedside table.

Nora's eyes lit up when she saw the package. "Is that it?" She turned off the TV.

"Gracie and I have been talking and—"

"Open it. Please."

Laura glanced at Gracie, then opened the package. She removed a thick plastic bag with a Velcro strap around the opening. Emblazoned across the plastic were the words, "Goodbye Bag."

Gracie scrunched up her face. "That's it? Looks like something you'd use to refrigerate leftover meatloaf."

"Nora, are you certain?" Laura asked. "Absolutely certain? Their webpage says the deprivation of oxygen is the most humane way to go. I don't buy it. Look at the bag and picture it wrapped tight around your head as you gasp for breath. Do you really want to suffocate to death? Gracie and I feel you'd be better off—"

"I'm as certain as I've ever been."

Laura searched for an out. "Don't you want your family here? Like, uh, cousin Cicily? Why don't we wait for cousin Cicily? I'm sure she would want to be here."

"I was never really very fond of cousin Cicily. She stole my recipe for German potato salad and published it in the *Methodist Women's*

Charity Cookbook as her own. Won first place. She said she changed it by adding more vinegar but she was fibbing. It was my recipe."

Gracie examined the Goodbye Bag. "What's to prevent her from ripping it off when she can't breathe?"

Laura checked the bottom of the box and removed a pair of plastic handcuffs with padded rubber wrapped around the cuffs to prevent chafing. Laura read from a package insert. "Once the Velcro is secured tightly around your throat you will have enough air to quickly handcuff both hands to the bedpost."

Nora smiled lovingly at both women. "Come here." They hesitated. "Please." Laura, then Gracie enveloped Nora in their arms, holding on tight, not wanting to let go. Nora turned to Gracie. "Perhaps you could handle the cuffs when needed." Laura reluctantly gave Nora the bag and Gracie took the cuffs.

Nora weakly gripped their hands and smiled with a serenity Laura didn't remember seeing before. "I love both of you very much. I've had a wonderful life and you both have been very important parts of it. Goodbye." She opened the bag and began to slip it over her head.

Gracie snatched the bag from Nora's hands, looped it over Laura's head, and tightened the Velcro. Laura clawed at the Velcro, but Gracie held on tight. Laura tried to scream but only sucked the plastic against her face and into her mouth. Her face contorted in stark terror. Gracie ripped the bag off Laura's head. "Humane, my bony ass."

Laura gasped for breath. "What . . . are you . . . doing?"

"Product testing."

"A warning would've been nice!"

"And ruined the validity of the results?"

"Validity of the results? Are you crazy?"

"Maybe we're doing something wrong," Nora interjected with a worried look.

"Forget the bag," Laura pronounced. No way are we going to let you torture yourself with that thing."

Tears filled Nora's eyes. "I was ready," she whispered.

"Pills. We need pills," said Laura.

"I asked the doctor for some barbiturates, but he was suspicious."

Laura handed her a tissue. "We'll think of something."

The route north from Nora's apartment up Cedar Boulevard toward Eastgate was so familiar Laura could've driven it in her sleep. A half-mile ahead on the right, Fairway Lane wound its way eastward to the Chesapeake Country Club. Today the grassy mounds surrounding the tennis courts would be filled with members watching the Ladies Doubles Championship. She and Helen won the championship two years earlier. A flood of memories washed over her. Good memories.

What the hell was she doing? She answered her own question—plotting the best way to help a wonderful woman kill herself.

My God.

She could make the turn onto Fairway Lane, find a seat next to her friends, and step back into her old life as if she'd never left. Her unusual behavior at the Orioles game could easily be explained by the stress from losing her husband. Everyone would understand. She hesitated, then eased off the gas, slowed for the intersection, and made the turn.

Her heart raced; she felt almost giddy driving up the lane. The leaves on the maples lining the road had already begun to yellow. In a few weeks they'd be brilliant red. The entrance road crested at a point above the tennis facility providing her a great view of the festivities. She pulled to the curb where she could see members packing the grassy knolls, sipping drinks, laughing, cheering the players down on the court. From her vantage point she recognized almost everyone. There was Alicia. Helen sat on the other side of the court in her tennis whites next to Gail Saunders. Gail must be Helen's new partner. Gail was okay at the net but couldn't serve worth beans. Laura had beaten her repeatedly during singles match events over the years.

All she had to do was park, then walk over, reconnect as if the incident at Orioles Park had never happened, and join the fun.

And then what?

She thought of Mickey. What would he say?

She surveyed the scene below her. A large group of friends laughing, enjoying their time together. Absolutely nothing wrong with that. But were they really her friends? She thought of Alicia and Helen standing on her porch with their Annie Oakley fast draw, icing her. And what happens tomorrow after the tennis matches, and the drinking and the gossiping and the fun was over? Something was missing. She realized she felt no emotional connection to the people in the crowd. Could she really go back to that life?

Her view blurred to a brash kaleidoscope of clashing colors and noises, and she was suddenly struck by the silliness of it all. Was that how she wanted to be remembered? Two-time doubles champion? Volunteer of the month? At the end of her life, looking back, was that really how *she* wanted to remember her time on Earth?

Laura was pretty sure she needed something more. She realized she wanted to find a better version of herself. Could helping Nora be the answer? She didn't know. But after watching the gathering of people she'd very recently consider her close friends, she wasn't certain she could ever return to the old Laura Beckman.

On the far side of the courts, Alicia raised her head, then froze. She'd spotted Laura. Alicia bent over and whispered something into Gail's ear. Gail looked up the hill toward Laura. Suddenly, both women stood as if on cue, pivoted, and turned their backs to her.

Laura smiled to herself. *Thank you, ladies.*

She drove up the road, looped around the circular drive in front of the clubhouse, and headed home.

She saw no reason why she would ever drive up Fairway Lane again.

CHAPTER ELEVEN

Brooke lit a cigarette, more than anything else to see the expression on the faces of the young couple at the end of the bar. She tried not to crack a smile as each of them twisted their heads back and forth, no doubt looking to see if anyone else was witnessing this blatant breach of the law. The couple weren't regulars. The girl wore expensive designer jeans with expensive designer tears across each knee. The tears in the frayed jeans of everyone else in the bar came from years of wear, as well as fish hooks, scaling knives, and the hundred other sharp edges found on a working boat. The couple quickly plopped down a few bills on the bar to pay for their unfinished drinks, and left.

Winkie Maddox, an old-timer sitting nearby, laughed. Brooke joined in. "Didn't take them long," he said.

Brooke topped off his beer from the tap. Winkie and her dad were friends, and several times a week Mickey would stop by for a quick beer on the way home. Winkie was a fixture, and the two of them would discuss the fishing conditions, or the latest Orioles trade, or the idiots in Washington. She missed her dad so much. Some days were worse than others, and this was one of those worse than others days. Maybe she'd tap herself a brew as well. Just one wouldn't hurt. Might help deal with her funk. Her mother would not approve, but who gave a shit? Still, she hesitated.

"Looks like you have a case of the deep blues."

Brooke turned to see Linda approach, carrying her guitar case.

"You're a little early," Brooke said.

"Thought I'd grab a quick beer to oil me up before the first set."

Brooke tapped a Bud into a frosted mug and set it in front of the singer. Linda took a deep swig.

"I feel better already. Join me?"

Brooke parked her cigarette in an ashtray, pulled another mug from the cooler, and reached for the tap. And stopped. Shit. She released the tap and used the dispenser to fill her mug with club soda.

Linda said, "On the wagon?"

"Long night ahead."

Linda lifted her mug. "To happy hearts and good sex."

Brooke laughed and clinked her mug. "I could use a little of both."

"So why the blues?"

"I guess I miss my dad."

"How's your mom doing?"

A very good question. How *is* Laura doing? "We don't have the best of relationships."

"Because of L.A.?"

"Mostly. I really fucked up."

"When it comes to love and family, at some point everybody fucks up." She drained half of her remaining beer and used the back of her hand to wiped the foam from her lips. " Did I ever tell you about Stan?"

"Boyfriend or husband."

"I used to be married. We started off great, but after a few years I knew Stan was running around on me. I threatened to leave him, but he begged for another chance. So we decided to go on this big western adventure trip, a dude ranch cattle drive, to get our marriage back on track."

Brooke took a deep drag from her cigarette. "And?"

"We're in this bunk house, Stan's upstairs playing poker with some other guys on the trip. I'm in bed downstairs. I tippy-toed across the hall to the room of our guide—this young, beautiful Marlboro Man—and screwed his brains out."

Brooke's laugh was so hard, it got caught up in the smoke and converted to a hacking cough. "Sorry," she said as she reached for a napkin.

"When we returned home nothing changed. One night Stan comes in late with whiskey on his breath and perfume on his clothes. So I told him about riding the cowboy, added a few embellishments about dick size which drive men crazy, and that was the end of that. Now, your turn. What happened in L.A.?"

Brooke paused. Did she really want to confide in Linda? She hardly knew the girl. On the other hand, maybe that was a good thing.

"We were so young—me, Tom. Jennie was only four. Tom worked hard to establish his practice and I think he felt guilty about the long hours, so he encouraged me to get back into music. Saint Thomas. I joined this rock band headed by a guy named—"

"Nail."

"Right. Real name was Willie Pringle. I knew he had a thing for me, but I had no interest in reciprocating. One night, Willie called and asked me to bring some straws to rehearsal. I found a box of bunny straws we used to con Jennie into drinking her milk."

"Think I know where this is going."

"I refused at first—no way I was going to snort coke. Christ, I was a mother."

"But . . ."

"But after a wild set where I wasn't only feeling the music, I was *breathing* it, I gave in."

"Let me guess. The sex really wasn't that great."

"All I remember was how, even through the coke fog, I felt guilty and unsatisfied."

"Hey, turned out the Marlboro Man was a pretty lousy lay, too. But you kept it up?"

"It wasn't the sex, it was the dream. Willie announced he was driving to Hollywood to meet with a record producer who all but guaranteed him a recording contract. He begged me to go with him. He promised I'd be out front, the face of the band. After a few successful records I'd go solo and be off to the races."

"Dreams can be dangerous."

A patron at the other end of the bar waved for a refill. Brooke lit another cigarette and headed his way. She knew the cigs weren't good for her. Laura was right about that. She'd picked up the habit in L.A. hanging around musicians and bars and booze. Everybody smoked. Wasn't so much to look cool, more a symbol of devotion to the music above all else—*don't matter if I die young, man, 'cause I'm makin' music that'll last forever.* What horse crap. She'd quit a couple of times, but then she'd have a drink or be sitting next to a smoker and the pull became too strong. The smoke relaxed her, made her feel good, smoothed out the edges. And there were lots of edges, like never being able to forget the worst day of her life.

She'd crept out of bed, careful not to disturb Tom. When they'd made love earlier she remembered feeling powerful, passionate, a passion no doubt fueled by the urgency of a last time. She'd buried her tears in Tom's shoulder. She probably would never feel his arms around her again. She almost stayed in bed, so warm, so comfortable, so . . . familiar. But she'd told herself that comfort was what she needed to leave behind, that comfort was a euphemism for a stifling, controlled life without life.

So she'd kissed her sleeping husband goodbye. When she bent over his face, surrounded by the smell of their lovemaking, she had to fight not to collapse on top of him. She'd tiptoed into Jennie's room, and her knees buckled. What kind of monster was she, abandoning this young child? At the time, she rationalized that if she didn't find her own identity she'd never be a good mother. Now she knew her rationalization was nothing more than unmitigated bullshit. Even after all these years she still marveled at her profound stupidity. She brushed Jennie's hair away and kissed her sleeping daughter on her rosy cheek. She had to bite her lip so hard to keep from breaking down that she drew blood.

She'd left a note on the kitchen table. Looking back, she didn't remember the words, but it didn't make any difference. Her family had been notified in her own handwriting that she'd elected to abandon them. No nice way to convey that thought.

After tapping a fresh Bud for the man at the end of the bar she returned to Linda. "Willie was late for everything, and there's no doubt in my mind if he'd been late that morning, I'd have run upstairs, ripped up my note, and crawled back into bed with my husband."

"But he wasn't late."

Brooke shook her head. "No. And of course L.A. was a bust. Willie chased his tail. Something could break any day now because he'd met some guy whose cousin worked someplace and they were looking for something and calls were going to be made and meetings were going to be scheduled. One spoonful of L.A. bullshit after another."

"Ever think about coming home?"

"All the time." But there always had been Laura. She often wondered if getting back at her mother could be part of the reason she abandoned Tom and Jennie. She knew Laura would be devastated and publicly embarrassed by her actions, and wouldn't be able to use her looks and charm to easily escape the wagging tongues of the people she thought were important.

Throughout Brooke's whole life, her mother had been a rules-follower—someone who could always be found on the side of conformity, of propriety. Brooke remembered once when she was a junior in high school responding to her mother's criticism that Brooke wasn't acting "appropriately" by asking, "Who says what's appropriate? Who sets the rules, Mom?" Laura had responded, "Everyone knows well the boundaries of acceptable conduct, some just ignore them. As long as you're living in my house, you will conform your behavior to appropriate norms." Yeah, thinking back, chasing a stupid dream was the reason she left, but rubbing Laura's "appropriate" bullshit in her face might've been a subconscious part of it, too.

She finally responded to Linda. "Let's say my mother wouldn't have welcomed me with open arms."

"Don't be too hard on yourself, kiddo. Remember—"

"I know, everybody fucks up."

"Exactly. And every woman has a Willie somewhere in her past."

Willie. What a jerk. She'd dumped him the first time he asked for money and took modest pride in the fact she'd never slept with him from the moment they'd left Maryland. Which didn't mean she'd behaved like a Girl Scout. She needed to survive, and working in a bar she got into things she shouldn't have, and hooked up with people she shouldn't have. And the booze. She'd stayed away from the drugs. Well, not weed, but who counted that anymore anyway. The hooch, however, was another story. She knew it had a hold on her and she was going to do something about it one of these days. Go to rehab or AA or something. She was going to do it soon.

"What brought you back?" Linda gently prodded.

The real question, Brooke thought wistfully, was what took so long? All those years wasted in L.A. Her daughter had grown without her. Tom had been an amazing father, and Laura quickly stepped in as a surrogate mother. Her dad traveled to L.A. in an effort to persuade her to return. Even Tom had called that first week offering to take her back and together they'd go to counseling. She'd been such an idiot—stupid, stupid, stupid—but she'd tearfully declined. She couldn't face her mother. Laura would've sliced her to ribbons, day in and day out. As a grown woman she was so afraid of her mother she not only threw her life away, but when given the gift of a second chance, she threw that gift away, too.

After that, no more chances. Even Saint Thomas had his limits. Her dad visited when he could, and sent money—without Laura's knowledge, she was certain—and passed on pictures of Jennie. Her old Frigidaire in the Encino walk-up had been papered with those pictures.

"What brought me back? Not really sure. I suppose I just decided it was time to come home."

"Tough?"

"I wasn't expecting a warm reception. Tom and Jennie barely acknowledged me. But it was worth it to see my daughter."

"Why did you wait so long?"

"I had this crazy hope that if I could find success in L.A. and come home a star, I could reclaim a little of the respect I'd lost. But, of course, it never happened."

Linda finished the beer and unsnapped her guitar case. "Want to join me for the first set?"

"No thanks. Maybe later."

"I'm going to hold you to that." Linda carried her guitar to the microphone and began fiddling with the audio equipment.

Winkie signaled for a refill. Brooke took another drag of her cigarette and headed down the bar to retrieve his mug, unable to shake the conflicting thoughts in her head about her mother. What Laura had done at the ballgame, so out of character. Was it possible her dad's death had changed her? And if so, into what? Brooke thought back to her less than triumphant return. She'd apologized repeatedly to Tom and Jennie and her dad. Her dad had accepted her apology, but of course not Tom or Jennie. She knew she would never deserve that, not after what she'd done and how long it had been. But had she apologized to her mother? She honestly couldn't remember. And if she hadn't, was it too late?

Maybe on the way to work tomorrow she'd stop by Eastgate Avenue and see if she noticed anything different about Laura Beckman. Perhaps it wan't too late.

CHAPTER TWELVE

Laura heard the Lamont before it came to a stop in her driveway. She peered out the window to see Gracie step away from the blue antique holding her phone in her hand.

Laura opened the door. "Ever think about fixing that muffler?"

Gracie ignored her. "Wrists."

"Most people have two and they come in handy connecting your hands to your arms. What about them?"

"I've been doing some research. Slitting your wrists is the most painless way to go."

"Is that right?"

"Absolutely." She pointed to her phone. "Research."

Gracie followed Laura into the house, then hurried past her to the kitchen where she removed a paring knife from the wooden block on the counter.

Gracie said, "Let's check out the tub. That's where she'd do it."

Before Laura could respond, Gracie was halfway up the stairs. Laura, momentarily stunned, didn't move.

Gracie called down from the second floor. "What are you waiting for?"

Laura took a deep breath and climbed the stairs to find Gracie already in Laura's bathroom.

Gracie studied the tub intently. "So much more humane."

Laura asked doubtlfully, "Do you do it with or without water?"

"In the movies I think they do it without water."

"Nora's a very clean person, I think she'd want to do it in water."

"So she'd be naked?"

"I guess she'd be naked," Laura said. "Who wants to get into a tub full of water with their clothes on?"

"But what about, you know, when they come to take her away? Would she want to be found naked?"

Laura said, "Good point. Maybe we forget the whole thing."

"No, we just forget the water. She lies in the tub fully clothed. Wearing something nice. A favorite dress."

"But she'll get blood all over it. Nora wouldn't want blood all over her favorite dress."

They both thought for a moment. Gracie said, "Okay, she wears her favorite dress. No water. She drapes her arms over the tub. We put a bucket under her hand. Then when she slits her wrist the blood goes into the buckets. No fuss, no muss."

Laura found the image of Nora bleeding out in a bathtub horrifying. "But what about the cutting? Do you think it hurts?"

"Maybe at first. A little bit. The experts say she should perform a quick plunge, and slash up through the line of the vein." Gracie demonstrated by slashing the knife in the air over her left wrist. "Cutting across the wrist is too easy to repair."

"Experts?"

Gracie shrugged and pointed to her phone.

An image of Nora lying in the tub with blood dripping from her arm into a plastic mop bucket flashed through Laura's brain. She stiffened. Every pore of her body iced over. *My, God, what am I doing?*

"Are you okay?"

No, no, no, no, no—

Laura?

Her voice lowered to just above a whisper, and she spoke more to herself than Gracie. "This is not a game. We're talking about taking the life of—"

"Anything I can do to help out here?" Laura turned to see Brooke standing in the doorway leaning against the jamb with a bemused look on her face.

Laura felt her face flush with embarrassment. "No." Her voice was sharper than she intended. She snatched the knife from Gracie's hand and bent over the tub. "Only trying to unclog the drain."

"Really?"

"Shouldn't you be at work? You didn't lose another job, did you?"

Brooke held Laura's gaze for a long moment. Were those tears in her daughter's eyes? Brooke pivoted without another word.

A few moments later Laura heard the front door slam shut.

CHAPTER THIRTEEN

October

If she had to pick, Laura would choose early October as her favorite time of the year in Annapolis. Warm during the day, and enough of a chill at night to call for a jacket. Last October Mickey had still been alive. Not only alive, but full of life. One year. God, where had the time gone?

She used a trowel to widen the excavation. The sun felt warm on her skin as she lifted the mums from the black plastic container and carefully set the shallow root ball into the six-inch hole next to the front porch stairs. On such a beautiful fall afternoon she would normally be socializing with her friends on the golf course. Laura found it both strange and comforting that she didn't miss it.

After covering the plant with soil and adding water, she carried the last container along with her portable radio to a spot on the other side of the stairs. The radio played a light jazz tune—something she would hear at the Sunday brunches she and Mickey would enjoy from time to time at the King of France Tavern at the top of Main Street. The station cut to a commercial, and she heard a familiar voice: *"Don't be sassy, come to Massey, Massey Mareenaahhhhs! Hi! This is Arlo Massey telling you that when it comes to marine storage—"* Laura quickly reached over and turned off the radio. Agitated, she picked up the trowel and returned to her digging, attacking the hole with the tool. What a jerk. How could such a crude man run a successful business? The place was probably on its last legs. She wouldn't store a rowboat—

"Hole's a little deep."

Laura jumped and checked over her shoulder. Gracie, standing behind her, nodded to the hole.

Laura said, "It's the perfect size." She placed the mum into the two-foot hole, and the entire plant sank below ground.

"Mind on something else?"

Laura ignored her. She removed the plant and swept most of the soil back into the hole. When she lowered the mum into the shallower excavation and filled in the soil, the plant remained halfway buried.

"Still too deep."

"That's the way you're supposed to plant them."

"Why are you so cranky?"

"I'm not cranky." Laura knew she was acting bitchy. Whether due to the image of Nora in a tub full of blood, or thoughts about Arlo Massey, she wasn't sure. Probably both.

Across the street her neighbor walked by with her snarling little dog straining on a leash.

"Do you think we'd get in trouble if we murdered that damn dog?" Gracie asked.

Mrs. van Arsdale and the dog passed a couple of teenage girls walking in the opposite direction. The dog lunged, screeching and howling as he tried to attack the girls. They screamed and reflexively tried to kick the dog away from them.

"Don't kick my Shane," Mrs. Van Arsdale shouted. "I'll have you arrested for animal cruelty. You could've killed him!" The girls ran away with Shane snarling and tugging at his leash to chase them. Mrs. van Arsdale and Shane passed out of sight.

"Justifiable homicide," Laura said, deadpan.

Gracie laughed, and Laura joined in.

Gracie turned serious. "We need pills, barbiturates. That way Nora can pass with dignity from the comfort of her own bed."

"If she's intent on going forward despite our attempts to talk her out of it, I suppose taking barbiturates is the most humane way to proceed." Listening to herself, Laura felt unnerved by the clinical tone of her voice. Like she was discussing how to deal with over-flow parking for the annual Ladies Association installation dinner instead of how to assist a beloved family member take her own life.

Gracie said, "Nora told me her doctor's suspicious and won't prescribe them."

"Maybe she could buy some over-the-counter sleeping pills and take the whole bottle. I see it all the time on TV shows."

"Those medicines are over-the-counter for a reason. What if they don't work? She could get violently sick and be rushed off to the hospital. The drugs could destroy her liver but leave her alive, and that's the last thing she wants. Why don't you call your doctor? Tell him your nerves are jangled and you can't sleep due to the loss of your husband."

"I already had that conversation with him the week after Mickey passed. He prescribed a very low dose of Valium and was quite stern about overuse. Only a few pills and no re-fills. I doubt if he'd pre-scribe anything stronger. What about your doctor?"

"Already tried." Gracie said.

"If we explain our dilemma to Nora, Perhaps she'd reconsider."

"We both know that won't likely happen. She'll try over-the-counter drugs, or some online Sleep-to-Peace concoction, and the chances of her botching it are high. She might try slitting her wrists or even buy a gun."

"God help us."

"Hey, maybe we drive up to to a sketchy neighborhood in Baltimore, find a drug dealer and buy from him."

"Brilliant idea. Best case we're arrested, worst case we're killed."

"We have to do something. Nora's counting on us, and we can't let her down."

Two days later, Laura and Gracie walked Elvis down Eastgate under the canopy of fall leaves brilliant in their russet and gold hues, taking in the large old homes with their wide lawns and inviting porches. Figuring she had nothing to lose, the previous day Laura had called Dr. Lowe's office and left a message with Phyllis, his nurse, explaining her increased anxiety living without Mickey. She'd asked for a stronger sedative. Ten minutes later Dr. Lowe called her back, quite concerned. She could tell by his tone he was suspicious. He strongly suggested she seek grief counseling.

She paused to let Elvis water the grassy strip between the sidewalk and the street, and took a deep breath. Usually the crisp fall air invigorated her after languishing in the heat and humidity of a typical Maryland summer. But today, even the usually reliable tonic of a beautiful October day could not lift the shroud of melancholy enveloping her. Sadness grounded not only in her memories of Mickey, but also in her belief she'd failed Nora.

Gracie said, "What if we take Nora across the state line to D.C.? Doctor-assisted suicide's legal there."

"I already checked that out. Nora would have to establish residency, a process that takes time. Besides, she doesn't want to move to D.C., she wants to die in her own bed here, where she's lived her entire life."

Gracie froze. "Better protect your ankles. Look who's coming."

Mrs. van Arsdale approached, leading Shane on a leash. "We should cross," Laura whispered.

As Laura struggled to reroute Elvis, Gracie muttered, "Too late."

"Mrs. van Arsdale, lovely afternoon, isn't it?" Laura said with false cheer. Gracie bent down and spread her hands to protect her bare ankles. But something was wrong. Actually, not so much wrong as different. Shane was not nipping, not yipping, not pulling, not snarling, not nothing. He was as meek and mild as . . . well, Elvis.

"Sit," ordered Mrs. van Arsdale with a smug expression, and Shane sat on the sidewalk with an obedience that would make the folks up in Westminster proud.

Never taking her eyes away from Shane, Gracie stood up slowly, warily lifting her ankle shield. "Watch out," she whispered to Laura. "It could be a trick."

Laura couldn't believe what she was seeing. "Mrs. van Arsdale, I can't help but notice how well-behaved Shane appears this afternoon."

"Bit the mailman again. He said if I didn't do something he was going to call animal control and take Shane to the pound. Do you know how long my Shane would last in a common dog pound with those, those *mongrels*?" She said the word "mongrel" as if she'd just sucked a lemon.

"I understand completely," Laura said. She avoided looking down at her particular mongrel. "But how did you modify Shane's behavior?"

"I took him to the vet and explained that Shane was a bit high-strung, which is quite common in dogs possessing superior intelligence. He, of course, being a professional, understood completely and prescribed Alprozalam."

Gracie's face wrinkled into a confused expression. "Alpro—?"

"Xanax. It acts as a sedative on dogs just like people."

Laura asked, "So the vet prescribed Xanax for a dog?"

Mrs. Van Arsdale huffed. "Shane's not just a dog."

"Of course not," Laura agreed.

"Vets prescribe people medicines for dogs all the time. Only the doses are different. I filled it at my regular pharmacy."

Laura caught Gracie's eye. They were thinking the same thing. She looked down at Elvis, fast asleep at her feet. "Behave yourself!"

Mrs. van Arsdale stared at her as if she'd lost her mind. And maybe she had.

CHAPTER FOURTEEN

The Tidewater Creek Animal Hospital examining room was small but clean. Elvis, wearing a muzzle Gracie found at PetSmart the day before, perched on the stainless steel table while Dr. Strong examined him.

"He doesn't appear overly aggressive," the vet said as he carefully removed the muzzle.

Laura glanced at Gracie. "You caught him in one of his quiet moments. Most of the time he's a wild, snarling beast."

"He'll rip your hand right off," Gracie added. She pulled her left hand from her pocket where she'd been keeping it hidden. The hand was heavily bandaged to a point two inches above the wrist. Dr. Strong's eyes widened and he hastily buckled the muzzle back over Elvis' snout. While he was distracted, Laura removed a tiny plastic bottle from her jacket and squeezed some drops of saline into her eyes. She replaced the bottle before the vet turned back to her.

"We don't want to put him down," Laura whimpered, the saline rolling down her cheeks. Gracie comforted her.

"There, there, dear." She turned to Dr. Strong and in a stage whisper, said, "My saintly niece recently lost her husband. She spent all her days taking care of others. Elvis is her last fragile tether to life. There must be something you can do. A strong sedative perhaps?"

"There are several medications especially formulated for dogs."

"That won't work," Gracie said.

Laura said, "What she means is, Elvis is much too wild for normal doggie medicine. Could there be, by chance, any human medication we might try?"

"For serious cases we've prescribed Alprozalam but, once started, you would have to keep him on it."

"Only if you think it best," Laura responded. She saw Gracie struggling to control her excitement.

Dr. Stong led Elvis to the scale. "Seventy pounds." He paused, presumably doing the math in his head. "The pills come one miligram each, so seventy pounds is thirty-two kilograms . . . no more than three pills a day. Give them to him with food." He wrote out a prescription and handed it to Laura. "This is a Benzodiazapine, powerful stuff," he warned. "Do not exceed three a day. I'm giving you one month's worth with one re-fill. And make sure you keep his meds separate from people meds. While the drug is prescribed for humans—"

Gracie interrupted. "Xanax." Laura shot her a double-dagger look.

"That's correct. But without a doctor's supervision human consumption could make you very ill, or even prove fatal."

That's the idea, Laura thought, part of her still not believing she was about to acquire the poison that would kill Nora Meyers. She heard the sound of loud snoring.

Elvis was curled up on the scale, fast asleep.

"Another chocolate?"

Nora strained to offer them the plate of chocolates from her bedside table.

"Thanks, we're fine."

Nora needed two hands to lower the plate back to the table without spilling its contents. Her coloring had sallowed since Laura last saw her only a few days earlier. Gracie fluffed up Nora's pillow.

"Stop fussing," Nora said. With Gracie's help she'd put on some makeup. A little powder, lipstick. The rouge was layered on so thick at Nora's insistence that the line between cheek color and circus clown clearly had been crossed. Laura and Gracie had regaled her with the story of their success with Dr. Strong. Nora was enthralled. "The bandaged hand and the muzzle and the fake tears. Very clever."

"Yep." Laura wasn't feeling particularly clever. In fact, her emotions were clashing so violently inside her brain that she was certain her head was about to explode.

Nora glanced over at the medicine vial sitting on the nightstand, then locked eyes with Laura. "Thank you."

"You're welcome." Laura glanced at Gracie who nodded her encouragement. "Gracie and I, we've been thinking. I know we had a pact but this is serious and you need to be absolutely sure."

"You look like you could last a long time," Gracie added.

"I don't want to last a long time." Nora calmly smiled at both of them. "I know this is a lot harder for you than for me. But I need you and . . . and I'm ready." She reached out and took Laura's hand.

"Oh, Nora."

"Are you sure there's no one else you'd like us to call?" Gracie asked.

"Just you two. Well, maybe Everett. He was part of our pact, too. There really is no one else. Allan's been gone twenty years now." She turned to a black and white photo of a handsome young man in his early twenties. "We were married when I was only seventeen. I still miss him." A guilty smile crossed her face.

"What are you thinking?" Gracie asked.

"Allan was the only man I ever . . . you know."

"Had sex with?" Laura asked.

Nora nodded, embarrassed.

Gracie's eyes widened. "Really? Only one? Ever wish you'd done it with another man?"

Nora blushed. "Wishing's a waste of time. That opportunity passed many years ago. It's too late."

Gracie focused on the handsome man in the photograph, and Laura could tell the wheels were turning. A sure sign of trouble.

Gracie said, "Okay, here's what I'm thinking. Mickey didn't get to run the bases until he was dead."

It took only a moment for Laura to see where this was heading. "Gracie, that's crazy."

"They have a Make-a-Wish service for dying kids, but nothing for adults, right?" Gracie turned to Nora. "Remember how you said chocolates were your only guilty pleasure?"

"Yes . . ."

"Well, you need to expand your horizons."

"I'm afraid I don't understand."

"I think what Gracie's saying—"

"Both of us. Right Laura? Both of us?"

She heard Mickey's soft, wistful voice in her head. *Wish I were ten so I could run the bases . . .*

Gracie plopped a chocolate into her mouth and grinned. "Nora, before you take those pills we're going to get you laid."

CHAPTER FIFTEEN

Gracie pounded the table. "What the hell happened to all the gigolos?"

Laura continued to scroll through the local yellow pages on her laptop while Gracie scrunched even closer so she could see the screen.

Gracie fumed. "Exotic dance clubs, escort services. They're all women performing for men. Damn men ran 'em out of town, that's what happened.

Laura stopped and leaned back in her chair. What the hell was she doing? Searching the internet for a man to perform sex for money? Had she lost her mind?

"Women should have a right to buy a roll in the hay just like a man," Gracie proclaimed. "Do you think other people know about this? It's discrimination."

"Write your congressman."

"Wait, what about that one?" Gracie pointed to an ad on the screen with an accompanying drawing showing three young women reaching up to touch the six-pack midriff of a young male dancer. He appeared naked, his groin covered by the strategically placed hands. The ad for The Stallion Corral proclaimed that only ladies were admitted until midnight, then "YEEHAWWW!"

Laura shuddered. "Yeehawww? Maybe the place is a little too—"

Gracie's eyes lit up. "Too what? You want a male prostitute? This is where we need to go."

Night fell as Laura drove Gracie and Nora down Route 301 into southern Maryland. They passed a sign welcoming them to Waldorf.

For the last hour she'd repeatedly mumbled under her breath, "It's not too late to turn back, it's not too late to turn back." But she'd kept driving.

"Why are you so nervous?" Gracie said.

"I'm not nervous."

"The speed limit's sixty-five and you're driving forty-five."

Laura accelerated another ten miles an hour. "I don't think I've ever been down this way before, and I'm unfamiliar with the roads, that's all."

Gracie said, "Back in the early sixties before completion of I-95, me and my friends would come down here all the time. Waldorf back then was like the wild west—gambling, prostitution, cheap booze. Even shoot-outs in the streets. And they never carded you. With a few exceptions, all that fun dried up once the interstate was built."

"Might one of those exceptions be the Stallion Corral?" Nora asked.

Gracie pointed ahead to a huge neon sign. "Looks like we're about to find out."

Laura drove into the Corral parking lot past the sign reading: "Welcome Beverly Pascali Bachelorette Party! No males till midnight, then Girls! Girls! Girls! YEEHAWWWW!"

"There's that 'yeehaw' word again," Laura said.

Gracie said, "It's not yeehaw. It's *Yeehawww!*"

Nora laughed. Laura purposely didn't give Gracie the satisfaction of a reaction. Why encourage the woman further? Through the rearview mirror she glanced at Nora in the back seat and noticed her eyes were bright, her cheeks flushed with excitement. Laura took a deep breath and reminded herself she was here for Nora. As long as Nora remained willing to go forward Laura would do her best to see their little adventure through. She drove around to the back and parked in the darkest corner of the lot.

"Why all the way back here?" Gracie asked.

"Because I'd rather not be seen entering an establishment called the Stallion Corral, that's why." She turned back to Nora. "Are you sure you're feeling up to this?"

"Don't have much feeling time left, so let's do it."

"Atta girl," Gracie said, giving Nora a thumbs-up. They stepped out of the car. Laura and Gracie each took one of Nora's arms and approached the building, a tired one-story cinderblock structure that no doubt had seen many different uses over its lifetime, most of them falling into the tawdry category. A line of twenty-something males, awash in testosterone, stood in front of an entrance marked Stallions only a few yards away from a second entrance marked Fillies. A young woman wearing denim shorts and a tight halter top with the "Stallions Corral" logo emblazoned across her ample chest sold beer to the boys in line.

"Can they do that?" Laura asked. "Isn't it against the law to sell alcohol outside a bar?"

Gracie shot her a "You've gotta be kidding" look.

Gracie and Laura helped Nora walk toward the Fillies entrance. They immediately found themselves surrounded by a crowd of rowdy girls from the bachelorette group. Judging by their breath and behavior, they'd already been imbibing. The girls teased the boys by shaking their butts in time to the blaring music piped through an outdoor speaker. One particularly tipsy girl lifted her t-shirt and flashed her boobs, drawing a barrage of whistles and catcalls before entering the bar with her giggling friends.

A male dancer dressed in nothing but a red silk jockstrap with the name "Chauncey" stitched in white vertically down the front, danced and gyrated through the crowd of women at the entrance, whipping them into a frenzy.

"Isn't he cold?" Laura asked.

"No," Gracie responded, "I'd say he's hot." Nora giggled.

"Yo, Mrs. Beckman."

Startled, Laura turned to see Arlo with a wide grin on his face standing in line with the horny boys. "Mr. Massey?"

At that moment, Chauncey thrust his pelvis back and forth hard into Laura's butt. She yelped and jumped away. Arlo wagged his finger at her. She quickly turned her back to him and spotted Gracie sidling up to Chauncey. Laura forced her way through the crowd, grabbed Gracie's hand, and pulled her away.

Gracie shouted over the music. "Wasn't that the rude man from the baseball game back there?"

Laura huffed, "I don't remember."

Though she hid a key and entered the Eastgate house during the day without knocking—growing up it was her house and she still considered it her house—at night Brooke made a point to knock. She rapped three times and waited for her mother to answer the door. Would her mother be willing to engage in an adult discussion? Not to clear the air—Brooke knew the air between them could probably never be fully cleansed—but perhaps they could start. She'd thought about calling first, but figured Laura would've come up with an excuse. She knocked again and when there was no response, strongly considered walking away. But she didn't.

She used her key and entered. "Mother?" No answer. She walked into the kitchen and saw Laura's computer opened. She tapped a key to clear the screen-saver and dropped her jaw when she saw the home page for the Stallion Corral. She couldn't believe it? Okay, her mother's adventure at the Orioles game was one thing, but Laura Beckman visiting a strip club? *Why Mother, whose behavior is inappropriate now?*

She had an idea. Why not have a little fun? She pulled out her phone and dialed. It took Everett only one ring to answer.

"Hello? Brooke?"

"I really hate to bother you, but it's about Mother."

"Oh, my God. What happened? Is she all right?"

"I don't know." Some tears at this point might add effect. She sniffled and whimpered into the phone. "I'm so embarrassed to tell you this, I know how fond you are of her."

"What, what?" Everett was approaching hysterical territory.

"I think she's gone to a—a male strip club."

Laura could best describe the wall color as whorehouse red. Music pounded. Magenta and turquoise lights flashed around the room as if projected from the bubble on top of a psychedelic police car. Rows of narrow wooden benches stained with who knew what were arranged on a raked incline surrounding a small stage. A battered eight-inch wide wooden railing that doubled as a cocktail table ran in front of each row of benches.

"Theater in the round," Nora marveled.

"Doubt if *Hamlet* ever graced this venue," Laura said. She jerked her hand away from a greasy railing and fished in her purse for a sanitary wipe. "When do you think they last cleaned this place?"

Young women filled the room, most taking turns rolling their heads back and gulping shooters of cheap liquor while their friends whooped and hollered. Like a football blocking back, Gracie led Laura and Nora through the crowd to a front-row bench where the three of them wedged themselves next to two half-drunk young women.

"Hi! I'm Carla, and this is Charmagne," said the bleached blonde. She nodded to the brunette with a pink stripe running through her hair. "Are you Bevvy's grammys?" She gestured toward a girl several rows over, the obvious center of attention.

"No," Laura responded. "We're definitely not Bevvy's grammys."

"We're here for the meat!" Gracie shouted. Before Laura could react, a male voice boomed over the loudspeakers.

"Ladies and *more* ladies!" The audience cheered. "A big Stallion welcome to a very special herd of fillies joining us tonight to celebrate the hitchin' up of Beverly Ann Pascali!" The girls cheered wildly as Beverly, already a bit unsteady, stood to acknowledge their applause. "And to start off Beverly's special night," the voice continued, "please welcome, Fast Eddie!"

The music volume rose even louder as a short, bleached-blond, well-built young man dressed as a western riverboat gambler danced down the stairs to the stage. His costume consisted of a bowler hat, spats, and several oversized playing cards protruding from his jacket. Four aces peeked out from his back pocket. He gyrated his hips suggestively, whipping up the girls, as he pranced around the stage before pausing in front of Nora. Eddie flashed a wide smile, then slowly peeled off his jacket and shirt, revealing rippled muscles and a well-defined abdomen. Nora gasped. "Oh, my."

Laura rose from her seat. "This is not a proper place for us. I don't know what I was thinking."

"Sit down," Gracie ordered. She nodded toward Nora who was beaming, transfixed by the show. Laura reluctantly complied, then watched Fast Eddie sashay over to Beverly and wiggle his butt. "Pick a card any card," he invited. Beverly yanked one of the aces from his pocket. Instantly his pants fell away leaving his spats and a white G-string with the ace of spades embroidered on the front as his only remaining clothing.

The girls went wild as he gyrated harder. Beverly reached out to tug down his G-string but he deftly turned away and danced around the stage until he was flush in front of Laura. He jutted his pelvis back and forth in time to the pounding music, the ace of spades face-high. Laura sat transfixed, then covered her eyes. The entire room broke out in laughter. Laura spread two of her fingers to take another peek at that crazy ace. Fast Eddie winked, then danced away to another side of the stage. Gracie climbed over the rail to follow him, but Laura and Carla hauled her back as the crowd booed.

A scantily clad, gum-chewing waitress approached. "Can I get you something, ladies?"

Gracie pointed to the dancer. "How about him?" The waitress ignored her. She'd obviously heard that one before.

"I'll have an iced tea," responded Laura. "Twenty buck mini-mum," said the waitress. "That's a lot of iced tea."

"Iced tea will be fine."

"Wild Turkey on the rocks," Gracie said.

"Make that two," added Nora. Laura raised an eyebrow. Nora continued. "Only I like my bourbon straight up." Gracie locked eyes with Nora, then both started giggling like a couple of girls who'd happened across their first Internet porn site. Even the waitress smiled as she made a note on her pad. No one watching would guess

Nora was very ill. Laura knew Nora had taken pain meds before coming, but her close to normal appearance still re-ignited Laura's misgivings. Maybe if Nora experienced a bit of excitement, she'd realize life could continue to offer interesting moments, and she'd keep fighting.

Laura turned to Charmagne. "Do the dancers ever . . . you know?"

"They're supposed to whip us into high heat so when the boys come in at midnight for the girl strippers, we're ripping their clothes off."

"That's when the joint makes its money," said Carla. "The boys get charged a hundred bucks a head minimum, and they pay it willingly."

"But what about the dancers?" Gracie pressed.

"They can get into a lot of trouble if they fraternize with the customers," responded Charmagne. "But—"

"But what?" Gracie asked.

"But for the right amount of money they'll meet a girl in her car during a break for a quickie," Carla explained.

"How does one go about—?"

"Slip the waitress an extra fifty and tell her the color and make of your car, then exit out that side door," added Carla, pointing to a narrow door in the back of the room, barely perceptible in the shadows. "He'll find you."

"But Eddie's only the first dancer," Charmagne said. "You need to shop."

Laura said, "Nora, coming to this tawdry place was our idea, so if you have even the slightest reservation—"

Nora beamed. "I love shopping."

An hour later, Nora and Gracie had developed a nice buzz. When Buffalo Bill whipped off his chaps and galloped around the stage,

Nora wrote something on a cocktail napkin and held it up: 8.5. The other girls around the room saw what she was doing. Encouraged by the support, as each new dancer performed the crowd would turn to Nora who would oblige by holding up a score. No one received a ten. The girls cheered, and Nora basked in the attention.

Laura suspected she was having the best time she'd had in ages. And maybe the reason was more than simply the scantily clad young men prancing around a ring. Being part of a happy crowd, the excitement, the cheering, the actual *joining in* on the fun.

Like going to a baseball game.

CHAPTER SIXTEEN

"Nor-a, Nor-a!"

Bevvy and her friends gathered behind Nora, and as each dancer finished Nora wrote a score on a napkin, then quickly covered the number with her hand. Nora teased, hiding her score until the chants reached a crescendo, then thrust the napkin high in the air triggering wild cheers. Even the dancers raised their game, so to speak, in an attempt to win a high score from Nora Meyers. Laura had long since given in, joining Gracie and the girls in cheering Nora on. Nora had yet to award a ten.

"That last one was a ten if I ever saw one," Gracie said.

Laura laughed. "You've said that for every dancer who's come out."

"They're all tens."

The announcer's voice boomed across the room. "All you lovely fillies out there, let's hear a loud 'whinny' for our newest wrangler, Stoney Hammer!" The girls, with Laura, Gracie, and Nora joining in, tried to whinny, but their alcohol-slurred attempts more resembled wheezing brays.

Dressed as a hard-hat construction worker, Stoney pranced onto the stage. Tall with an angular face, Stoney possessed a charisma not evident among his pretty-boy colleagues. Laura glanced at Nora. Her eyes shone even brighter. Stoney danced over to Nora and her

new friends, his eyes focused only on her. Nora could barely catch
her breath.

With a single motion, Stoney snapped away his jeans and tossed
them to the floor. Down only to his work boots, his tool belt, and
a tiny leather G-string, Stony bumped and thrust and jutted and
twisted and wiggled and undulated in front of Nora, moving to the
deep beat of the music, energized by the primal screams of the young
women. When he finished, Laura was sure Nora would expire right
then and there. Actually, not the worst way to go. Nora scribbled
on a napkin and didn't hesitate to hold it up high. A ten. The girls
squealed their approval and patted Nora on the back.

Nora wrote another note, folded the napkin, and passed it to
Laura. It read: "I want him."

The three of them sat in Laura's car, their eyes trained on the
side door of the Stallion Corral. "Do you think he received the message?" Nora asked for the third time.

"I saw the waitress give him the napkin," Laura reassured her.
She checked Nora in the rearview mirror. The vibrancy she'd shown
seemed to have drained away.

"There." Gracie pointed to the side door. It opened slowly.

"I think I may pee my pants," Nora said, eliciting laughter from
her friends.

But it was Fast Eddie, not Stoney, who emerged.

Laura and Gracie wiped the light condensation from the windshield. They saw Fast Eddie walk quickly over to a red, late-model
Mercedes sedan and step into the shadows.

Nora gasped. "He's taking off his clothes." Within seconds,
Eddie was completely naked.

Laura was transfixed. "How did he do that so fast?"

"He's a professional," Gracie responded.

Nora's jaw dropped. He's not wearing his . . . you know."

"Yes, Nora, that's known in the male anatomy as a penis, and a rather nice one I might add," Gracie said.

"I know what a penis is. I've seen a penis before," Nora responded.

They watched the car door opened and Beverly Pascali, scheduled to be the blushing bride in less than twenty-four hours, emerged and embraced Eddie. For a few moments she slowly rubbed her hips into his groin, then broke away and pulled him into the back seat of the car.

"The bride-to-be, I can't believe it," Laura said.

"Sure didn't have anything like that in our day," Nora added.

"Damn shame," Gracie said. "Seventy-six percent of divorces wouldn't have happened if the bride had gotten a little action the night before she tied the knot."

Laura said, "You made that up."

"Maybe I did, and maybe I didn't."

Nora pointed to the Mercedes. "Look at that." The car rocked up and down, moving faster and faster.

"Good suspension," Laura observed dryly.

Gracie nodded. "German engineering."

Nora's voice rose an octave. "There he is." Laura and Gracie turned back to see the Corral's side door open again, and this time Stoney emerged. He spotted their car. "He's coming, he's coming!"

Laura suddenly realized they had no plans for step two, when Stoney actually arrived at the car. She and Gracie would need to leave, of course. Should she pay before or after? Where would they wait? How could they make sure he didn't hurt her?

Stoney quickly reached the Lexus and stepped into the shadows next to the driver's side. Because of the tinted windows and condensation on the glass, he couldn't see inside. The ladies could barely make out his shadow. "He can't see us," Laura said. Part of her hoped he would go away.

"Is he taking his clothes off? I bet he's taking his clothes off," Nora said.

"We shouldn't look," Laura warned.

Paying no attention, Gracie quickly reached across Laura and rubbed away a peep spot in the condensation on the driver side window.

"Make it bigger," Nora whispered from the back seat. "I can't see."

Laura paused only a moment before carefully wiping more condensation away.

Stoney removed his signature leather G-string. He was now buck-naked. "Oh, my," Nora whispered.

Sweat beaded on Gracie's forehead. "That's . . . beautiful. Laura, you have to admit—"

"I don't have to admit—"

"Oh . . . " Nora interrupted.

"What?" asked Laura, alarmed.

"I think I just felt something, you know, down there." She giggled.

The door handle turned, and Stoney jumped into the back seat. His eyes widened. "Oh, sorry, wrong car." Mortified, he used one hand to cover his crotch and the other to open the car door.

"Wait," Laura said.

"It's the right car, sweetie," Gracie assured him. Stoney bore the frightened expression of someone staring at three hungry wolves.

Laura's voice cracked. "We would like to retain your services." Her attempt to sound business-like failed. Hardly surprising. She was about to enter a commercial transaction to purchase sex with a prostitute. She felt like she needed a shower.

"For who?" Stoney asked.

"For me," Nora replied.

Before Stoney could react, Laura grabbed the door latch. "Gracie and I will leave you two—"

"No," interrupted Nora. "Not here. Tomorrow night, my place. I need time to prepare."

A few minutes later, Stoney emerged from the car into the dark parking lot. Laura rolled down her window. "We'll see you tomorrow, then."

"Mrs. Beckman?" Arlo emerged from the shadows with a stupid grin on his face.

"Oh, God," she murmured under her breath.

Arlo glanced at Stoney, who was scrambling to put his clothes back on.

"You don't understand," Laura said. Hopefully the darkness prevented him from seeing the blood rush to her face. Where's a hole to crawl into when you need one?

Arlo wagged his finger. "Just remember, Mrs. Beckman, it ain't the size of the wand that brings the rabbit out of the hat, it's the magic."

Laura gaped at Arlo, unable to speak.

"Mother?"

Laura peered over Arlo's shoulder to see Brooke and Everett approaching. She closed her eyes and pinched the bridge of her nose, wishing she could magically transport herself somewhere, anywhere but the Stallion Corral parking lot in Waldorf, Maryland.

Brooke wore her expression of mock horror quite comfortably. She pointed to Stoney's bare butt, and emitted a theatrical gasp.

"Laura, are you alright?" asked Everett, assuming the posture of the hero arriving in the nick of time to save the damsel in distress. Stoney quickly slipped on his leather G-string, then his jeans. Without a word he grabbed his remaining clothes and hurried off toward the club. Everett puffed out his chest and challenged Arlo. "You're that rude fellow from the baseball game. I have half a mind to—"

"Half a mind's a terrible thing to waste."

Everett's head appeared about to explode.

"Look, pal, I'm an innocent observer here. Fact is, your friend will sleep well tonight 'cause she just had her field plowed." He flashed his idiot grin.

"That's not true," Laura said, her eyes burning into Arlo.

A loud clanging interrupted the standoff. Arlo checked his watch. "One minute to midnight. They're gonna open the doors." Without another word, he turned and jogged quickly toward the Stallion's door where the anxious boys were pushing and shoving to gain entrance. Laura, disgusted, watched him go.

"Yeehaw," she whispered under her breath.

Brooke couldn't contain her glee. "Mother, your behavior is not only highly *inappropriate,* but frankly rather disgusting and I, for one, question whether it may be time to discuss assisted living."

Laura glared at her, then rolled up the car window and started the engine.

"I'm not letting this go, Laura," Everett shouted. "I'll be in your kitchen tomorrow morning."

Laura closed her eyes and forced herself to take three deep breaths. She concluded any humiliation heaped upon her was deserved for trying to grant a ridiculous wish to a dying woman.

She drove home without uttering another word.

Everett brought the coffee pot over from the counter and filled everyone's cup around the kitchen table. It had been a late night, and all except Brooke were dragging. Laura hadn't been able to sleep. Everett and Brooke stared at her and Gracie as if they were a couple of truants. Laura had come clean about everything—Nora, the pills, the gigolo, everything. Everett was shocked, Brooke bemused.

"Wipe that smirk off your face," Laura snapped at her daughter.

"What smirk?"

"You know what smirk. And I don't even know why you're here."

"I wouldn't have missed this." Brooke lit a cigarette.

"Yes, I mind if you smoke, and thanks for asking."

Brooke stared at her defiantly, and kept on smoking.

Everett tentatively covered Laura's hand with his. "Laura, we're worried about you. I know we made a pact, but what you're doing, I think it may be illegal. Look what happened to that Kevorkian fellow."

She slipped her hand away. "Mickey suffered for months, stripped of the dignity to make the most important decision about his life, *his* life. We all remember what Nora went through the first time, and now that the end is inevitable she doesn't want to go through the pain and indignity a second time."

Brooke shook her head. "And hiring a gigolo to service an old woman, somehow that's okay?"

Her daughter echoed her own feelings, or at least feelings she experienced half the time. But she refused to concede. "What's not right to me is putting off doing that one thing you always wanted to do until it's too late." Brooke stifled a cough, triggering an instinctive concern in Laura's mind. "Did you ever have a doctor check out that cough?"

"I'm fine."

"When you get old and sick with lung cancer you'll have wished you'd listened to me and didn't start with the cigarettes."

"I said I'm fine, and by the time I'm old they'll have invented a cure and everyone will be smoking."

Everett was not to be sidetracked. "I was brought up to believe that suicide's a sin."

"Unbearable pain's a sin," Gracie retorted. "Having some stranger in a white uniform wipe your ass after you soil yourself, that's the mother of all sins in my book."

Brooke finished her coffee and stood to leave. "Part of me actually agrees with what you're doing, but . . ." She shook her head. "I don't know. I've done a lot of things in my life I'm not very proud of, but there's one thing I can still say."

"Please enlighten us," Laura said.

"I never murdered anybody."

Brooke headed for the door, and Laura didn't move a muscle. Brooke had abandoned her husband and small daughter, an unforgiveable offense in Laura's view, while she was about to do a good thing—helping a wonderful old woman escape lingering pain. Her daughter was trying to flip things around, assume the moral high ground. But it wouldn't work.

Laura felt herself shrink inside.

No! It wasn't murder . . .

CHAPTER SEVENTEEN

Nora sat up in bed, giddy as a seventeen-year-old primping for the prom. She held a mirror in her shaking hand as Laura applied some blush to her cheek while Gracie brushed out her thin hair. They'd applied color to it earlier, and Nora appeared pleased with the results. Cosmetics and hair products littered the bedspread.

"If you keep brushing, you're going to pull out what little I have left," Nora groused.

"I'm trying to give it some body. Now hold still."

Nora complied. Laura could see she loved being fussed over. Maybe it helped her forget the pain in her belly for a little while. Nora held the mirror closer. "Don't you think I need more blush? I don't want him to think he's, you know, with a cadaver."

"If I put on too much it doesn't look natural," Laura said.

Nora had called Laura with a shopping list. New bed linens—she'd been insistent Laura buy "those expensive ones and not white." Maybe cream or gold, she'd suggested. And new bed pillows; she didn't want him smelling old lady hair products on her pillow. And a nightgown. Not frilly, not red or black—she wasn't a harlot—but not an old lady gown either. Laura had done her best and an hour earlier they'd pulled off Nora's sensible white sheets and replaced them with butter-cream, 380 count Egyptian cotton. The nightgown had been a more difficult decision. Laura brought two gowns from Nordstrom for Nora to consider, and she fretted for fifteen minutes before electing a gold cotton knee-length with a flowered bodice. She made the choice because the gold complemented her new sheets.

Laura asked, "Did you take your pain meds?"

"Yes."

"Are they helping? Should you take more?"

"If I take more I'll be unconscious, which defeats the purpose. Now, what time is it? I can't see the clock. Gracie, move so I can see the clock."

Gracie didn't budge. "It's nine minutes to eight, exactly one minute later than the last time you asked."

"Don't be a smarty pants," Nora said. She watched her friends minister to her for another moment, then gasped.

"What?" Laura and Gracie said in unison as each stepped back, afraid that they might have somehow hurt her.

"Food. He's coming over at dinnertime, and I have absolutely nothing prepared." She tried to sit up, but Gracie gently pushed her back. "What's a gentleman to think when he arrives at dinnertime and I have nothing prepared?"

"Hush," Laura ordered.

"But he's a big man with a big appetite."

"I'm sure he'll eat before he comes," Gracie said.

"You think so?"

Both nodded.

"What time is it? Gracie, why is it you always stand in front of the—"

Gracie responded without turning. "Eight minutes to eight." She pulled her iPhone from her pocket. "Now, what kind of music do you want?"

"I don't know, something soft. Maybe Johnny Mathis. No, that's too old-fashioned."

Gracie tapped her phone, waited a moment, then said, "Okay, here's a list of the top ten most sensual instrumentals to play while you're having sex."

Nora said, "I don't have time for the whole list, what's number one?"

"Ravel's 'Bolero.'" Gracie tapped a few more times. "Here you go. London Symphony. Part of a full concert." She tapped once more, then set the phone on the dresser. "Where's the speaker?"

Laura handed her a small Bluetooth speaker she'd brought along for the occasion, and Gracie positioned the speaker next to the phone. In a few moments the soulful sound of a single clarinet filled the room. Gracie lowered the volume.

Laura found herself swaying to the music. "Beautiful."

"What if he doesn't come?" Nora said. "Of course, who could blame him. I mean, when you think about someone like him with someone like me—"

The doorbell rang. "He's early," Laura said. Nora remained frozen in place as Laura swept all of the hair and makeup paraphernalia off the bed into a wicker trash basket and carried it to the bathroom.

Gracie reached into her purse. "It's been a while, so I thought you might need this." She pulled out a tube of K-Y Jelly and set it on the bedside table.

"Thanks." The doorbell rang again. "Quick, get it before he leaves."

Laura hurried down the hallway to the living room and opened the door to find Stoney looking very nervous. "Come in."

Stoney entered, hesitant.

Laura closed the door. "She's in the bedroom."

"I almost didn't come. I mean, she's old enough to be my grandmother."

"So, why did you?"

Stoney shrugged, sheepish. "It's what I do. And your offer of a bonus, well . . . it's how I make my living."

To Laura, he seemed nervous, no longer the confident stud, gyrating almost naked in front of a gaggle of screaming women. "Follow me." Like a son obeying his mother, Stoney followed Laura to the bedroom. When Laura opened the door, they saw Nora sit up in bed, glowing. "Nora, dear, you remember Mr. Hammer?"

Stoney smiled broadly, turning on the charm. He was working now.

"Nora, you look lovely."

Nora beamed. "Did Laura offer you some refreshments?"

"Everything I need to satisfy me I'm looking at right now."

Nora's face flushed bright red.

Stoney eyed a plate of chocolates on the bedside table. "I should tell you I have a sweet tooth for chocolate."

Nora beamed and offered the plate of sweets to Stoney. She lifted the plate with one hand and, while not exactly steady, the hand only trembled a little bit.

"I think we can take it from here," Nora said.

As Gracie and Laura passed Stony on the way out of the room Gracie whispered, "If you hurt her, you'll have to answer to me."

His eyes widened, and Laura was certain he would bolt. "Don't pay any attention to her. You'll be fine." She pulled Gracie out of the room and quickly closed the door behind them.

For a long moment there was dead silence; neither of them moved. *Oh, my God, this is crazy.* Laura reached for the doorknob. "What were we thinking?"

Gracie gently tugged Laura's hand away. "Her life, her choice, remember?"

Inside the bedroom, the light from the bathroom leaking through the partially opened door offered the only illumination, but it was enough for Nora to see the tall young man standing over her. Stoney sat down on the bed, still fully clothed, and gently caressed her cheek with the back of his hand.

She cleared her throat. "Uh, Stoney, it has been some time since I—"

"Hush." He stood and removed his clothes. Not dramatically like on stage or slowly like a stripper, simply a man taking his clothes off.

Nora was glad to see he wore normal boxer shorts and not his leather G-string. Even in the dim light she could make out the musculature of his body. Not like one of those body-builders she would see in magazine ads. More like a swimmer. When he removed his shorts Nora turned her head away. She didn't know why. After all she'd glimpsed his private parts through the car window in the parking lot. He slipped under the covers next to her. She stiffened and could hardly breathe. A tiny voice in the back of her head took note of the fact that her pain had momentarily diminished. But she wasn't thinking about that. She wasn't going to think about death, only life.

Stoney gently rubbed her arm. Nora remembered the K-Y on the table and reached for it. Stoney gently pulled her withered arm back. "Let's wait a bit for that. He put his long, muscular arm around her and pulled her close so her head was resting on his shoulder. She stiffened. What was she supposed to do? It had been so long.

"Tell me about your life, Nora."

"I thought we were going to—"

"We will. But first, talk to me. Tell me about Nora Meyers."

She let out a deep sigh and relaxed. She felt like a child in her parent's protective embrace.

And so Nora told the story of her life from as far back as she could remember. She probably got a few facts and dates wrong, but it didn't matter. Stony stroked her arms as she spoke, while he listened intently. Then he told her about his life, and they nestled together like long-time lovers, comfortable in each other's arms. After almost an hour had passed, Stoney bent over and gently kissed her.

Nora felt her body slowly responding with sensations she hadn't experienced for years. She reached to her throat and untied the ribbon holding her new nightgown closed. He slipped it over her head. She reached her arm, fragile as a dry twig, around his back and found the strength to press against his rippling muscles. He carefully rolled on top, propped up on his elbows so not to allow any weight to fall on her.

"I won't break," she whispered. The guttural sound of her voice was not caused by her illness. As he enveloped her she silently gave thanks to her broken body for allowing her this last gift, a feeling of exquisite pleasure that for this one moment in time washed the pain away.

Laura checked the clock again, worry showing. "It's been almost an hour and a half. I was expecting four, maybe five minutes. If he hurt her—"

Gracie finished Laura's sentence. " . . . his hammer will lose its head."

They heard the bedroom door open and turned anxiously to see Stoney and Nora walking toward them. She was in her bathrobe, walking unsteadily. He had his arm around her, propping her up. She glowed as Stoney helped her to a chair. He gently kissed her on the cheek, then headed for the door. Laura dug in her purse and removed the white envelope containing his fee and handed him the envelope.

He gave it back and waved to Nora, his eyes welling up with tears. "Bye, Nora."

"Bye, Norman."

Stoney took a deep breath, wiped his eyes on his sleeve, and left.

Laura turned to Nora. "Norman?"

"Norman Pearlstein. Very nice young man." She sighed wistfully. "Sex is such an important part of life. We all should do more of it." She started coughing, then winced in pain.

Laura helped her up. "Come, we need to get you back to bed."

"I'd like to leave on Saturday. Would that be okay?"

Laura glanced at Gracie. "Of course, dear. Now, tell us about Norman."

"Details, we want details," Gracie said.

Nora reached into the pocket of her robe, removed the tube of K-Y Jelly, and handed it to Gracie. She grinned, and when she spoke Laura detected a note of pride in her weak voice.

"Didn't need it."

CHAPTER EIGHTEEN

Brooke left early for work so she'd have time to first stop by and speak to her mother about Nora. She drove down Eastgate and asked herself again why she even cared. If her mother wanted to throw her life away what did it matter? Her answer—her rationalization?—centered around Jennie. Though the girl probably hated her—with justification in Brooke's judgment—Brooke would do anything to spare Jennie more pain. If Laura went to jail for illegally assisting in a suicide, Jennie would be crushed, and Brooke could not allow that to happen.

She pulled into the driveway and spotted Laura rocking back and forth on the front porch swing, holding a glass of iced tea. *How do old people do that for hours on end?* Not that her mother was old; barely nineteen years separated them. The woman only acted old.

When Brooke stepped out of the car she felt a twinge of satisfaction at seeing her mother's surprised expression.

"Shouldn't you be at work?" Laura asked.

"Not due till six."

"Why don't you find a nine-to-five job like everybody else?"

"Everybody else doesn't work nine-to-five."

"You're a grown woman, do as you please. All I'm saying—"

"I didn't come over here to talk about my employment options."

Brooke forced herself to ignore her mother's "this oughta be good" expression, and sat down in the wicker chair across from the swing. She came straight to the point. "I don't want you to go through with it."

"Go through with what?" Laura's feigned expression of innocence was pathetic.

"You know very well what I'm talking about. Nora."

"Not looking for any advice, but thanks for the thought."

Brooke saw her mother's whole body tense up like a brittle twig where the slightest pressure could crack her open, and she consciously softened her tone. "I'm serious. Look, I know Nora says this is what she wants, but she's hardly in a state to make a rational decision. And even if she were, it's our job to protect her."

"Who knows what our job is? I witnessed, *you* witnessed your father die a long, painful death. Nora decided she didn't want her life to end that way. Do I feel comfortable helping her take her own life? Of course not. I have deep reservations, and both Gracie and I have continuously pressed her to make sure this is what she wants. It is. She only has a little time left and—"

"Says who?" Brooke heard her voice rising in violation of the solemn oath she'd made minutes earlier to keep things civil. A part of her knew her anger rooted from her own clashing emotions about her daddy. She hadn't wanted to to be cheated out of a single moment of his life, yet her desire to hang onto him no matter how much he suffered infused her with guilt as she remembered his lingering agony in painful detail. She took a deep breath and again forced a lowered voice. "So a few doctors say she'll die in six months. You know what they call the guy who graduates last in his class in med school? Doctor."

"Nora assures me her doctors are the finest in the area."

"She could live a year, maybe longer. New drugs come on the market every day. Who knows, in six months there could be a cure. And even if the docs are right and she dies in a few months, you want to take those months away from her? If she has problems with pain, up her meds, but don't kill her."

"Her life, her choice," Laura said, her voice catching.

"That's bullshit. Despite what she says, she's relying on you to do the right thing, and the right thing is not murdering her."

"It's not murder."

"Law says it is."

'You're offering legal advice now? Guess I must've missed your law school graduation."

Usually, her mother's biting sarcasm cut deep, but today Brooke saw Laura's response as defensive, like she was trying to ward off someone telling her what she herself was thinking.

"I thought I understood how much Daddy's death affected you," Brooke said, "just like it affected me. But I was wrong. His passing seems to have changed you. The old Laura wouldn't ever have considered running around the bases at Camden Yards. The old Laura would never have agreed to assist in a family member's suicide. As I've said, part of me likes the change away from tight-assed bitch to a woman living, if not on the edge, at least closer to the edge. But what you're contemplating goes too far, even for me." Brooke was tempted to ask her what happened in college to convert her from a young woman who apparently did live on the edge to the country club conformist, but doing so would breach the promise of confidentiality she'd made to Gracie. "Have you run your little scheme by Anna?"

"It's not a 'little scheme,' and . . ." Laura cast her eyes down to the slatted porch floora and lowered her voice. "I'd appreciate it if you wouldn't mention this to your little sister."

Brooke loved Anna, and had always been protective of her. No use bringing her into this mess. She nodded her assent.

Laura mumbled, "Thank you. "Now, you better get to work. Don't want to lose another job, do you?"

Brooke noticed the absence of her mother's usual caustic tone. Before Brooke could respond, Laura abruptly stood and wrapped her arms around her daughter, pulling her tight. Brooke was speechless.

Then, without another word, Laura entered the house and closed the door.

CHAPTER NINETEEN

Saturday morning. D-Day.

Laura drove with Gracie to Anchor Cove. D-Day, only here the D stood for death. Try as she might, she couldn't push Brooke's visit the day before from her mind. She found herself feeling bad about the conversation. Her daughter was only trying to help, and Brooke was right. What they were about to do was not only arguably immoral and probably illegal, but insane.

My God, she was about to provide the suicide weapon to a woman she dearly loved.

She thought of Megan, all alone in that L.A. walk-up. *C'mon, Megs, it'll be fun . . . just a taste . . . Laura, help me . . . so sorry, Megs . . . my fault my fault my fault . . .*

"Laura? You okay?"

"No I'm not okay. Of course I'm not okay. Listen, we have to try one more time to talk Nora out of this."

"Those are only words coming out of your mouth. You don't believe them." Gracie's tone suggested her own ambivalence.

"I'm not sure what I believe."

The tension inside the car smothered Laura. A car pulled out into traffic ahead of them. Laura leaned on the horn as if she were about to have a head-on collision with a sixteen-wheeler. "I can't believe it, did you see that jerk?"

Gracie didn't answer, and neither spoke for the next few miles.

Laura murmured, "Mickey used to say, talkin's always easier than doin'."

"Smart man."

They pulled up in front of Building A and spotted Brooke's ten-year-old Corolla parked at the curb. "What's she doing here?"

"She's Nora's niece, and I thought—"

Laura cut her off with a wave, then grabbed the brown paper bag from the back seat and hurried inside. Since when did children get the right to nose into every facet of their parents' personal business? Brooke should respect her mother's privacy and butt out.

They climbed the stairs to the second floor where Laura used the key Nora had given her and entered the apartment. Brooke stood alone in the living room, arms crossed and feet spread wide like a palace guard.

Gracie smiled. "Brooke, glad—"

Brooke interrupted. "I can't let you do this." Her eyes locked on her mother.

Laura purposely avoided her daughter's gaze, slipped around her, and headed to the kitchen. Her legs felt rubbery, and she realized she was holding her breath. She pulled a Mason jar half-filled with Wild Turkey bourbon from the paper bag and unscrewed the lid. They'd learned online that mixing Xanax with alcohol had a synergistic effect; each drug amplified the other. She'd been surprised how many sites existed advising on methods of suicide. Basd on what she gleaned, ten milligrams of Xanax combined with alcohol would be sufficient. They both decided the prospect of Nora surviving a botched suicide attempt was too horrible to contemplate and doubled the dosage to twenty milligrams.

Brooke followed into the kitchen and hovered over her mother. "Are you listening to me?"

"Her decision," she said in a quavering voice.

"No, it's *your* decision. *You're* the one who's going to kill her."

"You of all people have no right to lecture—"

"Enough," Gracie interjected. "How's she doing?"

"She's sleeping," Brooke responded. "Aunt Gracie, are you going to stand by and let her do this?"

Gracie's face turned white, her voice broke. "No, sweetie, I'm going to help."

"Mother, please."

Laura could hardly breathe. Gracie pulled a sandwich bag from her pocket and set it on the counter. The bag contained twenty milligrams of Alprozalam, crushed to a powder. The three women stared at the bag without speaking. Laura slowly inched her hand toward the bag. Brooke restrained her mother's hand with her own.

Brooke whispered, "Mother, no."

Laura gasped, her whole body shook. Through most of her life, she'd been the one to take charge. At the club, her friends teased her, calling her "General Beckman" because she could make a quick decision and move forward to implement it without hesitation or second-guessing. She didn't feel like a general today, and she would give anything to be somewhere else.

She's counting on me.

Laura took a deep breath and used her left hand to first gently squeeze her daughter's hand, then pry it away. She quickly opened the bag and poured the powder into the bourbon. The other two women stood dead still like mannequins in a diorama, eyes focused on the thin stream of powder falling into the amber liquid. Laura re-screwed the lid and shook the container, her eyes fixed on the contents. With an unsteady gait she made her way back to Nora's bedroom. Gracie and Brooke followed.

Nora's appearance had changed dramatically in just the six days since Stoney's visit. When Laura approached the bed she could barely hear tiny rasps of breath. Nora's skin appeared paper-thin, and her body seemed to have shrunken into itself.

Gracie must have been reading her mind. "She's decided she's ready. Her body knows she's ready. She only needs a little push."

Brooke's voice rose. "A little push? Do you understand what you're saying?"

"Shhhh, you'll wake her," Laura said.

Nora stirred. "Did you bring it?" Her voice was barely a whisper.

Laura showed her the Mason jar.

"Wild Turkey," Gracie said. "Just like at the Stallion."

Nora forced a smile. "Brooke, dear, thank you so much for coming. Could you please open the window?"

Brooke hesitated, indecision painted on her face.

Frustrated, Laura slipped past her daughter to the window opposite the bed and opened it. "She just wants a little fresh air, for God's sake."

Nora said, "It smells wonderful." She took a deep breath, and her body convulsed in a violent cough.

Brooke quickly retrieved a glass of water from the bedside table. She tenderly lifted Nora's head from the damp pillow and held the glass to her lips.

Laura took a deep breath, glanced at Brooke, and held Nora's hand. "Nora, I want you to listen to me. Your, uh, adventure with Stoney, there's no reason you couldn't have more of those, and other life experiences. Even if you do have only six months, which is only one doctor's opinion, why not enjoy the extra time?"

"I'm ready, dear." She smiled up at Laura, her pale blue eyes conveying the finality of her decision.

The door opened and Everett entered. His face blanched upon seeing the tableau facing him.

"I didn't expect you," Laura said.

"Nora's a friend and we had a pact, and never let it be said that Everett T. Tisdale does not keep his promises."

"Thank you for coming," Nora whispered.

Brooke moved close to the bed. "You don't have to go through with this."

"She's right," said Everett. "Nora, you must be sure. Life is precious, every moment."

"Not every moment."

"But you never know, tomorrow they could find a cure," Brooke added, desperation leaking into her voice.

"It's all right, I love you all."

"We love you, too," Laura said. She pulled a crumpled tissue from her pocket and dabbed her eyes. "Thank you for being such a wonderful part of our lives." Laura hugged her, then Gracie and Everett took their turn.

Nora smiled weakly up at Brooke. Brooke paused, then embraced her. "Please, Aunt Nora, don't leave us," Brooke whispered, her voice cracking.

Nora pulled her close. "You're a good person with a good heart. You both need each other. Don't . . . wait until . . ." Nora lost her strength to continue.

Laura overheard Nora's words, and her anxiety level ratcheted up one last notch. She wiped her eyes, took a deep breath, then handed Nora the Mason jar. Nora held it in her shaky hands and sipped from the straw. All except Brooke bowed their heads in silent prayer as Nora slowly drained the bourbon.

"Damn," Gracie whispered.

"What?" Laura asked.

"We need some music." She fished her phone from her pocket and taped furiously."

"Maybe we could sing something." Everett said. "A hymn."

Nora tried to speak. Laura bent down close so she could hear, then rose. "She says it's her birthday. Of course. I can't believe I forgot."

"That's why she wanted to leave today," Gracie said.

Gracie re-pocketed her phone. Laura clasped hands with Gracie and Everett. Everett offered his other hand to Brooke who paused, then reluctantly took it. Laura began singing "Happy Birthday," but slowly, softly, reverently, like a hymn. The others joined in. They sang it twice, the second round more slowly than the first, then all bowed their heads.

Moments later a musical voice pierced the silence with crystal purity. Brooke, her eyes closed, in her own world, sang another round of "Happy Birthday." Laura, Gracie, and Everett watched in awe as Brooke took the most simple, the most familiar of songs and, elevating an octave, deconstructed the tune much as a jazz impresario might do. She gently squeezed, pulled, and caressed each word, each note, as if it were a song unto itself, and the total effect was the most beautiful music Laura had ever heard. When Brooke finished her head remained bowed, her eyes closed. Not in prayer, Laura knew, but maybe in respect and affection for a departing soul.

Laura glanced up at Gracie and caught a momentary flash of wrenching grief on her aunt's face. Laura felt it, too, and bit her lip to stifle the wail fighting to be released. She attempted a smile—after all, Nora's death was supposed to bring the woman peace, a good thing, right? *Right?*

But the corners of her mouth wouldn't move.

CHAPTER TWENTY

St. James Episcopal Church, located in the rolling farmland of southern Anne Arundel County, dated back almost three hundred years. Nora had been baptized and married there. Now she lay in an open casket before a church full of mourners. Soon she would be buried in the small cemetery adjoining the church.

Brooke sat in one of the middle pews. She stared at the body while her mother, wearing the same black dress she'd worn to her husband's funeral, stood in front of a lectern finishing up the eulogy.

Nora had a slight smile on her face, as if she knew a secret. Peaceful. All the people who had come to the viewing had remarked how peaceful she appeared.

Brooke had wanted to shout, *she's not peaceful, she's dead!* Everyone's peaceful when they're dead because they can't move *because they're dead!* People were idiots.

And there was her mother up there prattling on about God and heaven and Nora smiling down on us bringing us this beautiful sunshiny day. Of course, if it had been raining we would've heard how the heavens were crying, joining us in our grief. What a racket. At one time, Brooke found the whole God thing harmless and actually marginally beneficial in that it helped ease the grief of loved ones. Lately she'd concluded that having to endure the sanctimony of those espousing this drivel was too high a price to pay.

For a brief moment on the drive home from Nora's apartment she'd actually considered reporting her mother to the police. She was pretty sure what they did violated the law. And even if technically it didn't, the negative publicity would be devastating. Let's see how Laura Beckman, everyone's Volunteer of the Year, liked being on the other end of the scorn machine for a while.

Except . . . except her mother had been booted out of the country club, and all of her so-called friends had abandoned her, leaving her with a seventy-year-old woman as her only gal pal. Laura had changed, and Brooke had to admit that change jarred her. It was so much easier to heap scorn on the Laura Beckman she knew prior to her daddy dying. Truth was, she could never really turn her mother in to the authorities. And Gracie would be implicated too. Nora wouldn't have approved, and Jennie definitely wouldn't have approved.

Okay, she couldn't take any more of this church bullshit. She stood up and headed for the exit. Her resistance built up over many years left her unaffected by the many sets of disapproving eyes following her up the aisle.

Laura closed the little notebook containing her remarks and noticed Brooke leaving the church. Laura's eyes reflexively darted to Jennie in the front row, but her granddaughter either hadn't noticed her mom's early departure, or more likely didn't care. She forced her wayward daughter out of her mind. Time to bring her remarks to a close.

She'd practiced the whole eulogy the night before. Her years of volunteer work and involvement with various club committees had given her plenty of opportunities to appear in front of groups, and she didn't feel uncomfortable at all speaking before the mourners.

" . . . and she departed this world surrounded by family and friends whom she loved, and who loved her. Nora's gentle wisdom will continue to remind us all of what's important in life. She will be deeply missed."

Laura, Gracie, Everett, and Jennie exited the church to a beautiful sunny day, temperature in the high fifties, air crisp and clean.

Anna caught up with them. "Returning to Annapolis for funerals is not a habit I want to continue."

Laura said, "We're still hoping when you get your doctorate you can move back here. There are financial firms in town, not to mention Baltimore and D.C."

Anna smiled and wrapped an arm around Laura's shoulder. "I'm trying to remember, but I think that's a subject we've discussed before." Everyone laughed. "I know you couldn't talk about it publicly, but last night, the way you explained Nora's choice to take her own life? I've been thinking about it and, knowing her and what she'd gone through, I think I understand now."

Laura glanced at Gracie and hoped Anna wouldn't notice her mother's discomfort. "Unique situation, honey."

Louise Cheney, the official church busybody who loved gossip almost as much as food, approached. "Lovely service. Will the refreshments be at your house?"

"Yes, Louise," Laura said.

"Poor Nora, except—"

"Except what?" Gracie asked.

"Lying there, she actually appeared to have a smile on her face. Rather strange."

"I'm sure it was the way the light played on the body," Laura said. Louise thought for a moment, nodded, then trundled off.

"She'll be first in line at the buffet table." Gracie said.

Stoney exited the church, and Gracie blew a kiss. He waved, then headed toward the parking lot.

"Who's he?" Anna asked.

"A friend of Nora's," Everett said, with a not too subtle conspiratorial wink at Laura.

"A very close friend," Gracie added.

Laura stared daggers at her aunt to shut her up. Big-mouth Gracie had told Brooke and Everett about Nora's date with Stoney, but fortunately it appeared Brooke hadn't passed on the information to her little sister.

Anna checked her watch. "Sorry, but I have to catch a plane back."

Laura didn't try to hide her disappointment. 'Can't you stay until tomorrow?"

"Brandon and I have this thing tonight . . ."

Her daughter was an adult now with her own life. A life passage—the child becomes an adult, the parent withers up and dies. "I understand." She spoke with a touch of melancholy in her voice. They embraced, and Anna hurried ahead to a waiting cab.

Laura, Gracie, and Everett reached the Lexus and spotted Brooke leaning up against her Corolla parked nearby.

Laura said, "I don't suppose you could've waited to leave until the service was over out of respect for Nora."

"Don't believe in churches. You know I don't believe in churches. Although I do agree with that one little rule. What was it again? Oh, yeah. Thou shalt not kill." She locked eyes with her mother, challenging her.

Lilly Melroy approached the group, looking quite stern. Lilly was one of those women who looked old no matter what her chronological age. Short and squat, she wore a gray and rose floral print that might've been stylish in the Fifties.

"Morning, Lilly," Everett said. "Lovely service."

In the back corner of the lot, a lift raised Lilly's brother, Russell, into a small disabilities bus. Slight of build even when healthy, Russell suffered from an advanced case of late-stage emphysema, and had to rely on an oxygen tank strapped to the back of his wheelchair to breathe. Unable to speak clearly, he communicated through a combination of slurred words and nuanced grunts that it seemed only his sister could translate.

Lilly ignored Everett. "I need to have a word with you, Laura."

Laura shrugged and followed her to a spot out of earshot from the others.

"It has come to my attention," Lilly said, "that you may have been complicit in Nora's death."

Laura's jaw dropped. She stammered, "I-I don't know where you could have heard such a thing." As soon as the words were out of her mouth Laura knew the answer. Gracie.

Lilly continued, "I am further given to understand that, in response to some bizarre last wish, you actually provided Nora with the services of a male *prostitute.*"

Laura never had been a good liar, and she capitulated, her words coming out in a rush. "Lilly, please, you don't understand. Nora asked me, as a friend—"

Lilly interrupted, her voice softened. "I don't think *you* understand. My brother, Russell, is terminally ill, in terrible pain, and he, both of us, were hoping . . ."

Laura's eyes widened in disbelief. Deep anger and the terror triggered by that anger pummeled each other in a battle to control her emotions. "No, no, no . . ."

Limbs shaking, she staggered away, her only goal to remain upright till she reached the car.

CHAPTER TWENTY-ONE

Two days after Nora's funeral, Laura drove down Muddy Creek Road, enjoying the morning rural landscape as the road wound south through the rolling countryside. Out of habit developed over many years, she only ventured into the sourthern part of the county for her weekly smoked bluefish fix. She'd never considered herself a snob, but "Annapolis people" rarely ventured across the South River Bridge bridge into "South County" where the "rural people"—translation, "rednecks"—lived. Thinking about it now, she figured she probably *had* been a snob.

She reached the Owensville Road intersection and turned left towards Galesville. She'd read in the *Capital* that residents in the town still walked to the post office on Main Street to retrieve their mail and chat with the post-mistress, who also ran a charter fishing boat. Few people locked their doors since crime was virtually nonexistent. Other than the market, the only time she'd visited the town was one night for dinner at the Pirate's Cove waterfront restaurant with members of the Association. She remembered the feeling among her group that these country folks were quaint bumpkins. She even recalled someone calling the place "Mayberry," and everyone giggling in derision. Looking back she felt ashamed. In truth, the peace and gentleness of the town were to be envied.

Her phone app indicated the marina was located off Church Lane. She turned right at the Methodist church and followed the winding road around to the end. There she was confronted with a huge sign in neon colors completely dissonant with the town's character: "Massey's Marina." She parked, grabbed the bag resting on the car seat, and stepped out of the car. She noticed the marina offered docking piers for both powerboats and sailboats. She headed to a small structure marked "Office."

She'd planned to mail the shirt back to him, and even had gone as far as wrapping and addressing the package. But she needed to make her Galesville bluefish trek anyway, so she decided to drop off the shirt in person and save postage. As she approached the office she felt a growing sense of unease—maybe this was a bad idea. Still, after struggling with Nora's death she needed a distraction. Not to mention her continuing battles with Brooke from which she needed a major distraction. And Arlo Massey, if nothing else, was a distraction.

She approached a grizzled yard hand coiling line outside the office. She remembered him from the baseball game. "Pardon me, how might I find Mr. Massey?"

"The lady from the Orioles game."

"That's me."

"Stiff Ripples."

"Excuse me?"

"The name of his boat. I saw him tightening his lines an hour ago so he should still be there. Pier B. Look for the Beneteau 423."

Laura caught herself finding the name clever, then immediately turned away in disgust both at the name and with herself. Sam pointed her toward the second docking pier. After a mumbled thanks, she walked briskly down Pier B, checking the names of the boats.

She had no idea what a Beneteau 423 looked like, but when she reached the largest sailboat on the pier she knew before checking. Sure enough, the name "Stiff Ripples," emblazoned in large gold and black lettering, ran from one side of the stern to the other. She knew right then she should've mailed the shirt. What was she thinking? She saw no one on deck and decided to leave the shirt on the boat, then depart quickly and quietly.

At the very moment she bent over to set the package on a deck chair the boat rocked hard away from the dock. She considered tossing the shirt onto the deck, but the movement of the boat might cause her to accidentally throw the package into the water.

She gingerly stepped onto the gunwale. As her foot touched, a wave again shoved the boat away from the pier, and her legs spread apart like a wishbone, straddling the water. She yelped, certain that she would fall between the boat and the pilings. She'd be crushed to death, and no one would even know. But the wave ebbed and the boat closed the gap again, and she stumbled down onto the boat deck.

Silence from the cabin. Thankfully, no one heard her. She rose to her feet and dusted herself off, then set the stupid shirt on a deck chair—the shirt had definitely achieved stupid status at this point—and took a step up to the gunwale to get off the damn boat.

"Who's there?"

Laura glanced at the closed cabin door. It was Massey's voice. Maybe if she ignored him—

"Identify yourself."

His voice was more insistent. She probably should comply. The cretin at the office recognized her. She stepped back onto the boat deck and cleared her throat. "It's Laura Beckman. I stopped by to drop off —"

"Come on in."

Laura stared at the closed cabin door. The Little Voice in her head told her to leave the boat and, based on many years of experience, the Little Voice was almost always right. "Just came to drop off your shirt," she called out. "I'll just set it here on the—"

"Come on in, I insist."

What was she afraid of? Entering an unknown enclosure containing a man she only knew as a lout who preyed on girls barely old enough to be his daughter, that's what.

"Mrs. Beckman?"

Okay, it was daylight, her car remained in the lot, and she'd make sure to leave the cabin door open just in case. After a deep breath to settle her nerves, she entered.

The cabin was much bigger than she would have guessed. Polished cherry paneling, a full kitchen, table for five. A bathroom with a stand-up shower. A kitchen—she knew the nautical term was galley—cluttered with beer bottles, a pile of egg shells, a greasy frying pan, and an open, half-used package of bacon. Laura wrinkled her nose. A narrow corridor led back to a closed door, probably the bedroom.

Should she leave the shirt on the table and quietly depart?

"Come on back."

His voice came from behind the bedroom door. Laura hesitated, then decided she was in his home of sorts and leaving without even saying hello would be rude. She walked through the passageway and opened the door and gasped. Straight ahead in a king-size bed Arlo Massey sandwiched himself between two beautiful young blond women who appeared to be twins. On his lap was a plate of half-eaten bacon and eggs. He wrapped his arms around the shoulders of the twins, and in each hand he held a bottle of beer.

Arlo greeted her with his stupid smile, and offered one of the beers. "Breakfast?"

Flushed, Laura quickly set the package on a dresser and turned to leave. "Didn't mean to interrupt."

"Hey, how'd it go with . . .?" He pulled his hands away from the twins and held them a foot apart.

Laura shook her head in disgust. "Sorry for intruding." She stepped back into the passageway.

"Intruding? Oh, you mean Heidi and—"

"Hilde," said one of the twins.

"Right, the Australian twins."

"Austrian," the other twin corrected, not showing the least offense.

"Right. Why don't you girls scat while I entertain my company?"

Laura's eyes widened. "Oh, no, no. I'm leaving."

"Stick around." He turned to the girls. "I think Tucker over in D-34's going out this morning and may need some extra hands." He grabbed them both under the covers. The girls giggled and jumped out of bed. Stark naked, they reached for bikinis. Arlo wrapped himself in a blanket and stood. The twins waved and scurried off.

Laura asked, "Isn't it a little cold for bikinis?"

"Nah. Besides . . ." he winked, "if I know Tucker, they'll be inside most of the time anyway."

Laura followed behind the twins. "Goodbye, Mr. Massey." She reached the kitchen with Arlo following in the blanket.

"You want some coffee?"

Laura ignored him.

"If I hadn't returned your license you'd be standing in line at the DMV for weeks. Not to mention you scalded me with a cup of boiling coffee."

"The coffee wasn't boiling." Laura paused. "Okay, one cup of coffee."

Arlo rummaged through a cupboard and emerged with a jar of instant coffee. He unscrewed the jar lid and examined the caked contents inside. "Don't think this stuff ever goes bad."

He opened the refrigerator, pushed aside six bottles of beer, and retrieved a carton of milk. He smelled the milk and tried to pour a little into the sink. A yellow glob slowly emerged from the carton and plopped into the drain.

"Black's fine," Laura said, holding her nose. "You live here full time?"

"Home sweet home. And please call me Arlo."

Stick-pins attached two photos to the paneling over the sink. One, eight-by-ten and grease-splattered, showed a skydiver freef-alling through the air. Though goggles covered his face, she could identify Massey from his stupid grin. The other photo showed a young boy, maybe ten or eleven, handling a small sailboat. Instincts honed from many years of engaging in obligatory small talk in un-comfortable situations tripped in. "And who is this good-looking young man?"

A shadow passed across Arlo's face. He peered out the small porthole down the West River. "That's Jake."

Arlo didn't add anything, and Laura could tell by his blank stare out the porthole his mind had shifted. Obviously the subject of Jake was one Massey didn't want to talk about. A child? Maybe a child who'd gone off the tracks, a subject with which she was quite familiar.

Laura turned to the skydiving photo. Without really caring, she asked, "Skydiving is a rather dangerous pastime, is it not?"

Arlo snapped back to the present. "Of course it's dangerous. You and I, we ain't exactly spring chickens so might as well go for the gusto." He flashed a toothy grin.

"Go for the gusto. A tired slogan taken from an old television commercial for beer if I'm not mistaken." Laura concluded she needed to leave. Immediately. "May I ask you a question?"

"Of course," he responded with a theatrical flourish of his arm.

"If one 'goes for the gusto' is there some requirement that one also must simultaneously act like a complete ass?" She headed for the door. "I must be on my way."

"What about the coffee?"

"Maybe another time."

"A rain check? I can live with that. But I need to return your husband's shirt."

Laura had almost forgotten about Mickey's pink shirt. She'd already given most of his clothes to Goodwill. "That's okay. If it fits, you can keep it." Arlo ingnored her and continued walking along the narrow corridor to to the back of the boat. She paused, then followed him. When they reached the bedroom she glanced up and noticed a large flat screen LED television mounted on the ceiling. She immediately diverted her gaze.

He mumbled, "Uh, not a lot of room in here."

Was that embarrassment showing on the man's face?

He rummaged in a dresser drawer. "Can't seem to put my hands on the shirt at this moment."

"Keep the shirt, Mr. Massey."

"Please call me Arlo."

She ignored him, pivoted, and moved quickly back down the corridor toward the kitchen, then up the steps to the outside deck. Arlo followed, still wrapped in the blanket. Once outside she stepped up on the gunwale.

Arlo took her hand. "Here, let me help you."

"That won't be necessary." She jerked her hand away and stepped off the boat as it lurched toward the pier. Her foot caught up in Arlo's blanket, pulling it from his body, and she went sprawling onto the pier deck landing on her left arm. She yelped in pain.

"Are you all right?" Arlo asked, apparently unconcerned that he was now completely naked.

Laura scrambled to her feet, holding her arm. To her horror, he began to climb up onto the pier. "Stay right there," she ordered, turning her back to his nakedness.

"But Laura, you're hurt."

"I'm fine," she said with her back turned. "And you do not have my permission to address me by my first name, although it makes no difference inasmuch as we will never see each other again." She turned and marched back toward the shore.

Arlo called after her. "What about my raincheck?"

She hurried away, calling back over her shoulder, "That check's been canceled."

CHAPTER TWENTY-TWO

November

Laura bent down to Russell Melroy's eye level. He slumped in the wheelchair, his eyes glued to the Demolition Derby on Laura's living room TV. He wore a black baseball cap and a black long-sleeve Dale Earnhardt T-shirt. The cap displayed a red "3" on the front and needed to be tightened. She cringed inside watching him wince in pain every three or four breaths despite being hooked up to an oxygen tank.

"Russell, are you sure I can't get you anything?" He shook his head.

She fluffed up the pillow behind his neck and returned to the kitchen. Lilly, Gracie, and Everett sat around the kitchen table sipping coffee and picking at generous pieces of Laura's famous German chocolate cake.

"Where'd you get that big bruise on your arm?" Gracie asked.

"I fell."

Gracie expression turned suspicious. "Where did you fall?"

Laura ignored her and sat down next to Everett. Everett immediately inched his chair closer to hers. Everett had been a family friend for years and she appreciated him being protective. She also knew he desired to be something more than a friend. On a couple of occasions she'd been close to disabusing him of any such thoughts, but in the end she never had the heart to do so. She cared for him, and as long as she didn't reciprocate she figured his sometimes clumsy efforts were harmless, and over time any romantic interest would fade away.

She turned to Lilly and saw the pain on her face. Laura knew how she felt—the anguish, the fear, the anger, and, most powerful, the guilt. Guilt from wondering if there was something she could've done but didn't do, guilt from wanting him to live just one more moment longer despite the pain, guilt from wanting him to die. And Lilly's anguish was about to get worse.

Laura softened her voice and took Lilly's hand in hers. "Due to your understandable persistence and Gracie being the total pain in the butt we all know she can be, I agreed to hear you out. I have done so and, I'm sorry, but the answer's still no."

Lilly appeared crestfallen. "Laura, you must reconsider," she pleaded. "He's in such pain."

"She could find herself in a lot of trouble," Everett said. "Perhaps if Russell considers this the best course, you might effect his wishes yourself."

"Don't you think I've thought of that?" Lilly responded tearfully. "But I don't know how."

Gracie glanced over at Elvis, asleep in the corner. "We could get you the pills."

"You're his sister. He trusts you," Laura added.

Lilly hung her head. "I'm not strong enough to do it alone. He's hurting, he begs me every day to help him go. And remember what you said at Nora's funeral? Her life, her choice? Laura, you inspired a lot of people, including me. You gave Russell hope."

After an uncomfortable pause Gracie spoke first. "Laura, it does feel right."

"I feel compelled to disagree." Everett spoke in his official second tenor voice. He sang first tenor in the church choir, but he'd once explained to Laura that from time to time he'd have to lay down the law to fellow choir members who weren't paying attention to the choir director, and he'd project authority by deepening his voice to second tenor. "Lilly's proposal is wholly inappropriate and I must insist—"

Laura lifted her open hand, cutting him off. Silence descended like a heavy velvet curtain. She closed her eyes and dropped her head. The others didn't move a muscle. What should she do? Had she truly done the right thing by helping Nora die? Or, as her daughter so artfully put it, was she a murderer? No, she wasn't a murderer. She didn't kill Nora; the cancer did that. Hadn't she simply done on her own what a hospice would do for a suffering patient? Well, no. More than a hospice. She needed to be honest with herself. But if helping a terminally ill person end his life on his terms was so vile, then why was it legal in eight states? Okay, admittedly only doctors were allowed to assist, and only then after going through a bunch of protocols to make sure the patient was both terminal and competent to make the decision. But Nora's case left no doubt either about her illness or her competence, and Russell Melroy easily satisfied those two criteria as well.

Images of Mickey and Nora flooded her mind. Mickey in such agony, Nora so peaceful. She should trust her heart.

After what seemed like an eternity, Laura lifted her eyes to Lilly and smiled. "What's his wish?"

Momentarily stunned by Laura's change of heart, Lilly clapped her hand over her moth and stifled a sob. "Let's go ask him." They stood, and she nearly crushed Laura in a ferocious hug.

Thinking back, Laura realized they'd never embraced in all their years of acquaintance. Suffering along with a loved one changes everything.

Everett straightened in his chair. "Laura, I must—"

She gently covered his hand with hers, cutting off his second tenor voice. His shoulders slumped, and he remained quiet.

They all trooped into the living room where Russell still remained transfixed by the TV. Lilly put her hand on his shoulder. "Russell, dear, Laura has agreed to help."

For the first time, he pulled his eyes away from the television. He managed a contorted smile and a raspy "thank you."

She squeezed her brother's shoulder. "They want to know your wish." He fumbled around in his pants, but his hand shook too much. Lilly reached into the pocket and removed a cheap orange flyer. She handed it to Laura.

Laura opened it for all to see. Emblazoned across the page were the words: "DEMOLITION DERBY! TUESDAY! CHESAPEAKE SPEEDWAY!"

Six days later, the dwindling daylight of November had all but disappeared. Laura, Lilly, and Gracie gathered in Laura's driveway, watching the county disabilities bus lower Russell's wheelchair onto the sidewalk. Russell wore his Dale Earnhardt NASCAR shirt and his ill-fitting hat. Brooke stood on the front lawn, arms folded, shaking her head.

Without Laura's knowledge, Gracie invited Brooke to join their trip to the derby. Her crazy aunt entertained the naïve belief Brooke and Laura's relationship might improve if Brooke were, in Gracie's words, part of the team. But when Brooke arrived she spent the entire time attempting to talk both Laura and Gracie out of helping Russell Melroy enjoy a last wish.

Lilly pushed Russell over to Laura's car. Laura examined Russell's wheelchair, mentally measuring it to make sure it would fit in her trunk. "We'll need to lift him into the back seat," Lilly said.

"It helps if one of us could come in from the other side, but it has to be someone who doesn't have a bad back."

Laura glanced at Gracie. That eliminated all three of them. "Brooke, perhaps you could give us a hand."

"You're mad, all of you. I'm sorry, but I will have nothing—"

"Bee!" Laura pointed at the front hedge in alarm. Brooke jumped back in fear and ran into the house. She was highly allergic to bee stings, had been since childhood. Laura recalled how more than once there'd been the wild ride to the emergency room, watching her child's breathing become more labored by the second. Then the drug companies came out with the EpiPen, a tubular device about the size of a cigar that easily allowed a person to self-inject a dose of epinephrine right through clothing if need be. Damned bees. Weren't they supposed to be gone by November? Laura turned back to Russell and the problem at hand. "Maybe if the three of us—"

A horn honked, and all turned to see Arlo Massey waving from an old van. The side panels displayed a photo of Arlo from the waist up. In the picture his arms wrapped around four smiling bikini-clad models, each wearing a sailor's hat bearing the marina's logo. He parked the van, then approached the group carrying Mickey's pink shirt.

Laura was shocked to see him. "Mr. Massey?" She pointed to the van. "What in God's name is that?"

"The famous Massey Mobile."

"It's hideous."

"I'll have you know I've drummed up a lot of business from people who've seen that van. So, how's your arm?"

Gracie caught Laura's eye and gave her an "Ah-ha!" look.

"We're rather busy."

"No problem. I happened to be in the neighborhood and thought I'd drop off your husband's shirt." He handed the shirt to Laura, then introduced himself to Lilly and Russell. "I'm Arlo Massey."

Lilly gave him a proper handshake. "How do you do? I'm Lilly Melroy and this is my brother, Russell." Russell grunted.

Arlo took Russell's hand and shook it vigorously, then pointed to his hat. "The Intimidator! Seventy-six wins, seven champion-ships. Hell on wheels, Russ, hell on wheels." Russell grunted his agreement.

Laura closely examined the pink shirt. "I see you didn't bother to launder it."

Arlo took the shirt from her, sniffed the armpits, then gave it back. "Hardly smells at all."

Laura couldn't speak.

Arlo turned to Lilly. "Where you off to?"

"Chesapeake Speedway,"

Arlo's eyes lit up. "Demolition Derby? Awright!" He held up his hand to Russell, who managed to raise his palm for a weak high-five.

Laura figured since he was here anyway she might as well take advantage. He owed her big time for his disgusting behavior on the boat. "While you're here, Mr. Massey—"

"When you were in my bedroom I asked you to call me Arlo."

Another "Ah-ha!" expression from Gracie.

Russell managed a smile, and gave Arlo a thumbs-up.

Laura felt her face blush. Why can't the human body control blushing? A clear design error. The blush morphed into a seeth.

Gracie took over. "Could you give us a hand getting Russell into the car?"

"Consider it done." Arlo lifted Russell out of his chair as if he were a baby, and gently set him onto the back seat of the Lexus. "By the way, Russ, your hat could use a little adjustment. May I?"

Russell nodded.

Arlo removed the hat, tightened the Velcro strap on the back, then replaced it on Russell's head. "Perfect fit."

"How nice of you," Lilly said.

"So virile," Gracie sighed.

Arlo asked, "You have somebody up there who'll lift him out?"

"No," Lilly responded.

Arlo folded up the wheelchair and put it in the trunk, then hopped into the front passenger seat. "I do believe my schedule's clear."

Laura's mouth moved, but nothing came out.

CHAPTER TWENTY-THREE

Black exhaust fumes hovered over the speedway like a cloud of doom making Laura's eyes water. Rickety bleachers filled with ten thousand rabid fans surrounded the dirt oval track. Though the temperature had dropped to the low fifties, most of the women in the stands, irrespective of age, wore revealing halter-tops. Arlo led them down to the pit area where the sound of two-ton machines colliding into each other at full speed only yards away from where they stood elevated the noise level to such a high degree Laura was certain she coud feel her bones rattle.

On the track, four remaining cars maneuvered around scattered disabled vehicles, trying to avoid being hit while at the same time crashing into one of the remaining opponents. Arlo explained that the last moving car wins. The vehicles in no way resembled the race cars Laura saw on TV. These junk heaps looked long overdue for their appointment with the landfill crusher.

They followed Arlo to a pair of filthy boots protruding out from under an orange junker with a crude "7" on one side scrawled in dripping white paint.

The man belonging to the boots crawled out. Slightly built with slick black hair, he wore jeans and a T-shirt covered with grease.

"Pardon me," Laura asked, "are you Earl?"

His eyes—Laura could think of no other description but "beady"—scanned each of them as if deciding between fight or flight. Apparently satisfied he was in no danger, he responded,

"Yeah, I'm Earl. You must be the idiots who called."

Arlo grinned. "That's us."

The orange car reminded Laura of evening news film footage showing what remained of a vehicle after a fatal accident.

"Is that it?" Lilly asked Earl, trying to keep the hesitation from her voice.

"Yeah, you bring the money?"

"Yes—" She jumped back almost tripping, startled by the deafening crash of two cars only yards from where they stood.

"You can still change your mind," Laura said.

Lilly gazed down at her brother, his eyes bright, smiling ear-to-ear. After only a moment's hesitation she reached into her purse, removed a thick envelope, and handed it to Earl. He turned away from her as if she might steal it back, and counted the money. "Cash, like you required. I can assure you it's all there."

When Earl finished, he nodded, folded the envelope in half, and stuffed it into his back pocket.

Arlo examined the car. "Sixty-eight Imperial?"

"Sixty-seven."

"I heard these old 64 to 68 Imperials have been so successful in derbies they've been banned," Arlo said.

"Yeah, the better tracks. Not here. Not too many rules here." For the first time, he smiled.

Laura counted a total of four teeth, five max. "What about safety?"

"Safety's number one."

Another loud crash exploded even closer to them. They turned to see two cars had smashed head-on into each other. A little bowling ball of a man in bib overalls and a plaid sports coat ran out into the field waving a yellow flag. The remaining cars stopped. Two shirtless guys wearing jean cut-off shorts and cowboy hats drove an old ambulance out onto the track and extracted an unconscious driver from each vehicle.

Arlo walked around the car with Earl trailing. "Good setup."

"The best. Fenders pounded up to keep tires from getting cut. Concrete poured into the door frames. Roll bars. All glass, headlights, tail lights, trim removed. Trunk and hood clamped down with threaded rods. Bars mounted over the grill to protect the radiator and across where the windshield used to be to keep the driver having his head sliced off by flying metal."

Laura, Lilly, and Gracie grimaced. Laura felt like she'd entered an alien world and wouldn't have been totally surprised if at that very moment Earl shed his skin to reveal a little green man from another planet.

Earl sized up Arlo. "You ever driven in a derby before?"

"I ain't the driver." He pointed to Russell, shriveled up in his wheelchair. "He's the driver."

Earl's jaw dropped. "You gotta be kiddin' me."

Laura stepped forward and handed Earl another envelope. "We have a release, signed and notarized. You're fully protected in the event of . . ." She glanced quickly at Russell. "In the event of an accident."

Earl opened the envelope and examined the release suspiciously. "I don't understand all this legal crap. For alls I know, this old fart here—"

"Name's Russell," Gracie said.

"As I was saying, for alls I know, if Russell gets himself killed you'd end up taking away everything I own."

Laura was about to say that she doubted that amounted to very much but held her tongue.

Earl handed the release back to Laura. "Ain't gonna happen." He reluctantly reached into his pocket to return the money.

Laura pleaded, "You don't understand."

Arlo gently laid his hand on Earl's arm. "Hold off a minute there, Earl. Walk with me." Earl hesitated, then shrugged and walked with Arlo beyond earshot of the others. After some whispering, Laura thought she saw Arlo reach into his own pocket and slip something into Earl's hand. When they returned, Arlo was all smiles.

"Earl here has reconsidered, and he's enthusiastic—" He turned to Earl. "I believe that's an accurate characterization, wouldn't you say, Earl?"

Earl nodded hesitantly.

"As I was saying, Earl is downright enthusiastic about giving Russell the thrill of a lifetime."

Laura wondered what Massey said to the disgusting little man. Probably slippped him more money. Laura wasn't quite sure how she felt about that. It was unseemly, but it achieved their goal. After a few moments she concluded she was thinking too much.

Arlo squatted for a heart-to-heart with Russell. "Look, Russ, Gracie told me you want to, uh, check out, and this is sort of your last wish, so to speak. But truth is, you could get all mangled up out there, and they'd take you to the hospital, and they'd keep you alive for who knows how long. You could be in a lot more pain than you are now. You sure about this?"

Laura was caught off guard by Arlo's show of compassion.

Russell put his hand on Arlo's arm and nodded. He gestured to Lilly, and his sister immediately bent her ear to his lips.

Lilly said, "He thinks you'll all understand if I take a second to tell you his story. As a boy, Russell loved cars. He studied to be an accountant but his dream was to save his money, someday own an auto repair business, and race on the side. But then he met Charlene at one of those seedy establishments where young women remove their clothing."

Arlo said, "His ex was a stripper?"

Lilly nodded. Russell shrugged.

"She lured him into marriage and then made it plain that she much preferred being the wife of an accountant to a grease monkey. By the time he dumped her, he was too old to start over. He's always loved cars and dreamed of racing for over sixty years. He wants a chance to live it now, even for a moment. No matter the consequences. The demolition derby is his only possibility."

Right on cue, Russell unzipped his jacket to reveal a red t-shirt emblazoned with the words, "Live Fierce."

Arlo paused, searching Russell's eyes. Then he smiled and whispered loud enough for Laura to hear, "Let's ride."

Arlo and Earl squeezed Russell through the open window and strapped him into the driver's seat. Arlo lifted the green oxygen tank from the wheelchair and positioned it inside the car next to Russell.

"You can't be serious," Earl said.

"No more dangerous than a gas tank," Arlo replied. "Now help me strap it in."

When the oxygen tank was secured, Earl bent down so Russell could hear him. " We're up next. Remember how your mama always told you to keep your nose clean? Well, same goes here. If you're gonna take a hit, cut it hard to take it on the side or back. Keep the nose clean. And remember—"

A crackling voice over an ancient PA system interrupted him. "Drivers on the track."

The first car to drive out was purple and bore the number nine. "Is that Crazy Otto?" Arlo asked.

Right on cue, the announcer said, " In car number nine, from parts unknown, Crazy Otto!"Loud cheers from the stands.

Spurred by the alarm in Arlo's voice, Laura focused on the driver. Crazy Otto pulled off his helmet revealing long, wild black hair. He was wall-eyed—his left eye seemed to wander around like it had a life of its own. Laura couldn't believe what she saw next. He loaded a pistol. "He has a gun!"

"Don't doubt it," Earl said. "He's as crazy as a shithouse rat. Don't think he actually killed nobody yet."

Laura couldn't let this go. "The man has a *loaded gun*. You must report him."

"Reporting's not something we do much around here." Earl pointed to car number three driving onto the track. "Course Crazy Otto ain't nothing compared to Psycho Bob."

The announcer's voice sounded even more excited. "In car number three, from, uh, Jessup, Maryland, Psycho Bob!"

Earl explained, "Jessup's the site of the state prison. Bob's on weekend work-release. Otto and Bob, they're the stars of the circuit so they always come out first."

Psycho Bob wore a Davy Crockett coonskin cap. He had one eyebrow that appeared to run from ear-to-ear. He blew his nose into his hand and rubbed the mucus on his cheeks like face cream, then gnawed on the steering wheel. Laura's jaw dropped. Maybe she really had entered a parallel universe.

Earl pointed to Russell. "Start her up, Russ."

Russell pushed the ignition, and the engine turned over. Lilly planted a big kiss on his cheek. Earl handed him a white towel tied in a knot.

"What's that for?" Gracie asked.

"If you don't want to get hit no more, toss the towel out the window. You're out of the race. The other drivers are supposed to leave you alone."

"Supposed to?" Laura asked.

Earl shrugged.

The PA system screeched. "In car number one, from Wilmington, Delaware, Mighty Mike O'Rourke, followed in car number two by . . ."

Earl turned to Lilly. "He got a nickname? He needs a nickname."

Russell beckoned to Lilly and whispered in her ear. "Death Wish?" she repeated.

Earl ran off to inform the announcer.

A few moments later the announcer cleared his throat. "And hailing from Annapolis, Maryland, driving car number seven, a rookie making his first derby appearance, Russell 'Death Wish' Melroy!" Loud cheers. Russell gave a thumbs-up and drove out onto the track.

The announcer continued. "And remember, folks, our feature race is sponsored by Lonnie's House of Love in downtown Elkton, where you can find all the love gear you need to guarantee sizzle in the sack. And if you ain't got a girl Lonnie can help you out there too." Loud cheers from the stands. "Lonnie also sells auto parts, specializing in pre-ninety-nine muscle cars. So let's hear it for our sponsor, Lonnie's House of Love!" Wild cheers from the stands.

Laura turned to Gracie. "Love gear?"

"They also sell sparkplugs."

The announcer continued. "And here to start the race is our favorite Lonnie's House of Love model, the beautiful Darla!"

Darla emerged from a black pickup and strutted out to the center of the field in six-inch heels and a pink string bikini. In one hand she carried a long-neck Bud and in the other a green flag. She blew kisses to the spectators and to the drivers, then held the flag high and brought it down hard. No one moved. She paused, then turned her back to the drivers, bent over, pulled down the back of her bikini, and mooned them.

"My God," Laura muttered.

The cars leapt forward, almost hitting Darla as she scurried off the field. The announcer shouted, "And they're off!"

Immediately, cars crashed into each other, causing reverberations so intense Laura could feel them standing in the pit. Two cars smashed into Russell, but at the last second he cut the wheels so the brunt of the impact was absorbed by the passenger side and the rear of the Imperial. Laura covered her eyes, then peeked through her fingers to see Gracie and Lilly covering their eyes as well.

Arlo shouted, "Yes! He's still going!"

Russell drove past the pit and waved. Laura pulled her hands away from her face and smiled to herself. She had to admit, Russell Melroy was having the time of his life.

After about twenty minutes, only three operating cars remained on the track—Russell, Crazy Otto, and Psycho Bob. Otto drove his car to one corner of the field while Bob maneuvered car number three to the opposite corner. Russell remained in the middle, stalled out. The sound of the cranking engine as Russell attempted to restart it could be heard above the screaming fans.

Without taking his eyes off Russell, Earl said, "Sorry."

Lilly became even more alarmed. "Sorry for what? What do you mean, 'sorry'? You can't say 'sorry' and—"

"The vets don't like a rook coming in and showin' them up," Earl explained. "Your brother there? Stuck in the middle? He's called 'bug juice.' You know, like when a bug hits the windshield and—"

"You have to stop them."

"Nothing I can do, lady."

It suddenly occurred to Laura that Russell planned to die in the car all along. "He wants them to kill him," Laura said out loud to no one in particular.

Arlo responded, "No, he intends to die in his bed. Right now what he wants is to win."

On the track, Otto and Bob zoomed toward Russell, who continued his frantic attempts to re-start the engine.

"He needs to throw the towel." Arlo said.

Lilly waved frantically at her brother. "Russell, throw the towel! The towel!"

Arlo spotted an old towel in Earl's truck bed. He ran to the truck, retrieved the towel, and waved it at Russell. "Russ! The towel, the towel!" Russell saw him and lifted the white towel so they could see it.

"He understands," Laura said, relieved.

"Thank God," both Gracie and Lilly said in unison. Their relief turned to horror when Russell flashed a goofy grin and tossed the towel back into his car.

"Old man's got balls, I'll give him that," Earl said.

The engine still wouldn't turn over. Russell was a sitting duck. Everyone watched in horror as Crazy Otto and Psycho Bob sped toward him from opposite directions, ready to crunch him up in a heap of mangled steel.

But a milisecond before he was about to become bug juice, Russell fired up the engine and peeled out, tires screeching. Otto and Bob slammed on their brakes but couldn't stop in time and crashed into each other head-on. The noise was so shattering, Laura was convinced the sound could be heard in three states. Both cars were completely disabled. Death Wish Melroy won the race.

Laura and Arlo sprang into the air, jumping up and down, waving their arms. "WOOOO!"

Earl and Lilly held hands and danced in a circle. All of the fans in the stands were on their feet, going wild.

Russell drove around the field triumphantly. Even the announcer seemed excited. "And the winner of the Lonnie's House of Love feature heat is . . . Death Wish Melroy!" The spectators roared louder.

Arlo and the ladies rushed out to him, Lilly pushing the wheelchair. Arlo detached Russell's inhaler from the oxygen tank, and with Earl's help, pulled him out through the window into his wheelchair. Hugs all around. Darla, accompanied by a photographer, hurried out as fast as her high heels allowed and handed Russell a cheap trophy with a mangled car on top. She posed next to him, and the photographer took their picture.

Off to the side, Laura couldn't help but smile down at Russell, clutching the trophy tight to his chest.

Death Wish Melroy was beaming, happy as a kid on Christmas morning.

CHAPTER TWENTY-FOUR

Laura and Gracie crossed through the small living room of the two-story colonial Russell shared with his sister in Crofton, a bedroom community near the county's western border. They passed Russell's trophy resting in the center of the mantel, and entered his bedroom.

Photos of NASCAR stars covered the bedroom walls, and several dozen model stock cars parked on a shelf next to the bed. Only a few weeks had passed since the derby adventure, yet in that short spot of time Laura could plainly tell Russell's condition had deteriorated significantly. His skin appeared milky, translucent, and though he was hooked up to his oxygen tank she could see him struggle with each breath.

Laura, Arlo, Gracie, Lilly, and Everett surrounded his bed. A glass of whiskey with a straw inserted rested on a bedside table. The women dabbed their eyes.

Through Lilly, Russell had expressed a desire to have Arlo present. Laura delegated the task of calling him to Gracie. The man made Laura feel uncomfortable, that's all.

When Laura saw him standing by the bed, she was surprised to see him clean-shaven, his hair neatly combed, wearing a dark navy business suit, blue dress shirt, and conservative maroon tie. Laura's first impression was how handsome he appeared. Then she summarily dismissed such foolishness. His somber expression and his body language left little doubt that he did not want to be there.

Everett spoke up. "Russell?"

"You'll need to speak louder," Lilly said.

"I feel compelled to advise you that what you intend to do here today is not necessary." Everett, raised his voice. "I'm sure we can find a doctor who will provide you with sufficient levels of pain medication to allow you to live for some time longer."

Russell emitted a sound that was barely perceptible. Lilly put her ear down to his mouth. He repeated the noise. She said, "He asks, 'Why?'"

"What does he mean, 'why?'"

"I think he means that he has chosen to check out now," Arlo said. "A few more days or weeks of either pain or stupor is not something that interests him. And he wants the final dignity of making his own decision. 'Live Fierce.'"

To Laura, Arlo appeared troubled. Could this be the same boorish man who dated girls in their twenties, sometimes two at a time?

Arlo left the room.

"Where's he going?" Gracie asked.

Arlo reappeared with the Derby trophy. Russell's eyes showed a tiny glimmer of light. Arlo wrapped Russell's hand around the trophy. Russell managed a crooked smile, and nodded toward the whiskey.

"I think he's telling us it's time," Laura whispered. One by one, they embraced Russell and whispered a few words in his ear.

Lilly held her embrace the longest. "You have been more than a brother to me. You've been my dearest friend. I love you. Sleep well."

Laura carefully removed the trophy from Russell's grip and laid it in the crook of his arm. She placed the glass in Russell's hand, then backed away. After talking with Lilly, Laura had mixed the drugs into Old Grand Dad whiskey, Russell's favorite. He wrapped his lips around the straw and drank. It didn't take long for him to drain the glass. When finished, he let the glass fall from his hand. Laura quickly replaced it back on the table. Russell gave a slight nod to Lilly, then closed his eyes.

They all held hands. Gracie started singing "Amazing Grace" in at least three different keys. Laura glanced at Arlo. Again she was struck by how he seemed shaken, distant, not his normal self. Before Gracie had finished singing the hymn for the third time, Russell was gone.

Lilly sobbed quietly into a lavender colored hankie. The others left her to be alone with her brother.

They crowded into the tiny living room. Arlo appeared a bit forlorn. Laura asked, "Are you okay?" He didn't respond directly, but instead mumbled something that sounded like "dodgeball." Without meeting her eyes, he squeezed past her, his hand lightly brushing her hip, and left.

"What's with him?" Gracie asked.

Laura was sure the hip touch was an accident caused by the tight quarters.

Gracie pressed. "Laura?"

Before she could respond, Lilly entered from the bedroom carrying the empty whiskey glass. "Laura, I can't thank you enough for leading the way. He went so peacefully."

"To be honest with you, I'm still not sure we're doing the right—"

The front door banged open and a large woman burst in. About seventy-years-old, wild platinum-blonde hair, and makeup so heavy it caked on her skin. She clearly had work done and whoever performed the surgery should've been indicted.

Lilly was shocked. "Charlene?"

"Came as fast as I could," Charlene responded. She had one of those screechy voices that caused human bones to vibrate.

Lilly dabbed her eyes. "I'm sorry, but he's gone."

"Gone? Why isn't my husband in the hospital getting the care he needs?"

"Ex-husband," Lilly corrected her.

"He's not 'ex' in my heart." Charlene released a run of tears that appeared about as genuine as her silicone breasts.

"Listen, Charlene," Lilly said, "Russell couldn't stand the pain anymore, and he . . ." She shot a glance toward Laura, then cut herself off.

Charlene's expression turned on a dime. "What are you saying? Suicide? You forced him to commit suicide?"

Laura said, "We didn't force him to do anything."

"Don't you know the insurance company—?" She quickly caught herself. "Why didn't you stop him?" Charlene's eyes fell on the empty glass in Lilly's hand and eyed it suspiciously. "You haven't heard the last of this." She stormed out in a huff.

No one spoke for a long moment.

Gracie asked, "What do you think she meant when she said, we haven't heard the last of this?"

Lilly said, "Charlene's the most vindictive person I've ever met, particularly when money's involved. I hope I haven't caused you both any trouble."

Only minutes earlier Lilly had witnessed the death of her brother. The last thing she needed was an added layer of stress. Laura said, "I'm sure everything will turn out okay."

A chill shivered down Laura's spine, and her stomach twisted in a knot. She was all but certain everything would not turn out okay.

CHAPTER TWENTY-FIVE

Laura entered her kitchen from the backyard, taking a break from raking leaves, and sneezed again.

Mickey always liked raking the leaves, and she'd let him do it. That way she could avoid the allergens and give herself more time to—*what?* Play with her friends at the club? Looking back, maybe Mickey didn't really love raking leaves all that much. Maybe she let him know she had no time for such things because she had an important meeting here, or a tennis date there. A wave of guilt washed over her. How could she have been so blind?

She rummaged around in the fridge for the lemonade and saw a lone bottle of beer sitting in the back. Must've been there forever. Beer made her think of Arlo Massey. She wondered if he liked raking leaves? She shook her head and chastised herself. Why was she thinking about him anyway? Since Russell's passing, she hadn't seen or heard from him. Not that she expected to. Or wanted to.

Her thoughts were interrupted by the muffled sound of a car door slamming. She walked to the living room and peeked out the window. Two men dressed in coats and ties climbed the porch steps—one a tall African-American, the other a short, swarthy-looking fellow.

She opened the door just as the short guy was about to ring the bell. "Good afternoon."

"Good afternoon, Mrs. Beckman," said the taller man. "I'm Detective Will Jefferson." He flashed an ID. This is my partner, Chaz Olivetti."

"Has someone been in an accident? Gracie? Everett Tisdale?" She gasped. "Not Jennie, please tell me it's not Jennie."

"There's been no accident, Mrs. Beckman," Jefferson said.

Olivetti spoke up with an edge in his voice. "We're from homicide."

She froze.

Jeffrerson asked, "May we come in?" Laura didn't move. "Mrs. Beckman?"

"Uh, yes. Certainly." She led them into the house, closed the door, and gestured toward the living room. "Please, have a seat." *Homicide?* Her legs felt rubbery and she grasped the back of Mickey's caramel–colored leather chair to keep from collapsing. "May I offer you a refreshment? A cold drink?"

"No thank you," said Jefferson.

They sat on the sofa. Jefferson was a handsome man, early forties, close-cropped hair with a few flecks of gray at the temples. His soft brown eyes conveyed a gentle weariness that she figured came with the job. Olivetti was built like a cube—broad shoulders, no neck, little waist, shaved head, moustache, and an agitated expression.

"How can I help you?" Her raspy voice didn't sound like her own.

Olivetti spoke with no trace of warmth. "We're here investigating the deaths of Russell Melroy and Nora Meyers."

Laura hoped the two officers wouldn't notice her shaking hands and knees.

"Are you all right, Mrs. Beckman?" Olivetti asked, hardly trying to mask a smirk.

"I'm fine. It's not every day police detectives enter your home to ask about the deaths of two people, one of whom was a friend, and the other a family member held very dear."

"We understand," Jefferson said.

Laura glanced at Olivetti. She didn't think he understood one bit. "Nora and Russell, their deaths were suicides. I know, I was there."

Olivetti fished a notebook from his jacket pocket. "Mr. Melroy's wife . . ." He flipped through the notebook pages. " . . . Charlene Melroy—"

"Ex-wife," Laura corrected him.

Olivetti ignored her. "It seems Mrs. Melroy suspects that you, in concert with others, may have unlawfully assisted in Mr. Melroy's suicide. And then there's the 'coincidence' of your sister-in-law's death." His inflection of the word "coincidence" didn't escape her.

She clasped her hands together in a grip so tight all the blood drained away. "Charlene's after Russell's life insurance. He never changed the beneficiary, and if his death's ruled a suicide, Charlene doesn't collect a penny."

"Both Mr. Melroy and Mrs. Meyers died from an overdose of a benzodiazepine," Jefferson said.

"We're interested in knowing what happened in Mr. Melroy's and Mrs. Meyers' bedrooms," Olivetti said.

Laura's voice froze.

"Mrs. Beckman?" Olivetti persisted.

Jefferson turned to his partner. "Uh, Chaz, do you think we need to Mirandize her first?" Olivetti's dirty look left no doubt that Mirandizing Laura was absolutely the last thing he was interested in doing. Jefferson ignored his partner. "Mrs. Beckman, these allegations are serious, so maybe you should contact a lawyer before we go further."

"Christ, Will, that's her choice."

Jefferson intoned, "You have the right to remain silent—"

"I think I'll wait and talk to a lawyer," Laura interrupted.

Olivetti didn't hide his displeasure. With an exaggerated sigh, he stood, removed a card from his pocket, and handed it to Laura. "After you consult with your attorney, I suggest you call me. It'll go better for you in the long run."

Laura showed them out. Jefferson lingered until Olivetti was out of earshot. "This is very serious, Mrs. Beckman," he cautioned in a voice barely above a whisper. "I'm not saying you're doing anything, but you better stop it now." He held her gaze for a long moment then walked out onto the porch and down the steps toward his car.

Laura closed the door and gasped. She lost the strength in her legs and had to lean against the door for support. What had she done? What was she going to do? Who was she going to call? Alicia's husband had always done their legal work, not because Laura found him particularly brilliant. He'd been Mickey's friend, and looking back she realized she had no say in the matter. But there was still one person she trusted. She reached for her phone.

Gracie got straight to the point. "Are we going to the slammer?"

Their position buried deep in the plush sofa cushions required that they looked up at Tom Marshall sitting tall in Mickey's leather chair. Laura felt like a child who'd been caught doing something bad, and her stern father was about to pronounce punishment. Laura knew most of the attorneys in town, but none she trusted more than Brooke's former husband. He'd done an amazing job raising her granddaughter, Jennie, and over the years her respect for him continued to grow. She'd been pleasantly surprised when he'd agreed to see them.

Like a child in the hot seat Laura tried to put off the inevitable by delay. She made a move to get up. "It's almost five. Why don't I fix a plate of—"

"I'm not hungry."

"Maybe a glass of lemonade, or a beer. I know I have a beer because the other day I was looking in the fridge for—"

"Laura, I'm fine."

Laura sank back down, trying to make herself as small as possible. Tom's voice was neither angry nor friendly. Part of her hoped he would yell at her and get it over with.

"I don't understand it," he said. "New, life-saving discoveries occur every day. You helped to deprive a sick person of the chance, even if it's a tiny chance, to get better."

Laura figured if she were speaking with a completely disinterested attorney he wouldn't scold them like that. But Tom's rebuke was oddly reassuring.

Laura took a deep breath and straightened up. "People must be given all the information available that relates, even remotely, to their illness. They should obtain a second and a third opinion. They should talk to family and clergy. But in the end, everybody needs to be free to make the final decisions about their own bodies, their own lives. And their own deaths."

"Laura, I have to say I'm surprised by your involvement. When Brooke and I were married, you came across to me as—" He searched for the words.

"As shallow and superficial?"

"I'm not here to judge, but I wouldn't have guessed you'd have selected a cause that could put you in such jeopardy."

"I've not selected a cause, Tom. Not like before anyway, where I volunteered for the charity of the month. This is—different. It *feels* different." How could she explain it to him? Her eyes lowered. How

could she explain it to herself? Her voice softened. "I guess I've simply come to realize that my life has not been well lived." She lifted
her head and held his gaze. "I'm trying to change that."

No one spoke.

Finally, Tom took a deep breath. "Okay then, here goes. Assisted
suicide is considered homicide and a conviction could result in sub-
stantial prison time. The Supreme Court back in '97 ruled there's no
Constitutional right to commit suicide with the help of a physician,
much less someone who's not a doctor. The decision was unanimous, and given the political split on the court you can imagine
how rare a unanimous decision is."

"We *are* going to jail," Gracie lamented.

"Suicide does not in and of itself constitute a crime," Tom continued. "It may implicate moral or religious issues, and can often
be grounds to deny a life insurance payout. But if a person takes his
own life, that is, if he's the one who actually pulls the trigger, there's
no crime. And as a practical matter there's no one to prosecute
anyway since the person's dead."

"What if you, uh, give him the gun?" Laura asked.

"The key is, he must pull the trigger. Let's say the person's weak
and has trouble pulling the trigger, and asks his friend to help. The
friend, out of love, helps him pull the trigger. The law says the friend
committed murder."

"Oprah was right, the law's an ass," Gracie said.

"I believe that quote comes from Dickens' *Oliver Twist*," Tom
said.

"Maybe they both said it."

Tom leaned forward. "Nora and Russell died from an overdose
of a Benzodiazepine."

"Alprozalam. Xanax mixed with alcohol,' Laura said.

"You witnessed these deaths?"

Both nodded.

"Did you provide the drugs?"

After a pause, they nodded again.

"I see." He thought for a moment. "Well, if they drank the booze on their own, took the glasses in their hands and drank without any assistance from you, then—"

"They did," Laura confirmed.

"Then you're likely in the clear as far as a homicide charge goes. That leaves the drugs. Alprozalam's a schedule four controlled substance. Dispensing drugs without a prescription and obtaining a controlled substance illegally violates both state and federal laws."

Laura and Gracie gulped in unison.

"I've dealt with Olivetti before. He's like a bulldog that's sunk its teeth into your leg. He's not going to let go."

"You're right, he's not a pleasant man," Laura said.

Tom stood to leave. "I know you both thought you were doing the right thing. Who knows, maybe on some level you were. But you put yourself square in the law's crosshairs. You've already at the very least violated state and federal drug laws. As your lawyer, I must advise you to refrain from any further such activities. Otherwise you're putting yourselves in serious jeopardy."

Laura asked, "So what do we do now?"

'Nothing. Hopefully, the police will find more pressing crimes that deserve their time and resources. If you are contacted again, call me immediately, and politely inform the detectives that I've advised you not to speak to them without me present."

He stood, and Laura walked him to the door. "Don't worry, we've learned our lesson. And thanks."

Gracie nodded vigorously. "Definitely learned our lesson."

"One more thing," Tom said. "Do not discuss your . . . passive presence at Nora's and Russell's suicide with anyone. Got it?"

Both responded in unison. "Got it."

Tom hugged them both. "I don't want you to get hurt."

When the door closed, Laura couldn't stop shaking. *Prison? My God.* She turned to see Gracie smiling at her conspiratorially. "What?"

Gracie pulled her hand from behind her back and proudly displayed her crossed fingers.

Laura scowled. "Are you out of your mind? You better uncross those fingers, old woman. I'm not going to jail."

"We only go to jail if we get caught. Remember Russell's t-shirt? 'Live Fierce.' Now, I believe I recall you saying something about a beer?"

CHAPTER TWENTY-SIX

Brooke drove down West Street heading for work, unable to shake from her mind thoughts of her ex-husband. When she'd been away, they'd had little contact. Every now and then he'd pick up the phone first when she called Jennie and there'd been the frosty, uncomfortable exchange of hellos. Very little other than that. When Tom's mother passed away some years back, she'd called him to convey her condolences. She'd always gotten along well with Harriet, certainly more so than her own mother, but after a clipped "thank you" and an awkward silence, the call ended quickly. She'd forced him out of her life and willed him out of her mind.

Okay, maybe that wasn't completely true. Every now and then Tom's image snuck back into her head, usually at the strangest times. Like when she was dating that musclehead. What the hell was his name? Al or Sal, something like that. He'd been jumping her bones in his tiny Venice apartment, and she'd called out Tom's name at an awkward moment. The musclehead asked her afterwards who this Tom guy was. She smiled to herself as she remembered her answer. She told him "Tom" was not a man's name, but a Buddhist chant—"Tommmmmm"—which meant exquisite pleasure. The idiot, completely taken with his chiseled body and sexual prowess, actually believed her. Since she'd come back, what little contact there'd been all related to Jennie. She heard he'd been dating a woman for a while, some lawyer, and Brooke was genuinely happy for him. But seeing him at the club after her daddy's funeral opened the door a crack, the door she had promised herself to keep closed.

She reached for a cigarette. Keeping one eye on the road and one hand on the wheel she fumbled in her purse for her lighter. The car lighter broke months ago, and she never bothered to fix it since she always carried her own. Where was the damn thing? The lighter was the only keepsake she'd retained from her past life. Sterling silver. Tom gave it to her on their first anniversary. He engraved it, "I will love you forever." Actually, if she were perfectly honest with herself the idea she'd willed Tom from her mind was total bullshit. Every time she used the lighter to smoke a cigarette she thought of him.

She turned her purse upside down and glanced at the contents on the passenger seat out of the corner of her eye while she rummaged through her stuff with her right hand. No lighter. She spotted the familiar dog-eared photo she kept in the bottom of the purse, and held it up in front of her so she could still see the road ahead. The picture showed a young woman in a polka dot dress holding hands with a smiling young girl in a periwinkle outfit. The girl held an Easter basket.

On many occasions over the years she dug the picture from her purse with the clear intent of tossing it in the trash. But for some reason she couldn't do it; the old photo always seemed to find itself back inside her bag. All that time. So much lost, never to be recovered. She sighed and dropped the photo back into her purse.

Oh, yeah, the lighter. She probably left it at her mother's house. Eastgate was on the way, and she had the time before her shift started. She eased into the right lane to make the turn.

Laura and Gracie, both dressed in shorts and sweatshirts, attempted with only moderate success to execute crunches on Laura's living room rug while a blonde tight-body on TV crunched and counted, never losing her sunny smile. Behind her, a sign in bright gold lettering ordered: "Tighten up with Tessa!" At that moment Laura dedicate herself to hunting down and strangling that smiley face with her bare hands. Tessa finally came to a stop. Laura and Gracie collapsed back onto the rug.

Gracie panted like a fat dog in July. "Alls I'm saying is, listen to yourself, what you tell other people, what you told Tom. You know, their life, their choice."

"How can you . . . talk and . . . do this?" Laura asked between gasps of air.

Tessa's cheerful voice filled the room. "Okay, girls, let's roll over onto our tummies and lie flat."

Gracie said, "If I roll over on my tummy it's impossible to lie flat." But they both rolled to their stomachs and followed Tessa's direction anyway.

"Okay, girls, let's finish up with a nice stretch. Up on your hands, arch your back like a kitty cat, and feel that pull in your lower back. Now move those hips up and down. Oooo, now doesn't that feel good?"

"Ow, ow, ow, ow," the ladies responded in unison.

"Why do we watch this bimbo?" Luara asked.

"It was your idea."

"News flash. I'm not always right." The words echoed in her head, along with an image of herself wearing an orange jump suit.

With music pounding a heavy beat in the background, Tessa waved. Laura reached for the remote and turned her off in mid-wave. They both collapsed onto their backs spread their arms wide, then pulled their knees up and gently rolled back and forth to stretch their lower backs.

Gracie continued. "As I was saying—"

"How could you even think about doing it again? Didn't you hear Tom? Were you listening when I told you about the police coming here, right in this very living room? They were from the homicide division. Let me say that again in case you didn't hear me. They were from the *homicide* division."

"So what? We haven't done anything wrong. In fact, we've helped two very nice people."

"We violated drug laws, and some, including my own daughter, would say we didn't help them, we killed them."

"We didn't kill anybody. They were dying, like Mickey, and wanted to end months of pain. They knew what they were doing. They had a good life and we gave them a last wish that brightened that life a little at the end. And then *they* made the final decision, *they* drank the cocktail. We didn't pour it down their throats."

They'd both stretched to the point where their knees reached the floor on each roll. Laura couldn't wash the image of the orange jump suit from her mind. "It's a moot point anyway, since thankfully no one else has approached us for help." Gracie remained silent. Laura froze. "What? Are you telling me there's someone else?"

The door opened and Brooke entered. She glanced at them on the floor with their arms spread and their feet flat on the rug. "I get it. The crucifixion. But aren't you missing the star of the show?"

The ladies climbed to their feet. "That's sacrilegious," Laura said.

"It certainly is. Now, have you seen my lighter? I think I might've left it over here."

"Special lighter?" Gracie asked.

"Tom gave it to her on their first wedding anniversary," Laura said. "It's engraved, 'I will love you forever.'"

'Wow, you don't even bother attempting to hide the sarcasm from your voice," Brooke said.

"You shouldn't smoke anyway."

"You shouldn't poison people, so we both have our little faults don't we?"

Laura sighed. "The lighter's on the counter."

Brooke headed for the kitchen.

"Speaking of Tom," Gracie said, "he was in this very living room this very afternoon." Laura shot her a dirty look.

Brooke stopped and turned. "What was Saint Thomas doing here?"

"Attorney-client privilege," Gracie responded, pursing her lips.

"I see. Hopefully, he advised you not to murder anybody else, at least not this week." Brooke disappeared into the kitchen.

"That's not funny," Laura called after her, then glared at Gracie. "You had to open your big mouth."

"I think she and Tom should—"

"Should what?" Brooke asked as she came back into the room.

Laura lifted her chin. "Nothing." She was proud of her level tone. Things were under control now. Nora and Russell were gone. She couldn't force herself to feel bad about that. But there would be no more, and hopefully Tom was right. The cops would busy themselves with more important matters.

"Nothing. That about sums it up." Lighter in hand, Brooke headed straight for the door. "Try to stay out of jail, Mother. Don't want you to sully my reputation."

Watching her daughter leave triggered a response in Laura she wasn't expecting. "Brooke..." Her daughter stopped and turned. "I . . . I understand your concerns, and I share them." Laura held Brooke's gaze. "And I didn't mean to make fun of your relationship with Tom."

No one spoke.

Finally, Brooke stammered, "G-goodbye . . . Uh, have a nice . . ."

She left, and Laura noticed her daughter made sure the door closed softly behind her.

Gracie said, "Don't know what caused you to do it, but that was a nice thing to say to her."

Laura shook her head. "She's always known how to get my goat."

"Wonder where that saying came from." Gracie followed Laura into the kitchen. "I think back in the olden days somebody had his goat stolen and said, 'Gaylord got my goat' and then it passed down through history."

"Gaylord?" Laura handed Gracie a bottled water from the fridge.

"But why not a cow? I'm sure he'd be just as mad if Gaylord had stolen his cow. In fact, a cow was probably more valuable than a goat. But you don't say, 'She really gets my cow,' so it had to be a—"

"Gracie!"

"I was only wondering, that's all."

"Stop wondering."

"You're cranky because Brooke told you not to help anyone else."

"I'm not particularly interested in spending the rest of my life in jail. We helped two very nice people, that's enough. In fact, that's more than enough." Gracie pulled a piece of leftover cake from the fridge. "What would Tessa say about that cake?"

"She can't have any."

Laura smiled and cut the piece of cake in half. She pulled two forks from the drawer and handed one to Gracie. "Fork?"

"Fork Tessa."

Laura couldn't help but laugh as they sat down at the table.

Gracie's expression turned contemplative. "I'm serious, Laura. What we've done is a good thing, and there are many other people out there who're hurting as bad as Nora and Russell. You told Tom your life hadn't been well lived. So how are you going to spend the rest of it? Now that you've done your good deed, are you going back to running for queen of the Spring Fling?"

Laura's appetite immediately disappeared and she pushed away the cake. "Since when did you become my conscience?"

"Remember how Nora called chocolate her guilty pleasure? You provided her a last wish, a last pleasure. So I was thinking we could call your service the Chocolate Shop in her honor. You know, like a code name?"

"My service?"

"You can help others."

"Why don't you continue the service yourself? You can use Elvis to get the pills."

"You're the leader, I'm the follower."

"This discussion's moot. No one's come forward anyway, so—" Gracie's Cheshire Cat expression stopped her in mid-sentence. "What?"

"Remember Mildred Harper from the garden club?" Gracie walked over to the side table and opened her purse.

"Yes, but she resigned last year due to—"

"Serious illness." Gracie pulled a slip of paper from her purse. A phone number was written on the note. "She called, begged us to help her."

"How could Mildred have known about Nora and Russell?"

Gracie looked away. "I don't know, maybe Lilly said something."

"You're a lousy liar." Gracie didn't respond. "Don't you understand the more people who know, the more dangerous it is for us."

"What I understand is, Mildred's hurting and we can help."

Laura leaned back in her chair and closed her eyes. How *was* she going to spend the rest of her life? She believed, no, she *knew* helping Nora and Russell had been the right thing to do. If she assisted more people was that really so bad? But then again, who was *she* to play God? And the fear of spending the rest of her life in prison snapped the hairs on the back of her neck to attention. With the police involved, things had changed. Was it worth putting herself and Gracie in jeopardy?

Her mind moved to her last days with Mickey. She trembled, recalling the heartbreak and pain. She raised her head and scanned the room until her gaze reached the dining room trophy wall. Is that the life she wanted? Safe. Balanced. Appropriate.

She slowly surveyed all of the plaques and photos and trophies until her eyes fell upon the empty place she'd been saving for her Symphony Ball plaque. It had seemed so important.

"Laura?"

Live fierce.

After a long moment she stood and walked to the utility room off the kitchen. She dragged out a large white plastic trashcan.

"Laura?"

She pulled the trashcan to the dining room and parked it in front of the trophy wall. Her eyes surveying every item on display. These trophies were what mattered? This was her life? With a wide flourish of her hand she swept all of her trophies and plaques and certificates of appreciation and commemorative photos into the trashcan, shelf by shelf, until all the shelves were completely barren.

Stunned, Gracie said nothing.

Her back still facing Gracie, Laura said, "I'll see her, but that's all I'm promising."

Gracie reached for her phone.

CHAPTER TWENTY-SEVEN

December-February

Laura, with Gracie walking along side, pushed Mildred Harper in her wheelchair over the bumpy cobblestones leading the annual Christmas parade through Annapolis. Following them were the majorettes and cheerleaders from Four Rivers High School and the Fighting Tartans high school band. Directly behind the band, Mortie Stein, dressed as Santa Claus, tossed out candy canes to onlookers from his seat on the back of a bright red fire truck. Mortie was Jewish but once explained to a local reporter that Santa had come to be more like the Thanksgiving turkey, an American holiday icon who transcended religion. He omitted the fact that all those candy canes were wrapped in cellophane bearing the words: "Stein's Hardware."

Mildred wore her old Tartan plaid drum major uniform—Laura had let it out in the waist an inch or so—though most of the uniform was covered by the heavy blanket tucked across her lap. Mildred held a baton high in the air, crisply waving it in perfect time, leading the musicians down the street.

The decision to help Mildred had not been easy. Laura knew Mildred through the garden club but never considered her a close friend. She fully expected to deny Mildred's request. On the drive over to the assisted living facility she'd rehearsed how, after expressing her deepest, heartfelt sympathies, she'd gently inform the woman she couldn't help. But Mildred also must've rehearsed, as she was ready to make her case.

Mildred produced three separate medical opinions confirming her terminal prognosis. She constantly drifted back and forth between constant pain and, when she took an extra pill to dull that pain, unconsciousness. She'd considered simply taking the whole pill bottle but read too many stories of people who'd botched the job. She needed professionals, she had no real family, and she wanted to have her last wish fulfilled while a tiny bit of strength remained in her ninety-one-year-old body.

Laura melted; Mildred won her case. Gracie had a strong hunch how the decision would turn out and brought along a plastic bag filled with chocolate cookies to commemorate the decision. Laura couldn't help but notice Mildred's smile as she took her first bite. And so here they were, marching in a *parade* of all things, so Mildred Harper could have one last chance to twirl her baton.

The parade terminated at the end of Main Street where Christmas shoppers tightly packed the city dock, and the band somehow assumed the formation of a Christmas candle on the narrow street while playing "Hark the Herald Angels Sing." The festive crowd sang along, then clapped and cheered when the song was finished. Laura surveyed the crowd and glimpsed Brooke watching her like a disapproving schoolteacher.

Laura remembered that Mickey took Brooke to the Christmas parade every year when Brooke was young. Had Brooke been attending since she'd returned from L.A.? Why didn't she know? Laura was the parent, and parents remain parents no matter the age of the child. Without thinking, Laura raised her arm and waved to Brooke. Startled, Brooke froze for a moment before hesitantly returning the wave.

Two young trumpet players dressed in Tartan kilts marched up to Mildred and helped her out of the chair. She stood, propped up on each side by the two young men, and Mortie bellowed—his bellow was one of his strongest Santa qualifications—"Ladies and gentlemen, the Four Rivers High School Marching Tartans are pleased and honored to welcome back their drum majorette from 1946, Mildred Jones Harper!"

Mildred and Mortie waved, the crowd cheered louder, and she basked in the warmth of their welcome. At Mortie's signal Mildred held her baton high and brought it down on the beat to begin a rousing rendition of "We Wish You a Merry Christmas." Laura didn't know Mildred all that well, but she doubted the woman had been this happy in a long time.

Gracie, caught up in the moment, borrowed a pom-pom from a cheerleader and pranced around, waving it in time with the music. When she danced in front of a trumpet player, she playfully flipped up his kilt. He was naked underneath. The boy's eyes bulged, but he chose to trooper on and continued attending to his musical responsibilities. A gaggle of mommies in the front row squealed, and covered the eyes of their children. Mildred laughed as she deftly led the band and the audience through three repetitions of the Christmas classic.

Laura relaxed in her kitchen, enjoying her third cup of coffee, this one decaf. She stared down at the note Gracie left: "Chocolate Shop—Eddie Shanski." Almost two months had passed since Mildred led the Christmas parade. She arranged to pass on New Year's Eve. As she explained, "Out with the old, in with the new." A deeply religious woman, Mildred anticipated a new adventure in the after-life. She insisted that once they said their goodbyes, Laura and Gracie should leave the drink on her bed table and depart. That way they wouldn't be anywhere near Mildred when the drugs were consumed.

Of course it hadn't happened that way. Mildred had no family and Laura couldn't abandon her to die alone. So she held Mildred's hand while Gracie again showed her the large color photo from the front page of the *Capital* depicting Mildred, baton held high, directing the band at the Christmas parade. Laura dissolved the pills in a glass of champagne, and the three of them toasted the new year. Laura comforted Mildred as she passed and at the time had no misgivings.

Since then she'd lain low. Gracie brought her two more potential "clients"—Gracie's word, but in both cases the "applicants" expressed a desire to save family members the financial strain of keeping them alive. While sympathetic, in Laura's view neither justified the services of the Chocolate Shop.

But Eddie Shanski was a deserving case. Russell's lodge brother, Eddie had been "referred" to her by Lilly who described his story. As a teenager Eddie lied about his age and joined the army to fight the Germans in World War II. He became a highly decorated veteran of the 101st Airborne Division "Screaming Eagles," and parachuted behind enemy lines into Nazi occupied France on D-Day in June, 1944. He broke his left arm when he landed in a tree, but continued on without complaint as they fought their way up Hell's Highway to Bastogne and the Battle of the Bulge. Somehow, he survived.

Eddie's biggest thrill had been shaking Eisenhower's hand in England shortly before the D-Day jump—a Pfc. talking to the Supreme Allied Commander. No one back home believed it until a photo of the handshake appeared six months later in the *Capital*. Now in his nineties and given only a few months to live over a year earlier, his body, riddled with bone cancer, had stubbornly decided to hang on. His medications only partially addressed the constant pain. He begged for Laura's help, and she agreed. Her grandfather had been an Omaha Beach survivor, and she felt she owed Eddie. But his last wish required some help. That meant calling Arlo Massey.

She remembered the greasy photo in his boat's kitchen and figured Arlo could probably assist. She hadn't seen him since he'd walked away after Russell passed, but she'd caught his marina commercial a few times on TV. It was really awful and reminded her this was the man who named his boat *Stiff Ripples*. Disgusting. Still, she had no real choice.

Laura stopped her car at the entrance to Massey's Marina. She spoke to Gracie without turning her head. "Wipe that smile off your face."

"What smile? How do you know I'm smiling when you're not even looking at me?"

"I know you're smiling, and not a cheerful or a happy smile either. More like a smirk."

"Is that right? I'll have you know there is no smirk on my face and there hasn't been a smirk on my face since you told me we were using Arlo on this case."

"We're calling them cases now?"

"Sounds more professional. And as for Arlo, thou do-ist protect too much."

"If you're going to quote Shakespeare, at least try to—" Laura turned to face Gracie. The woman's grin was so wide the corners of her mouth seemed to touch her ears. Laura closed her eyes and shook her head.

Gracie climbed out of the car. "Here comes your boyfriend."

"Where do you think you're going?"

"Back seat."

"I don't want you in the back seat, I want you up here with me where I can keep an eye on you."

Gracie ignored her and climbed into the back seat as Arlo arrived.

"Good morning, ladies," Arlo said, full of cheer. He climbed into the front seat. "Glad you called on me, Laura. Love being part of the team."

Laura's words were as much a message to herself as to him. "There is no team, Mr. Massey. This is not a game. It involves heart-wrenching moral, ethical, theological, and legal issues. You are here because we need access to a jump plane. That's it. What we're doing is very, very serious."

Laura expected the usual snappy responsive quip, but Arlo surprised her. At first, he said nothing. He finally spoke in a quiet voice devoid of inflection.

"I know."

It took the full extent of the drive and Gracie's incessant chattering for Arlo to warm back up to his normal form. Laura concluded there might be a few layers to Arlo Massey hidden underneath the obnoxious jerk.

Single and in her mid-twenties, Mary Shanski had been living alone. She tutored kids for SAT exams during the day while finishing up her masters in the evening at the University of Maryland. When her great-uncle invited her to live with him and help out a little around the house, she jumped at the chance to save rent money.

Mary assisted Eddie down the steps toward her car. What a beautiful morning to fly, she thought. Clear blue sky, a few puffy clouds, a gentle breeze. Perfect. Very few WWII vets were still alive, and it was highly unlikely many of those men could fit comfortably into their old uniform. Eddie had the opposite problem. He'd lost so much weight that the olive drab tunic now draped over his slight frame. Her uncle was frail and his breathing labored. She could not believe he was actually thinking about parachuting out of an airplane. But the cancer had ravaged his body, he was in constant pain, and if this little adventure brought him a few minutes of joy, she was okay with that.

As they approached the car, she heard the faint sound of the phone ringing from inside the house. "You want me to run in and get that?" she asked.

"Nah, probably a sales call. Some guys with foreign accents are always calling, trying to sell me Viagra." Eddie folded his body into Mary's small compact, anxious to get going.

Mary smiled and slid into the driver's seat.

"You sure you called Randy?" he asked.

"Yes, I called him. That's the third time you asked me that. He'll meet us at the plane."

The phone continued to ring as they drove off.

It took forty-five minutes for Mary and Eddie to reach Tipton Field, a modest private airport in the western part of the county. She helped Eddie out of the tiny car, and they slowly made their way across the tarmac to the plane.

"A de Havilland Twin Super Otter," Eddie said.

"Looks fat." Her uncle knew planes and enjoyed any opportunity to discuss them. With Mary, it was a one-way discussion.

"Perfectly designed for jumping," Eddie explained. "The plane only requires a short take off and landing strip and handles well at slow speeds. See the extra large door? It's located in the front so the plane's center of gravity won't be affected when jumpers exit. Notice anything unusual about the tail?"

"Looks like an airplane tail."

"It's designed higher than normal so no jumper is accidentally blown into it when he leaps from the plane." Eddie spotted Laura, Arlo, and Gracie climbing the stairs to the plane and waved.

"Who are they?" Mary asked.

"Other jumpers. And there's Randy." He waved to a strapping young man in his early twenties standing at the top of the stairs."

"Sure you want to do this?"

"Never been more sure of anything in my life, Sweetie." He turned and hugged her. Mary was surprised. Her uncle had never been a hugger.

"I love you," he whispered. "Thank you for taking care of me."

"I love you, too. Now, Promise me you'll do what Randy says."

"Promise."

Randy, a former Navy SEAL and an experienced skydiver, descended the stairs and gave Mary a quick hug. With his thick shock of red hair and his easy smile, the young man was the spitting image of his grandfather. Eddie lived vicariously through Randy's stories, usually pressing the young man to repeat his account of a jump in excruciating detail.

"Take care of him," she said.

"Don't worry, I will." He helped Eddie up the stairs.

Randy's expression seemed odd. Sad? No, more complicated than that. She couldn't quite put her finger on it.

At the top of the stairs, panting heavily, Eddie blew a kiss to Mary, then he and his grandson disappeared inside the plane.

CHAPTER TWENTY-EIGHT

Laura watched Eddie try to mask a grimace as the plane bounced through another air pocket. They'd been flying for about forty-five minutes sitting on uncomfortable jump seats, conversation all but completely drowned out by the deafening turbines.

She shouted across the narrow aisle. "Are you okay?"

Eddie grinned. "Couldn't be better." His eyes were bright, alive. Much different from when they'd first met three weeks earlier for his "interview."

Eddie sat between Randy and Arlo, across from Laura and Gracie. In addition to the pilot, Arlo had arranged for a jumpmaster named Ty to join them.

Laura and Gracie had been chilly, so Ty, a handsome blond-haired young man in his thirties, provided them both with warm diving overalls. Laura originally assumed Arlo could handle Eddie by himself, but both he and Eddie had insisted that she and Gracie accompany them on the flight. Arlo appeared to be back to his old self. He smiled at Laura with an expression that suggested he had something up his sleeve.

"Getting close, Arlo," Ty said.

Arlo walked to the rear of the cabin and returned with three parachutes.

Laura sat up, alert. "Why three?"

"Ty's going to jump with us."

Laura was visibly relieved.

Randy strapped on one of the chutes, then helped Eddie to his feet.

"Where are we?" Gracie asked.

"Caroline County on the Eastern Shore," Ty answered. "Our club has a deal with a farmer who lets us jump on his property in the winter months when nothing's growing."

"Isn't it pretty cold out there?" Laura asked.

"It's unseasonably warm on the ground for February. Mid-forties. Sunny. Up here at thirteen thousand feet it's colder, but everyone's dressed warm enough."

"Approaching." the pilot called back from the cockpit.

Laura stood and gave Eddie a long hug. His body seemed frail and brittle, even under his thick tunic and jumpsuit.

"Thank you," he whispered.

Gracie opened a plastic bag filled with chocolate cookies and passed them around. "Our little tradition."

Ty said, "Thought you'd never jumped before."

"Different tradition."

Eddie took a bite, then hugged Gracie, Arlo, and Ty. He removed a battered tin flask from his pocket. "High school sweetheart gave me this after my first jump. Sort of a good luck charm."

"Whiskey?" Ty asked.

Eddie held Laura's gaze and smiled. "Johnny Walker Black. But before I drink, we have a little surprise for the girls."

Laura didn't like surprises, and she had a sinking feeling she particularly wasn't going to like this one. She was right.

"You're going with us," Eddie announced with glee.

"No way," Laura responded. Gracie shook her head.

"Come on, it'll be fun," Arlo urged.

"I never jumped before," Gracie said.

"Don't worry," Arlo said. "You won't be jumping by yourself. You'll be strapped real tight to Ty."

Gracie appraised Ty as she would a thick cut of tenderloin, then turned to Laura. "I'm game."

"Are you nuts?"

"She'll be fine, Mrs. Beckman," Ty assured her. "Think of it like a ride at an amusement park. And she'll be triple buckled. She couldn't be more safe." He handed Gracie a helmet, goggles, and gloves.

"Suit yourself." Laura returned to her seat. "I'll meet you on the ground. Hopefully you'll be in one piece."

Randy helped his grandfather put on a helmet, goggles and gloves, then strapped him tight to his own body."

Laura locked eyes with Randy. Eddie had shared his plans with his grandson. While resistant at first, the young man came around and promised to keep Eddie's plan secret. She knew Eddie's wish had to be hard for Randy, and she witnessed a wide range of emotions on the young man's face. But she could tell by the way that they looked at each other that Randy felt a special bond to Eddie. He clearly loved his grandfather very much.

Eddie turned to Laura. "One last thing. You're going, too."

"That's ridiculous. Besides, there's no one for me to . . ." Arlo flashed his devilish smile and it hit her. "No way. Absolutely not."

"If you don't go, I don't go," Eddie said, trying to stand up straight to convey the resoluteness of his position, but with only marginal success. "This is my wish, and you're part of it. I want you both to experience the joy of flying through the air. That's it. No debate."

Laura was speechless.

"You heard the man," Arlo said. He offered Laura a harness. "If you need assistance, I'd be happy to help you put it on."

Laura paused for a long second, then snatched the harness out of his hand. "I can do quite nicely on my own." The others clapped. Arlo handed her a helmet, goggles and gloves.

"Get ready," the pilot called out. Laura quickly put on the gear.

"Good job, Laura," Arlo said. "Come here."

She was slow to move, so Arlo took a few steps behind her, and yanked her tight against him. She let out a tiny squeal. The others laughed. "Gotta spoon real close. Don't want you falling out of the harness."

Laura's eyes widened, and she scrunched her butt back against Arlo's hips. "If you say one word, I'll push you out of this plane without a chute."

"My lips are sealed," Arlo replied. He quickly buckled her in.

"We're here," the pilot announced. Ty pulled a lever and the cargo door opened. A blast of cold wind smacked them in their faces.

Laura rubbed her goggle lens. "My goggles fogged up, I can't see."

"They'll clear in a second," Arlo explained. And sure enough, the fogging disappeared.

"Hold up," Eddie said. He lifted the flask to his lips and drank it dry. "Good-bye, everyone."

"Don't say goodbye, Eddie," Ty said. "We'll see you on the ground."

Eddie held Laura's gaze for a moment in silent acknowledgement of his decision.

She looked to Randy, and even through the goggles she could tell he was struggling to contain his emotions.

"Go!" Ty shouted. Eddie waved to everyone one last time, then Randy jumped through the door and disappeared.

"Where'd they go?" Laura asked, alarmed. Ty pointed down, and she spotted Eddie and Randy tumbling through the air.

Laura cried out, "His chute's not opening!"

"He's free-falling. The chute will pop at fifty-five hundred."

"Closest any human being will ever get to flying," Arlo said. "The greatest feeling in the world." He paused. "Well, not the greatest feeling, more like the second greatest feeling in the world. Right, Laura?"

Laura knew he was winking or smiling or had some idiotic adolescent expression on his face, but fortunately he was wearing his helmet and was directly behind her so she was spared seeing it.

"You ready, Ms. Lujack?" Ty asked.

"Anyone holding me this close can call me Gracie."

Ty jumped out into the wind with Gracie waiving her arms and legs like child throwing a tantrum. Laura anxiously watched Ty extend his limbs to stabilize, then pulled them in and dove. When he reached Randy and Eddie, he spread out his arms again and locked hands with Eddie. Laura was horrified.

"Don't worry, they'll pop the chute in plenty of time. Ty's the best," Arlo assured her.

Laura reached to unbuckle her harness. "Okay, Eddie's gone and Gracie's gone so now we really don't need to—"

Arlo wrapped his arms around her and jumped through the door into the crisp February air.

"Geronimo!"

Laura tried to scream. In fact she was certain she did scream, but the roar of the wind through the helmet ear holes drowned out any sound. She felt the skin on her face and neck ripple. She'd squeezed her eyes tight. Slowly, she opened them and saw the sun, a beautiful blue sky, a few puffy clouds, and the earth below. Far, far below.

"Breathe, Laura," Arlo yelled into her ear hole. She realized she was holding her breath. She took a quick gulp of air, then another, then her breathing settled down to that of a person suffering normal hysteria. Off to her right she glimpsed Randy and Eddie, spread-eagle, Eddie holding hands with Ty, Gracie hanging under him, circling lazily in the air.

Laura felt the falling sensation give way to a sense of floating. For a moment she allowed herself to actually enjoy the experience. Then Arlo pulled his arms in close to his body and assumed the position of a diver. She again felt the rush of air as they shot down like a human bullet.

They reached the others in a few seconds. Arlo joined hands with Eddie and Ty. They formed a human ring and were as giddy as kids on their first roller-coaster ride. Laura opened her eyes a tiny bit and saw Gracie grinning at her. Laura couldn't tell whether her aunt was smiling with excitement or grimacing in fear. Maybe both.

The six earthlings circled through the air like hawks gliding on a canyon updraft. Laura gathered the courage to open her eyes wide and take it all in. Looking down on the Earth below with its tiny inhabitants and their tiny insignificant problems, she sensed she was flying, not falling. Soaring above it all. Omnipotent.

Ty pointed to the altimeter on his wrist. The single hand on the dial approached fifty-five hundred feet. Eddie and Arlo nodded and the three men broke away. Eddie saluted, then reached for the rip-cord but he was too weak to pull it. Randy covered his grandfather's hand with his and pulled. The chute blossomed out like a beautiful yellow flower.

Ty and Arlo pulled their cords almost simultaneously. Laura felt a jerk, then she was carried upward. Above her head she saw the billowing parachute canopy with the words, "Massey's Marina" emblazoned across the orange silk in big white letters.

Laura realized she probably wasn't going to fall to her death, and she allowed herself to relax. She waved and Gracie returned the wave. Off to her left she watched Eddie, cradled in his grandson's arms, drift down softly toward earth. From her vantage point Eddie appeared to be suspended from a single puffy cloud, drifting away in the breeze. She couldn't tell for sure whether he'd passed yet, but he would soon enough. She knew now his last moments were about as perfect as a human could experience before departing this life—the air whistling across his helmet, the crystal blue sky, the brilliant sun—floating away to eternity.

In many ways Eddie had been easier than the rest. He'd lived in pain much too long; the cancer was eating him alive. When Laura asked about family he'd told her about his grandson and his wonderful niece, Mary, and promised to leave her a note. But he didn't want to die in a bed. This is where he wanted to be. Now, having herself experienced this amazing combination of excitement and serenity, she understood completely.

Laura closed her eyes, took a deep breath, and experienced a level of peace and contentment she hadn't felt for a long, long time.

CHAPTER TWENTY-NINE

Jefferson was so deeply engrossed in the file on his desk that he didn't hear his partner come up from behind and slap two newspapers infront of him, one after the other.

"Look at that."

"Good morning to you, too." Jefferson saw both papers had been folded over to the obituary page. Olivetti had drawn arrows pointing to two pictures: Edward Lee Shanski and Mildred Eileen Harper.

"Yeah?"

Olivetti laid two other documents on top of the newspapers: each a coroner's report.

"How?" Jefferson asked, but he thought he knew the answer and he was right.

"Benzodiazepine," Olivetti announced. "Mixed with champagne for Harper and scotch for Shanski."

"I assume I don't need to ask about the presence of one Laura Beckman and one Grace Lujack at the suicide event."

"Bingo."

"How'd they go down?"

"The Harper woman led the band in the Christmas parade. Some last wish thing."

"I remember the picture in the paper."

"She died New Year's Eve accompanied by Beckman and Lujack. The drugs were in the champagne. The M. E. says time of death was probably right at midnight."

"So she has a final New Year's Eve toast with her friends, and goes out with the old year."

"Yeah, but she didn't come in with the new."

"Poetic, when you think about it."

"Poetic, my ass."

"What about Mr. Shanski?"

"A little different," Olivetti answered. "Seems he was this WWII hero, a D-Day paratrooper. He decides to check out with one last jump. The black widows join him. He drinks the spiked whiskey, jumps, and passes out of this life on the way to the ground."

"Again—"

"It ain't poetry, Will, it's murder."

"Any evidence Beckman and Lujack held the drink to Shanski's or Harper's lips?"

Olivetti paused. "Not directly," he said grudgingly.

"Look, my stack's not getting any shorter. These old people chose to end their life on their terms a few months, maybe even a few weeks or days before they would've died anyway. Now you tell me where we should spend our time. They were already dying."

Olivetti pulled a sheet of paper from his jacket pocket, and with a smug expression, handed it to Jefferson. "Not exactly."

Tom, Laura, and Gracie sat across from Olivetti and Jefferson in an interview room. The rough-hewn table was heavily stained with cigarette burns. The police had called them in for a meeting. Laura wasn't enthused about going, but after giving the matter some thought Tom decided it might be a good way to "fish around," find out what the cops were up to. Both she and Gracie had been given strict orders not to say anything unless Tom okayed it.

Tom spoke first. "We're here solely on a voluntary basis. I've instructed my clients to say nothing."

"We understand," Jefferson said. "Thank you for coming."

Laura guessed that Jefferson had decided to take the lead given Olivetti's penchant to antagonize. Olivetti opened a folder and removed copies of the obituaries for each of Laura's "customers" and placed them on the table.

Jefferson said, "We know of your . . ." He glanced at Tom ". . . *presence* at the suicides of each of these individuals. Mrs. Beckman, I know you think you're doing the right thing, but we've asked you here to impress upon you the gravity of your situation."

"Yeah, like spending the rest of your life in a room with no view," Olivetti said.

Jefferson glared at his partner and continued. "Both of you need to understand, you're facing possible second-degree murder charges."

Laura and Gracie gasped simultaneously. This was nothing different from what Tom had said, but coming from the police made it sound much more real.

Laura couldn't help herself. "But all we're doing—"

Tom put his hand on her arm to cut her off, then turned to Jefferson. "Detective Jefferson, both these decedents took their own lives. They made an informed decision to avoid excruciating pain. My clients know where the line is, and they didn't cross it. Both of these people faced certain death in a matter of months, maybe weeks."

Jefferson cast his eyes down, and Olivetti grinned. Laura didn't like the expression on his face.

"Tell 'em, Jefferson," Olivetti said.

"The doctor's office called as Mary and Eddie left for the airport, but Eddie didn't answer," Jefferson said. "The doctor was calling to report Eddie's most recent test results. He was in remission. The cancer was in remission. He likely had a year or two left, maybe more."

Laura was too stunned to speak.

Jefferson added, "His niece is beating herself up since she actually heard the phone ring before they left for the field, and she believes she should've insisted he answer it."

"We've assured her it wasn't *her* fault," Olivetti interjected.

"You're saying he wasn't dying?" Gracie asked.

"That's exactly what we're saying," Olivetti said. "You killed a healthy man."

Tom pounded the table angrily. "That's outrageous! No one killed anybody. This changes nothing. Mr. Shanski made the decision to take his own life. It appears now he made that decision based in part on incorrect information, but that has nothing to do with my clients."

Olivetti stood up, then bent down and got in Tom's face. "We'll see about that."

"Chaz!" Jefferson barked. Olivetti paused, then slowly straightened up. "Why don't you go get yourself a cup of coffee."

Olivetti glared at Jefferson, then slammed the door as he left.

Jefferson sighed with a weariness that infected his every feature. "Mrs. Beckman?"

Laura was in shock. Eddie hadn't been dying. She couldn't bring herself to believe it. Olivetti was right. She'd been responsible for killing a man who could have enjoyed a few more years of life.

"Mrs. Beckman?" Jefferson repeated.

"Laura." Tom tried to reach her. After a long pause she barely nodded.

"Mrs. Beckman, I'm not completely unsympathetic to your efforts here. My mother suffered months of needless pain before she passed, and once all hope was gone, I will admit the thought of giving in to her wishes and pulling the plug was very tempting. If it were up to me, your case would be shoved to the bottom of the pile. We have more than enough bad guys in this county to keep us busy. But it's not up to me, so I will do my job. We'll be watching, so please, no more. Do you understand what I'm saying?"

Laura stared off into space.

"Mrs. Beckman?"

"Are you sure?" she whispered.

"Sure? Sure about what?"

"Eddie, he wasn't going to die?" she asked in hushed anguish.

"Sorry."

"He wasn't dying," Gracie whispered to herself. "Jesus."

Tom stood. "We better go."

As soon as they reached the street, Laura's knees gave way, and Tom had to catch her. Gracie bent over and took deep breaths. Laura leaned her head back, faced the gray overcast sky and emitted a high-pitched sound, more a wail than a scream.

A moment later, the tears came.

CHAPTER THIRTY

Even with Gracie holding her arm, Laura felt unsteady as they walked down the wide steps of St. Anne's Episcopal Church. Laura knew the church well having attended various weddings and funerals over the years. Built in 1704, the church was the oldest and most prominent in Annapolis. The majestic structure had seen more than its share of funerals over the centuries, and its services were unfailingly moving.

Laura felt awful, and the weather didn't help. February was her least favorite month in Annapolis—a cold, damp blur of gray until late March. The funeral didn't help either. Randy's moving eulogy assured there were no dry eyes in the church. Laura's own tears arose as a result of a much deeper trigger than the death of a fine man: she'd killed Eddie Shanski.

"Excuse me?"

Laura turned to see Mary Shanski approaching with a stricken expression. Oh, my God, she knows. Not only did I kill her uncle, I also brought untold heartache to this young woman.

Mary said, "I recognized you both from the airport. You were with Uncle Eddie on the plane."

All Laura could do was nod.

Gracie said, "He was a fine man."

"You were probably as surprised as all of us when you learned he committed suicide," she continued.

Gracie dug her fingernails into Laura's arm.

"He thought he was dying," Mary continued. "But you probably didn't know he was mistaken. Uncle Eddie was in remission."

Laura couldn't speak.

"What a tragedy," Gracie said quickly, acting surprised.

"I asked Randy if Eddie had said anything as they glided down to Earth. He said, no. Too windy to hear anybody talk. Since you were the last people to see my uncle before he jumped, I was wondering if he, you know, said anything to you?"

Gracie glanced at Laura, then jumped in. "Yes, he did. He said how much he loved you, and what a long, wonderful life he'd led, and how blessed he felt, and how much pain he was in. And the skydiving, well, he seemed very happy at the end."

"Thank you, that means a lot."

"I'm Gracie Lujack, and this is Laura Beckman."

Laura allowed Mary to take her hand and shake it. "Sorry for your loss," Laura mumbled. Then she could hold back no longer. Her eyes brimmed with tears and she gasped her words. "I'm so . . . so very sorry."

Mary hugged her. Laura had to clutch the young woman to keep from collapsing.

"Uncle Eddie was lucky to have been with people like the two of you at the end," Mary said. "Thanks for coming." She waved and walked off.

Laura felt battery acid drizzling into her stomach.

"You look like crap," Gracie observed.

"Did you see her?" Laura struggled to stop the gush of bile rising in her throat. "That sweet girl. Not only did I . . . God, if only he'd answered the call from his doctor."

"You need a drink."

"Alcohol only makes matters worse." Laura pulled a tissue from her purse and dried her eyes as they walked toward the parking lot.

"C'mon, a glass of wine and a sandwich will do you good."

"Laura?"

She turned to see Arlo approaching. She'd seen him slip into the back of the church during the service but pretended not to notice.

Gracie said, "So, Arlo, we're going out for a drink and sandwich, want to join us?"

Laura said, "I'm not really—"

"Hungry?" Arlo interrupted. "With all due respect, Laura, you look a little wan."

"Wan?"

"Wan," Arlo repeated.

"Very wan," Gracie added solemnly.

Arlo took Laura's arm. "The food will do you good. Now, where shall we go?"

"What about the place Brooke works, the Slippery Clam?" Gracie said. "It's just down the street."

"Don't think the food's very good," Laura mumbled.

"How would you know?" Gracie said. "You've never been there."

"A quick sandwich," Arlo said. "That's all."

"And alcohol," Gracie said.

Arlo added, "To toast Eddie."

Too tired to resist, Laura allowed herself to be gently guided down the street toward the harbor.

Brooke enjoyed the soothing draw of the smoke as she polished the short glasses. The Clam finally received its first smoking citation based on a complaint by some D.C. do-gooder. She could see banning smoking in restaurants. Okay, fine. But *bars*?

The door opened, and she almost dropped the glass when her mother walked in. Goosebumps bubbled up Brooke's arms. What the hell was she doing here?

Arlo and Gracie led Laura to a small booth. Brooke checked her watch. Almost four. The place was virtually deserted. Wait help wouldn't arrive for another half hour, so she had no choice but to serve the group herself. She crushed out her cigarette, grabbed menus, and approached the table. "Welcome to the Clam. Didn't know you knew where it was, Mother."

Laura ignored her.

"Brooke, honey, we decided to grab a sandwich after the funeral," said Gracie.

"Oh yeah, the parachuter. Read about him in the paper." She paused, then it hit her. "Don't tell me. He was another one of your—" She stopped mid-sentence. No need to tip off Arlo to what her crazy mother was up to. Although for all she knew he was part of the gang.

Arlo said, "I used to come in here years ago when it was Orvie's Bait Shop. Back there, in the corner under the Bud sign, that used to be where Orvie kept his blood worms."

"Hopefully the food has improved," Brooke said.

Arlo and Gracie laughed.

Brooke passed out the short menus. "Can I get anybody a drink?"

Laura set the menu down on the table unopened. "Ice water would be fine," she said without looking up at her daughter.

"She'll have a glass of Chardonnay, and so will I," Gracie said.

"Gimme a Bud, no glass," Arlo said. He quickly perused the menu. "And I'll have a crab cake sandwich with extra chips."

Gracie said, "Your mother and I will split a turkey sandwich. On wheat, lettuce, tomato, and mustard. And not the yellow mustard. We both like that Gray Pom Pom stuff, right, Laura?"

"Grey Poupon," Brooke said.

"Whatever's easiest," Laura responded in a dead voice.

Brooke knew something was wrong. She left to get the drinks and take the food order to Mike who was working the grill in the tiny back room kitchen. When she returned she easily could hear the conversation in the booth.

"She looks good," Arlo said.

"Very pretty girl," Gracie added. "Like her mama."

Did Gracie just wink at Arlo? What was going on? Were Arlo and her mother an item?

"I would take them to be sisters," Arlo said. Laura didn't flinch. "Uh, Laura, I'm at a loss here. I thought you'd be happy. You gave this guy a wonderful last wish, and you allowed him to escape a painful death. Well, maybe happy's the wrong word, but—"

"He wasn't dying." Laura's voice didn't rise above a whisper but it was loud enough for Brooke to hear.

"But no one knew," Gracie added hastily. "The phone call from his doctor came as he was leaving for the airport. He was in a hurry and didn't answer."

Brooke's eyes widened. Oh, my God. No wonder the Queen Bee's in such a blue funk.

Arlo reached over and put his hand on Laura's arm. "No one knew," he said softly. "Eddie made his choice even though it was based on faulty information."

"That's what Tom said," Gracie added.

Brooke approached the booth from behind Laura with the drinks. She saw her mother slowly pull her arm away from Arlo.

Gracie said, "His life, and he chose to live fier—"

"I don't want to hear it," Laura hissed. "If it weren't for me, he'd still be alive. It doesn't make any difference whether he knew or not. I'm responsible."

Laura turned at the sound of Brooke's gasp and cringed.

"I need to go home," Laura whispered. "I'm not in the mood for a string of 'I told you so's' from my daughter."

"Mother, wait . . ."

Arlo tried to dissuade her. "Laura, listen—"

Laura interrupted him and locked eyes with Gracie. "Now."

Gracie shrugged and slipped across the bench. Laura purposely bumped into Arlo so he'd get up and let her out.

"We'll come back another time, honey," Gracie said to Brooke.

"You want me to come with you?" Arlo asked.

Laura shook her head.

Brooke didn't think she'd ever seen her mother in such anguish, even when her father died. Laura's semi-apology the day she stopped by to retrieve her lighter had haunted Brooke. In many ways having a firm wall between them, while hurtful, had been simpler to deal with. Seeing her now so vulnerable was unnerving. As Laura passed by, Brooke instinctively reached out her hand and squeezed her mother's shoulder.

Laura stiffened in surprise at her daughter's show of compassion.

"It'll be okay," Brooke whispered.

For a moment Laura's features softened. She reached up and covered Brooke's hand.

Then she left without another word.

CHAPTER THIRTY-ONE

May

In the weeks and months that followed Eddie's funeral, Laura kept to herself. At the beginning, Gracie came by regularly for what she called a cheer-up, but over time those visits became much less frequent. On her way out the door after her last visit she said, "I'll come back when your pity party's over." Laura didn't care what she said. She didn't care much about anything.

Everett appeared one afternoon and brought what he proudly described as his grandmother's famous pineapple-pork casserole. He explained he had toiled for hours making it himself from her secret recipe. He offered to come in and warm it up for a sample tasting, but Laura—probably a little too firmly she realized even then—told him that wasn't going to happen. She muttered a "thank you" for the food then closed the door, leaving the crestfallen man standing on her doorstep. She carried the casserole to the kitchen and unceremoniously dumped it down the disposal. The smell was toxic. Didn't Everett tell her once his grandmother died of food poisoning at the age of fifty-two?

Arlo called, but Laura politely put him off. He stopped by a few times unannounced with an invitation for dinner; Laura declined. She wasn't in the mood. He never gave up, calling once or twice a week, but after a brief exchange Laura always terminated the call.

She spent most of her time reading, or watching mind-numbing television. She only ventured out of the house when necessary. She slept late and was in bed by seven thirty, eight at the latest. Despite her inactivity, she lost weight from lack of eating. She existed simply by existing—minute-to-minute, hour-to-hour, day-to-day.

Brooke came by a few times and surprised Laura by not haranguing her, although Laura knew Brooke had been right all along. She was a murderer.

Brooke tried talking to her, even assuring her that while she continued to disapprove of her actions, she did not believe Laura was any more responsible for Mr. Shanski's death than for the deaths of the others. A part of Laura welcomed the quiet, soothing assurances from her daughter, but in the end nothing helped. Anna periodically checked in from Chicago, mostly to keep Laura up to date on her growing relationship with her boyfriend, Brandon. Anna had no knowledge of the Chocolate Shop so when Anna asked why Laura sounded so glum on the phone, Laura claimed she was suffering from spring allergies.

Jennie stopped by regularly, and these visits were the only times Laura seemed to perk up. Maybe it was the optimism of youth that could not help but infect those within its reach. To the best of her knowledge, Jennie wasn't aware of the Chocolate Shop. Her young granddaughter regaled her with breathless updates of her school and social life—her favorite teachers, her dance classes, an upcoming recital, how she's been begging her dad for a puppy—each element of the utmost importance in her young life. But when the girl left, Laura easily slipped back into what Brooke called her blue funk.

And so it went through March and April. For the most part, everyone left Laura alone to deal with her demons. She no longer bothered to dress in the morning, and instead shuffled about in her housecoat and slippers.

One warm evening in early May, Laura answered a knock at her door to find Arlo standing on the porch with that stupid grin and a bottle of wine.

"I was just in the neighborhood . . ."

She was instantly aware she wore only a tattered housecoat, and she clutched the collar tight around her neck. "I thought I made it clear I'm not in the mood for visitors."

"No problem, no problem at all. But it's such a nice evening I assume you won't mind if I sit out here on the swing." Without waiting for a response, he pivoted and made himself comfortable on the porch swing. Laura was too stunned to move. He said, "And I wonder if I could trouble you for a corkscrew. Oh, and a wine glass. A wine glass would be nice."

Laura stepped back inside the house and closed the door. She wasn't an idiot. She knew what he was trying to do, and she wasn't going to fall for it. She returned to the kitchen and her television show, something on the house and garden channel about installing a skylight. Every few minutes she'd stand up and peek out the front window. Arlo continued to rock back and forth. Finally she decided the only way to get rid of the man was take him his stupid corkscrew and insist after his one glass of wine she expected him to vacate the premises. *One* glass.

She found the opener and pulled a wine glass from the cupboard. She hesitated, then took a second glass. The thought of adding a touch of make-up or running a brush through her hair briefly crossed her mind, but there was no reason anymore to care about her appearance, and the last thing she wanted was to give Arlo Massey the wrong idea.

Fifteen minutes later Arlo rocked gently on the swing, sipping his wine while Laura sat in a porch chair saying nothing.

Arlo said, "You haven't touched your wine."

"Not thirsty."

"Look, Eddie might've technically been in remission, but given his age, let's face it, he was on his last legs."

Laura mumbled, "Time. Even a few extra months could've allowed a new treatment, a new drug to come to market."

"That's true, but the likelihood is remote, and what would this new drug have done to improve the life of a man in his nineties? Maybe reduced the pain? Add a few months of failing health? Who knows?"

"That's the point. We don't know, and now we'll never know."

"Let's assume Eddie answered the phone and learned he was in remission. What would he have done? Even in the best of circumstances the chances of him being physically able to fulfill his last wish later were remote. So given a choice between lying in bed for a few extra months, or going out on his own terms, what would he have chosen? I don't think there's any doubt he would've gone forward, and climbed the stairs to that plane."

After a long moment Laura stood and spoke without inflection. "You're free to finish your wine, then please leave. I'm going to bed."

She entered the house and closed the door firmly behind her.

Laura stood at the kitchen sink scraping most of a fried egg from a small breakfast plate, the same one she used for lunch and dinner. Over the several days since Arlo's visit, her mind had been filled with thoughts of Eddie Shanski. And Arlo Massey. What would Eddie have done if he'd answered the phone? Was Arlo right? Would Eddie still have gone ahead?

A part of her knew she needed to eat, but she had no appetite. She'd felt light-headed for several days, and even she had to admit her mind wasn't as sharp as it should be. The night before she'd awakened twice, convinced she'd seen Mickey standing at the foot of the bed. Two days earlier she was certain Arlo Massey dropped off a package on her porch dressed as the mailman.

She glanced out her window at the backyard. Something caught her eye. While she'd always been told her gardens were the envy of the neighborhood, in her mind at that particular moment the five shrubs bordering the back fence appeared as giant weeds, rogue invaders bent on destruction. Where had they come from? Who planted them there?

She immediately dropped the plate in the sink, and rushed out the door to the garage, still in her housecoat and slippers. She found the yellow-handled shovel hanging on the tool rack. Resting the shovel on her shoulder like a rifle, she marched out to the backyard, crossed the lawn, and confronted the enemy lined up against her fence—five majestic snowball viburnum. The shrubs bore dark green leaves, and large white snowball shaped flowers that emitted a beautiful fresh fragrance. Mickey once had described the fragrance as the "smell of spring." The five plants created a spectacular backdrop for her garden. Yet to Laura, they now appeared alien, invading her yard and her home. They had to be eliminated, and she was the only one to do it.

She plunged the spade deep into the roots of the first viburnum with singular determination. The work was hard. The plants were over ten years old and deeply rooted. But nothing was going to deter Laura Beckman from ridding her yard of these hideous interlopers.

Two hours later, covered in sweat and grime, Laura stood triumphant over five *Viburnum Opulus*, formerly gorgeous, but now in the last throes of death. Her pink slippers were filled with dirt.

Her housecoat was splattered, her hair tangled, and her face appeared like she'd just finished a mud-wrestling match and lost.

"Laura?"

Laura turned to see Arlo standing at the gate, viewing her as he would a creature from a distant world. She stared at him for a moment, then her eyes lowered to her housecoat. She was too stunned to speak.

Arlo let himself in. "Are you all right?"

Laura found her voice, although it sounded a bit strange to her after days of not having heard it. "I'm fine, and I thought I made myself clear the last time you called."

"I was worried about you."

"There's nothing to worry about. As you can see I'm very busy."

Arlo gently took the shovel from her. "What are you trying to do here?"

Laura's eyes surveyed the pile of shrubs she'd removed as if seeing them for the first time. Who had pulled out her beloved viburnum? And why was she covered in soil?

"Laura?"

"Oh my God," she whispered as the realization of what she had done hit her. She felt faint and wobbled on her feet. Arlo caught her as she was about to fall, and he held her close. Some part of her brain registered that she was covered in mud, but the strong embrace of this man trumped those thoughts, and she melted into his arms.

They heard a car door slam shut. A few moment later Anna's excited voice preceded her as she came around from the front of the house. "Mother?"

Laura pulled away.

Anna, with Brandon, in tow, reached the gate and stopped dead in her tracks.

Arlo jumped in. "Your mother slipped in the mud."

"Who are you?" Anna asked.

"Arlo Massey. I'm a friend of your mother. And you must be her other daughter."

"Anna, and this is Brandon Carter."

They shook hands.

"Mother, you pulled up your prized viburnum."

Arlo said, "Pull up? No, we're transplanting, right, Laura?" Laura stared at the pile of shrubs. "Your mother was about to go inside to clean up. Maybe you could give her a hand. In the meantime, Brandon, why don't you and I finish up the transplanting." He tossed the shovel to Brandon.

Brandon reached over his shoulder to make an awkward catch. "Uh, sure."

Through her haze Laura realized her youngest daughter was standing in the backyard. Should she have known Anna was visiting? Anna had called several times over the past weeks, but Laura never had the interest or energy to engage in conversation, and always cut the call short. Was Anna here to cheer her up? Why was everyone trying to cheer her up? But there was something wrong. Maybe not wrong but . . . something. Like the young woman was about to burst. Laura asked, "Are you okay?"

"More than okay. Brandon and I are engaged!" She ran to Laura brandishing her left hand. A stunning princess-cut diamond ring sparkled on her finger. "I wanted you to be the first to know."

For a moment, Laura was stunned. Then her face broke into a wide grin. "Baby." Anna opened her arms for a hug but Laura shied away, embarrassed by her appearance. "I'm covered in—"

Anna wrapped her arms around Laura and held her close. "I love you."

For a moment, Laura didn't respond. Then the floodgates opened, the tears poured out, and she squeezed her daughter so tightly Anna could barely breathe.

"Mother?"

Laura instantly released some of the pressure and then, for some reason, they both started laughing. The laughter felt so good and the laughs continued and Laura didn't know whether her tears were laugh tears or cry tears but she didn't much care as she and Anna spun and danced around the muddy yard in their own little world.

CHAPTER THIRTY-TWO

June

Laura stood at the kitchen counter, her hands deep in a huge steel bowl of cold steamed shrimp. Through the open window she could see and hear most everything going on in her backyard.

The viburnums didn't make it, the roots too damaged. After their death was assured, she'd immediately replaced them with mature, fully grown hydrangeas—expensive but worth it. Thanks to her attentive, even admittedly compulsive care and the warm June sun, a blanket of flowering balls framed by rich green foliage now draped the back fence, each ball a separate bouquet of tiny pink and purple petals. Laura had to admit the tapestry of color exceeded in brilliance even her prized viburnums in their prime.

The caterers busied themselves unloading food from their truck out front and setting up tables on the back lawn. Everett stood high on a ladder in front of the back porch, a hammer in one hand, a nail in the other. He was draped in a large banner, attempting to attach it to the cross trim. The ladder wobbled.

Gracie called up to him, "Get your balance."

Everett's voice was partly muffled by the banner covering his head. "I can't see. Hold the ladder."

"You want me to get up there and do it?"

"No, I want you to hold the ladder."

Gracie took hold of the ladder and the wobbling stopped. "You ain't exactly on top of the Empire State Building. Hammer the nail through that little hole in the corner."

"It's called a grommet. You didn't even know it was called a grommet?"

"I don't give a damn what the hole's called; it's a hole. You hammer a nail through it and the thing the hole's in hangs from the nail. I'm coming up there."

"You'll tip the ladder!"

Gracie climbed three steps up the ladder. It only wobbled once before tipping over sending Everett, Gracie, the ladder, and the banner, on a quick descent into Laura's skip laurels bordering the porch. The shrubs cushioned their fall, contusions to egos the only injuries.

Everett and Gracie were sent to the sidelines, and fifteen minutes later two of the caterers quickly hung the banner proclaiming: "*Anna and Brandon—Engagement Celebration!*"

Laura chuckled and continued to efficiently peel away the shells, then transfer the cleaned shrimp to a porcelain dish.

Brooke watched from her seat at the table. Her eyes wandered to the dining room.

"What happened to your trophy wall?"

"I'm no longer a club member, so . . ." W*hy couldn't she tell her daughter the truth?*

"Don't suppose the Chocolate Shop had anything to do with it?"

Laura didn't respond, her eyes focused on the shrimp in her hand.

"Look, I don't care. It's your life, and if removing all of your plaques and shiny trophies means you are truly shedding your past, count me as a supporter. Doesn't mean I fully agree with your new role as arbiter of how long a person should live. Wouldn't you call that playing God?"

"I'm *not* playing God. And you'll be happy to know I've put—*that*—behind me."

"The Laura Beckman Gang has hung up its spurs?"

Laura needed to change the subject. "Could you please find me a lemon?"

Brooke shrugged, walked to the refrigerator, and pulled a lemon from the bottom drawer. "I thought the caterers were doing the food."

"They are. But Anna specifically asked for my shrimp salad, so that's what I'm going to give her."

Brooke set the lemon next to the mixing bowl.

Laura noticed her eldest daughter had lost weight. Probably the smoking. Right on cue Brooke shook a cigarette out of a pack. "Not in here," Laura ordered.

Brooke paused, then replaced the cigarette in the pack. She ambled over to the liquor cabinet in the dining room. "It's five o'clock somewhere." She opened the cabinet. It was empty. Laura didn't try to hide her smug expression. Brooke walked deliberately to the closet under the stairs. She rummaged around, and retrieved her father's fishing tackle box, then made a big show out of carrying it back into the kitchen.

"What are you doing with that?" Laura asked, suspicious.

Brooke opened the box, removed a quart bottle of vodka, and with a defiant expression took a huge swig.

Laura automatically responded to her daughter's defiance with a familiar scolding edge to her voice. "Remember what happened at your father's funeral reception. Please don't ruin this special day for Anna."

Brooke froze, and her eyes welled with tears. She poured the vodka down the sink, emptying the bottle, then turned to leave. "Tell Anna I said congratulations."

Laura said nothing. Brooke reached the door.

Laura froze. An image ran through Laura's mind—a little five-year-old girl, bouncing down the stairs every morning. She'd take her mother's hand, and they'd skip around the kitchen island singing . . .

We're off to find the morning glories,
Sparkling with sunlight and dew,
We're off to find the morning glories,
Look! I see them!
A good morning glory to you.

The little girl would point to her mother, then her father, then her little sister . . .

And you, and you, and you!

Laura emitted a tiny gasp. Why had that memory appeared out of nowhere? Why now? It only took a moment to answer her own question. The Chocolate Shop. She'd been experiencing firsthand the fragility of life, too much of which was wasted, immersed in pain and recriminations. Laura slumped into a chair.

"Brooke, wait."

Brooke warily walked back into the kitchen. "Yes?" After a few seconds had passed. She mumbled, "I have to be—"

"I'm sorry." Laura's voice barely rose above a whisper. "For everything." Her whole body felt like she'd just stepped under an icy shower. A trickle of sweat drizzled down between her breasts. *How can you be cold and sweaty at the same time?* She took a deep breath. "My recent, uh, activities have made me think a lot about death, including my own. When you think about your own death you have no choice but to consider your life. How you lived it. I've come to realize I'm not particularly proud of my life, especially my . . . parenting skills. In short, they sucked." She took a deep breath. "And . . . and I want to formally apologize for my shortcomings in that department."

Brooke sat down across from her. "Mother—"

"Let me finish. Do those shortcomings completely justify you throwing four years of your life away by abandoning your husband and child? No, not by a long shot. But you have years of life left to live, and you have a wonderful daughter, a great sister, and..." Laura swallowed to clear the lump in her throat. "... and if you let her, a mother who loves you very, very much."

Brooke was speechless.

Laura bowed her head and closed her eyes. No tears. She was several layers below tears. After what seemed like an eternity, she took another deep breath and returned to the counter. "If you like," she said matter-of-factly, "you may give me a hand with these shrimp."

In a daze, Brooke walked to the sink and washed her hands before dipping them into the shrimp bowl. For a moment, their fingers touched. Both of them froze. Then Brooke slowly curled her pinkie around her mother's pinkie. Laura bit her lip. Brooke released her finger and the two women, their eyes glistening, finished peeling the shrimp without another word.

Four hours later, close to a hundred guests mingled outside in the beautiful June evening, enjoying the food, music from a string quartet, and lively conversation. Brooke had showered and changed at Laura's house, and now appeared in a stunning tangerine cotton dress and short-heeled white sling-backs. Laura and Jennie, wearing a light turquoise dress that contrasted beautifully with her deep tan, watched as Brooke cheerfully helped the caterers keep the food table replenished. Laura couldn't recall ever seeing her eldest daughter so radiant.

"How did you keep her from drinking?" Jennie asked with a sour expression.

Laura was surprised and saddened by her eight-year-old grand-daughter's grown-up question. But if your mother leaves you when you're four years old and stays away for years, she supposed the girl's maturity was understandable.

"She's your mother. Mothers make mistakes."

"Yeah. Like abandoning me and Dad."

"Listen to me. Time's precious. Grudges steal too much of it. Your mother loves you."

"But—"

"Let it go."

Jennie's eyes glistened. Her lower lip quivered. Laura crouched down so her face closed to within a few inches of her granddaughter.

"I know it will take a while to get over your mom going away—"

"For four years."

Lauara wrapped her arms around the girl and pulled her close so Jennie's head rested on Laura's chest where she could feel the girl's quiet sobs.

Laura stroked Jennie's hair and whispered into her ear. "I know, baby, I know." She pulled the girl tighter to her body. "Honey, maybe you could do me a huge favor and think about forgiving her. Not all at once. I understand that's probably asking too much. But everybody makes mistakes, and some mistakes are real doozies like what your mom did. If you take a chance on her, I have a strong feeling you won't regret it. She loves you so much."

"Did you forgive her?"

This time Laura was speaking to herself more than her granddaughter. "Yes, but I waited way way too long. Don't make the same mistake I did."

CHAPTER THIRTY-THREE

Brooke watched their conversation from across the yard. Her daughter and her mother. Not only did they look so much alike, their personalities came from the same template. She didn't mind the comparison. Laura was, if nothing else, a strong woman and there were a lot worse examples of humankind in the world for her daughter to emulate.

She spotted Tom off in the corner talking to Anna and Brandon. When the couple walked away to greet newly arriving friends, Brooke poured two cups of punch and carried them over to Tom.

"Thirsty?" She handed him the punch.

He sniffed it.

"Don't worry, no booze."

"Thanks," he responded coolly, taking a sip. "Anna seems very happy."

"And I couldn't be happier for her. I love her so much. She deserves a wonderful life."

Neither spoke, the tension claiming their voices. Finally, he nodded in Jennie's direction. "She looks beautiful."

"You did a great job raising her, Tom. Of all the things I owe you, that's one I'll never be able to repay."

His fae hardened, and his voice took on an edge. "Ever hear from . . . I'm sorry, the guitarist?"

"Nail."

"How could I forget?" Tom didn't try to hide his disdain.

"I was an idiot."

"You were."

"What I'd give to rewind those years."

Tom held her gaze and the circuits connected for a moment. "Me, too." The wariness didn't leave his eyes.

"Daddy?"

They turned to see their daughter approach. Without acknowledging Brooke, Jennie took Tom's hand.

"Come on, I want you to meet Ella. She's here with her parents and we're in the same dance class and Jilly's still my best friend, but Ella's my new second best friend." Jennie led him farther away, leaving Brooke holding her cup of punch.

Tom stopped. "Maybe your mother would enjoy meeting Ella as well." His voice was hesitant, clearly uncertain about the invitation. Both adults fixed their gaze on Jennie. Brooke held her breath. After a long moment, Jennie nodded. Smiling nervously, Brooke quickly joined them, and the three moved off together to meet Jennie's new second best friend.

The next two hours were both the happiest and scariest Brooke could remember. They mingled with friends, old and new. She took a nervous delight in watching the expressions of people who knew them as a couple—the women particularly were unable to completely mask their surprise, and Brooke had no doubt eyebrows would rise and chatter intensify the moment she and Tom moved on to another group.

The two of them parted frequently to do this or that, but somehow found themselves returning to each other's side, albeit at a respectable distance. Her feelings in his presence were at once both awkward and comfortable, and she sensed his feelings mirrored hers. Very wary. Very weird. Wonderfully weird.

As the party drifted toward conclusion and only a few guests remained, Brooke and Tom helped the caterers begin the cleanup. Brooke lit a cigarette and sucked the soothing smoke into her lungs. She glanced across the yard to Laura, who gave her a disapproving stare. "I'm almost thirty years old and she still makes me feel like a teenager."

"Look at it this way. It shows how much she cares. And—"

Brooke knew what he was going to say.

"And Jennie—well, all of us—wouldn't mind seeing you stop smoking. You're young, but if you keep it up, someday . . ." He didn't have to finish the sentence.

Brooke took a long last drag, then stubbed out the cigarette on a dirty saucer.

Laura stood at the gate with Anna and Brandon saying good-bye to her guests. She stole a glance toward Brooke and Tom. There seemed to be something different about them this evening. Something . . . fragile? Possibly a re-start? That would be too much to hope for.

The shrillness of Gracie's voice cut through her thoughts. "So why didn't you invite him?"

Laura turned to see Gracie standing next to her.

Anna asked, "Invite who?"

"Please ignore her," Laura said. "You probably weren't aware, but Gracie's been living in the fruit cellar and we only let her out for the evening."

"Her boyfriend," Gracie said.

"Mother? You have a boyfriend?"

Laura said, "I'm going to have to excuse myself to minister to my dear, deranged aunt." She turned to Gracie and raised her voice an octave as if talking to a two-year old. "Come along, Gracie. Be a good girl and come with Laura. Time to put the little pink pills on the choo-choo and let them ride into the tunnel."

Laura led Gracie to the punch table. "Have some punch, you'll feel better." At that moment a catering assistant removed the punchbowl and headed off.

"Laura?"

They both turned to see Alvin Olson approach. Alvin was slightly built, wizened, but managed his eighty-plus years very well. Alvin had owned the Dancing Crab restaurant next door to Mickey's store, and over the years they'd become fast friends. His wife, Mary Ellen, confined to her wheelchair, waited near the gate. Always vigorous and athletic, she'd been very ill and now seemed withered and frail and . . . uh-oh. Laura had a bad feeling.

"So glad you both could come."

"Thanks, Laura. Hi, Gracie. Great party. Anna and Brandon are super kids."

"Yes they are," said Laura. "So if you'll excuse us, we have to get back to the other guests."

"Uh, Laura, there's something I need to talk to you about."

"Why don't you give me a call over the next couple of —"

Gracie interrupted. "What is it?"

Alvin went on. "You know that Mary Ellen is terminal, and Lilly told me how you helped Russell. There've been rumors that you've helped others." His voice lowered to a whisper. "You know, the Chocolate Shop?"

Laura had to end this right here and now. "Mary Ellen's been a good friend, but I'm afraid we're not offering assistance anymore. I'm very sorry."

"The cops are investigating," Gracie whispered loudly, "and we can't have any trouble."

Laura glanced at his wife and couldn't help asking. "How is she?"

"Constant pain, despite the medication," Alvin answered. "I've always provided for her but now, when she really needs me . . ." He choked up, unable to finish.

Oh my God. The poor woman. She pulled a napkin from a nearby table and handed it to him. *No. She couldn't.* She swallowed hard and spoke in a tinny voice. "Again, I'm very sorry."

Brooke and Tom gathered up the folding chairs across the yard. Brooke noticed Alvin Olson speaking with her mother. "I know Mrs. Olson's very ill. I hope Mother's not reconsidering," Brooke said.

"I warned your mother, but it's her life," Tom replied.

Brooke walked to the fence and retrieved the last lawn chair. She felt a sting on her leg. "Ouch."

"Bee?"

A large red welt spread across her calf.

"Where's your Epi?"

"Damn. I left it in my other purse."

Tom and Brooke hurried across the yard to Laura. Brooke was in obvious distress.

"She's been stung," Tom said. "Do you have an Epi pen here?"

Laura crouched down to examine the sting. She shook her head. "I'll take her to the emergency room. Let me grab my purse."

Brooke's breathing became more labored. "I think I better go now."

Tom said to Laura, "You watch Jennie. I'll take her." Without waiting for a response, he helped Brooke toward the gate, almost running into Everett who moved aside.

Laura watched the couple leave. Brooke needed to get to the hospital quickly or her throat could completely close up.

"Should I call an ambulance?" Everett asked anxiously.

"By the time an ambulance arrives they'll already be at the hospital."

The pain in Brooke's leg caused an unsteady gait, and Tom had to wrap one arm around her to keep her from falling.

"Are you sure?" Everett asked.

"Don't worry," Laura said. "She's in good hands."

Brooke sat on a bed in a curtained emergency room cubicle. Tom stood behind the doctor as he moved the stethoscope from Brooke's chest to her back. She'd received a shot of epinephrine as soon as they'd arrived, and the result was almost instantaneous.

"You'll be fine," the doctor said. "But you must keep your EpiPen with you at all times."

Brooke responded with a hacking cough.

"As an ex-smoker, I'd recognize that sound anywhere."

"I'm going to quit."

"I recognize the sound of that, too," he chuckled. "Let's have you breath deeper this time." He moved the stethoscope to her right side below her armpit. By now the cold metal had warmed and she didn't flinch. "Breathe. Hold it. Breathe." He moved the sensor to her back. "Breathe again." He replaced the stethoscope in his pocket and frowned. "I'd like to get a quick chest x-ray while you're here."

"What's wrong?" Tom asked.

"Probably nothing. But the combination of her reaction to the sting, and the cough . . . She's here anyway. Won't take long."

"I'm fine." She coughed again. "The sting triggered it. Catching my breath, that's all." She coughed harder.

"She'll do it," Tom said.

Brooke drew comfort from Tom stepping forward and taking charge. She couldn't remember the last time a man had done that. If it took a lousy chest x-ray to encourage his newly discovered protective instincts toward her, that was a small price to pay. She nodded to the doctor.

Three hours later, Brooke sat in stunned silence as Tom drove along the narrow Annapolis streets.

"I still think you should drop me off at my mother's so I can get my car."

"I'm taking you home. Don't want you driving tonight."

"I'm fine, really." But she wasn't fine. She was about as far away from fine as she could be.

"Remember, the doctor said there were many benign explanations, and lung cancer in a woman of your age is exceedingly rare."

"Seven percent—not too rare."

"You want me to say anything to Jennie?"

"Let's wait until the bronchoscopy."

"What about Laura?"

"Guess I'll handle that."

They pulled to a stop in front of Brooke's townhouse. "I can stay for while. Might help to talk."

"No, you go on. I'll get Mike to pick me up on the way in to work tomorrow and drop me off to get my car."

He turned to face her and took her trembling hand is his. "Don't worry. Remember, there's a ninety-three percent chance you're clean. But hopefully this little scare will persuade you to stop smoking. If you keep it up, when you're fifty or sixty those odds will turn around on you big time."

"Saint Thomas."

"I hate it when you say that. Nothing could be further from the truth. Come on, I'll walk you to the door."

Before she could respond he was out of his car and opening the passenger door. They walked up the steps and he took her arm. It seemed so natural.

On the stoop she unlocked the door and gave him a quick peck on the cheek. "Thanks, Tom."

"Call me." His smile, usually so overpowering, was not enough to conceal the concern in his eyes. He squeezed her shoulder, then turned and walked back to his car.

She watched him open the car door, then turn for a quick wave. She gasped. Her whole body shook, and her shoulders heaved as she sobbed uncontrollably. Tom cleared the seven steps in two leaps and wrapped her in his arms. She melted into him, her body convulsing in sobs. "Oh, Tommy—"

He squeezed her tight and didn't let go as he led her into the house.

Chapter Thirty-Four

Brooke sat in her car parked in front of the Eastgate house. The last four days had been a blur. After they'd returned from the emergency room Tom stayed for almost two hours, sipping coffee and talking. Actually she did most of the talking, and he did most of the listening. She hardly recalled what she'd said. Mostly babbling on about her life and her regrets. Tom listened, speaking only to remind her of strong reasons to be hopeful: the doctor said there were many benign explanations for the shadows detected on the edges of both lungs; she had a strong support group; and given her age the odds were heavily in her favor. She'd considered asking him to stay the night—not for sex, but to have a warm body to snuggle up against. She didn't, and in retrospect she was glad she didn't because he would've said no in as kind a way as possible, and then she would have been more devastated.

The previous afternoon he'd taken her to the hospital where she'd undergone the bronchoscopy. Tissue samples were extracted, and a biopsy performed. Tom was amazing, like he'd temporarily shelved away all of the pain she'd caused him. Last night he'd invited her over for a spaghetti dinner with Jennie. Her daughter remained cool towards her. Brooke sensed Jennie had assumed the role of woman of the house and viewed Brooke as competition. Brooke knew she would have to remain respectful of her daughter's position and understood

Jennie wouldn't be anxious to throw it all away just because her mom popped back in town and showed up sober a few times. But after a great meal and a game of Monopoly her daughter warmed up considerably. At the end of the evening Jennie voluntarily gave her a hug. Feeling her daughter's smooth thin arms wrapped around her neck had been beyond wonderful. Tom also embraced her and whispered that everything would turn out fine.

Everything didn't turn out fine. The doctor called an hour earlier. Once he said the word "cancer" she didn't hear the rest of the conversation. She'd immediately called Tom, and after a moment of shocked silence he did his best to cheer her up. Medical science has come a long way, great health facilities in the state, the best doctors in the world, we have to fight, and so on.

Now she needed to tell her mother. Tom told her not to drag it out. He was right. She stared at the front door, took a deep breath, and stepped out of the car.

Ten minutes later, she sat at the kitchen table, eyes downcast, ignoring the cup of coffee resting in front of her. She'd taken Tom's advice and told Laura right out of the box. Laura stood frozen in place. An absurd image flooded Brooke's mind of her mother standing in one of those museum tableaus, next to a Pilgrim or a caveman, with a wet dish in one hand and a towel in the other. *Americanus Housewifus.*

Laura's face unfroze, and she threw the towel at Brooke. "It's the cigarettes and the booze and practically living in smoky gin joints and inviting God knows how many men to . . ." Her mother couldn't finish, breaking down in tears, her body collapsing in on itself.

Brooke, drowning in a mix of terror and guilt, struggled to keep it together. "Sorry," she whispered. She stood and walked toward the door.

"Don't you . . . don't you dare walk away from me when I'm . . . when I'm . . ."

Brooke stopped and turned. After an instant that seemed to last forever, they fell into each other's arms, squeezing tight. As Laura's sobs blended with her daughter's, Brooke felt Laura's fists weakly pounding against her back.

Like most Marylanders, Brooke grew up learning all about the Johns Hopkins Medical Center. Hopkins, a successful Baltimore businessman who understood the meaning of work from his youth toiling in the tobacco fields of his family's southern Maryland plantation, died three years before the institution bearing his name opened its doors. At the time of his death in 1873, his bequest of $7 million to the university and hospital was the largest philanthropic bequest in the nation's history, equal to over $114 million in today's dollars. Almost from the beginning, the Hopkins Medical Center in Baltimore consistently ranked at or near the top of all such institutions in the world.

Brooke rode with her mother through its huge east Baltimore campus and remembered a conversation she'd witnessed between her parents. Mickey was frustrated with paying Maryland taxes. *They should change the state motto to, 'If you can dream it, we can tax it.'* He'd talked about moving to Virginia. Brooke strenuously objected. She didn't want to leave her friends. And her mother resisted with a long list of reasons. Topping the list were the club, her house and garden, and their proximity to the exceptional health care services at Hopkins. Brooke had come to learn the hospital held an almost mythical status in the minds of Marylanders. So while the biopsy had been performed in Annapolis, the results, along with Brooke's x-rays, were forwarded to Hopkins for analysis.

They moved quickly through check-in. Brooke received her official orange Hopkins access card, and within twenty minutes they sat in the office of Dr. Bruce Bryant, deputy head of Hopkins' Oncology Department. Dr. Bryant was tall, with big ears, large soft hands, and a deep, reassuring voice. Brooke took strange comfort in the absence of the usual certificates and diplomas hanging on the walls that one came to expect when visiting a physician. Dr. Bryant knew who he was, and his position in this institution said all that needed to be said about his competence.

He pointed to the chest x-ray illuminated by the light box. "Right here in the left lung, see that mass?"

"It looks so small," Laura said.

"Four centimeters. The mass in the right lung is smaller, three and a half centimeters. Certainly not the worst I've seen." His expression and tone remained studiously nonjudgmental. "How long have you been smoking?"

Brooke glanced at Laura before answering. "I started in high school." She watched as her mother cringed, but wisely held her tongue.

"You have what we call non-small cell lung carcinoma," Dr. Bryant continued in his warm baritone.

"Is that the good kind or the bad kind?" Laura asked.

"I'm afraid when it comes to cancer of the lungs, there really is no good kind."

"Why do they call it non-small cell cancer. Why not large cell cancer?" Brooke asked.

Dr. Bryant smiled. "In all my years of practice I can honestly say no one's ever asked me that, and the truthful answer is, I don't know."

"Who cares what they call it?" Laura said impatiently. "We need to know how bad it is."

"It's serious, but we have a number of tools in our toolbox to treat it."

Laura paused. "I understand there are different stages of cancer."

"Because the cancer is in both lungs and has breached the right lung, it's categorized as stage four."

Brooke's chin dropped to her chest. She shook her head in disbelief.

Dr. Bryant continued. The irony is that lung cancer in a person of your age is very rare, but when it does occur we're seeing more cases of stage four level than in the general population."

Brooke felt the oxygen being sucked from the room.

Dr. Bryant leaned forward for emphasis. "Listen, it's a number. Doctors are infatuated with numbers. Is stage one better than stage four? Of course. But the lines between theses levels are fuzzy, so don't dwell too much on the number."

Laura jumped in. "So we know we're not dealing with a hangnail here. Now, what can we do to get my daughter better? She's not even thirty years old. Can't you cut it out?"

"Given its location, unfortunately, no. However, we will start a regimen of chemotherapy and radiation therapy at once. We've made great strides in dealing with the side effects of chemo, so many patients don't experience the level of discomfort once routinely associated with this treatment. I'm afraid you'll likely lose your hair, and experience fatigue, but the most debilitating side effects—the nausea, vomiting, mouth sores—there's a good chance we can lessen them."

"Who cares if she loses her hair?" Laura said. "Hair grows. What I want to know is, after going through this, is she going to get better?"

"It's still too early to make any reasonable prognosis. Let's start with the treatment and then we can make an assessment down the road."

"What's the survival rate?" Brooke asked, her voice a monotone.

"Again, I wouldn't get caught up with statistics," Dr. Bryant responded. "Everybody's different."

Brooke pulled her phone from her back pocket. "I'll look it up online. What's the rate?"

"Twenty-five percent last a year."

Laura gasped.

Brooke persisted. "And five years? Out of every one hundred patients who have what I have, how many make it to five years?"

"Two."

Both Brooke and her mother sat expressionless.

Dr. Bryant leaned forward. "Brooke, remember what I said. Those are only numbers. Everybody's different, every case is different. Those stats don't factor in such things as lifestyle, nutrition, adherence to treatment, family support, emotional strength, and a bunch of other factors. Now, before I send you next door to set up your treatment schedule, are there any other questions?" Brooke stared at her feet and shook her head.

He stood and took her hand. "We've got a lot of real smart people here working day and night on some exciting stuff, so you've got to keep fighting."

"Don't worry, Doctor," Laura said, "she will."

On the drive home both women were quiet. Laura caught herself gripping the steering wheel so tight she feared she would snap it in half. She tried to turn on a smooth jazz station to fill the silence, but her hands shook so much she couldn't manage to find the right button. As they crossed the College Creek bridge she couldn't hold back any longer. Her mouth felt like it had been stuffed with balls of cotton, and her voice came out dry, raspy.

"We're blessed to live so close to Hopkins, you know. Gracie showed me in *U.S. News & World Report* that Hopkins was ranked number one in cancer care. Not only in the U.S., but in the whole world."

Laura pulled up in front of Brooke's house and stopped.

Brooke opened the car door and stepped onto the sidewalk.

"I'm coming in with you," Laura said.

"Thanks, but I'll be fine."

"We're packing you up. You're moving back to my house where I can keep an eye on you."

"There's no need—"

"Do what you're told, young lady."

Brooke's smile struggled to overcome the look of fear frozen on her face.

"What's so funny?"

"After all the pain we've caused each other, it takes me dying to finally have something resembling a normal mother-daughter relationship."

"Number one, you're not dying, and number two, people are idiots. Let's go."

Brooke dutifully followed her mother up the stairs.

CHAPTER THIRTY-FIVE

September

The next four months blurred by and, while in most respects quite horrible, in some ways they were the best days Brooke could remember. She moved into her old bedroom. On the second day her mother dragged out a large cardboard box from deep inside the closet. The box contained her bedroom things from over a decade earlier—stuffed animals, rock posters, high school memorabilia—and Laura distributed them around the room. Despite her mild protests—a mature young woman with a young daughter should not wake up in the morning to the sight of a teen idol not old enough to shave staring her in the face—she quickly gave in.

Despite Dr. Bryant's assurance that modern medicine had found ways to soften chemo's side effects, Brooke figured her body must not have received the memo. She felt sick constantly. She'd quit her job immediately after the diagnosis, and at the beginning spent most of her time in her room. But that didn't last long; Laura wouldn't let her mope. Her mother routinely burst into the room with a smile on her face and a "Get up, we're going out." And so they did. To the mall, to the movies, even to dinner. So long as Brooke took her pills right before she ate, the nausea dissipated for a while.

When her hair first started falling out in the shower, Laura was there to comfort her.

"It's only hair," she kept repeating. "It'll grow back and you'll have a beautiful head of hair for the next sixty years."

Brooke soon looked like some comic book warlock with a few long clumps hanging from the side of her head, so she shaved the rest off with Laura's help.

"You have a beautiful head, no bumps," Laura assured her.

When Brooke viewed herself in the mirror she wondered if she would ever have hair again.

Anna visited immediately when she heard the news and, upon returning to Chicago, called every day. Her little sister's support meant a great deal to Brooke, and the two Beckman girls found themselves closer than ever.

Anna, in town for the weekend, joined Laura to make big deal about shopping for a wig. Brooke found their enthusiasm so infectious she looked forward to the outing. That morning the three of them ate a quick breakfast, showered, and put on their best shopping outfits.

Brooke refused to wear a head-scarf like some old lady babushka. It so happened "flapper hats" were the current rage, and Brooke had found a cream-colored linen flapper with a turned-up half rim at Nordstrom the week before. That flappers happened to be in style at the moment was a positive sign in Laura's view. She concluded Fate, having dealt Brooke such a powerful blow, had now decided she'd suffered enough. Brooke wasn't so sure Fate spent a whole lot of time focusing on women's fashion, but the thought seemed to make her mother feel better.

Laura decided the hospital's wig shop would be too depressing, so they drove to Washington and found the perfect place in Georgetown. Shelves along three of the cream-colored walls contained rows and rows of wigs—all colors, all lengths, all styles.

Mirrors covered the fourth wall. They arrived mid-morning to discover they were the only customers in the shop.

The owner, a small, dark-haired woman in her early sixties with
a kind, understanding face, dragged a pink and cream paisley chair
in front of the mirror. Brooke sat like a queen on her throne as
Laura, Anna, and the owner brought her one selection after another
to try on.

"Haven't you ever wanted to be a blonde?" Laura asked as she
handed Brooke a short, pageboy-style selection.

Brooke chuckled. "I've been a blonde, I've been a redhead, I've
colored my hair black and purple and green. In fact, there probably
isn't a color I haven't tried in my life."

Without breaking a smile, the owner asked, "Have you tried
fluorescent orange, dear?" She handed Brooke a spiked mohawk
wig in the same color as traffic cones. It took a while for everyone
to stop laughing.

After two hours, they couldn't decide among six selections so
Laura bought them all. The owner threw in the orange mohawk for
free.

They enjoyed a late lunch at Clyde's and left early enough to
beat the rush hour traffic. When they arrived home, Brooke was exhausted and went straight to bed. Later, Laura brought her a tray of
soup, crackers and ginger tea, and Brooke spontaneously wrapped
her arms around her mother's neck.

"Thank you for a wonderful day."

Recovery from each chemo treatment sometimes took a week
or more, but the periods between chemo recovery and the next
treatment were almost normal. Brooke called them her "cherries
'n chocolate" times, named after her favorite indulgence. Tom vis-

ited daily. During these few weeks of normalcy he'd take her out to dinner or a movie, usually not both because she would get too tired. Often Jennie would go along. Laura was always invited, but wisely begged off, and often provided babysitter service. Strange as it seemed given her prognosis, these cherry 'n chocolate periods were some of the happiest Brooke could recall.

One of the most difficult hurdles she faced was quitting smoking. Should've been a no-brainer, but if you're addicted to the taste of poison, *really* addicted, those little white sticks are your friends who comfort you in times of stress. You don't automatically dump your pals because one day you discover they're chomping away at your lungs. She wanted to stop, but often when the pull was strong she'd give in, rationalizing that she was doomed anyway so why not enjoy her limited time?

One day when she rebelled and offered the "might as well enjoy my last days on earth" argument, Laura promptly collected Tom and Jennie. The three of them conducted a house search that would've made the CIA proud and confiscated all of her stashes. After that she stopped, popping chocolates or gumdrops into her mouth whenever the urge to hang with her skinny white pals hit her.

Brooke wanted so much to be intimate with Tom, but she couldn't read him. His kindness toward her probably was only that, kindness to the mother of his daughter—nothing more. He always offered his arm when they walked together and hugged her when he left. But was it a sympathy hug? Or something more?

On Labor Day, Laura organized a little backyard picnic. Only family and a few friends. The weather was perfect, and Brooke enjoyed a wonderful day. She had to go in for another chemo treatment, and they'd become progressively more difficult to tolerate. Worse, the length of her cherries 'n chocolate periods continued to shrink, so she wanted to stretch as much out of her last day as possible. She decided the time had come to force the issue. What was she waiting for, next year? No courage potion was stronger than a smack in the face with your own mortality.

Everyone had left except Tom. When he came to say goodbye, she told him she felt tired and asked if he would help her upstairs. He, of course, agreed. After all, he was Saint Thomas. At the door to her bedroom, he gave her his usual ambiguous hug, then turned to leave. She held his hand in a gentle restraint. A look into his eyes and a tiny tug of her hand sent her message loud and clear.

"Brooke, I'm not sure—"

She dropped his hand like a hot potato. "I'm sorry, I . . . well, I'm not really sorry . . . I mean I'm sorry you're declining, and I'm sorry if I embarrassed you, but I'm not sorry—"

Her words were cut off by the urgent press of his lips against hers. He swept her body up into his strong embrace, and in two strides carried her into the room, then kicked the door closed. He set her down gently on the bed and unbuttoned the first few buttons of his shirt.

"No, let me," she said in a voice made husky by her want. She undressed him slowly, savoring each moment as if she were carefully unwrapping a new present. When she finished, she leaned back and viewed him in the dim light. So strong, his body had gained little fat in the last few years. Just a slight rounding in the love handle region. He was a man, not a boy, and she wanted him so much she ached.

"My turn," he said. Brooke lay back and watched as he undressed her, moving much faster than she had. He slipped onto the bed beside her.

"Saint Thomas," she whispered, as she traced her finger lightly across his chest and down his belly.

He stiffened. "Please don't call me that."

"Sorry." She didn't want anything to pierce the mood.

"I'm far from a saint." Much to Brooke's chagrin, he'd become distracted.

She tried to kiss him back to business. "You were always so—"

He pulled away. "Brooke, there's something you should know."

To Brooke, her knowledge could as easily be augmented in a couple of hours without any real, long-term impact upon her overall understanding of the universe. "Whatever it is, we can talk about it later."

"I had an affair with Patti Coggins."

"Patti Coggins? Peppy Patti?" Patti Coggins had been a paralegal in Tom's office. She joined the firm right out of the University of Maryland where she'd been a cheerleader. Brooke half-believed Patti's constant cheefulness resulted from drugs, but Pattti claimed life itself made her joyous. *Ick.* Brooke remembered laughing with Tom about Peppy Patti. So many years had passed. But she did recall Patti putting a smiley face inside the "P" when she wrote her name. Double *Ick.*

"It was while we were still together," Tom explained. The words had been locked up for so long that once the door opened, they came tumbling out. "That's why I never objected to you being away all the time practicing your music. The moment you left for a rehearsal, I would drive over to Patti's house."

"So before Willie and I—"

"I was the first to break the vows, Brooke, not you. I'm so sorry."

A broad smile spread across Brooke's face. Tom's affair in no way excused her abandonment of her child, or even of him, not really. But it did ease the guilt a bit. Yes, it did. She felt giddy as she rolled over on top of him, straddled his belly, and covered his face with kisses.

"Thank you, thank you, thank you."

"Brooke, I just admitted to you—"

She kissed him again. This time much more slowly, lightly dragging her lips across his, barely making contact, then pressing hard against his mouth. She scrunched her hips back, and wrapped her arms around his neck, melting into him.

At that moment all the bad things disappeared.

CHAPTER THIRTY-SIX

November

Two days before Thanksgiving, Laura received a call from the chief nurse at Dr. Lowe's office.

"Phyllis? My physical's not scheduled for another two months."

"It's not about your physical, Laura. I want to give you a heads-up that a detective Olivetti left here a few minutes ago. He was with some crazy woman."

Laura felt her stomach flip. It had to be Russell Melroy's ex-wife. "Charlene Melroy?"

"I believe that's right. Anyway, this detective was not pleasant, not pleasant at all. The brutish man comes right up to me in front of a waiting room full of patients and says he needs to see a list of all prescriptions written for you in the past year."

"Did you give him the information?"

"Absolutely not. I spoke with Dr. Lowe, and he said unless they have a subpoena or a written authorization from you those medical records are private."

Laura would have to thank him next time she saw him.

"This detective didn't much like that answer," Phyllis continued, "and the crazy woman—"

"Charlene."

"Right. She liked it even less, and started yelling, 'Cover-up! Cover-up!' Scared the you know what out of our patients. Even the detective must've been embarrassed because he left real quick. But he did say he'd be back."

"I can't thank you enough."

"No problem, and if he does come back with a court order it might take me a while to find those records."

"No. If he complies with the law, I want you to comply as well. I'll not have you and Dr. Lowe getting into trouble on my account."

"Is everything okay, Laura? Are you in some kind of jam?"

"I don't know, but the good news is, there will be no more cause for the authorities to be concerned in the future." Laura again thanked her and hung up. She wished she could simply admit to the police she was wrong and did a bad thing and promise she wouldn't do it ever again. But Tom advised her to keep her mouth shut, and he was probably right. Besides, if she confessed to a controlled substances violation, Gracie would get into trouble as well, and she couldn't accept that. She fervently hoped if she kept her head down the police would get caught up in all of the street crime she read about every day and put her case on the bottom of the pile.

Charlene was the wild card. Russell Melroy's crazy ex-wife would be determined to do whatever was necessary to gain control of Russell's life insurance proceeds, and for that she needed to show Russell's death didn't qualify as a true suicide. Laura couldn't see her voluntarily going away. Hopefully, Charlene would become such a pain in the butt to the police that they'd eventually stop paying attention to her.

Despite the heavy weight of Brooke's illness, not to mention Laura's potential exposure to criminal prosecution, she was determined to make Thanksgiving special and the weather cooperated—

clear sunny day, crisp air, and a few inches of snow on the ground from a surprise snowfall the night before.

As project foreman, Laura supervised a crack crew—Brooke, Jennie, Anna, and Gracie—preparing food in the kitchen. Brooke assumed responsibility for the mashed potatoes, something she could do while seated to conserve her energy. Anna made a cornbread stuffing, Gracie snapped green beans. Jennie combined chunks of orange, including the peel, into the Cuisinart along with whole cranberries and a ton of sugar. She'd learned this simple recipe in kindergarten and every Thanksgiving since, tradition called for Jennie to make her cranberry relish.

Laura peeked into the living room. Tom, Brandon, and Everett focused intently on the TV where the 'Skins battled their dreaded rival, the Dallas Cowboys. Tom and Brandon were deeply engrossed in the football game, while Everett sat in the wing chair with his brow furrowed, examining the TV screen as he would a biology specimen.

Laura smiled to herself. The women happily fussing in the kitchen, the men watching football. What a wonderful normalcy. Well, not completely. There was, of course, the eight-hundred-pound monster in the room eating her daughter's lungs. Still, Brooke appeared quite at peace sitting at the table peeling potatoes—a contentment Laura attributed in large part to Tom's spending the last weeks in her daughter's bed. Tom's all night visits brought with them the added bonus of Jennie staying in the guest room. Laura loved having the girl in the house. Jennie's youthful energy went a long way toward keeping Laura from slipping down the blue funk chute to a deep depression.

She checked the clock, then pulled the turkey from the oven. After carefully lifting the foil, she sucked up the juice in the bottom of the pan with her baster and dribbled the liquid over the bird.

Next she sprinkled a generous amount of oregano across the turkey breast. Laura discovered oregano-flavored turkey recipe on a ski trip with Mickey to Snowmass, Colorado, ten years earlier. When she started adding the spice to her own Thanksgiving bird, guests raved, and begged her for the secret. She politely demurred; everyone should be able to claim one or two secret recipes.

"So where's your boyfriend?" Gracie asked her.

Jennie didn't hide her surprise. "Grandma? Do you have a boyfriend?"

"No dear. Aunt Gracie's just acting like a big silly."

"Arlo Massey, that's her boyfriend," Gracie said.

It was Brooke's turn. "Mother, you've been holding out on me."

"You must forgive poor Gracie. Alas, she's in the early stages of dementia."

"Alas, my alas ass."

"Sad, so sad. We must try hard to look past her delusional ravings and show her the compassion a person in her condition deserves."

"Arlo Massey," Anna said. "He's the guy who Brandon helped transplant the viburnum. I remember we saw him later on TV."

"The man's a lout and has the mentality of an eighteen-year-old frat boy."

Gracie, Anna, and Brooke sang in unison, *"Don't be sassy, boat at Massey, Massey Mareeenahhhs!"* Everyone laughed except Laura.

"You all are living proof that watching TV kills brain cells. This discussion is closed."

Forty minutes later, they were all seated around the dining room table.

Laura said, "Everett, would you please say grace?"

She saw the man beam with pride having been selected from all those at the table to undertake such an important assignment. Everyone clasped the hands of the persons on either side of them.

"Let us pray," Everett intoned.

Laura noted that he employed his deepened second tenor voice to convey the solemnity the occasion deserved. All bowed their heads except Brooke.

"Our heavenly father . . ." Everett proceeded with the prayer, dutifully giving thanks for a long list of things ranging from "the freedoms bestowed upon us by our great nation" to "the new chef at Lisella who makes these delicious Italian pastries."

After only a few words, Brooke released Laura's hand. Laura peeked up to see her daughter staring into space.

Everett added a special plea at the end for God to relieve Brooke of her illness, and concluded with, ". . . and thanks for the opportunity to share parts of our lives with Mickey Beckman. A great father, husband, and friend."

Laura pressed her eyes tight. *Oh, Mickey, I miss you so much, and I wish you were here to help save our daughter.*

After the "amens," Laura dabbed her eyes with a napkin, then turned to Tom. "Might I ask you to carve the turkey?"

Tom picked up the cutlery and expertly undertook his given task. Everett frowned. She'd considered granting the coveted turkey carving assignment to Everett, but Tom was again a member of the family.

Laura had to admit the food tasted better than she could ever remember, and seeing Brooke talking, laughing, acting so *normal,* was a true gift.

Anna stood. "Let's all pitch in and clean up so we can get to the seven o'clock show."

Hollywood studios released their holiday blockbusters over the Thanksgiving holiday, and it had been a tradition in the Beckman household over many years for everyone to attend the movie theater after Thanksgiving dinner.

Brooke insisted on helping clean up, and with all of them working the table was cleared and the dishes washed and put away in record time. Brooke begged off the movie, and prodded Tom to join the others. Everett offered to stay and keep Laura company, but she told him she needed to rest. At Jennie's personal urging Everett joined the movie party, and off they went, leaving Laura and Brooke alone.

Laura could tell Brooke was weakening and helped her daughter up the stairs to her bedroom. At the door, Brooke spontaneously gave Laura a big hug. "Thank you," she whispered.

"For what?"

"For a wonderful Thanksgiving." Brooke paused and turned away. "It may be my   "

"Don't say it," Laura interrupted sharply. "You'll have many, many more. Now go to sleep, you need your strength."

"I'll lie down, but not sure I want to go to sleep."

"Why not?"

Brooke didn't answer and moved to close the door. "'Night, Mother."

Laura held the door from closing. "Why don't you want to sleep?"

For some reason Brooke appeared embarrassed.

"Brooke?" Laura pressed.

"Good night, Mother." She pushed the door closed.

Laura's first instinct was to open the door and demand to know what was causing her daughter to miss her sleep. Sleep was important to her recovery. If the meds kept her awake, they needed to talk to the doctors. But something told her to back off.

They would talk in the morning.

The tiny ceiling crack ran from the far corner of the room to a point directly above the dresser. Brooke was surprised she'd missed it earlier during her exhaustive nightly surveys of the ceiling while lying in bed trying to stay awake. Two hours had passed since she'd said good-night to her mother. She watched mind-numbing TV for a while and kept the table light on while reading the latest Lee Child thriller, but even Jack Reacher couldn't keep her eyes open forever.

Each night during her ceiling surveys she'd ordered her brain to stay away from the topic of the big D, but her brain had stubbornly refused to obey. Would she see a white light like those people who reported near-death experiences? Would she even know she was dying? The idea of an after-life was plain silly, and she viewed modern Judeo-Christian religion no differently than ancient Romans and Greeks who worshipped Jupiter and Zeus. A society, no matter how primitive or how advanced, needed to believe in a higher power to explain the randomness of life. And of death. So she had no illusions that there'd be a happy reunion with her dad and grandparents dancing among the clouds. When she checked out, that would be it. The end. *Finito.*

Her eyelids felt like lead curtains. She re-opened her book. Jack was about to walk into an ambush. That would hold her attention for a while.

She couldn't allow herself to fall asleep.

She was afraid she'd never wake up.

CHAPTER THIRTY-SEVEN

Laura was too distraught to sleep. After a couple hours watching *Seinfeld* reruns—she found she could quote many of the lines before hearing them spoken— she decided to take a walk. Anna, Brandon, and the others hadn't returned from the mall yet. More and more stores were opening Thanksgiving night offering pre-Black Friday sales, and the group probably decided to do a little shopping.

The temperature hovered in the high twenties, so she dressed quickly and put on the blue fleece vest Mickey bought her years earlier on one of their ski trips. At the sidewalk she turned left, passing the familiar homes where most residents had dutifully cleared the snow from the sidewalk in front of their houses. However, there were a few, including Mrs. van Arsdale, who probably didn't even own a snow shovel.

Church quiet. No wind. The stars out in full force. She took a deep breath of the cool air and exhaled slowly. Brooke needed her to be a rock. She was Brooke's mother, and a mother has the ultimate responsibility.

Lost in her thoughts, she didn't hear the vehicle come up behind her. The sound of the door slamming shut made her jump. She turned to see Arlo exiting the Massey Mobile.

"Arlo?"

"Good evening, Laura." He appeared rather subdued. "Great night for a walk," he said.

"Yes, it is."

"Mind if I join you?"

"Public sidewalk." She turned and continued walking. He strode next to her, close but not touching.

"Have a nice Thanksgiving?" he asked politely. Too politely.

"Yes, thank you. And you?"

"Didn't really have a dinner or anything. Most of the restaurants and bars were closed. I finished off a couple of beers and a family-size bag of Cheetos watching the 'Skins kick some Cowboy butt."

"You couldn't find any company? What about the Austrian twins?" Laura knew she was being catty, but part of her didn't care. Which left the other part, a part that confused her. "Sorry, that was unkind."

"Actually, I've sort've sworn off, you know, the female companionship thing for the last few months." As if realizing his words might be misinterpreted, he hastened to add, "Not that I don't like women or I'm not capable of performing or anything." He quickly changed the subject. "I heard about your daughter."

"Aunt Gracie has a big mouth." Laura turned left onto Bay Street to make the circle back home.

"She's worried about you with this coming so soon after your husband's passing."

Laura stopped in her tracks and turned to face him. "Please listen to me. My daughter's not dying. I won't permit it. And I'll entertain no further comment on that subject, if you please."

"My apologies. You're right."

There he was with that politeness again. It seemed unnatural. They continued walking, Arlo continued talking. "Boy, that demolition derby was a kick, wasn't it?"

"Except the police are watching us, and if Russell's ex has her way we'll all end up in jail." They approached Laura's house. She glanced up and glimpsed Brooke watching from the upstairs window.

"You have to do what you think is right."

"Okay, I give up. As I recall, I'm not in your target demographic. Why are you being so nice to me? Why do you even care?" To Laura, he appeared like he was struggling to decide how much to open up. "Arlo?"

He finally asked, "You ever play dodgeball as a kid?"

His question puzzled her. "Yes, of course."

"See, some people, they think of death as this skinny old guy in a black hood carrying this sharp blade on a stick."

"A sickle."

"Yeah, a sickle. Well, I always pictured him as a playground rec director."

"Doesn't sound very scary."

"He's dressed in black, and he has this huge smile on his face. He's out on the playground, and there are a zillion people in the game, and he throws the ball and whoever he hits, dies. But you don't care because there are so many people the chances of you getting hit are really low. You run around and live your life, and in the meantime ol' Death, he keeps throwin' that ball. And you're vaguely aware that people are falling but you don't pay much attention because you're caught up in your own little corner of the playground.

"Then one day, you reach a certain age and you look around and you happen to notice there's not that many people left on the playground. And you can see Mr. Death and he can see you. He smiles and throws the ball, and you dodge, and the ball hits someone else. Now there's one less person on the field, and he throws again and again, and you keep dodging and . . . well, you wonder how long it will take before you get hit. So maybe you run a little faster and play a little harder because the next throw might smack you right in the face." Arlo paused. "And it seems so random because sometimes the ball hits somebody who's only been on the playground a few years."

Laura was a bit taken back by Arlo's introspection. "A colorful metaphor, Mr. Massey, but I'm still at a loss to understand what that has to do with me."

"I was watching how you dealt with death, how you took away the pain and gave Russell and the others one last bit of fun. Like, okay, you knew death was coming, but by taking control of how people passed, by doing it on their terms, you thumbed your nose at death and shouted, 'Hey, we're still in charge here.' That took a lot of courage, and maybe made it a little easier for me to deal with the fact that the ball can hit anybody, and that someday, I'm going get smacked myself. So my interest in you, I don't know, it's either because of that or—"

"Or what, Mr. Massey?"

His expression snapped back to a puckish grin. "Or because your ass ain't half bad."

Reflexively, Laura slapped him. Arlo ducked and the momentum from Laura's swing caused her to lose her balance. She grabbed at Arlo, but they both slipped on the ice and fell, Laura landing on top of Arlo in the snow. "Get off me!"

"You're on top of me."

Laura struggled to get up but slipped again and fell back on top of Arlo. This time he wrapped his arms around her. She resisted for a moment, then collapsed into his embrace. The dam burst and the tears gushed out. Unable to stop, she cried there in his arms. Neither said a word.

After a couple of minutes, Laura struggled up and helped Arlo to his feet. They were both covered in snow. She felt overwhelmed with embarrassment. "I'm sorry."

"Listen, maybe you'd like to walk down the street and get a cup of hot chocolate."

A sense of panic washed over her. "No. I mean, thanks, but, no. I must go." She turned quickly and almost jogged up the path to her front porch, leaving him standing in the snow. When she opened the door, Brooke stood at the top of the stairs with her arms folded, her expression that of a mother who'd caught her teenage daughter with her clothes disheveled and her boyfriend zipping his fly.

"Mother, I'm shocked, shocked."

"Brooke?"

Brooke couldn't hold her faux frown any longer, and her face broke out into a huge grin. "Making snow angels with the infamous Arlo Massey, I see. Aunt Gracie's been keeping me up to date."

"I'm giving you a direct order to ignore everything that old woman says. Now go on back up to bed." Maintaining the knowing smile, Brooke walked slowly up the stairs. "And wipe that stupid smile off your face. You look like an imbecile."

"Yes, Mother." Brooke widened her smile as she disappeared up the stairs.

Chapter Thirty-Eight

December

A week after Thanksgiving, Laura answered the door to find Arlo standing on the porch. He'd called a few times asking how Brooke was doing, and on each occasion he invited Laura to dinner. She politely declined.

"So, I was heading downtown to grab a bite and wanted to see if you might join me."

Brooke, wrapped in the quilt, shuffled into the foyer from the living room. "Hi, Arlo."

"Good to see you. How are you feeling?"

"Having a pretty good day. Would you like to come in?"

"Actually, I stopped by to see if your mother might want to join me for dinner."

Laura said, "Thank you, but—"

Brooke interrupted. "She'd love to."

Laura turned to give her daughter a dirty look. "I was fixing dinner for Brooke, and I don't think—"

Brooke pulled Laura's coat off the rack and shoved it into her arms. "Go. I think I'm competent to warm up tomato soup in the microwave."

"But I'm not dressed to go out."

Brooke and Arlo spoke in unison. "You look beautiful."

Three hours later, Arlo walked her up the steps to the front porch.

During an amazing dinner at the Treaty of Paris restaurant, Laura had been surprised to discover she actually enjoyed herself. Arlo kept the conversation light and civil—the weather, the traffic, local politics, favorite old movies. She'd been tempted to ask about his son but didn't want to puncture the façade of normalcy by veering into serious family matters. Still, the pretense could only last so long. She couldn't hold back the guilt of being away from her gravely ill daughter. Brooke needed her full attention. When he asked if she wanted dessert, she'd demurred and requested he take her home.

At the door, Laura found herself feeling awkward, like a teenager on her first date. She said, "Thank you for dinner. I admit it felt good to get away for a few hours."

"My pleasure. You need to allow yourself a break more often. Not only is it good for you, but in the long run good for Brooke. You're doing her no good by smothering her."

Laura felt the blood rush to her face. "Smothering her? I'm sorry, but I don't appreciate receiving advice from you or anyone else on how to care for my own daughter. And at the moment, I'm frankly not focusing on 'the long run.'"

"I apologize. You're right. None of my business."

She needed to get inside.

"Good night, Laura. Please give my best to Brooke. And I hope we can do this again real soon." He took her by the shoulders and kissed her on her cheek.

Cheek kisses were supposed to be the same as a handshake. Aunts and uncles and friends cheek kissed. So why did this kiss seem different? His lips barely grazed her skin. Okay, she needed to nip this in the bud, whatever "this" was.

"Arlo, I appreciate your interest, and dinner was enjoyable, but I think it best if we don't . . . socialize any more, at least until Brooke is fully back on her feet. She deserves my complete attention."

He held her gaze, not saying a word. Why did her spine snap into freeze-lock? She was standing outside on a winter night, that's why.

Finally, he nodded. "Okay, if that's what you want. Good night." He walked down the steps to the sidewalk.

The door opened a crack. Brooke's voice. "Not too late to call him back and invite him in for a nightcap."

Should she? She felt a touch of guilt. Why? Had she betrayed Mickey? No, of course not. She'd done nothing wrong. Besides, it was a cheek kiss, that's all. Or was she feeling guilty about not feeling more guilty? Laura hesitated too long. Arlo turned onto the sidewalk and disappeared into the night.

The twenty-third of December brought a wonderful early Christmas present. Brooke's tumors had shrunk. The change was not dramatic, and the doctor cautioned against over-optimism, but Laura could tell Brooke was feeling better. She could see it in Brooke's coloring, and her appetite was returning. Laura, Brooke, Tom, and Jennie were so happy they went out to dinner at Lewnes's Steak House to celebrate receiving the most valuable Christmas present of all—hope. But hope had a price. The doctors, encouraged by the positive results, decided the best chance to knock out the cancer completely was to increase the treatment intensity. Which meant more sick days, and fewer cherries 'n chocolate days. Nevertheless, motivated by the positive report, Brooke would persevere.

Christmas day was one of the coldest on record—single digit temperatures, freezing wind, five inches of snow. The weather continued into the next week, and moving about the house Laura had to bundle up in a thick sweater. Replacing the insulation in the old house was another one of those things on Mickey's to-do list that never got done.

On the Saturday before New Year's, Laura left Brooke's room with a tray full of empty dishes and a smile on her face. She'd made beef barley soup, one of Brooke's favorites, and her daughter scarfed up every last drop. What a wonderful change from only a few weeks earlier. She ran into Anna coming up the stairs carrying a large fabric sample book. Anna's weekend visits seemed to perk Brooke up, and Laura was glad both her daughters were home together.

"How's she doing?" Anna asked.

"Much better. Her appetite's back. What do you have there?"

"Linen swatches. The wedding planner let me borrow the book."

"The big day will be here before you know it."

"Don't remind me." Anna paused and held her mother's gaze. "I've told you before, and I'll say it again, we can postpone the wedding. Brooke's recovery is all that's important right now. The wedding will be a distraction and—"

"Exactly. That's what Brooke needs. A distraction."

Anna nodded. "By the way, you have company." Before Laura could inquire, Anna entered Brooke's room and closed the door.

Laura carried the tray into the kitchen and was startled to see Alvin Olson, along with Gracie and Everett, seated at her kitchen table, drinking coffee and nibbling cookies. They must have arrived while she was with Brooke. "Alvin?"

"I called them here for a meeting," Gracie said.

"A meeting about what?" Alvin's presence made it pretty clear that this meeting would have a one-item agenda. The Chocolate

Shop. Gracie confirmed her suspicions by offering a chocolate cookie from the platter.

"First of all," Everett asked, "how's Brooke?"

"Is the tumor still shrinking?" Gracie asked.

"We go back in two months. The new protocol's rough on her. Anna's upstairs keeping her spirits up. So, Alvin, how's Mary Ellen?"

Before Alvin could respond, Gracie jumped in. "That's why we're here. Alvin called me and asked us to reconsider."

Alvin said, "She's in so much pain. The doctors say she could still linger for months, and I was hoping—"

"I'm sorry, you shouldn't have come." The tone of Laura's voice sounded colder than she meant it to be, but she was not going to start up again. No way.

Everett nodded his agreement. "I concur fully. When Gracie called and said she was inviting me to give an opposing viewpoint, I, of course, agreed. Never let it be said that Everett T. Tisdale shirks the tough decisions. Alvin, if Laura and Gracie do what you ask, they'll face grave consequences from the authorities."

"Maybe we could do one more," Gracie said. "We do it quietly, who's to know?"

"The police will know immediately upon review of the obituary," Everett said, looking pleased with his quick logic.

"What if her death was ruled due to natural causes?" Gracie asked. "Then there'd be no red flag."

"So now you're going to add a doctor to the list of police targets? I will not put anyone else in jeopardy. I'm so sorry. Please give Mary Ellen our best and tell her she's in our prayers."

Alvin, his head hung in defeat, slowly got to his feet. "I understand," he whispered. "Thank you for at least considering. I can see my way out."

Laura felt overwhelmed with helplessness. She'd experienced first-hand the level of anquish Alvin was now going through. But helping Alvin and Mary Ellen would likely buy her and Gracie a one-way ticket to prison. She couldn't. *She just couldn't.* No one said a word as he shuffled out of the kitchen, the portrait of a broken man.

When they heard the front door close, Laura re-directed her frustration at Gracie. "I can't believe—"

"Don't get mad at me. The poor woman's in pain, and we can do something about it. I'm not going to apologize. In fact, I may do it myself. I'll need you to fill the prescription."

Everett moved closer to Laura, leaving no doubt as to which side he was on. "It would be insane to offer the service with the police watching. I support Laura's position completely. We will have no part in your efforts, Gracie, and I strongly advise you to rethink your ill-conceived position. However, no matter what course you decide to pursue, suffice it to say that Laura and I—"

From behind them, Brooke's voice cut him short. "Let's do it."

Surprised, they all turned to see Brooke in her bathrobe leaning against the door jam, looking gaunt but resolute.

"Baby?" Laura whispered. "Where's your sister?"

"In the bathroom. She'll be down in a minute." Brooke held Laura's gaze and smiled with a look of wisdom Laura had never seen before. "I understand now. You were right. A person should be able to make his or her own end-of-life decisions. Being confronted with your own mortality can change your perspective pretty quickly."

"I don't think you understand the risks."

"Fuck the risks. Live fierce, remember?"

"Honey—"

"Let's do it . . . together. You and me and Gracie."

"Brooke—"

"Let's re-open the Chocolate Shop."

Laura, followed by Gracie and Brooke, walked through the front door of Alvin and Mary Ellen's apartment.

Alvin welcomed them. "Come in, come in. Let me take your coats. She's in the bedroom waiting for you."

Standing there, Laura reflected on how easily she'd given in to re-opening the Chocolate Shop. Her immediate change of heart had been reflexive, instinctive, triggered by the image of Brooke standing there, staring death in the face—the evil rec director?—and effectively saying, "Hey, we're still in charge." Fortunately, Anna hadn't heard the conversation and returned to Chicago. Laura didn't want to worry about her youngest daughter if things broke bad. She'd gone over with Brooke and Gracie three times the legal line they could not cross. Neither appeared to pay her much attention. She knew she would have to be the one to enforce adherence to the rules, and she fully intended to fullfil that responsibility.

While Alvin hung up their coats, the three women scanned the small living room. The space signaled that the occupants were warm, caring people. Alvin had sold his small chain of drug stores to a national corporation fifteen years earlier, and could afford about anything they wanted. But the furnishings appeared comfortable, not pretentious. Several black & white photos of a young woman racing downhill on skis sat on the mantel.

"Is that Mrs. Olson?" Brooke asked.

Alvin didn't try to hide his pride. "Cortina d'Ampezzo, Italy, 1956."

"The Olympics? She was in the Olympics?" Brooke inquired, suitably impressed.

"Fifth in the downhill and seventh in the slalom," said Alvin. "She said it was the greatest thrill of her life. Other than meeting me, of course."

The women chuckled politely.

"Follow me." Alvin led the women down the hall to a bedroom.

When they entered the bedroom, Mary Ellen was struggling to sit up in bed. Alvin rushed to her side, fluffed up a big pillow, and wedged it carefully behind her back. Even in her dissipated condition, Laura cold tell she'd once been a strong, beautiful athlete. Medicine bottles covered the table next to the bed, and Laura could hear the woman's labored breathing across the room.

"Thank you all for coming," Mary Ellen said. Laura could see her struggling, willing her voice to project. In anticipation of their visit she'd put on lipstick and a touch of blush. "Alvin, have you offered our guests some refreshments?"

"We're fine," said Laura.

"Thank you so much for agreeing to help." Mary Ellen tried unsuccessfully to hide a wince as she spoke.

"You need to be sure," Laura said.

"I'm sure."

Gracie pointed to the table full of medications. "Why don't you dump all those pills in a tall glass of Old Grand-dad and have one last cocktail?"

Mary Ellen glanced at Alvin.

"We already tried that," he said. "I crushed up her pain meds and mixed them in a glass of peppermint schnapps. She'd always had a glass of schnapps after a day of skiing, and it brought back wonderful memories. We said our goodbyes, and she drank the schnapps. She became violently ill, vomiting, shaking, twitching. I couldn't stand to watch so I called the paramedics, they pumped her stomach, and here we are." He turned to his wife. "I'm sorry, I couldn't bear to see you like that."

She squeezed his hand. "You did it because you love me."

"Mary Ellen wanted to make sure I didn't get in trouble, so she convinced the authorities she suffered from dementia and didn't understand the dosage. So that's why we're turning to the professionals."

"We're far from professionals," Laura said. Our services are offered in friendship, and things could go just as badly working with us." Laura still had a full prescription of Xanax from the vet sitting in her medicine cabinet. "We'd be happy to provide you the drugs, and you both could go forward on your own."

"We trust you, Laura," Mary Ellen said. "We really want you to handle it."

Gracie jumped in. "Do you have any last wish, something you want to do before you leave us?"

A broad smile crossed Mary Ellen's face. "As a matter of fact, I do."

CHAPTER THIRTY-NINE

January

Charlene Melroy was in a foul mood as she walked down Main Street to her hair appointment. Beckman and Lujack killed Russell, the old fart, and the damn cops were doing crap. Why the hell didn't her dearly departed ex pay a few more bucks for an insurance policy that paid in the event of death by suicide? The ungrateful cheapskate. She'd shown the insurance company the string of suicide obituaries along with a statement from Detective Olivetti certifying that the two murderers admitted attending all of them. But the company was trying to weasel out of paying. *We're terribly sorry for your loss, Mrs. Melroy, but there's insufficient evidence to support your claim the insured was the victim of foul play.* Insufficient evidence, my ass. She was between jobs at the moment. With the insurance money she could open a place of her own. Not a strip joint, a small nightclub. Understated, classy. She'd gone 'round and 'round thinking of a name but kept coming back to "Charlene's."

And the idiot owed her. So he'd walked in on her screwing their neighbor's eighteen-year-old son, so what? She viewed it as mentoring, nothing more. Christ, she even apologized. But sister-bitch forced Russell to divorce her, and now Beckman and Lujack were trying to cheat her out of her rightful inheritance. She'd appealed the benefit denial to keep the case alive while she tried to dig up more evidence that the two bitches poisoned the imbecile. She'd come to realize if she were to be successful she'd have to do the cops' job for them.

She was about to enter the salon when she spotted a familiar face on the other side of the street. The Lujack woman. What the hell was that crazy old biddie up to? Charlene positioned herself behind a parked truck so she wouldn't be seen. Gracie entered Sun & Snow, a shop that sold surfing gear in the summer and ski equipment in the winter. Charlene decided to stay put. Patience and persistence, that's what her daddy said you needed to get ahead in life, and Charlene Sue Sutter Melroy had both.

In less than twenty minutes, Gracie emerged from the store carrying a shopping bag. After making sure she wouldn't be seen, Charlene crossed the street and entered the shop. She headed straight for a young salesgirl replacing jackets on hangers.

"May I help you?" the girl asked.

"Thank you, but I was supposed to meet my sister here. Gracie?"

"You just missed her."

"Oh, my." Charlene feigned a look of disappointment. Good thing she'd taken those acting classes years ago. "We were going to meet and pick out a gift for a relative."

The salesgirl appeared confused. "Your sister gave me the impression the outfit was for her. I mean she tried it on to make sure it fit." She pulled a fluorescent pink one-piece ski outfit with faux fur trim from the rack. "This is what she bought. A little wild for me, but she loved it."

"Sis probably didn't tell you she was color blind. Did she mention where she was going to wear it?"

"She said a group of friends planned to take this sick lady skiing up at White Elk tomorrow. Didn't make sense to me. Why would you take a sick person skiing?"

"An excellent question, my dear, an excellent question."

Charlene sat across a small conference table from Jefferson and Olivetti. She was pissed and didn't care if they knew it. "I called you yesterday afternoon, and I do not appreciate having to wait until now to see you."

Jefferson tried to keep his cool. "Mrs. Melroy, we're talking about less than twenty-four hours. I'm sure you can appreciate that Detective Olivetti and I have other cases."

Charlene saw it was time to push the tear button. Instantly her eyes watered and tears drizzled down her cheeks. "They killed my husband." She sniffed and reached for the tissue she had placed in her pocket for this very occasion. "And I can't stand by in good conscience and watch them rip the heart out of another poor family."

"I understood Mr. Melroy was your *ex*-husband," Jefferson said.

"So what? He still loved me and wanted to provide for me, but thanks to Beckman and Lujack, the insurance . . . Well, that's not important, of course. It's the threat to others that should be our only focus."

"Lujack said they're taking a sick friend skiing?" Olivetti asked. "Don't make a whole lot of sense."

Of course it does, you idiot. "I believe the sick friend is about to become their next victim this very afternoon and thought you might want to stop them before they killed again. Isn't that what you people are supposed to do? Prevent cold-blooded murder?"

That morning Laura sat at her kitchen table, staring at the phone as if it were radioactive. Standing behind her, Brooke and Gracie egged her on.

"Do it," Gracie said.

"Call him, Mother."

"There's has to be another way."

"To transport the five of us plus gear?" Brooke said.

Of course there was another way. She could rent a U-Haul van. But the truth was she'd come to trust Arlo and rely on his discretion. "Okay, on one condition. You both wipe those idiotic grins off your faces." Brooke and Gracie instantly changed their expressions to exaggerated frowns.

Laura threw up her hands in defeat and reached for her phone.

CHAPTER FORTY

The day before, Sam had sent over two new brunettes—"mouse meat," the term applied to first-time wharf rats—looking for a winter sail and a good time. But when Arlo opened the cabin door and saw them standing together all bundled up, giggling, anxious, each with the familiar "I'm open for anything" expression, he sent them away as he'd done with other female opportunities in the past months. The woman sitting next to him in the Massey Mobile was the reason. Laura Beckman was physically attractive, but he knew that didn't explain it. Maybe that was the point. He felt a connection to her that was deep, visceral. Something he hadn't experienced since his early days with Lorraine. Laura didn't want to change him, but she made him want to change himself to please her.

He drove west along Route 40 through snow-covered mountains blanketed by an overcast sky. Gracie and Brooke occupied the seat behind them. Alvin and Mary Ellen huddled together in the third seat. Brooke slept comfortably, wrapped in a blanket Arlo found for her.

His thoughts dwelled on Laura. While she'd warmed up to him, even to the point where he thought she now considered him a friend, it was pretty clear that's all he was, and probably all he would ever be. Not that he blamed her. He'd come across to her as a shallow jerk, an old fool chasing younger women in a vain attempt to make himself feel young again.

Laura Beckman still loved her late husband and was tethered to her memories of their life together. Her attention was fully consumed with her daughter. He knew there was no room for him in her life, and there shouldn't be. Yet here he was. Unexplainable.

"Awfully nice of you to help out, Arlo," Gracie said. "The van's perfect."

"When Laura called, how could I say no?"

Gracie continued. "And what a fortunate coincidence that you happen to know someone at the resort who will help us, isn't that right, Laura?"

Laura ignored her.

Gracie pressed. "Laura?"

"We certainly are grateful that Arlo decided to help out," Laura said. "Now why don't you check out the wonderful scenery you've been missing because you've been flapping your trap since we left Annapolis."

"No need to be rude."

"I've already told Arlo we appreciate his help."

"Glad to do it," Arlo said. "Hopefully, Freddie will come through."

"How is it you know this young man?" Laura asked.

"Freddie heads up the ski patrol. He worked for me last summer at the marina. We had a little incident, nothing really, but let's say he feels he owes me one."

The van passed a sign that read: *White Elk Resort, 45 Mi.*

Arlo glanced in the rearview mirror to check out the Olsons in the third seat. Mary Ellen, appearing tiny in a heavy coat, snuggled up next to Alvin under a blanket. "How are you two lovebirds doing back there?"

"Wonderful," Mary Ellen said. Alvin kissed her tenderly.

Out of the corner of his eye he caught Laura watching him. He turned for a second and held her gaze, feeling the connection. Did she feel it, too?

Gracie interrupted his thoughts. "You two are missing the scenery."

Jefferson increased his speed on the interstate. "I still don't understand why you wouldn't let me call the Staties or Garrett County to go check it out. In case you haven't noticed, we're out of our jurisdiction."

"It's our case," Olivetti said. "When we make the collar, we'll call the county boys for back-up. Although I doubt if they'll give us much trouble."

"Chaz—"

"Don't know why you're so nervous. We're investigating multiple homicides and trying to prevent another."

"Suicide more likely."

"The church says suicide's a sin."

"The state of Maryland says it's not, as long as someone else doesn't pull the trigger, and so far all we have is a lot of smoke, no fire, a few old souls who were soon to die anyway, and a desk full of real murder files stacked a foot high."

"They'll still be there when we get back. All I'm saying is, if one of those women so much as helps her drink one sip, it's second degree, and I'm taking them down." Olivetti crossed himself, then gazed heavenward, his expression reflecting his certainty of divine approval.

By the time the Massey Mobile reached the resort the clouds had cleared, leaving a sunny blue winter sky. Arlo offered to help Mary Ellen into her wheelchair, but Alvin said he could handle it, and Arlo gave way. After Mary Ellen was settled in, Alvin tucked Arlo's blanket around her lap.

"How's that, El?"

"Fine." Mary Ellen's voice sounded weak. She took in a deep breath of the crisp air. "Smell that air, Sweetie. Heavenly." She breathed in deeply again but this time the quick intake triggered a hacking cough that sounded as if it would dislodge all her internal organs.

Laura removed a small knapsack from the back of the van, and slipped her arms into the straps. Gracie locked eyes with her, neither spoke.

Gracie's skis were old when she last used them over thirty years earlier. With Arlo's help, she untied the skis from the rack on top of the van, slung them over her shoulder, and followed the Olsons as they made their way toward the resort center.

Laura turned to Brooke. "Wait here, Honey, and I'll go find you a wheelchair."

"I can walk with a little help."

In an instant, Arlo was at her side. "Arlo Massey, pedestrian support at your service." He wrapped his left arm around her back and they started walking slowly. Brooke turned to Laura with a puckish grin. "Arlo has another arm that I'm sure he would be willing to make available."

Arlo waved his right arm.

Laura hesitated for a moment. She could almost feel his arms wrapped around her, pulling her tight, as they flew across the sky over the Maryland countryside. Then an image flashed in her mind of Thanksgiving night, lying together in the snow on her front lawn. She slipped her arm through his and they proceeded to the resort center, a large square surrounded by shops and restaurants bustling with activity.

A group of six young men in tight ski pants passed them, laughing and jostling each other. Gracie stopped in her tracks. "We've reached the promised land."

Arlo helped Brooke to a bench. "I need to find Freddie. Can I get you anything?"

"I'm fine. What a great place for people watching." She seemed to be truly enjoying herself. Alvin pushed Mary Ellen next to the bench, then walked across the square to a kiosk selling hot chocolate.

Brooke patted Mary Ellen's knee. "How are you doing?"

Mary Ellen beamed as she took in her surroundings. "Everything, the smells, the sounds, the air, the mountains, I couldn't be happier."

Arlo pointed to a ski rental shop in the corner of the square. "Laura, when was the last time you skied?"

"I'm sure it's like riding a bike."

By four o'clock most of the skiers had headed in for the day. Laura and Gracie rode the lift to the top of the Pine Tree ski run, an intermediate trail as indicated by the universal blue square on the sign. The others had come up the mountain on two snowmobiles. When the lift chair slowed to the unload point, Laura saw the others waiting for them in the flat gathering area at the bottom of the short lift dismount hill. Laura was determined to dismount without falling. As soon as their skis touched the surface, Gracie sped off without incident. Laura skied down toward the two waiting snowmobiles and for a moment felt in control. Then her left ski caught an edge, and she fell, rolling butt over teacup, and landed at the feet of one Arlo Massey. He reached down to help her, but she shook off his arm. She wanted to get up on her own.

"I'm fine." She crawled to her feet and her skis immediately shot out from under her. This time she allowed Arlo to help her up.

Gracie smirked. "Fall off your bike much?"

Alvin tucked his wife into a sled attached behind one of the snowmobiles. The sled was used by the ski patrol to transport injured skiers off the mountain. Brooke, all bundled up, sat on a nearby bench sipping hot chocolate. Alvin kneeled next to the sled and handed his wife a pill.

"This should help with the pain for a little while."

She swallowed the pill, then pecked his cheek. "A little while's all I need."

Freddie, short, tan, with bright eyes, a brighter smile, and curly black hair, wore a patch on his red and white jacket signifying his positon as the head of the White Elk ski patrol. He checked his watch. "You have about an hour of daylight left. The rest of the skiers and boarders are off the mountain, so you'll have things to yourself. I'll keep this lift open for you."

"Thanks, Freddie," Arlo said. "Can you open the lift to Screaming Eagle? We might give it a try a little later."

"That's a double diamond expert run."

"I know."

Freddie shrugged. "You got it, but please be careful. It's icy up there this time of day." Freddie tossed Arlo a walkie-talkie. "Here, in case there's a problem."

"Thanks."

"Hey, I owe you. When the police raided—"

Arlo interrupted him. "I see no reason to relive ancient history."

Freddie skied over to Mary Ellen and pointed to a wooden lever that served as a hand brake. "Make sure the brake's engaged when you're stopped to prevent the sled from slipping back and forth." He bent down to Mary Ellen. "Hope you enjoy your ride."

She smiled up at him and took his hand. "I will and thank you so much."

Freddie waved, then zipped down the hill.

Arlo turned to Mary Ellen. "Ready?"

Mary Ellen managed a smile. "Can't wait."

CHAPTER FORTY-ONE

The weakness of Mary Ellen's voice made hearing her difficult, but her sparkling eyes communicated quite clearly her excitement and anticipation.

Arlo jumped onto the snowmobile's wide seat. "Release the brake." Alvin released the brake, freeing the sled, then climbed onto the other snowmobile. Arlo beckoned for Laura to join him. "Jump on."

"No, no, I'm fine, I can ski . . . ouch." Gracie had jabbed her in the kidneys with her ski pole. Gracie continued prodding her toward the snowmobile. "Stop that prodding. Do I look like a cow to you?" Laura undid the bindings on her skis, slid the skis into the side brackets, then gingerly threw her leg across the seat of the snowmobile and sat down behind Arlo. She tried to maintain space between her body and his, but the size of the seat and the thickness of their ski jackets made that impossible. She turned back and returned Marty Ellen's wave.

Gracie zipped past them down the moderate slope of the intermediate run with the smooth grace and precise tight turns of a downhill racer. "Follow me!" she shouted, her ski form approaching instructional video level.

Arlo started the engine, and Laura instantly felt the heavy vibration between her legs.

"Ready?" Arlo had to shout back to Mary Ellen to be heard over the sound of the engine. She gave him a thumbs-up from the sled.

Laura asked, "Where do I hold on?"

Without responding, Arlo clicked the engine in gear and the snowmobile shot forward. Laura yelped and instinctively grabbed around Arlo's waist to keep from falling off. "That's where you hold on," Arlo yelled over his shoulder. He shot over the hill's crest and headed down the mountain, traversing the slope, back and forth, like a skier.

Laura held on for dear life. Occasionally, she glanced over her shoulder to check on Mary Ellen in the sled. The woman, her expression one of pure joy, gleefully stretched her arms skyward as if she were riding on a roller-coaster careening down the track. Alvin appeared much less confident driving the snowmobile as he followed Arlo down the slope. Brooke remained on a bench at the top of the hill enjoying the view. When Arlo reached the bottom he stopped, turned and caught Laura smiling.

Arlo said, "You have to admit, that was fun."

She felt guilty for enjoying herself given Mary Ellen's "situation." But then again, this outing was the fulfillment of Mary Ellen's wish, and everyone enjoying themselves was a big part of it. She spoke loudly so Mary Ellen could hear. "Yes, actually, a lot of fun."

Arlo shouted over the noise of the engine to Mary Ellen in the sled. "How are you doing back there?"

Mary Ellen's voice barely registered above a whisper. "Again . . ."

Arlo had difficulty hearing her but Laura interpreted.

"You got it!"

He drove the snowmobile straight up the slope and took his two passengers down three more times. After each run, Mary Ellen's voice became even weaker, and Laura continued to act as translator. Mary Ellen's message was the same: "Faster!" Arlo readily complied.

With each run, Laura held on tighter to Arlo. She had no choice, she told herself, she didn't want to fall off and break her neck.

For the next few runs, Laura joined Brooke on the bench, watching as Arlo, pulling Mary Ellen in the sled, and Alvin raced down the slope. Alvin won and everyone, including Alvin, knew Arlo let him win. But no one cared.

Laura noticed Brooke seemed to be really enjoying herself. Her coloring was better, and her eyes sparkled. Her daughter appeared genuinely happy. The treatments were working. If Laura could continue to keep the fight in Brooke alive, those monstrous little cancer cells would be dead and gone in short order.

Gracie found some red and blue bamboo poles stacked up against the side of the lift and used them to set up an alpine racecourse down the slope. Mary Ellen seemed to have rallied a bit and offered her expertise on the spacing.

Once the course had been set up, Gracie challenged Mary Ellen to a race. Arlo encouraged Brooke to join him on the snowmobile and with gentle prodding from Laura, Brooke agreed. Afraid she would not have the strength to hold on, Arlo let her sit in front of him so his body created a protective cocoon. Alvin stood next to Laura at the top.

Laura yelled, "Go!" and the racers were off. Even though the snowmobile had tremendous power, it was more cumbersome and took more time to navigate in and out of the blue gates while Gracie zipped down the red course, winning by a few seconds. Good-natured boos rained down on Gracie.

"Sore losers!" she shot back, and everyone laughed.

Determined to make the course more fair, Arlo insisted that the snowmobile needed much wider gates, and so the course was modified. This time Alvin, taking a cue from Arlo, positioned Mary Ellen in front of him on the seat and the Olson team beat Gracie by a whisker. Loud cheering from everyone, including, after a few seconds, even Gracie.

The group continued playing on the mountain like a bunch of carefree children—switching riders, racing, teasing, laughing, having the times of their lives.

At 5:30 the sun had sunk low on the horizon. Mary Ellen, too exhausted to speak, waved Laura over and rasped, "I think it's time." Laura squeezed her hand. "And remember," Mary Ellen continued, "I want to see the sun set from the top of the mountain."

Laura turned to the others. "We should go up before the sun sets." The mood changed instantly.

"Alvin and I will drive Mary Ellen and Brooke up Screaming Eagle," said Arlo. "You and Gracie can take the lift."

Down at the resort center, Jefferson and Olivetti flashed their badges to Freddie. "Tell us where they are," Olivetti ordered.

"We have thousands of skiers and boarders, sir," Freddie said, the picture of innocence. "I don't know these people you're talking about. The lifts closed awhile ago, so they've probably left. Or maybe they're in one of the shops or restaurants. You're free to—"

Olivetti interrupted him. "Cut the crap. I can see one of the lifts running at the top of the mountain."

"That's for the sweepers," Freddie answered.

"Sweepers?"

"At the end of the day, the ski patrol sweeps all of the runs to make sure there's no one hurt who didn't come down."

Olivetti got into Freddie's face. "Kid, I've perfected a bullshit meter that tells me when the best liars in the world are spinnin' me, and you're a rank amateur. So let me lay it out for you in terms so simple there's a good chance even you'll understand. If you don't help us and there's a murder, you'll go down hard as an accessory."

"Murder?" Freddie was surprised and a little scared. "They told me—"

"What did they tell you?" Jefferson asked.

"That this old lady, she was dying and she was this famous skier when she was younger, and she wanted to ride down a mountain one last time before . . . you know."

"What's the fastest way up there?" asked Jefferson.

Freddie, unsure of what to do, hesitantly nodded to a snowmobile parked near the bottom of the first lift.

Olivetti ran to the snowmobile.

Jefferson hesitated, then followed his partner. A moment before they pulled out Olivetti spotted Freddie lifting a walkie-talkie to his mouth. "Hey, Bozo. You warn them we're coming, expect an automatic accessory charge laid on your sorry ass."

On top of the Screaming Eagle run, the highest point of the mountain, everyone gathered around Mary Ellen's sled. Gracie passed out chocolate cookies. Mary Ellen smiled, and whispered to Gracie, "Very clever." She took a bite and let the rest drop into her lap.

Alvin bent down and took his wife's hand. They were at the top of the mountain, and the sunset had painted the snow a warm orange hue. To the right, the Screaming Eagle run shot steeply down the mountain. To the left, a sheer cliff dropped to a rocky gorge almost a thousand feet below. Red danger signs marked the crest of the cliff and ropes sealed it off even to expert skiers.

"Push me over there, near the crest," whispered Mary Ellen. "I want to see the sun setting." Arlo unhooked the sled from the snowmobile, then he and Alvin carefully pushed the sled near the red ropes. Alvin had to steer the back of the sled to steady it on the icy surface. Arlo pulled the hand brake tight, safely anchoring the sled. The others gathered around.

"Thank you all so much," Mary Ellen whispered.

"You will be terribly missed," Laura said.

Alvin, struggling to keep it together, hugged his wife. He whispered to her. "I love you, El. You've been my life." He kissed her.

"I love you too, Allie," she said, her voice barely audible. After a long moment, she turned to Laura. "I'm ready."

Laura glanced toward Brooke, who nodded her approval. Laura removed from her backpack a plastic bottle containing the treated cocktail—peach schnapps mixed with a little orange juice—and inserted a straw. She held the bottle in her open hand.

Mary Ellen feebly reached for the bottle. "I have to take it from you, I remember."

The group heard the roar of a snowmobile in the distance but were too focused on Mary Ellen for it to register. Mary Ellen took the bottle with a shaky hand, and quickly drank from the straw.

Laura heard the snowmobile before she saw it. She turned just as it shot up and over the crest of the Screaming Eagle run and sped toward them. She caught Mary Ellen's eye. Mary Ellen saw the cops and nodded. She beckoned a tearful Alvin down to her. "Thank you for this wonderful gift. Good-bye, my darling." She kissed him. Laura could tell the Xanax cocktail was already having an effect as Ellen appeared woozy, swaying her head back and forth. Then, without warning, she somehow summoned one last ounce of strength and flopped her upper body hard against the hand brake. Before the group could react, the sled slid down the ice.

"Grab it!" Arlo shouted.

Alvin dove, but missed the sled. All they could do was watch.

The cops arrived, and a moment later the sled shot under the ropes and off the cliff carrying Mary Ellen Olson on her final run into the warm embrace of the glowing sunset.

Three hours later, Laura and her group remained confined to a small conference room in the resort's administrative offices. On one side of the room, Laura, Gracie, and Brooke continued to console Alvin. On the other side, Arlo dealt with Olivetti, Jefferson, and a big, ruddy-faced detective from Garrett County named Stuart.

"I repeat, you witnessed it yourself, detective," Arlo said. "Mrs. Olson disengaged the brake on her own."

Olivetti did not attempt to hide his frustration. "Yeah, and what are we going to find in the autopsy?"

"You'll find a lethal dose of barbiturates, which all of us will confirm were voluntarily ingested by Mrs. Olson shortly before she alone disengaged the brake."

Olivetti sneered. "I'm gonna take a wild guess that the victim didn't have a prescription for the meds. So why don't you save us all a lot of time and tell us where they were obtained?"

"I honestly don't know," Arlo replied.

"And what's your interest in this again?"

"Friend of the family."

Jefferson pulled Olivetti aside. "Come on, Chaz, we have nothing."

"From what I see, he's right," Stuart added.

Olivetti stared out the window at the darkness. He turned and addressed the group. "I know you think what you're doing here is somehow humane, maybe even heroic. It's not. It's wrong. It's murder, and I'm not gonna let this go." With a nod of his head,

Olivetti signaled to Jefferson it was time to leave. "You're free to go," he announced to the group.

As Olivetti passed Alvin, he mumbled, "Sorry for your loss."

CHAPTER FORTY-TWO

February

When Laura first stirred awake every morning, she mouthed a quiet prayer asking God to keep Brooke's cancer in remission. So far, her prayers had been answered. The doctors told Brooke she was one of the lucky ones. Thanks to Laura constantly stuffing her daughter's mouth with food, Brooke gained weight, her color returned, and she seemed healthier every day.

Given Brooke's progress, a few days into the month Tom invited her to move in with him. Laura was hungry to soak up the time lost with her daughter and selfishly hoped Brooke would decline for just a little while longer. But she also wanted Brooke to be happy, and Tom Marshall made Brooke Beckman Marshall very happy. Brooke surprised Laura by electing to stay until after Anna's wedding, a compromise Laura heartily endorsed. They both viewed the remission as a gift, a second chance, and together vowed to live every minute to the fullest.

Laura was glad to see Brooke's medical reprieve also converted her into a relentless advocate for helping the terminally ill make their own decisions about how and when to depart this world. So Brooke became Robin to Laura's Batman. When word of the Chocolate Shop spread, as Laura knew it inevitably would, a steady stream of potential new clients applied. Brooke's job was to screen each case, to make sure the potential client was both truly terminal and competent to make a life-ending decision.

Time moved steadily through the month of February, and each day seemed better than the last. Laura's relationship with her daughter deepened, and Brooke's condition continued to improve.

One day late in the month, Stan and Sally Marchand contacted Laura. Sally's dad, Virgil Conway, lived at Anchor Cove. They heard about the Chocolate Shop through one of Virgil's friends who knew of the services Laura and Gracie had provided to Nora. Laura invited them over to join Gracie and Brooke for iced tea in the living room. Laura guessed they were in their late forties. Stan reminded Laura of a bowling ball with droopy hound-dog eyes. Sally was the opposite—tall, scrawny, with short curly hair dyed coal-black. Both had dressed up for the occasion.

"Dad's been sick for so long. Liver cancer," Sally said, dabbing her eyes.

Stan added, "Terminal."

"I'm so sorry," Laura said.

"He's in constant pain," Sally said. "He's told us repeatedly he's ready to pass, but his doctors say their job is to keep him alive no matter what."

Gracie frowned. "Bastards."

Brooke said, "You understand we'll need to speak with Virgil ourselves to be sure he understands the service we're offering."

Sally replied, "Of course."

Gracie asked, "Does he have a last wish?"

"A final boat ride," Stan said. "Virgil loves the Bay."

Laura smiled. That was an easy one.

Two days later, Laura and Brooke walked through the Anchor Cove main building past a pool where a water aerobics class was in full swing and made their way to Virgil Conway's room. The door was open, but they knocked anyway.

"Come in."

They found Virgil sitting in a chair wearing a t-shirt and sweat pants. He struggled to remove a pair of socks. The man appeared gaunt, scrawny like his daughter, maybe mid-seventies. He still had half a head of silver hair and wore thick, horn-rimmed glasses. His skin bore a yellowish tint, a typical sign of liver disease.

"Mr. Conway, I'm Laura Beckman and this is my daughter, Brooke Marshall."

"Oh, yes. Sally told me she might be bringing visitors over. May I offer you something to drink?"

Laura said, "No, thanks."

"Can I give you a hand with those socks?" Brooke offered.

"Thanks. Something we take for granted by the age of four now becomes a daily ordeal. Getting old ain't for sissies."

While Brooke bent down to help him remove his socks, Laura got down to business.

"Virgil, you know why we're here. Your daughter and son-in-law told us about your condition. The liver cancer."

"Yeah, a real bitch. You go through life, trying to live up to the don'ts."

"The don'ts?"

"Don't smoke, don't eat too much fat or cholesterol or sugar or carbs. Don't drink too much, don't forget to exercise. There are a bunch more of them but in the end they *don't* make much difference. I sometimes think about all of the bacon cheeseburgers and chocolate ice cream I passed up."

Laura smiled briefly, then sobered. "We understand, because of your condition, you desire to end your life."

"Who wouldn't think about it? I've discussed the subject with Sally and Stan—they handle all of my doctor stuff—and they suggested you folks might help. Sorry, but I've forgotten your names already."

Brooke said, "Mr. Conway, you must be sure about your decision, and we'll need evidence of your condition."

"I'm sure. If I'm going to die soon anyway, why not do it now?"

Laura, Brooke and Gracie sat around the kitchen table for their morning staff meeting. Laura turned to Brooke.

"Any problems with Virgil Conway? He seemed like such a nice man."

"Yes, I'd say there's a problem."

The day after their visit, Sally dropped off copies of several medical records and Brooke examined them closely. Virgil Conway definitely had been diagnosed with liver cancer, but the details were sketchy. Before they'd left his room, Brooke asked him to sign a consent form Tom prepared for all potential clients giving Brooke the right to examine the applicant's medical records to confirm a terminal diagnosis. Brooke decided to follow up with Virgil's oncologist, and while she didn't speak with him directly, she spoke to one of the nurses familiar with Virgil's case.

"Yes, Virgil has liver cancer," the nurse said. "But it's in its early stages with a forty-three percent five-year survival rate. Plus, he's on the list for a liver transplant."

Gracie shook her head. "I'll be damned."

Brooke continued. "Virgil was a successful businessman and has a sizable estate. I checked back with the Cove administrator. After we left his apartment, Virgil went directly to the pool and joined his water aerobics class. It seems Virgil also has been dating one of the other residents at Anchor Cove. I'm guessing Sally and Stan are afraid they won't receive the pile of money they expected and decided to hasten Virgil's demise. Virgil has early onset dementia, and he relied on his daughter for doctor reports."

Laura was thankful Brooke had done her job, and going forward she vowed they'd be even more careful. "All in favor of denying the request of Virgil Carter presented by his money-grubbing, despicable children, raise your hand." Three hands rose. "Unanimous."

"Then I'll can the Marchands and inform them of our decision," Laura said. "And if you agree, I intend to add a piece of my mind for what they tried to do to poor Virgil."

Gracie and Brooke again each raised a hand and spoke in unison. "Unanimous."

Gracie and Brooke recommended that Arlo be granted admittance to the Chocolate Shop staff as a "junior associate," and Laura didn't object. After a few cases, Laura grudgingly admitted his help proved invaluable. That Laura enjoyed his company was a fact she gradually permitted herself to concede. Even Tom pitched in once or twice, although he limited his participation to the make-a-wish department. Laura was convinced Brooke had twisted his arm, but that was okay. Now, based upon her doctors' reports, it appeared she would have an opportunity to twist arms for a long, long time.

The shop's make-a-wish department, of course, was the most fun. One client, Elaine Rockaway, who was no longer ambulatory, always dreamed of going hang-gliding. The Chocolate Shop crew drove her down to Nags Head, North Carolina and strapped her onto a makeshift sled that Arlo had put together. They connected the sled to a hang glider and pushed her off the highest sand dune, not far from where the Wright Brothers made history. The chilly breeze was perfect. She only needed her hands to maneuver the glide wing, and she sailed through the air for a long time before landing the sled softly on the sand. Again and again Elaine sailed off the dune, like a kid repeatedly going back to the top of a snowy hill to sled down to the bottom.

Another client, Maggie Harlow, had been a Rockette who'd danced at Radio City Music Hall some sixty years earlier. She wanted to see the Rockettes one last time.

Arlo couldn't go, and Brooke prevailed on Tom to join them. Arlo insisted Laura take the Massey Mobile to make it easier handling Maggie's wheelchair. So Laura drove everyone to New York in a van with scantily clad women painted on the side. Every few miles driving up the Jersey turnpike, cars would honk as they passed. The honks were usually accompanied by catcalls or whistles, and on two occasions, they were mooned. Everyone laughed, especially Maggie, who marveled at Laura's sense of fun and lack of inhibition. Laura felt a strange empty spot due to Arlo's absence, a sensation she rationalized as nothing more than missing the outrageous antics of the class clown.

Thanks to Tom's efforts, when they reached their destination they gained access to the backstage area. Maggie was giddy as they wheeled her to the wings of the stage. She carried in her lap a framed photograph of herself sixty years earlier. The photo showed a beautiful Rockette kicking her leg high in the air.

They watched from the wings and witnessed the excitement and energy of the show as the dancers performed much as they had since the show opened in 1932. Maggie sat transfixed, her eyes bright, color returning to her pale complexion. She munched on a chocolate cookie Brooke offered a few minutes earlier. Tom nudged

Brooke and discreetly pointed to Maggie's feet. They were tapping in time to the music, and every once in a while she would raise one leg and then the other a few inches off the chair, mimicking the dancers' world-renowned high kicks.

At the end of the show the curtain came down to loud applause. In the wings, Maggie clapped enthusiastically. As the Rockettes paraded off the stage, each one paused to give Maggie a quick hug. She was overwhelmed. The dancers in the wings listening to the applause until the curtain rose, then filed back onto the stage for the curtain-call. The last dancer in line winked at Laura, then took the handles of Maggie's wheelchair and pushed the startled woman onto the stage. The lead dancer stepped forward.

"Ladies and gentlemen, thank you for your kind applause. Before we go, we'd like to introduce you to one of our alumnae, Maggie Harlow!"

The applause was thunderous. First, a few people stood up in the front row, then a few more, and in a matter of seconds Maggie Louise Harlow, Rockette, was receiving a standing ovation at Radio City Music Hall.

Laura glanced away from the stage to her daughter pressing against Tom. His eyes glistened. Laura bit her lip, feeling the pressure of unspilled tears. Brooke was fine now, she reminded herself. Just fine.

CHAPTER FORTY-THREE

The New York trip had been exhilarating, but after returning home Brooke was so exhausted she slept almost until noon. When her mother opened the bedroom door with a breakfast tray, Brooke couldn't remember the aroma of coffee smelling so good.

Laura rested the tray on Brooke's lap and flipped open the legs to hold it steady.

Brooke's appetite had almost fully recovered, and the breakfast looked delicious—scrambled eggs with a touch of cheese, toast lathered in almond butter, and coffee.

Laura sat on the edge of the bed. "How are you feeling?"

The last thing Brooke wanted was being constantly reminded of her cancer, and she'd laid down strict orders not to raise the subject, particularly now when, fingers crossed, it appeared the treatments were working. "You know the rules. You're not allowed to ask me that."

Laura chuckled. "I've been breaking a few rules lately, so what's one more?"

Her mother's comment reminded Brooke of her talk with Gracie about Laura's wild past and the mystery surrounding what changed her into the woman Brooke knew virtually her whole life. She'd promised Gracie she wouldn't mention the conversation to her mother, but what the hell? Brooke was a rule-breaker, too. She took a bite of egg and spoke while chewing.

"So, I understand you were a bit of a hellion when you were young."

Startled, Laura paused for a few moments. "I see you've been talking to Gracie."

"Secretly putting itching powder in cheerleaders' briefs? Beautiful. What did you call them? The peppies?"

Laura smiled. "Perkies. My best friend Megan and I, we called them perkies, because every time you saw them in class, in the hall, everywhere, they were so . . ."

"Perky. The itching powder caper must've been a blast."

"You should've seen them. Big game, gym filled, and they start their routine. At first they tried to disguise their discomfort. I remember the head cheerleader squeezing her thighs together, rubbing them back and forth while trying to maintain her smile. But it didn't take long. A minute after they started their dancing, all of the girls reached under their skirts in front of all those people and frantically scratched their crotches. The fans hooted in laughter. The perkies ran off the floor in embarrassment. Megs and I, we laughed our butts off. The one week suspension was well worth it."

"Then what happened?"

"What do you mean?"

"The rebel, the wild girl. What happened to her?"

Laura's expression clouded, and she lowered her eyes. "She grew up. Happens to everyone."

"Okay, granted, everyone matures. I get it." She took a sip of coffee. "But, Mother, let's face it. Your change from young rebel to, sorry, uptight straight-arrow bitch was too abrupt to explain away as simply growing up. Gracie said . . . she said something happened, something that changed you. She didn't tell me what it was."

Laura took a deep breath and closed her eyes. Brooke could almost see the wheels turning in her head. Finally she spoke, her voice lowered to a near whisper.

"Megan Foster was my best friend since sixth grade. Almost from the first day we met, we were inseparable. And I suppose both of us had, using your word, the rebel gene. We always seemed to find ourselves in the principal's office for misbehaving. We viewed rules as a challenge, a game. How many can we break without getting caught? Our parents were ready to kill us. We were more sophisticated in high school. We smoked pot regularly, and on a couple of occasions even tried cocaine. While we weren't the official class sluts, Meg and I did more than our share of partying."

Brooke tried with only partial success to keep a straight face. The idea of Laura Beckman, the official arbiter of appropriate behavior, snorting coke and sleeping around was almost too much to absorb.

"We both attended Bollen College, a small liberal arts school in southern Virginia. Bucolic, picture-postcard beautiful. From our first day, Megs and I had a blast. We took to the college party scene like fish to water. And continued our rule breaking."

"Like . . .?"

"Like the time we painted boobs on the statue of the college founder, Horatio Bollen. Never got caught, and a photo of the statue made the inside cover of our yearbook."

"Then . . .?"

"At the beginning of my second semester I met your father at a ski resort. After high school he'd worked in his dad's furniture store for a couple of years before going to college, so he was several years older. I fell head over heels in love. At first Megs felt left out, but we continued to party, the only difference being Mickey was with us. The three musketeers. A year later, right before Christmas, I found out I was pregnant. I considered terminating the pregnancy, but Mickey proposed, and despite warnings from everyone that we were way too young—and they were right, of course—we married that April. I was only four months into the pregnancy, and at your grandmother's insistence, I wore a white empire-waist gown that covered my bump."

"And I was that bump. Wow."

"You were born in September, right before the start of my junior year. I took the first semester off, but after that, with a little bit of creative scheduling, your father and I did a pretty good job of balancing school with baby care."

"I never knew I was a knock-up kid."

"On the rare occasions over the years when the subject of our wedding came up, we deflected the conversation. And let's face it, kids are so caught up in their own lives, they have no real interest in the early lives of their parents." Laura paused, then with an anxious expression asked, "Is that important to you? The knock-up kid thing?"

Brooke tilted her head and considered. "Not even a little bit." Laura sighed, as if a weight had been lifted from her shoulders. Brooke motioned with her hand. "Finish the story. Being married with a kid must've curtailed your partying."

"Only partially. Mickey was a great sport, and we were both wise enough to know that for the marriage to survive, we each needed some space to act like a typical college kid. So once a month we'd take turns watching the baby while the other one went out and had fun. Only two ironclad rules—no drugs, and no sex."

"Sounds very enlightened. But I gather something happened during one of these girls' nights out."

Laura's face changed to an expressionless mask. Her eyes remained opened, but she wasn't seeing. At least she wasn't seeing Brooke in bed with scrambled eggs on her lap.

"Yes, something happened. A kid in my psych class told me about a party that night at the Beat house. Beta Epsilon Tau. He was a guitarist in the band. According to the guitarist—I've long forgotten his name—only members, dates, and special guests could attend. I thought it would be a fun challenge to see if we could crash the party. Megs didn't want to go, but I egged her on . . ."

"C'mon, it'll be fun."

Laura paused at the top of cracked concrete steps and made sure Megan was following her. The Beat house, a red brick three-story with white trim, and white pillars, featured a wide front porch extended almost the entire width of the building. Band music pounded through the open door and windows. Partiers filled the porch. Guys reclined in rockers with girls on their laps, and couples lounged against the thick railing. Everyone held a red Solo cup.

Megs asked, "How do you plan on getting in? All I see are couples."

"We'll claim we're a couple."

"Not sure the troglodyte Beat boys are into the lesbian scene."

Laura undid the top two buttons of her blouse, then reached over and did the same on Megan's sweater. "There. A little fucking cleavage can go a long way."

"Not sure this is a great idea."

"We probably won't get in, so nothing to worry about."

At the entrance a big fellow wearing a gray sports coat with a Beta Epsilon Tau coat-of-arms patch over the breast pocket stopped them.

"Evening, ladies. Who are you with?"

Laura responded, "The band."

"Their dates are all inside. And tonight is couples only."

Laura immediately wrapped her arm around Megan and pulled her close. "You're not prejudiced against gay people, are you?"

He scanned each of them up and down, pausing at their chests, then swept his arm toward the door. "Go right on in, and have a good time. I recommend the grape punch."

Brooke straightened and plopped another pillow against the headboard to support her back. "I have a feeling where this might be going. The grape punch."

Laura nodded. "Good guess."

The place was a madhouse.

"Looks like the party's been going on for a while," Megan shouted over the pounding music. She nodded to the four-piece band squeezed into a corner of what must've been an expansive living room before the furniture had been removed. "They're awful."

"One Hole Whistle" was painted on the bass drum. Laura waved to the guitarist. "He confided to me in class he dreams of becoming a rock star someday."

"Best of luck with that."

"After a few drinks, everything sounds good. Even fucking One Hole Whistle."

"Speaking of drinks . . ."

They found their way to the crowded kitchen. Bottles of cheap bourbon lined the counter, and beer partially submerged in crushed ice filled the sink.

Laura asked, "Beer or booze?"

"Beer's fine."

"I don't see any grape punch?"

A male voice behind them. "On the back porch."

They turned. The greeter smiled and pointed to the back screen door.

Megan said, "Thanks, but a beer's fine."

"You have to try the punch. I helped make it myself. And I know the last thing a couple of party crashers want is to appear rude."

They both shrugged and followed him out to the porch.

"My name's Steiner, by the way."

Laura asked, "First or last?"

"First. And you are . . .?"

Meg and Laura exchanged glances. "Laura said, "I'm Karen, and this is . . ."

"Sylvia," Meg said.

They followed him out onto the back porch. A tall guy with a black beard and smooth smile—he could've easily been a jock—stood next to a galvanized mop bucket resting on a bench next to a stack of Red Solo cups. The bucket contained a dark liquid.

Steiner said, "This is Karen, and this is Sylvia. They're . . . a couple and want to try some grape punch."

"Looks like the water after you mop a dirty floor," Laura said.

"The bucket's brand new," the jock said," and we washed it thoroughly to make sure." He dipped a Dixie cups into the bucket and held it out to Megan.

Laura asked, "What's in it?"

"Actually, no grapes. A little raspberry vodka, a touch of peppermint schnapps, a lot of club soda, fruit punch."

"None for me, thanks," Megan said.

C'mon, Megs, try it . . ."

Steiner smirked. "I thought your name was Sylvia."

Laura took the cup from Steiner's hand and gave it to her friend. "Try the damn grape punch."

Megan shrugged. "Just a taste." She took a sip. "It's okay." She offered the cup back to Laura.

"No, go ahead and finish it."

Megan hesitated, then drank some more. "Actually it's not bad. Hardly can tell there's any alcohol in it." She drained the cup.

Steiner handed another cup to Laura, and she tasted the dark liquid. "Definitely too sweet for me, but thanks." She returned the nearly full cup to Steiner.

"Want a refill?" Steiner asked Megan.

"Go ahead," Laura prodded. "Maybe it'll make the band sound better."

Steiner dipped Megan's cup in the bucket and pulled it out, filled almost to the brim.

Megan giggled. "I kind of like it." She chugged the drink in one long swallow, egged on by the applause of Laura, Steiner and the jock.

The two friends returned inside. Both grabbed a beer from the sink, then made their way through the crowd into the living room to hear the terrible band. A few minutes later, they each danced with guys wearing gray blazers. Ten minutes after that, Megan was in deep make-out mode with her dance partner, a stocky blond guy with a baby face. Laura politely rebuffed the kid she was dancing with, but had no reservations about Megan enjoying herself. She was single and had no ironclad rules.

On the way back to the kitchen for another beer, Laura saw baby-face leading Megan upstairs. Her friend appeared more than willing, although she did seem a little wobbly. Laura felt a bit light-headed herself. She'd only taken a single sip, but there was probably more vodka in the grape punch than Steiner had let on.

Back in the living room, she noticed several of the frat boys, including the jock, whispering among themselves. One by one, they left the living room and headed up the stairs. Wonder what—?

"Hi, want to dance?"

A skinny guy in a gray blazer smiled at her. What the hell? She took a long swig of beer, set the bottle on a side table, and danced to the mostly steady beat of One Hole Whistle.

When the song was over, she felt a little woozy. From one beer? Oh, shit. She hurried to the stairs and had to grasp the hand-rail to keep herself steady as she climbed. On the second floor, the first door on the right was closed. Four guys in gray blazers lined up outside. She moved toward the door.

The first guy in line, chubby, wearing glasses, shot out his arm across the door. "You're not allowed in there." He smirked. "Why don't you wait for your . . . partner . . . downstairs." He flitted his tongue in and out of his mouth. "Unless you want to make it a three—"

Laura bit down hard on the hand attached to the arm blocking her path. Chubby screamed and jerked the arm away. Laura burst into a room smelling of dirty socks and froze.

Megan Foster, her very best friend in all the world, lay naked on a bed, semi-conscious, lolling her head back and forth, while Steiner humped her hard. The jock stood off to the side zipping up his pants. Megan's dancing partner waited his turn, naked from the waist down.

Megan saw her. " . . . aura . . . elp me . . ."

The jock said, "Hi, Karen, want to join—?"

Laura spotted a trophy resting on top of a dresser and grabbed it. She had no idea what accomplishment the trophy represented, but it was heavy and hard. She swung the trophy with all her strength at Steiner's face, catching him flush. He screamed and fell back, blood spurting from his mouth. The jock saw Laura coming toward him. She swung and missed, driving him back.

He screamed, "What the hell are you doing, you muff-diving bitch! She wanted it!"

"You fucking drugged her, you sorry piece of shit!"

Laura pulled Megan to her feet and helped her slip into her jeans and t-shirt. "You better find yourself a good lawyer, assholes, because rape qualifies you for a twenty-year stay in an eight-by-ten!"

She half carried, half dragged her friend out of the room. No one tried to stop her.

"Oh, my God, Mother. What happened?"

"Nothing." Laura sighed. The emotionless mask Laura wore while recounting her story suddenly cracked, and a mixture of grief and regret painted her face. "Nothing happened." She bit her lip, trying with only partial success to stem the tears. "I begged Megan to go to the cops, or at least to the university administration to report the assault, but she refused. Remember, this was thirty years ago, long before #metoo. Times were different. Women were conditioned to believe unless a weapon or a brutal physical beating were involved, the presumption was, they asked for it. Back then, no meant yes. So Megan blamed herself. And though she never told me directly, she blamed me. She was right, of course. I was the one who pushed her to attend, to drink the punch. She stayed away from class, and two weeks after the 'incident'—her word—she slit her wrists. Her roommate found her in time and she recovered, but a few days later she left school. I tried to stay in touch, but she never answered my calls. She moved to L.A. and succumbed to the drug scene. Never saw or spoke to her again."

"What ever became of her?"

"About ten years later I heard she died from a drug overdose in an L.A. flea-bag off Ventura Boulevard."

Brooke covered Laura's hand with her own. "So sad, but you have to know what happened to her wasn't your fault."

"If I hadn't pushed her to go, prodded her to drink the punch, if I'd acted more responsibly, the incident wouldn't have happened, and she'd be alive today."

"So you smothered the rebel gene for thirty years and swung as far as you could back in the other direction."

Laura wiped her eyes with the back of her hand. "I know it's difficult to understand, but even years later, if I ever considered coloring outside the lines, the image of Meg being raped in that frat house flashed into my head. I guess after a while the safe path became ingrained, and that's how I lived my adult life. Safe."

"But it's impossible to change your DNA, a DNA you passed down to your first born. And now you're acting . . .?"

"I don't know." Her still glistening eyes conveyed an unfamiliar impish expression. "Responsibly irresponsibly?"

Brooke smiled. "Yeah. Responsibly irresponsibly. I like that." She reached across the tray and hugged her mother. "I love you."

Laura whispered, "Love you, too, baby."

CHAPTER FORTY-FOUR

Charlene Melroy was fed up with the incompetent cops. She decided she needed to get herself a mouthpiece. Since her resources were not as flush as they should have been due to what she considered the criminality of the Beckman bitch and her cohorts, she needed to find a lawyer who would take her case on contingency. She found her man in Benny Bosco.

Benny's office could be found in a rundown two-story strip mall located along Route 3, the main artery between Annapolis and Baltimore before Interstate 97 opened. The strip mall consisted of a car wash, a Vietnamese manicurist, and a Mexican restaurant called Jose's Taco City. Charlene grabbed the eight-by-ten manila envelope from the passenger seat and climbed the back stairs to Benny's office on the second floor above Jose's.

Letters had fallen off the cheap door sign. It read "enny osco, Attorney at Law." Who gave a crap about spelling anymore anyway? That's what computers were for.

The door stuck, and Charlene had to ram her shoulder into the edge nearest the jamb to open it. Benny sat behind his desk. The desk was positioned such that Charlene could see porn on his computer screen. His hid his left hand under the desk.

He rushed to clear screen. "Mrs. Melroy, I presume." Benny was quite short, and his age fell in that gray area between fifty-five and seventy. He wore heavy black-rimmed glasses, and his suit was so shiny Charlene believed she could see her reflection in his lapel. His hairpiece qualified as his most memorable feature. If purchased from a catalogue it might've been called the "Seventies Elvis"—a shiny black pompadour that sat on top of his head like a curled-up ferret.

Thankfully, Benny offered his right hand and kept his left in his pocket. She shook his hand, then quickly sat in the lone dinette chair in front of his desk without being asked.

Benny nodded to the envelope in Charlene's grip. "I believe you said something about an insurance policy on the phone."

She handed him the envelope. "Do you think you can help me, Mr. Bosco?"

Benny opened the envelope. He perused the first page of the policy. "That would of course depend on the—" His eyes fell on the policy amount. He smiled from ear-to-ear. "No doubt, Mrs. Melroy, no doubt at all."

CHAPTER FORTY-FIVE

With Arlo's help, the Chocolate Shop arranged a paddock pass for a client, a former jockey, at the John B. Campbell stakes race at Laurel Park. The race ended in an exciting photo-finish, and the client had the time of his life.

That evening, after returning the ailing man to his sister's house where the second phase of the Shop's services would be performed the next day, on a whim Laura asked Arlo if he wanted to stay for a glass of wine. She briefly wondered if describing that horrible night so long ago at the college frat house to Brooke triggered the "whim." Gracie and Brooke quickly made their excuses, leaving Arlo and Laura alone on the porch.

It was uncharacteristically warm for the end of February—mid-fifties. They sipped their wine in a silence Laura found surprisingly comfortable. Laura sat next to him on the glider, and for a few minutes they quietly enjoyed their tea, rocking back and forth.

"I'm sure I can find you something stronger to drink."

"The tea's fine."

"Thank you for all you do to help us with our, uh, enterprise. It's difficult to think of how we'd get along without you."

"Truth is, I can't remember when I've had so much fun. Well, not the other part, that's not fun, but—"

"I understand." After a little more rocking, Laura decided to satisfy her curiosity. "Tell me about Jake." Arlo didn't respond for what seemed like forever. Had she crossed a line to forbidden place? "Please, forgive me. I had no right to pry."

"Jake is . . . Jake was my son. He died."

"I'm very sorry. How did it happen?"

Arlo paused, reflective. "Jake had bugged me for permission to take out the seventeen-foot Sunny by himself. We'd used it to teach him sailing, and after a while that little boat became his second skin. It was the middle of summer, a clear day, no bad weather forecast. Lorraine would have protested, but she was in Virginia visiting her parents. Jake reminded me his eleventh birthday would arrive in a couple of days, and soloing in the Sunny was all he wanted for a birthday present. I gave in, conditioned on him remaining in the West River and not venturing out into the bay. And he had to be back in half an hour. He was so happy. Gave me a big hug and kiss, then sailed off." Arlo stopped speaking, his eyes distant, no doubt reliving the most horrible day in his life.

"I know this must be very painful for you so please, you don't need—"

"I watched him turn the bend. He waved, then disappeared. It was the last time I'd ever see my boy alive. Jake sailed the boat all the way to the mouth of the river. You know kids, you give 'em a rule and they push it to the edge. The water where the river current meets the bay is always pretty rough, and Jake capsized. He'd been wearing a life vest, and it was a weekend so there were lots of other boats around. A thirty foot Grady picked him up quickly, but apparently when he fell out of the Sunny his head hit one of the cleats. He died of a freak head injury, not drowning. Just like that, he was gone. Waved goodbye, sailed around the bend, and disappeared from my life."

Laura could feel the weight of his anguish, not to mention a touch of guilt herself. After all, her child had confronted death and survived. She squeezed his hand. "I'm so sorry. And his mother?"

"Lorraine blamed me and she was right, of course. She left the day after the funeral. Divorce by mail. Last I heard she was in Oregon someplace."

"Arlo, I know I've been hard on you, and if I'd known about Jake . . . well, I want to apologize."

"No apologies necessary. Actually, you've kind of re-charted my course a bit. Since Jake passed, I'd been pushing things to the edge. I guess I thought if life's so fragile, you need to—"

"Go for the gusto?"

He chuckled. "Don't know where the right balance is, but I think maybe what I'm looking to do is live my life . . . I don't know . . ."

"Responsibly irresponsibly?"

"Yeah, I like that." He sighed and took in the surroundings. "You have to understand, not too long ago the idea of simply sitting on a porch and listening to the sounds of the evening would have bored me to death."

"And now?"

"Now I can't think of any other place I'd rather be."

Laura felt herself flush. The death of his son had jangled things up, but she didn't want to respond to him out of sympathy. "Sunday nights after *Sixty Minutes* Mickey and I, we used to sit out here, rocking back and forth, watching the world go by." She sensed an instant change in Arlo, an involuntary pulling back.

"You must think of Mickey all the time," he said, looking away.

Laura answered truthfully. "Not all the time."

Arlo's face lit up. He inched next to her and put his arm across the back of the glider.

They both set their tea down on the table.

He dropped his hand to her shoulder, and the touch of his fingers instantly sent a gentle hum through her whole body. How could that be? He just touched her shoulder and suddenly her body responded as if it had a mind of its own, pressing closer to him on the swing. He leaned toward her, and his lips pressed softly against hers.

No. She couldn't allow herself to be distracted away from her daughter. Her body tensed, chilling the moment. She stood, took his hand, and lifted him to his feet.

"Good night." She brushed his lips with hers, then turned for the door.

"Laura . . .?"

She looked back to see him standing next to the porch rail, forlorn, confused, his hands deep in his pockets.

He wasn't the only one who was confused. Laura admitted she was attracted to the man, and that attraction made her feel guilty. Was it about Mickey? And how could she give even a moment's thought to any kind of relationship with Arlo when her daughter needed her.

She entered the house, closing the door softly behind her.

CHAPTER FORTY-SIX

Jefferson and Olivetti entered the captain's office Monday morning to find Benny and Charlene seated at the small conference table.

"I believe you know Ms. Melroy," said the captain. "And this is her attorney, Mr.—"

"Morning, Benny," Jefferson said. "Thought you were disbarred."

Unflustered, Benny didn't miss a beat. "On temporary status pending appeal. How's it goin', Jefferson, Ovaletti?" Benny left no doubt he mispronounced Olivetti's name on purpose.

Charlene scowled, and her face blew up like a puffer fish. "Captain, how dare these public *servants* disrespect my attorney."

"My sincere apologies, ma'am. Detective Jefferson is no doubt distracted by the distinct possibility he may be transferred to the traffic division, so his rudeness, while inexcusable, is nevertheless understandable."

Benny wiped his hand on his shiny mustard-colored trousers, then rested it on Charlene's shoulder. "We're all on the same team here. We simply want justice for my client's late husband, and for all of the others who have fallen victim to this serial killing machine."

Jefferson couldn't help himself. "That's an exaggera—"

"Shut up, Jefferson," the captain said. "Perhaps you both could bring us all up to date on your progress."

Jefferson turned to Olivetti, but his partner knew when to keep his mouth shut. "As we've reported, after the incident at White Elk we consulted with the Assistant State's Attorney, and she concluded there was insufficient evidence for a probable cause finding. We found no evidence of Beckman and her group helping the victim drink the cocktail, and we both witnessed the victim releasing the hand brake without any assistance."

"They're more clever than you," Charlene said.

"What about the drugs?" Benny asked. "Can't you get them on controlled substances?"

"The docs aren't cooperating." Jefferson knew what he was going to say next likely would result in a one-way ticket to meter-maid status, but he couldn't help himself. "Besides, we thought our time would be better spent on higher-priority cases, like last week's drive-by shooting on Clay Street."

Charlene jumped in immediately. "Christ, those people are always killing each other, so what else is new?"

It was all Jefferson could do to control himself. He lowered his voice to a near-whisper. "La Keisha Smith was an eight-year-old girl outside playing hopscotch when a car drove by and some punks with assault rifles tried to take out her brother. Instead, the auto-matic gunfire literally cut this innocent child in half. That means two pieces, Mrs. Melroy. A fate you might find unacceptable even for *those people.*"

Charlene turned ashen. Benny stepped in. "My client meant no disrespect, Detective, no disrespect at all, did you, dear?"

Charlene shook her head, afraid to speak.

"We know you all are busy, don't we?"

Charlene nodded.

"But we're trying to prevent another murder like these two tragic cases." Benny opened his briefcase and carefully set on the table two excerpts from the obituary pages of the *Capital*. Circled in red were the photos of Margaret Harlow and Willie Beck, a former jockey. Jefferson and Olivetti read quickly. In each case the story identified the cause of death as suicide by drug overdose.

"If we can't catch them administering the drugs," the captain said, "we need to pursue the controlled substances violations. Call over to the D.A.. Tell him we need a subpoena for their medical records. Tell him I'm asking personally."

"You got it, Cap," Olivetti said.

"Jeez, Chaz," Jefferson said with an exaggerated look of concern. "Glad to see you've recovered from your severe bout of laryngitis."

The last day of the month fell on February 29, leap year. That extra once-every-four-years day was supposed to bring either good luck or bad luck. In the Beckman household, the leap year luck wasn't bad, it was horrible. First thing in the morning, Phyllis Kesler called Laura to say they'd received a subpoena for Laura's medical records. Phyllis whispered into the phone, "Don't worry, Dr. Lowe's record keeping's a mess. Not everthing's been uploaded to the computer yet, so it will take a long time for me to find them."

"Thanks, but as I told you before, I want you to fully comply with the order. We both know I have nothing to hide."

After Laura hung up, she checked out Elvis, asleep under the kitchen table. What were the chances of the police discovering the vet prescriptions? She quickly decided she couldn't worry about it because of much more concern, Brooke's condition seemed to have slipped. The fatigue and shortness of breath returned. Laura was certain this change was nothing more than a mild reaction to all of the medications Brooke had been taking, but in an abundance of caution, after lunch she drove her daughter up to Dr. Bryant's office for an x-ray.

An hour after the test was completed, she and Brooke followed a nurse through the waiting room door to the mysterious "back area." Laura tried to read the nurse's expression to no avail. She wondered if in nursing school they taught a class in blank expression. *Mental note: never play poker with a nurse.* The nurse led them to Dr. Bryant's office. Clearly they didn't teach the blank expression class in med school. Laura and Brooke had barely sat down before he spoke.

"I'm sorry, Brooke, but the cancer has returned."

He said a lot more, but the words were all a blur.

CHAPTER FORTY-SEVEN

The car ride home was quiet. Brooke appeared small in the passenger seat, as though she were shrinking before Laura's eyes. Laura resolved that she simply would not, *could not* allow anything bad to happen to her daughter. She was the mother, and that simply was that.

Laura said, "To tell you the truth, I never thought that highly of Dr. Bryant. And Elaine Masterson? Well, her son, Sid, he's a radiologist, you know, and he told her there are lots of doctors who think Hopkins is highly overrated. As soon as we get home, I'm calling Elaine and we're going to find you—"

"Sid Masterson tried to feel me up at my own wedding. Not to mention that his license was suspended for gross malpractice."

"That was years ago."

"Mother, I said no! Just . . . no."

Despite biting her lip, Laura cried quietly as they drove the rest of the way home in silence.

That night Brooke lay in bed, her breathing labored. It was as if the doctor's news, in and of itself, had accelerated the disease. Tom sat next to her, holding her hand. "Laura's right, we need a second opinion."

"We received a second opinion. Dr. Bryant showed the test results to three of the other oncologists at Hopkins, and they all agreed."

"Then we need a fourth."

Brooke squeezed his hand to cut him off. "You don't know how happy you've made me these last months."

"So much wasted time before then."

"I was such a fool."

"When you left, I thought I hated you. But the truth was, I never stopped loving you. And now you're going to leave me again." He gasped, but held back tears.

Brooke smiled warmly. "You'll be fine. Someday you'll have grandchildren to keep you busy, and you'll meet a wonderful girl and . . . and—"

Jennie's entrance stopped her breakdown before it could start. Tom kissed Brooke tenderly, then got up and hugged his daughter. He kissed Brooke again. "I'll see you later." Tom closed the door softly behind him.

Jennie sat on the edge of the bed, sniffling away tears. "It's not fair. Everything was starting to get great with you and Dad."

Brooke attempted a serene smile and squeezed Jennie's hand. "Shhhh, you'll be fine. You have a wonderful father, and someday you'll meet a great guy and live a full, wonderful life. And you have Grandma."

"I want you."

"I know, baby, I know."

Jennie cast her eyes down, she hunched her shoulders drawing into herself. "I'm so sorry, you know, for the way I treated you."

Brooke pulled her daughter to her breast. "I deserved every bit of it and more," she whispered. "I was selfish and hurt the two people in this world I treasure the most. People are so stupid." Brooke had come to accept her premature death. What choice did she have? But the idea of leaving her daughter released a slow trickle of tears she'd been struggling to contain. She reached for a tissue. "Why don't you climb next to me for a little while?"

Jennie slipped off her shoes and crawled under the covers. Brooke held her daughter close and stroked her hair. Neither said a word. Neither had to.

Laura entered Brooke's room carrying several loose pages in her hand. Jennie had gone back downstairs, and Laura found her daughter alone, staring at the ceiling.

Laura said, "I've been doing some research. Look here. At the Moffitt Cancer Center down in Tampa, there's this doctor who specializes in—"

"Stop."

"But it says—"

"I said *stop!* I don't give a fuck what it says! Jesus, stop trying to help! I'm dying. Deal with it."

"It's natural for you to be upset. The Moffitt Center also provides state-of the-art counseling—"

"Counseling?" Brooke's laugh was hollow. "Little late for that, don't you think? I come back from L.A. with my tail between my legs, and instead of being there when I need you most, you—what did your ladies group call it?—iced? You iced your own daughter. If you'd forgiven me, maybe Jennie would've forgiven me, too. All those lost years, I was an object of disgust in the eyes of my own daughter. And I was an embarrassment to you. Do you know . . . can you even *conceive* what it feels like to be a pariah to your own parent? Now, all of a sudden I'm dying and you're trying to be mother-of-the-year. Who knows? Maybe somebody will give you a plaque for that."

Too stunned to speak, Laura turned and left the room. She'd reached the top of the stairs when she heard Brooke call out.

"Mother . . .?"

Laura returned to find her daughter crying.

Brooke said, "So . . . sorry. Didn't mean—"

"No. You were right. I was selfish and . . . and I was a lot of things that make me feel more ashamed than you'll ever know. But I never stopped loving you. Oh, baby, I'm so . . . so sorry."

"Come here."

She sat on the bed and they melted into each other's arms.

An hour later, Laura returned to Brooke's room carrying a brown paper bag.

"What's in the bag?"

"New medicine I thought we ought to give a try." Laura pulled from the bag a gold foil Godiva Chocolate box. Brooke opened the box, and inside were two layers of chocolate-dipped cherries. Her eyes brightened. "And to wash it down . . ." Laura removed a bottle of Cristal champagne from the bag.

"You pushing me off the wagon?"

"We'll jump off together." Laura climbed up onto the bed next to her daughter and leaned back against the headboard. She set the box of chocolates between them, then fussed with the champagne cork.

"Give it here." Brooke took the bottle and loudly popped the cork, spraying champagne over both women. They laughed easily. Each ate a chocolate-covered cherry, then took a deep drink of champagne from the bottle.

"Did Sid Masterson really feel you up on your wedding day?" Laura asked.

"Yep. Ran into him on the way to the restroom, and he wanted to kiss the bride. Jammed his tongue down my throat and squeezed my left boob."

"Pig." They both laughed again and took another swig of champagne.

"So, what's the deal with you and Arlo?"

"We're friends."

"You slept with him yet?"

"No."

"He's crazy about you. It's obvious to everybody who sees you two together."

"I'm long past the point where—"

Brooke interrupted. "Remember what Nora said? Sex is a good thing, and we should do more of it. Come on, you must've had some sexual fantasy."

"No."

"Fess up, code of truth."

"Brooke."

"Okay, I'll tell you mine. Good thing about dying is you don't worry anymore about being embarrassed."

"You're *not*—"

"Flannel PJs."

"Doesn't sound very exciting."

"Exactly. I've slept with maybe forty men."

"Forty?"

"Give or take. And yet what I really yearned for was making love to a man while I was wearing flannel PJs. We'd kiss forever. He'd gently slip off my bottoms, and we'd make love tenderly, slowly, and it would last and last and last . . ."

Laura's face flushed. She felt her breathing get heavier. She grabbed the champagne bottle and took a deep swig. "Where's a man when you need one?" They both giggled.

"I told you mine, so what's yours? Or did you satisfy all of your fantasies in your rebel gene days?"

Laura paused. The alcohol was definitely getting to her. She sighed. "Redi-Whip."

"Whipped cream? Your fantasy is making love covered in whipped cream?"

Laura simulated spraying whipped cream all over her body. "Pssssttt . . ." They both giggled, and it was difficult for Laura to catch her breath. "It . . . it comes in low cal." They laughed so hard Laura had to press her thighs together to keep from peeing her pants.

Brooke snuggled up close to her mother. "Why didn't we do this when I was younger?"

"I didn't think you wanted anything from me. You were always your father's little girl. I was simply . . . there."

"You're so wrong. You probably don't remember, but when I was little, I'd come down the stairs in the morning and—"

Laura sang. "We're off to find the morning glories . . ."

Brooke joined in. "Sparkling with sunlight and dew,

We're off to find the morning glories,

Look! I see them!

A good morning glory to you, and you, and you!"

Laura found a tissue on the bedside table and blotted her eyes.

Brooke said, "All through my sorry life, all through the crap, there's something I kept with me. There, in the drawer."

Laura stretched across the bed and opened the drawer to the bedside table. She removed a faded photograph taken years earlier. Brooke appeared to be eight or nine and was holding Laura's hand.

In her other hand she carried an Easter basket. Laura wore a polka dot dress. "Easter Sunday."

"So long ago. I was looking for pictures of us together, but . . ." Her voice trailed off. They both knew there weren't any later photos of them together except for Brooke's wedding to Tom. "I didn't think you wanted me close to you."

Laura's eyes filled with tears. "I was so foolish."

"I always kept the picture with me, even at the lowest points. A few years after it was taken, I gave up church, but I always had good memories of Easter Sunday."

"Now might be a good time to re-acquaint yourself with the church."

"Sorry, don't buy it." Brooke's voice changed to singsong as she mimicked, "I mean, like, you know, there has to be a God and a heaven 'cause someone as important as me, you know, should live forever." Her voice returned to normal. "Truth is, our lives are nothing more than stepping into a puddle. When we die, we step out, the water closes over, we disappear, and it's as if we were never there."

Laura couldn't speak and pulled her daughter tight.

Brooke whispered, "Mother?"

"Yes, honey?"

"I've decided on my wish."

CHAPTER FORTY-EIGHT

March

Jefferson held the phone to his ear, waiting on hold to follow up a lead in the La Keisha Smith slaying. He had a daughter her age, and this was one case he wasn't going to let slip through the cracks. He watched Olivetti at his desk, scouring each page of Laura Beckman's medical files for the second time.

"Have to hand it to them," Olivetti said. They're doing a good job coverin' their tracks. Ain't nothin' here. Either the doc's writing prescriptions on the side, or they're getting the stuff on the streets. So what do you think? They scorin' the drugs on the street?"

"Damn." Jefferson's source had hung up on him. He turned in exasperation to Olivetti. "No, they're not buying the drugs on the street."

"How can you be so sure?"

"I'm sure." He stood to leave. The snitch insisted they talk by phone, but he should have known better. He was going to find the little bastard and shake him down for whatever he knew. As he headed for the door, he almost collided with the captain entering the room.

"Jefferson. You made progress in those assisted-suicide cases?"

"Uh, Olivetti's taking the lead there. I'm following up on La Keisha Smith."

"Understood, but listen. Benny called the mayor, and the mayor called me. Turns out Benny's the cousin of the mayor's wife."

Olivetti piped in. "Don't worry, we're on it."

Winkie Maddox had never seen anything quite like it before. He sat at the bar on his usual stool, sipping his usual beer, nibbling his usual crab cake sandwich as he had every Saturday afternoon for as long as the Clam had been open for business. His longevity gave him special privileges, in this case meaning he was the only customer permitted in the room. The government bureaucrats telling him he couldn't have a smoke with his beer was bad enough, but this? He shook his head. What the hell was the world coming to? All of the tables and chairs had been pushed back into the corner, and the owner had turned the whole damn bar into a damn dressing room for a bunch of damn women.

Brooke, from her wheelchair, watched as her sister Anna pirouetted in her white wedding dress, a strapless matte satin gown with a beaded sweetheart neckline and a beaded asymmetrical dropped waistline. A sweep-length train flowed out from an A-line skirt.

Brooke, Jennie and two other bridesmaids—Anna's friends from Chicago— wore strapless charmeuse light periwinkle short dresses. The Chicago girls primped in front of the bar mirror. Except for Winkie's little corner, the entire length of the bar was covered in enough makeup and hair concoctions to start a small salon.

"You look beautiful, Aunt Anna," Jennie said.

Brooke turned to Winkie. "As one of only two males in the joint, what do you think?"

"She looks like one of them models in the magazines."

"Thanks, Wink. Pour yourself another one on the house."

Mike, the owner, emerged from the tiny kitchen. Brooke reached up and hugged him. "I can't thank you enough."

"Shaddap. How often do we have a blushin' bride in here? Never, that's how often. And where the hell else were you going to do your women stuff with the wedding across the square? At the Rusty Pike? That joint's so filthy even Winkie won't go there."

"Except for two-for-one night," Winkie corrected. Everyone laughed. He glanced out the window, "There's a gang of guys in tuxedos comin' this way. You want I should lock the door?"

The excitement in the air ratcheted up even higher.

"I think they're ready," said Brooke. "Are you ready?"

Anna grinned. "Never been readier." Even Winkie laughed as he slid off his stool to open the door.

Laura sat on the aisle of the first row. Mother nature had cooperated by offering an unseasonably warm day and a cloudless sky. A portion of Market Square had been cordoned off, and rows of folding chairs set up for the guests. Beyond the ropes, tourists and residents alike mingled, waiting for the wedding to start. Husbands and boyfriends kept checking their cellphones and nudging their women, but the ladies held fast. There was going to be a *wedding*, for goodness sake. How could you not stay and watch? Apparently, many of the men didn't share the same level of enthusiasm. Most abandoned their ladies and straggled, alone or in groups, across the square to the string of bars bordering the harbor where they could catch a March Madness college basketball game and grab a cold one.

She'd originally pushed for a church wedding, but Brooke had reminded her sister that she'd grown up by the Bay, and a waterside wedding in the heart of town would be truly unique. Laura considered enlisting the groom's parents to persuade Anna. Not long ago, she would have thought nothing of pressing her point, but not long ago now seemed more like a century away. So she backed off. After considering a number of sites, Tom offered to pull in a few favors and arranged for Market Square at the head of Annapolis Harbor to be blocked off several hours.

Laura's initial instincts were to dive right in and manage the affair. After all, she was the mother of the bride. But Brooke had assumed the lead, and Laura was thankful for the diversion. Watching her two daughters planning the event had warmed her heart at a time when heart warming was sorely needed. She sat in the folding chair waiting for Jennie to make her entrance, and realized she rather liked not being in charge. Of course, she'd insisted the reception take place in her backyard, and the Brooke-Anna team readily agreed.

The rows of white chairs faced the water. A lectern and a small altar with huge displays of flowers on each side had been set up near the water's edge. To the right, a string quartet played softly. Brandon's parents had strongly insisted that a man of the cloth perform the marriage, and a minister from St. James Episcopal agreed to preside.

Laura scanned the crowd, and her eyes stopped at the statue of Alex Haley sitting on a bench nearby reading to three children of different ethnicities. The memorial commemorated Haley's ancestor, Kunta Kinte, a seventeen-year-old African slave who first arrived in America at that very spot in 1767. Haley's book *Roots* had won a Pulitzer Prize and been depicted in a miniseries on television way back in the seventies that some considered a seminal event in the history of race relations in America. Haley himself had since passed away. The circle of life. And today the circle would continue on the same spot with a wedding of two young people who, Laura knew, would do their part to make the world a little better. Funny. The way the statue was positioned, it appeared Haley was simply another guest waiting patiently for the wedding to begin.

Arlo sat next to her, then Gracie and Everett. Gracie made eyes at the minister, despite his attempt to studiously avoid eye contact with her.

Laura whispered, "He's a minister, for God's sake. Not to mention he's half your age."

"Remember what Benjamin Franklin said."

"And what did Benjamin Franklin say?"

"That women age from the tips. Which means the middle, where you find the good stuff, always stays young."

"Have I mentioned before that you're hopeless?"

All told, there were about 130 guests. The minister gave a signal. Everyone turned to see a line of handsome young man in white tuxedos escort Brooke, Jennie, and the other bridesmaids from the Slippery Clam, move across the Square, and walk down the aisle between the rows of white folded chairs. Some of the tourists watching clapped. Laura's eyes locked on Brooke. She walked with the help of her young escort. Brooke glowed, and no one who didn't know could tell she was ill. Brandon and his best man disembarked from Arlo's boat and walked to the front of the gathering. Arlo had docked the boat in the harbor and made it available to the wedding party. At Laura's insistence, he tied a sheet over the stern to cover the boat's name. Somehow the words, "Stiff Ripples" didn't quite fit the sanctity of the occasion.

The string quartet immediately transitioned into Wagner's "Bridal Chorus," and everyone stood as Tom escorted Anna across the square. Laura felt Arlo take her hand. She took comfort from his gesture and gave his hand a little squeeze. Her attention returned to Anna. Laura believed a man should walk the bride down the aisle, and Tom had volunteered. Anna's dress was stunning. The onlookers outside the ropes applauded enthusiastically. One of the male tourists whistled loudly, then bent over in pain when his wife jammed an elbow hard into his ribs.

Halfway down the aisle, Tom and Anna stopped abruptly. The music continued playing, but both guests and onlookers were stunned. What was going on? Did the bride suddenly have second thoughts? Brooke whispered in her escort's ear, and he guided her over to Laura. Tom and Anna, grinning from ear-to-ear, extended their arms to Laura, beckoning.

Brooke whispered, "Go."

Laura slowly rose from her seat and allowed Brooke to lead her back to the bride. Tom stepped aside into an aisle and Laura, her eldest daughter following close behind, led the bride down the aisle to the altar, stepping in time to the music.

The minister intoned, "Who gives this woman to be married to this man?"

Laura was so choked up she could barely speak. "I do." She paused and took Brooke's hand. "No, *we* do."

Everyone clapped, even the onlookers.

Laura didn't think people were supposed to clap at this stage of the ceremony. She decided she didn't care and hugged her two daughters tight.

The applause grew louder.

CHAPTER FORTY-NINE

The reception was in full swing.

Brooke asked Linda Taylor to front for the band, and she'd readily agreed. Linda stepped to the microphone on the small bandstand set up in the corner of the yard next to the hibiscus. "Ladies and gentlemen, may I have your attention please?" The guests quieted, well aware of what was coming next. "It is my honor to present to you for the first time as a married couple, Mr. and Mrs. Brandon Carter!" The guests cheered, and the band played as Anna and Brandon exited from Laura's house, crossed the back porch, and walked hand in hand down the steps to the festive, welcoming crowd that packed the backyard.

Laura stood with Gracie by the buffet table. Everett walked by, dutifully recording the event with his old video camera. Laura had pressed for a professional videographer, but Everett insisted. She'd relented only after confirming that his video could be converted to digital.

Gracie whispered, "Why is it Mr. and Mrs. Brandon Carter? Why not Anna and Brandon? They've only been married a couple of hours, and already the woman's lost her identity. I'm gonna go tell that singer she's a woman and should know better." Gracie's move toward the bandstand was brought up short by Laura's horse-collar grip on the back of her blue taffeta dress.

"You'll do no such thing. And don't worry about Anna losing her identity. Remember her gene pool."

"Good point," Gracie conceded. "Now let go of my damn dress." They watched with pride as Anna greeted the guests and saw the bride quickly become adept at performing a half- piroutette lean-in to pose for selfies.

Anna approached Brooke sitting in her wheelchair at a small table, holding hands with Tom. Brooke and Tom stood, and the three of them embraced in a group hug. Rather than letting go they clinched tighter, rocking gently back and forth as one. Gracie handed Laura a napkin from the table and took one herself. While Laura dabbed her eyes, Anna gently broke away and walked toward her mother. Laura stepped into her daughter's outstretched arms.

"Baby."

"I love you," she whispered. "Thanks for everything."

Linda's voice interrupted them. "Ladies and gentlemen, please clear the dance floor as Mr. and Mrs.—"

"Her name's Anna!" Gracie shouted. Silence. Then everyone laughed.

"My apologies," Linda said with a deep bow in Gracie's direction. "Please clear the floor for Anna and Brandon to enjoy their first dance as hus—" She glanced at Gracie. " . . . as wife and husband."

"I think that's my cue," Anna said. She found her husband, and they danced gracefully around the portable dance floor in the center of the yard.

Arlo approached. "She looks as pretty as her mama."

Laura greeted him with a dismissive wave of her hand. "Don't try that syrupy stuff with me, Arlo Massey. I'm not one of your bikini bimbos."

"It's true." Arlo plucked a hors d'oeuvre from the buffet table. "And for your information, I've completely given up on the younger ladies. Not to say I've quit looking. Always going to look."

"No harm in looking," Gracie added as her eyes followed a young waiter carrying a tray of stuffed mushrooms. "I have a hankering for a mushroom."

Laura asked, "Is hankering even a real word?"

"Of course it's a real word." Gracie took off, trailing the waiter like a bloodhound.

"Can I get you a drink?" Arlo asked.

"Thank you, nothing alcoholic." Laura said. "At least not yet." Arlo went off to the bar. He passed Mrs. van Arsdale standing at the edge of the crowded dance floor, frowning and licking a cracker. She clutched her purse close to her chest. Shane popped his head out from the top of her purse. Laura waved, and Mrs. van Arsdale quickly covered the purse flap over the tiny dog, then turned her back.

Gracie returned holding a mushroom on a toothpick. Laura said, "I thought you were allergic to mushrooms."

"Who told you that pack of lies?" She dropped the mushroom in a trash receptacle.

Brooke waved them over. With Gracie in tow and Arlo following with a drink in each hand, Laura made her way to Brooke's table. "Is everything okay, honey?"

"Feeling a little tired," Brooke responded. "Maybe we ought to do this now."

"Do what?" Tom and Arlo asked in unison.

Laura and Brooke grinned at each other conspiratorially. Laura turned toward the bandstand and got Linda's attention. Linda gave her the thumbs-up. The music stopped and she grabbed the microphone.

"Ladies and gentlemen, may I have your attention please?" It took a few moments for the crowd to quiet. Linda continued. "We have a special treat this evening. The sister of the bride has agreed to favor us with a song." Everyone turned toward Brooke.

Tom didn't try to hide his concern. "Are you sure you're feeling up for this?"

Brooke nodded confidently. "Help me up on the damn stage." Tom hesitated for a moment.

"You better do what the lady says," Laura advised with a twinkle in her eye. Tom and Arlo helped Brooke out of her chair and carefully walked her to the stage steps. Tom attempted to follow her, but Brooke stopped him.

"I think I can take it from here." Tom and Arlo gently released her and she faltered, then quickly grabbed the standing microphone for support. When Tom and Arlo made a move to assist, she waved them off. "I'm fine, guys, honest." She turned her attention to the audience.

"Again, thank you all for coming and helping us celebrate my little sister's wedding to a wonderful young man. In my mother's toast, she thanked Brandon's parents, Adrian and Marge, and I want to say we already consider them part of the family." The crowd applauded politely and turned to acknowledge the parents of the groom.

"When my sister and I were young, like all little girls we were fascinated by weddings. She made me promise that when she grew up and got married, I would sing at her wedding." Brooke turned to Laura. "As some of you know, I haven't been feeling too well lately, but this is my special wish. To keep my promise. My mother has made sure I've received lots of rest. Then she sprayed my throat with this awful-tasting stuff and made me gargle some concoction made of honey, lemon, oregano and—"

"Old Granddad!" shouted Gracie to instant laughter.

Brooke smiled. "Thanks, Mom." She nodded to the band and they struck an A minor chord. Brooke turned back to Anna who'd made her way to the front of the stage. She took a few quick shallow breaths, then began to sing Joe Cocker's "You Are So Beautiful" to her sister. Her voice, roughened by the cancer, projected a mournful, earthy Janis Joplin sound. Linda backed her up on the chorus. Laura was hopelessly biased, but judging from their expressions, she wouldn't be surprised if the guests agreed it was the most moving rendition of the song they'd ever heard.

When Brooke finished, there was complete silence. Then the whole place erupted in thunderous applause. Brooke appeared energized from the response. She glanced down at Tom and Jennie. Tom whistled, Jennie squealed, and they both applauded even louder than the rest. Jennie mouthed, "I love you." Laura thought she was going to burst wide open. Arlo embraced her, and she hugged him right back.

Someone in the crowd shouted, "More, more!" and the other guests picked up the chant. Brooke's smile captured her entire face. She let go of the microphone stand, then whispered to Linda. She turned back and held up both hands to quiet the crowd. "Well, maybe one more." The guests shouted their approval.

Laura glanced over at to make sure Everett was recording.

Brook said, "This is an old song by Pink I used to sing when I was . . . on the road." The band struck up "So What?" Brooke, using the microphone stand as her anchor, performed a mild prance across the stage as she belted out the song with Linda and the drummer backing her up. Tom moved to assist her, but Laura held him back.

"She's going to collapse," he said.

"No, she's not."

The guests began to dance, not only on the dance floor, but everywhere. At Laura's insistence, even the wait staff joined in. Arlo pulled Laura onto the one remaining corner of the floor. Tom danced with Jennie. Gracie danced around the mushroom waiter as if he were a flagpole until he conceded and joined in.

Everett set down his camera, approached Mrs. van Arsdale, and asked her to dance. She appeared momentarily shocked, but only momentarily. She glanced around quickly, spotted unofficial church busy-body Louise Cheny stuffing two cheese balls in her mouth at once, and looped her purse over Louise's neck.

"Keep an eye on Shane, will you?"

Louise screamed as Shane popped his head out of the purse and snatched the last cheese ball from her plate. Mrs. van Arsdale dragged Everett to a small grassy corner and boogied so violently other dancers cleared space in fear of catching a foot or flying elbow.

On stage, Brooke grabbed the mic from the stand and pranced and danced and sang her heart out.

Family and guests gathered along the front walk waiting for the newlyweds. Anna and Brandon huddled with their families on the porch. Brooke, back in her wheelchair, reached up to embrace her sister. "I love you, baby."

"Love you, too. And thanks for the song. You were the star of the evening."

"No, the bride's always the star." Hugs all around.

"Thank you all for everything," Anna said to the group. "We had the best wedding anyone could have imagined. And don't worry, Mom, I'll call and tell you everything."

Brandon's brow furrowed. "Well, maybe not everything." Everyone laughed. The bride and groom proceeded down the porch steps and were greeted with a gentle rain of rice. Then into a limo, and off they went.

Laura addressed her guests. "Still plenty of desserts left, so everyone back to the party!" Louise led the crowd back through the gate to the desert table.

Tom bent down to Brooke. 'I'm so proud of you, but you look tired, and I think it's time to get you back to bed."

"Good idea," Laura said. "Oh, wait. She hurried inside, then quickly returned with a package and handed it to Tom. He opened it.

"What's this?"

"Flannel pajamas."

"Little warm for flannel, isn't it?"

"No, it's the perfect temperature," Brooke said.

Tom shrugged and handed the package to Brooke. He easily lifted her from the chair and carried her across the threshold.

Then Brooke Beckman Marshall, sister of the bride, disappeared inside the house with her man.

CHAPTER FIFTY

April

In the weeks after the wedding Brooke's health faded fast. Laura read how very sick people, through sheer force of will, often hung on until a special target date—Christmas, a birthday, a graduation, a birth, a wedding—the signposts of life. Brooke's target date seemed to have been the wedding of her sister, and now that the wedding had come and gone she could relax and let fate take its course. Laura had other ideas. She would not permit her daughter to die, no matter what the doctors said. She watched stories on TV seemingly every day about people who'd been given weeks or months to live but beat the odds, and she was going to do whatever was in her power to make sure Brooke would be able to tell her "doctors were wrong" story for years to come.

Laura decided Brooke needed a new target date. She reasoned that by setting one target date after another, she could keep Brooke alive indefinitely, or at least until there a medical breakthrough occured. She opened Brooke's bedroom door carrying a tray of tomato soup and saltines, primed to implement her plan.

Brooke appeared to have shriveled smaller even over the last twenty-four hours. Laura put on a cheery face, folded down the tray legs, and set it across Brooke's lap. "Campbell's Tomato Soup made with water, not milk, just how you like it." She fluffed up Brooke's pillows to support her back. "Scooch up a little bit, honey." Brooke winced as her body moved.

"Not sure I'm hungry."

"How's the pain? Are the pills helping?"

"A little."

"Take more of them."

"Then I'll be unconscious, which sort of defeats the purpose."

Laura remembered that was the same thing Nora had said. "You have to eat. You need to keep up your strength to fight."

"Why bother fighting? I'm practically dead anyway."

"I'll tell you why, so you can see your first niece or nephew, that's why."

Two days earlier Anna had confided that she thought she was pregnant, and Laura had been saving this pitch for a few days, waiting for the right time. If she could persuade Brooke to buy into hanging on for nine more months, well, a lot could happen in nine months.

Brooke smiled weakly. "That would be nice, wouldn't it? Anna will be a great mother." She took Laura's hand and held her gaze. "I need the Chocolate Shop."

Despite wishing otherwise, Laura was hardly shocked by Brooke's request. And she came prepared. "Absolutely not. First, it would be unethical to provide the service to a close family member. That's why doctors don't operate on their own kids."

"What about Aunt Nora? And those doctor's kids could easily go to another doctor. Where else can I go?"

Clearly, the cancer hadn't yet affected her daughter's brain. "And second," Laura continued, "you wouldn't pass the client vetting process—a procedure, by the way, that you helped devise—because Dr. Bryant has yet to officially state that death is imminent."

"Uh, mother, he told us both I have weeks, maybe a few months, but not years left."

"That's right, *months,* maybe lots of months. And during those months anything can happen. Now, I'm your mother, and I'm telling you to focus every ounce of mental energy on living to see that baby." Laura squeezed her daughter's hand. "From this minute to the next. From today to tomorrow, then from tomorrow to the next day. Force yourself alive for one minute at a time, and before you know it you'll be holding—"

Brooke's body convulsed, then shook. She coughed so violently Laura was convinced pieces of her lung would spew from her mouth at any moment. Blood spattered over the food tray as Laura grabbed the phone and dialed 911.

Laura sat in Brooke's hospital room, reading another article in a medical journal, this one about potential promising research at the Cleveland Clinic. She'd lost track of time; the routine of her hospital visits had caused one day to run one into another.

Brooke had been fading in and out of consciousness for the last two weeks. Watching her, it was impossible for Laura to block from her mind the images of Mickey lying in bed almost two years earlier. Not only the images, but the smells and the sounds, including the soft beeping of the life support monitor. So much had happened since Mickey's death—some good, some not so good, and some downright awful.

Brooke moaned. Laura watched her daughter struggle to breathe through the tube sticking down her throat and wondered, not for the first time, if Brooke's illness was God's way of punishing Laura for facilitating the suicides of so many people. Laura believed she had done the right thing, but—

Brooke groaned louder, and her eyes opened. Laura set the journal down on a side table, making sure the publication remained open to the Cleveland Clinic article, and approached her daughter. With the breathing tube, Brooke couldn't speak.

"Baby?"

" . . . ai . . ."

"Pain?" Laura asked.

Brooke nodded.

"Already asked. Two more hours. Listen, honey . . ." Laura retrieved the medical journal. "Says here how up at the Cleveland Clinic there's a promising new treatment being tested on mice, and they think—"

Brooke groaned louder, her face grimaced in pain. She was struggling to speak, shaking her head back and forth. Laura gave her a pad and a Bic pen. She wrote "Shot. Give me shot."

Brooke coughed, her eyes pleading.

"They will, honey, in a few—"

Brooke's eyes brimmed with tears. She wrote, "Not enough never enough."

Laura took her hand, shrunken and scabbed from the IVs. "You must hang on."

Brooke responded with huge letters taking most of the page. "NO MORE!!!!" She flipped to the next blank page. "Please . . . take me home."

Laura's eyes welled up. She gazed down at her suffering daughter, her first child, her baby.

Could she do it? *Oh, God . . . please help me help her . . .*

The tears flowed freely now.

She stood, reached over, and slowly closed the journal.

CHAPTER FIFTY-ONE

The gentle lapping of the bay water against the hull had a hypnotic effect, no doubt aided by two glasses of chardonnay.

"Sure you're ready for tomorrow?" Arlo asked.

The warm night breeze softly tossled Laura's hair. "Of course not."

He'd invited her for a night sail to get away from Eastgate Avenue. Tom and Brooke wanted some time alone, so Laura reluctantly agreed. Now she was glad she'd accepted the invitation. They'd sailed for a while before Arlo anchored in a quiet deserted cove. No other boats and only a single house set back some distance from the shoreline. He'd piled a stack of green-striped bolster pillows on the top deck in front of the mast along with flat seat cushions. They lounged in comfort, side-by-side, staring up at the overcast sky.

"This is very nice," she said. "I have a feeling I'm not the first female who's lounged on these green-striped cushions."

"Well, it's been a while—"

She squeezed his hand and chuckled. "I don't care. I mean, I really *don't* care." She glanced up at the house in the distance. "Do you think they can see us?"

"With this overcast sky, no way."

She scrunched closer, and the heat of his body warmed the full length of her. Another deep breath. She felt like she was floating—not on a boat in the Chesapeake Bay, but floating through the air. Life was so arbitrary, she thought. Between the moment you're born and the moment you conceive a child, there were a million things that happened—paths you choose, and paths chosen for you by the randomness of life. If I hadn't attended *that* college, if I hadn't decided to go to the gym *that* morning, if my friend hadn't fixed me up *that* night, if I'd never even met *that* friend. Any single change, any tiny deviation and that *particular* child would never have been born, its unique existence never even been imagined. Then there was the completely haphazard timing of conception, the chemistry between two people at that single millisecond in time creating a gene mix that can't be duplicated. Even identical twins have different personalities, different biologies. There would never be another Brooke Beckman Marshall. The recipe for that singular biological soup results in only one serving.

"What are you thinking about?" he asked.

"Life. So fragile, so . . . precious."

Without thinking, she rolled over on one elbow and kissed him full on the lips. He responded, and she felt her entire body flush. She hadn't had sex for over two years, and before that with no one other than Mickey for almost thirty.

Time to change that.

She sat up and peeled off her top, unsnapped her bra, then slid off her shorts and underwear. In a moment she lay back, completely naked. She expected Arlo to jump on top of her, but was glad he didn't. Instead he quickly undressed and slipped his arm under her neck. Together they rested there, side by side, her head nestled against his chest. Neither said a word.

The clouds parted, revealing a rich tapestry of stars and a full moon that illuminated the cove like a heavenly spotlight.

Arlo whispered, "The folks in the house. They can probably see us now."

She felt enveloped, strangely comforted by the thick blanket of stars. Her voice was rough, almost hoarse. "I . . . don't . . . care."

He moved to roll over on top of her, but she held out her hand and gently pushed him back. She slipped her knee across his thighs and mounted him. She bent over so her breasts fell just enough to brush his lips. She moaned and adjusted her hips, then slid down on him and gasped as he filled her completely. They timed their rhythm to the slow, steady sound of the black water slapping the hull.

Laura lifted her eyes to the heavens, to the moon and the distant stars, and felt the warm breeze caress every pore of her body.

Life—so fragile, so horrible.

So . . . wonderful.

CHAPTER FIFTY-TWO

Jefferson hung up the phone and was about to make another call when Olivetti stopped at his desk. "Let me guess," Jefferson said. "The suicide cases."

"How'd you know?"

"You have that glint in your eye."

"Cap says he's getting heat from the politicos again and wants to see some progress."

"Benny Bosco must be paid up on his campaign contributions."

"Aren't we Mr. Cynical this morning?"

"Chaz, can't you follow up? I'm swamped."

"This won't take long. Bosco says his client came into certain information that there's gonna be a 'service' at the Beckman house today."

"And how did poor widow Melroy happen upon this information?"

"Seems that Charlene and the Lujack woman share the same hairdresser, and the hairdresser reported that Lujack said—"

"I think you're already up to triple hearsay. You going for a record?"

"Let's check it out. If there's nothing there, there's nothing there."

Jefferson raised his hands in surrender.

Twenty minutes later they drove down Rowe Boulevard, past the Naval Academy football stadium. Olivetti pulled into the parking lot of a strip center. "What's up?" Jefferson asked.

Olivetti retrieved a slip of paper from his pocket and passed it over. "The pharmacy, there? According to her medical records that's where Laura Beckman fills her prescriptions."

"I thought there wasn't any evidence of prescribed controlled substances in her medicals."

"There wasn't. But her pharmacist might know something." Olivetti stepped out of the car and walked away from the pharmacy.

"Where you going?"

Olivetti pointed to a bagel shop at the end of the row of stores. "No time for breakfast this morning. Want anything?"

"Yeah, I want to get back to work on a real case."

"This is a real case."

Jefferson sat in the car for a moment, then reluctantly stepped out and entered the pharmacy.

The place was small, not like the big chains where drugs are mere incidentals. Jefferson made his way to the counter and, based upon his name tag and Jefferson's finely-honed detective skills, determined that the man standing behind the counter was the pharmacist. Jefferson flashed his badge.

"Good morning. We're conducting a routine check into possible controlled-substances violations in the area."

The pharmacist appeared offended. "Detective, I can assure you that I take my responsibilities very seriously, and subject to approval from my attorney, I'd be happy to show you my compliance records for as far back as you wish."

"We have no reason to believe you to be involved in any way. Actually, we were interested in one of your customers, Laura Beckman."

"Laura?" He laughed. "You've got to be kidding. Laura Beckman is the straightest arrow in town."

"I'm sure she is. But we were wondering if there happened to be any prescriptions that you filled that might not have come from her primary care doctor."

"All specialist prescriptions are supposed to be copied to the primary."

"And nothing might've fallen through the cracks?"

The pharmacist scowled at the affront. "I'll have you know, sir, nothing in this pharmacy 'falls through the cracks.' Our professionalism is what distinguishes us from the chains and, but for that, we would be out of business."

Jefferson could see this was going nowhere, and frankly he couldn't care less. He'd done his job and that was that. "Thank you for your time." He turned to walk away.

"I assume you know about Elvis."

Jefferson stopped and turned back. "Yeah, about six feet tall, black hair, wears a lot of sequins, hasn't been seen around much lately.

"I'm speaking of Laura's dog."

"Does he sing?"

"No, but I've been filling prescriptions from his vet."

"For what?"

"Alprozalam. Xanax."

"Damn," Jefferson uttered under his breath. "You have this vet's name?"

"I'll write it down." He flipped through several screens on his computer, then wrote out Dr. Strong's name and address on a slip of paper and handed it to Jefferson.

In the car, Jefferson stared at the slip of paper while he waited for Olivetti to emerge from the bagel shop. What should he do? Obviously, the dog was the source of the suicide drugs. Laura Beckman had violated federal and state controlled substances laws, and he had an obligation—*shit*. The idea of arresting Laura Beckman and Gracie Lujack for helping terminally ill patients control the end of their own lives was heartbreaking. He thought of his own mother and the months of needless pain she suffered at the end. What if his mom had been one of Beckman's clients? Would he have arrested her? Easy answer. Hell no. He would've thanked them.

The car door opened and Olivetti got in while balancing a cup of coffee in one hand and a bagel-egg sandwich in the other."

"Want me to drive?" Jefferson asked.

"I'm good," Olivetti responded. He set the coffee down in the grimy cupholder and started the car. "Any luck with the pharmacist?"

Jefferson curled his hand around the slip of paper and dropped it into his pocket.

"Jefferson?"

"Possibly. Let's see how the day goes."

CHAPTER FIFTY-THREE

Brooke lay in bed wearing her new periwinkle-striped flannel pajamas. Surrounding the bed in a respectful half-circle were Laura, Arlo, Gracie, Everett, Tom, Jennie, Anna and Brandon. The chocolate cookies had been passed out and consumed. Brooke managed one bite.

She breathed heavily. She'd declined to take the prescribed dosage of the pain pills sent home with her from the hospital because they rendered her unconscious. She refused to smother what little was left of her fading senses. The cancer would win in the end, but she would determine the time and place, thank you very much. The place was here; the time was now.

At first she'd considered simply consuming all of the remaining pills in the vial, but she was fearful it wouldn't work. Besides, she trusted her mother. She reached out feebly for Jennie's hand. Her daughter sobbed uncontrollably.

"Don't cry, baby."

"I . . . I don't want you to die."

"I know, I know. But you're going to be fine. Better than fine. You listen to your daddy and your grandma, and there's no doubt in my mind you'll turn out to be the most amazing woman in the whole world." She hugged her daughter and bit her lip to stifle the sharp pain in her back.

She turned her attention to the others, and when she spoke her voice came out as a raspy whisper. "Thank you . . . thank you for coming . . . want you all to know how much . . . how much I love you. Tommy, Mom, Anna . . . and the baby. Sorry I won't be around to see him."

'Her," Anna said, fighting to keep it together. 'We're hoping for a girl and were going to name her Brooke Laura Carter."

Will Jefferson drove down Eastgate Avenue and parked in front of the Beckman house. When he and Olivetti stepped out of the car, they saw both Charlene Melroy and Benny Bosco were there to greet them.

Before either of them could speak, Charlene began to read from a small book, modulating her voice like an evangelical preacher.

"Saint Augustine writes, and I quote, 'It is never licit to kill another, even if he should wish it, indeed if he request it because, hanging between life and death, he begs for help in freeing the soul struggling against the bonds of the body and longing to be released; nor is it licit even when a sick person is no longer able to live.' End quote. The Gospel of Life, number sixty-six."

Bosco jumped in. "Thank you, Sister Melroy, for those soaring words. We enlighten you gentlemen with the wisdom of the saints to remind you this is no time for sympathy, no time for false compassion, no time for—"

Jefferson pushed him aside. "No time for this crap." With Olivetti trailing, Jefferson quickly made his way to the front door and rang the bell. He turned to Bosco. "Wait here."

Bosco puffed up his chest like a bantam rooster. "Sir, my client has a right—"

Jefferson's glare cut him off.

"Very well, we shall wait. We have no interest in interfering with the swift exercise of justice."

Jefferson closed his eyes tight and counted to ten.

All of the witnesses gave Brooke a last hug. She whispered good-bye to each with few personal words. Then she turned to Laura. "I'm ready."

They heard the doorbell ring. Brandon slipped out of the room. Gracie handed Laura the glass of vodka. Laura had laced the alcohol with crushed Xanax. She stared at the glass for what was only a few seconds but seemed like minutes, emitted a tiny gasp, then caught her breath and set the glass on the bedside table. She was about to ask Brooke if she was truly sure she wanted to go through with it, but she knew the answer. And she agreed with the decision.

Brooke moved closer to the side of the bed near the table. The effort exhausted her and she had to catch her breath. After close to a minute she tried to reach for the glass but was too weak to lift her arm.

Suddenly Jefferson and Olivetti filled the doorway.

"What the hell?" Tom exclaimed. "You have a warrant?"

"Don't need one," Olivetti responded. "We were admitted voluntarily, and now we are witnessing a crime being committed."

Brandon blanched. "I'm sorry, I opened the door and they—"

"It's okay," Laura said.

Olivetti gestured to Jefferson. "Grab the drink."

"Hold up," said Tom. "You entered without a warrant and under false pretenses."

"Why don't we let the lawyers figure that out?" Olivetti responded. "In the meantime we have an obligation to stop a crime from being committed before our very eyes."

"What crime?" Tom asked. "A dying woman wants to drink a little vodka." He turned back to Brooke. "You have to take the glass voluntarily, honey."

Olivetti shoved his way into the room, then froze, transfixed. Brooke's whole body convulsed and her face constricted in excruciating pain as she tried, without success, to reach for the glass. Tiny rasping cries mixed with her tears.

"Jesus," Jefferson whispered.

Brooke locked eyes with Laura. "Help me."

Laura reached for the glass. She'd been unsure whether Brooke would be able to consume more than a single swallow and had quadrupled the dose.

"No," Tom said sharply. "She must do it herself."

Brooke's body shook again as she attempted a pathetic lunge for the glass that fell way short. She gazed up at Laura, her eyes beseeching.

"Mommy . . . please . . ."

Olivetti took a step toward the bed.

Laura stepped into his path. Her eyes on fire, she spoke in a chilling whisper. "Don't you fucking touch my little girl."

Olivetti stopped short. Laura snatched the glass from the table, took a deep swig of the vodka into her mouth, and held it there, her cheeks billowing out. Everyone froze.

Laura bent over her daughter and tenderly kissed her. When their lips touched, Laura slowly passed the vodka from her mouth into Brooke's. Brooke continued to swallow, and when she was finished her head sank into the pillow, and she closed her eyes. Laura was crying freely now and didn't care.

Tom turned to the two cops. "If you're planning on making an arrest . . ."

Neither detective spoke; each had his eyes glued to the tableau on the bed.

Jefferson finally turned to his partner. "Chaz?" Olivetti didn't respond. Jefferson lowered his voice to a whisper. "I didn't see anything. How about you?" Olivetti remained transfixed by the tableau in front of him. "Chaz?"

After a long pause, Olivetti responded, "Not a damn thing." He crossed himself and mumbled a brief prayer. "Sorry for your loss." They both turned and exited quietly.

Arlo signaled to the others in the room, then led them out and closed the door behind him.

Laura crawled into the bed and carefully pulled her daughter close. For a while, the only sound in the room was that of Brooke's ragged breathing and Laura's quiet sobbing.

Brooke whispered, " . . . love you . . ."

"I love you, too, baby."

"I'm goin' off to find . . . to find the morning glories . . ."

Brooke said something else, but Laura couldn't hear, so she tilted her ear closer. "What, honey?"

"Redi-whip." She smiled one last time, then closed her eyes.

Time passed. Laura had no idea how much. Then a few tiny gasps, and her daughter was gone.

Outside the house, Charlene and Bosco confronted the two detectives as they descended the stairs from the front porch.

"Well?" Charlene asked. "You arrest anyone?"

"What for?" Jefferson responded.

"Unassisted suicide," Olivetti added. "Tragic."

Bosco jumped in Jefferson's path. "We have a right to—"

Jefferson pushed him aside. Bosco tripped over Charlene's feet and fell flat on his butt.

"Sorry," said Jefferson in a tone that made plain he was anything but sorry.

"That's assault!" shouted Bosco. "And what about the illegal drugs?" he sputtered.

"You ain't got a case, Benny," Olivetti said. "And you're not going to make a dime on this woman. We're closing the file."

Bosco paused as the truth of Olivetti's statement sank in. He turned to Charlene. "Adhering to the highest moral canons of my profession, it would be unethical for me to continue as your attorney. Therefore, I hereby relinquish my representation." He turned his back on Charlene and hurried off.

"You can't . . ."

Jefferson pulled the slip of paper containing Dr. Strong's contact information from his pocket. He tore it up and dropped the pieces into a nearby trash receptacle.

"What was that?" Olivetti asked.

Jefferson glanced up at the Beckman house. "Nothing. Absolutely nothing."

Laura snuggled her daughter close, cradling her. An image, nearly thirty years old now, flashed in her mind. Of a young mother, lying in a hospital bed. Of a smiling nurse nestling the newborn into the mother's arms for the first time. Of the excitement, the unbridled joy. A new life. So much promise. A blank slate ready for a life story. Wondering with happy anticipation how that story would turn out.

Funny how the mind works. Laura kissed her daughter's cheek. The story turned out to be way too short. Yet in the end . . . Laura noticed something clutched in Brooke's left hand. She gently unfolded her daughter's fingers and, through eyes blurred with tears, stared down at the photo of Brooke in her Easter outfit.

And Laura in her polka-dot dress.

CHAPTER FIFTY-FOUR

Laura gazed out over the church full of mourners as she concluded her eulogy. She wore a navy and white polka-dot dress she'd found at Nordstrom. On a table in front of her, Brooke's ashes filled a simple silver urn. An old family photograph of Brooke, Tom, and Jennie taken many years earlier rested in front of the urn. The minister who'd conducted the service sat next to the podium. Laura smiled to herself as she noticed that a few of the mourners had traces of chocolate on their mouths. At the outset of the service, Arlo and Tom walked down the center aisle, passing trays of chocolate-covered cherries to all in attendance.

"…and so, in closing, probably like most mothers and daughters, Brooke and I disagreed on a few things. She didn't really buy into the existence of heaven. I wouldn't be in this building if I agreed."

She saw a sickly looking elderly man dressed in an oversized blue suit seated in a wheelchair parked next to the first pew. He cast his eyes heavenward and mumbled to himself. A prayer? Behind him Will Jefferson listened intently.

Laura caught Arlo's eye, then continued. "Brooke also said living life was like stepping into a puddle. When you leave, the water immediately closes over, and you disappear like you were never there. Again, she was wrong. Brooke, all of us, when we step out of that puddle, we leave footprints in the water. Impressions that impact and influence the lives of all who knew us and loved us. Footprints that last forever."

It was a beautiful spring day outside the church as the mourners paused to offer their personal condolences to Laura and Jennie, who clutched the urn close to her body.

Louise approached. "So sorry for your loss. Will the refreshments be at your house?"

"No gathering today, Louise. We'll do something next week."

Across the lawn, Gracie gave Laura the high sign. Laura picked up a large shoulder bag by her feet and found Arlo. They joined Gracie, who escorted an old woman pushing the wheelchair carrying the sick man in the blue suit. The group made their way across the lawn, through the parking lot, to an open field.

Arlo took over for the old woman and pushed the sick man into a tight, square enclosure where a burly fellow waited for them. The woman, Laura, and Gracie followed. The burly man secured the enclosure.

"So, how are you holding up?" Arlo asked Laura.

"Pretty well, thanks." She paused, struggling to keep her expression neutral. "Say, I was thinking, since we're going to be on the Eastern Shore anyway, maybe we might think about staying for a few days."

A broad smile crossed Arlo's face. "I don't have a change of clothes."

"Probably not going to be a problem," she said. He kissed her. They heard clapping and turned to see Gracie applauding wildly.

"Took you long enough."

After the burly man adjusted the gas, he nodded to an assistant who unhooked the tethers. The hot air balloon rose slowly at first, then more quickly. Everybody in the basket waved to the mourners gathered in front of the church below.

The balloon drifted up into the cloudless blue sky. Laura smiled at the wonder and glee in the sick man's eyes as he experienced his last wish. His wife bent down and kissed his cheek, and his gnarled hand found hers.

Laura squeezed closer to Arlo and glanced down at the shoulder bag sitting at her feet. Two cans of Redi-Whip peeked out over the top.

"You never told me what your last wish would be," he said.

Laura gently caressed his cheek with the back of her hand, then reached her arm up around his neck and pulled him close. She whispered, "I've decided to live the rest of my life so in the end there will be nothing left for me to wish for."

"Responsibly irresponsibly."

She smiled and kissed him again, this time holding it longer.

Because the sky was so clear, the balloon could be seen for a long time before it finally disappeared over the eastern horizon.

Notes and Acknowledgements

As of this writing, physician assisted suicide is legal in seven states and the District of Columbia. I hope the number of states will increase, and indications are that the public is becoming more comfortable with the concept. Oregon has had PAS laws on the books since 1997, and as of January, 2018, legal lethal prescriptions had been written for over 1900 patients, and about 1200 people had died from ingesting those drugs. I find this discrepancy reassuring, because it means 700 patients who were provided the opportunity to end their lives elected to change their minds. That's a good thing. Our lives, our choices.

"Make-a-Wish" for seniors is in its infancy, but there are nascent efforts now underway. Wish of a Lifetime is a non-profit organization operating out of Colorado that, by most accounts, appears to be doing good work in this field.

There are way too many people to thank for their assistance in creating this book to list here, but I must acknowledge the amazing editorial contributions of John Paine, Rebekah Orton, Jenna Brownson, and Lucy Marker, as well as the tremendous help and support of the Women's Fiction Writers Association. And thanks to David Hillis for his medical advice.

And, of course, the ultimate acknowledgement must go out to you, my wonderful readers. Thank you. And remember—

Live Fierce!

J. J. Spring
Belleair, Florida, 2019

CPSIA information can be obtained
at www.ICGtesting.com
Printed in the USA
LVHW090812080719
623417LV00006B/52/P